A journalist by profession, **Douglas Jackson** transformed a lifelong fascination for Rome and the Romans into writing fiction. His first two novels were the highly praised and bestselling *Caligula* and *Claudius*, while his third novel, *Hero of Rome*, introduced readers to a new series hero, Gaius Valerius Verrens. Eight more novels recounting the adventures of this determined and dedicated servant of Rome followed, earning critical acclaim and confirming Douglas as one of the UK's foremost historical novelists. His most recent novel, *The Wall*, is set during the final years of the Roman Empire. He has also written adventure thrillers under the name James Douglas.

Douglas Jackson lives near Stirling in Scotland. You can follow him on Twitter @Dougwriter

Praise for Douglas Jackson

'A novel steeped in history . . . his battle scenes are as bloody and violent as any Tarantino movie. Yet he does this in a matter-of-fact way. There is no horror for horror's sake . . . exhilarating reading . . . full of incident and adventure, the product of the author's fertile imagination and knowledge of the period.'
ALLAN MASSIE, *SCOTSMAN*

'A tour de force that . . . cements his reputation as not just one of Scotland's best historical fiction writers but one of our best writers . . . an all-conquering triumph.'
DAILY RECORD

'Superb battle scenes . . . I was gripped from start to finish.'
BEN KANE

'Superbly written and packed with historical detail and action.'
SUNDAY EXPRESS

'One of the finest wri   re.'
FO

T0112812

Also by Douglas Jackson

CALIGULA
CLAUDIUS

The Gaius Valerius Verrens series
HERO OF ROME
DEFENDER OF ROME
AVENGER OF ROME
SWORD OF ROME
ENEMY OF ROME
SCOURGE OF ROME
SAVIOUR OF ROME
GLORY OF ROME
HAMMER OF ROME

A Marcus Flavius Victor novel
THE WALL

THE BARBARIAN

Douglas Jackson

PENGUIN BOOKS

TRANSWORLD PUBLISHERS
Penguin Random House, One Embassy Gardens,
8 Viaduct Gardens, London SW11 7BW
www.penguin.co.uk

Transworld is part of the Penguin Random House group of companies
whose addresses can be found at global.penguinrandomhouse.com

First published in Great Britain in 2023 by Bantam
an imprint of Transworld Publishers
Penguin paperback edition published 2024

A CIP catalogue record for this book
is available from the British Library.

ISBN
9780552178228

Typeset in Electra LT Std by Jouve (UK), Milton Keynes.
Printed and bound in Great Britain by Clays Ltd, Elcograf S.p.A.

The authorized representative in the EEA is Penguin Random House Ireland,
Morrison Chambers, 32 Nassau Street, Dublin D02 YH68.

Penguin Random House is committed to a sustainable future
for our business, our readers and our planet. This book is made
from Forest Stewardship Council® certified paper.

This one's for Keir and Tom,
the two bright new stars in our growing universe.

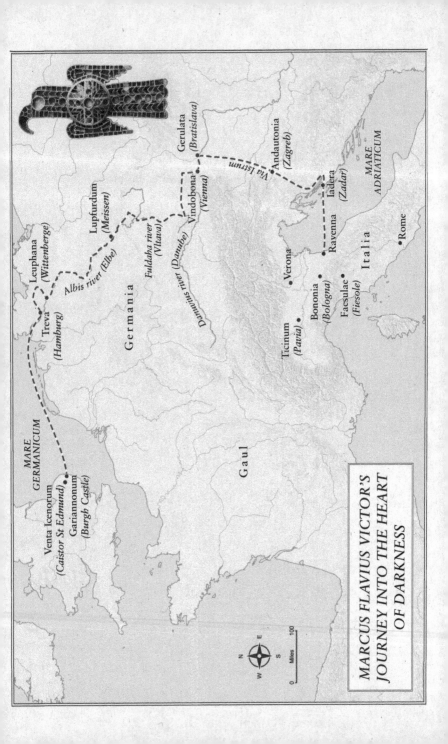

MARCUS FLAVIUS VICTOR'S
JOURNEY INTO THE HEART
OF DARKNESS

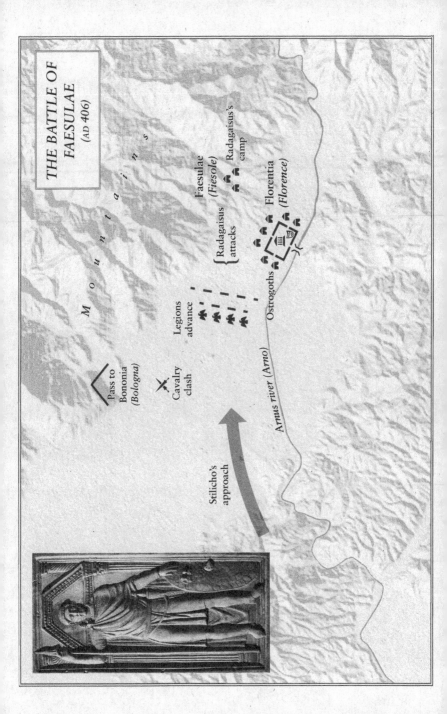

THE BATTLE OF
FAESULAE
(AD 406)

M o u n t a i n s

Faesulae
(Fiesole)

Radagaisus's
camp

Florentia
(Florence)

Radagaisus
attacks

Legions
advance

Pass to
Bononia
(Bologna)

Cavalry
clash

Ostrogoths

Arnus river (Arno)

Stilicho's
approach

There marched under Roman leaders and banners the onetime enemies of Rome, and they filled with soldiers the cities they had not long ago emptied by hostile plundering. The Goth, the Hun and the Alan responded to their name.

Latinus Pacatus Drepanius, AD 389

I

East coast of Britannia, AD 406

The invitation to cut his own throat arrived in the wolf hour when the Saxons usually came; that time just before death surged screaming out of the darkness, while the guards were half asleep and dreaming of a warm bed and the comforts of a warm woman.

'You want to watch this one, lord.' Luko, Marcus's standard-bearer, glared at the courier, hand on his sword hilt. 'Appeared out of the dark like a shadow, bold as you like, and said he would see you and only you.'

Marcus studied the still figure waiting in the flickering torchlight by the gate of the fortified villa outside Venta Icenorum: the most ordinary man in the world. He'd met them before, these almost formless creatures who could blend in to any background and move from place to place without leaving the faintest memory of their passing. Medium height, medium build, anywhere between thirty and forty. A workman's clothes, or a poor trader down on his luck, sweat-stained leather cap covering whatever hair he had. The bland features empty and impassive. Whip him, feed him, stick a knife in him, he didn't particularly care. His job was to be here, and here he was.

'You have a message for me?'

The man reached beneath his cloak.

'Careful,' Luko hissed.

Just the slightest hint of a smile on the thin lips. 'If I was here to kill someone, they'd already be dead.' He drew an object from beneath the patched folds of rough cloth and stepped forward to place it in Marcus's hands.

A leather pouch, oiled to keep the elements at bay and affixed with not one seal, but two. Marcus saw that the first bore an image of the Emperor Honorius wearing a jewelled crown. It covered the flap of the pouch and proved the contents hadn't been tampered with. The second was a personal seal, but one that carried with it even more power than the one above.

By the time he looked up the courier was already moving towards the gateway. 'Will you not stay for an answer?' he called. 'Or at least some food?'

'I was told there would be no answer.' The man paused in the shadows. 'And that it was best none should know of my coming but those you trust with your life.' A faint glint of white teeth in the gloom. 'Your man on the west wall was asleep, soldier. I could have been inside and away and you wouldn't even have known I'd been here.'

Luko grimaced at the jibe. 'Just give me one—' But he was wasting his breath. The gateway was empty.

'Have Falco's beer stopped for a week.' Marcus's mind was already on the possible contents of the pouch. 'And get a servant to bring some bread and cheese to my quarters.'

Luko nodded. 'The lady Valeria . . . ?'

'Nobody else is to know about this, for now.'

As Marcus turned away, he heard Luko's mutter: 'And we know what that means, don't we? Nothing but trouble.'

Of course the invitation to commit suicide didn't say so in so many words: General Flavius Stilicho, *magister militum*, and commander in chief of the Roman Imperial army in the west, was much too subtle for that.

2

Marcus read the letter for the second time by the light of the oil lamps, searching for any nuance he might have missed. It was a lengthy missive for a soldier renowned for his parsimony with words, but the familiar voice snapped out in short, economical sentences. A hurried message if Marcus was any judge, perhaps dictated on the move, or in a snatched moment in the midst of other, much more important business. Marcus had fought side by side with Stilicho eight years earlier against the Picts, Saxons and Scotti when the barbarians threatened to overwhelm Britannia. The campaign had formed a bond between them that would never be broken.

'*Marcus, friend and comrade, forgive this sudden intrusion into your life, but I believe the situation warrants it. Word of your exploits reaches me even here in Metulum and though others have taken credit for your victory at Longovicium, be sure that your old friend still has your interests at heart.*' Marcus read the name Longovicium with an accustomed pang. Though his part in the battle was grudgingly acknowledged, he'd never quite received the laurels that might have been expected for a man who had smashed the power of the Picts for a generation. '*You will be aware, even in far off Britannia, that the Empire has never been in more peril. The names Alamanni, Burgundians, Quadi, Goths, Marcomanni and Suevi will mean little to you, but believe me when I tell you that each of these tribes is as powerful and dangerous as your Picts. All wish to sup from the Roman cup, though for now the Rhenus and Danuvius stand between us, and our army of Gaul and barbarian allies help keep them at bay. Yet I fear still greater danger lies in the east where pressures beyond my knowledge force ever larger numbers – a veritable flood of barbarians – against our frontiers. One day that flood will break. It is to guard against that dread day that I find myself playing politics in this backwater when I should be preparing for war. But I must return to the true purpose of this letter. If the Empire is in peril, then it pains me to tell you that Marcus Flavius Victor is in greater peril still. I am sure that, the occasional rashness apart, you do your duty assiduously as always. Yet word has reached the ear of our Emperor Honorius that one Marcus is plotting to set himself up as usurper in Britannia,*' *perhaps to challenge him for the western Empire itself.'* Now Stilicho had Marcus's attention. His deception at Longovicium had created the illusion of just such a conspiracy. If Honorius truly believed his sources this could kill him. *'And who could that be, but the erstwhile Lord of the Wall, a commander without an army, a soldier without a cause, now languishing discontented and chasing shadows among the reeds and mudflats on the Saxon Shore? The roots of such a calumny lie somewhere in Britannia, perhaps closer than you think, but the conduit is our old comrade, the Hero of Longovicium, Dulcitius, whose renewed presence in the court of Honorius has proved such a trial over the last two years. Nevertheless, he has provided no evidence and I believe I have persuaded Honorius that he cannot, in all conscience, act without it. Yet the Emperor is less malleable at twenty-one than he was at sixteen and our relationship is not what it was. I fear some torturer's cellar in Londinium is even now being prepared to receive you. Some men might resort to despair at hearing this news – your family, naturally, would also be implicated – but I know you to be made of sterner material. I also know your loyalty to the Empire is as strong as my own. To that end I would urge another course of action. Should the opportunity arise, join me either here or at the Emperor's court. If you profess your loyalty to him in person, I am certain your transparent honesty,'* Marcus could imagine the wry smile that accompanied the words, *'and soldierly bearing will win his trust. He has enemies aplenty without creating imaginary ones. Should you avail yourself of this offer, a regimental cavalry command awaits you. I cannot surround myself with enough men I trust, and I would trust you with my life, old friend. At need, the enclosed warrant and attached seal will provide you with safe passage and a change of remounts as long as I hold any power in this land. I remember you once professed a desire to see Rome before you die; join me and perhaps we can visit the city together.'*

Marcus sat back and let out a long breath. A heady brew, indeed, and one to be treated with care unless you wanted a sore head. Or worse. On the one hand, stay where you are and eventually the men with the red-hot knives will come looking for you. On the other, join me and all the riches of the Empire will be at your command. But there was much more. This was a letter that contained murky depths where many less obvious dangers lurked.

'The roots of such a calumny lie somewhere in Britannia,' perhaps closer than you think . . .'

Was Stilicho warning of someone in the provincial bureaucracy or in Marcus's own entourage? The first he could accept, the second didn't bear thinking about. These were *his* men. Almost all of them had fought at his side at Longovicium and stayed with him during the years of virtual exile that followed. Luko, his standard-bearer, forced to do guard duty because they were so short of manpower. Valeria, his sister and second in command, and her husband Zeno, once *medicus* to the Emperors of the East, now a more than valued comrade. Senecio, the Numidian bowman. Julius, whose twin Janus now ruled the Picts of the High Lands. And Leof, who Marcus swore could smell his fellow Saxons at a bowshot's distance. Valeria would have her opinion about the letter's contents, but he decided not to wake her for now.

He turned his attention back to the letter. 'Yet the Emperor is less malleable at twenty-one than he was at sixteen and our relationship is not what it was.' And 'I cannot surround myself with enough men I trust, and I would trust you with my life, old friend.' What did this tell him about Stilicho? That the general's credit with Honorius was running low. That his position and even his life was in danger. He considered what he knew of Stilicho's relationship with the Emperor. Stilicho was the son of a Roman officer, but part-Vandal on his mother's side, which perhaps explained some of what he was reading. On his deathbed, Emperor Theodosius, Stilicho's uncle, made Stilicho guardian to his two sons, Arcadius, then eighteen, and eleven-year-old Honorius. A more ambitious man would have arranged a suitable accident for the boys and might have reunited the Empire. Instead, Stilicho honoured his vow to Theodosius and allowed Arcadius to return to don the purple of the eastern Empire in Constantinopolis. Honorius he placed on the throne in the West under his guiding hand, and appointed himself the young Emperor's commander in chief. From what Marcus had heard, in his inner heart Stilicho might have had reason to regret his decision.

Was there anything else?

'He has enemies aplenty . . .'

Of course. Stilicho had married his daughter to the young Honorius to cement his dynasty, and raised his son high in the Emperor's service. In Marcus's memory he was scrupulously honest, but could also be utterly ruthless. It was well known he had sacrificed friends and allies to ensure his own and his family's advancement. Which meant Honorius's court was a snake-pit of intrigue and conspiracy, a situation that could only induce an atmosphere of paranoia and distrust. And Marcus, the accused usurper, and a man who had not so long ago raised an army capable of taking Britannia for himself, was to stand in front of the notoriously unpredictable Emperor and profess his loyalty?

The thought made him laugh aloud, bringing a look of confusion from the servant standing against the wall to his left. Should he take up Stilicho's offer? Of course he should. It was the offer of life itself.

But how?

Marcus couldn't just gather his men and ride to the nearest port. He was under the orders of Chrysanthus, the province's *vicarius* and Rome's most powerful official in Britannia. Chrysanthus would never give permission, and to leave without it was to invite accusations of treason. No, he had to have a proper plan.

'Marcus?'

He slipped the scroll inside his tunic as Valeria, tall and slim and wrapped in a thick cloak against the chill, entered the room with that wraith-like ability she had to move in complete silence.

'Don't you ever knock?'

The dark eyes gleamed beneath a tangle of russet hair and she hugged the cloak tighter. 'I just wanted to remind you that you should be leaving for Londinium in three hours.'

'How could I forget?' Marcus smiled. It was so like her to check and double-check every detail. In battle or in the council chamber he could always rely on the finely honed blade and the piercing intellect of his warrior sister. 'It's less than two weeks since I sent Chrysanthus my last report. Now he says he wants to see me in person.'

'You think that's significant?'

'Who knows.' He frowned. 'But the timing is strange, with so many reports of Saxon ships just over the horizon.'

'You can trust us to give them a warm welcome.'

'I do.' Valeria would hear within the hour if a Saxon raider dared to come closer. Marcus had watchers on every coastal estuary and a system of couriers to report their sightings.

'And think of the possibilities,' she said cryptically.

'Yes,' he agreed. They were so close. One more decent capture and everything would fall into place.

Brenus.

II

Londinium (London)

Approaching Londinium after a three-day ride from his base on the coast east of Venta Icenorum, Marcus was struck as always, not by the scale of the walls, which were undoubtedly impressive, but by the lack of soldiers manning them. He guessed that barely one in three of the towers was properly garrisoned and the parapets themselves lay bare of any military presence. Growing up in the north, for him the city had taken on an almost mythical status, the epicentre of Britannia's wealth and power. Yet, even then, the days of its greatness had likely lain far behind it. Certainly the reality was a pale and slightly grubby shadow of the city of his boyish dreams.

He was well enough known for the gate guard to nod him through with his escort. Instant transformation from the watery sunshine of a late-winter afternoon to the gloom of the narrow streets and their towering, all too often crumbling, three- and four-storey *insula* apartment blocks. The tall buildings didn't just block out the light, they created a permanent repository for the latrine-room stench that pervaded almost every part of the city from the broken drains and festering dungheaps. At street level most of the *insulae* were host to shops and workshops, but many of the stores were either boarded up or abandoned altogether.

Men, conspicuously lacking jobs and hope, haunted the doorways in groups – the predations of Saxon pirates had left the factories, warehouses and moorings on the Tamesa empty – and their women stared hungrily at passers-by from the shadows of the darkened windows. Look a little further and the next stage of their journey was etched on the pinched faces of the ragged beggars who sat shivering on every street corner. Yet turn a few of those corners and the contrast could not have been more noticeable. In the Forum, well-fed bureaucrats from the *vicarius*'s staff and lawyers in silk-edged tunics and fine-spun cloaks went about their business among marble columns and painted busts of the Emperor Honorius and his predecessors, Theodosius and Gratian.

What would Brenus think of it all? A needle of anguish seemed to pin Marcus's heart at the thought he'd never taken the opportunity to show his son the true glories of Rome.

After the battle at Longovicium he'd intended to return home with the Ala Sabiniana to their fort at Hunnum, and then find a way to sail to Saxonia and search for his son. Brenus had been taken in a Saxon slave raid against the Brigantes, along with Marcus's mother, Venutia. Poor Venutia. When he remembered her, it was the iron will and the calm clarity of her thinking he missed the most. She had been a Brigantian princess and matriarch not just of the family but of the entire tribe. She must be dead by now, he guessed; she'd been old and sick when the raiders came. But, according to a Saxon Leof had questioned, Brenus had still been alive in the spring. Praise God that he lived still. He had been eight or nine when he was taken, a sickly child whom Marcus had never forgiven for the death of his mother in childbirth.

For the first years of his son's life, he'd ignored Brenus. Then, when it became clear he would never be a warrior, actively spurned him, barely able to look at the boy. When Brenus realized his father wanted nothing to do with him, he retreated to the arms of his grandmother which, if anything, made Marcus dislike him more. Yet since Brenus had been taken, each passing day increased the burden of regret that he'd never chosen to know his own son. He understood it was partly self-pity, but he knew that if he did nothing, he would have a gaping hole where his heart should be for the rest of his days. At first, it had been little more than a vague and ill-thought-out urge to find a ship and make a headlong dash to Saxonia. Fortunately, circumstances intervened to prevent what would undoubtedly have been a disaster.

First his old enemy Julius Dulcitius, *dux Britanniarum* and military commander of the north, insisted Marcus and his cavalry regiments should join him in the pursuit of the fleeing Picts. Since Marcus had no intention of catching the surviving invaders, now under the rule of his former comrade Janus, this turned out to be a protracted and fractious affair which did nothing to endear him to a man who already suspected him of being a traitor to Rome.

When Dulcitius eventually released him to return to Hunnum, he found his responsibilities as Lord of the Wall diminished. Units that had been under his control for years were grouped together under subordinate commanders. His authority over others was dramatically reduced. A senior official, the *magister officiorum*, appeared without warning to carry out an inquiry into certain dealings involving the Lord of the Wall and hitherto enemies of Rome, the Selgovae king, Corvus, and Coel, king of the Votadini.

By now two years had passed and Marcus's frustrations built to the point where they threatened to destroy him, and would have, were it not for Valeria's wisdom. Still, he had no option but to comply when he was called to Londinium six months later to temporarily assume the duties of the Count of the Saxon Shore, who had drowned crossing a river during a storm. There it quickly became obvious that all was not well at the heart of Britannia's administration, and that he, Marcus, continued to be under suspicion for the events that preceded Longovicium.

Yet, to his astonishment, all was not in vain, for his unwanted transfer resulted in a development that would never have occurred had he remained on the Wall. Not only did he discover Brenus's location, he also knew the name of the man who held him.

Marcus led his escort on the cobbled road along the edge of the enormous basilica and then turned south towards the bridge that spanned the river. It was here, on the north bank between the bridge and a sometimes noxious stream, that Chrysanthus lived amidst the decaying magnificence of the governor's palace. The palace was a sprawling affair of several dozen rooms, with its foundations set firmly in the Empire's glory days. A series of lovingly tended terraces overlooked the river, with views to the fields and woods of the south bank beyond.

His relationship with Chrysanthus, an elderly nobleman of impeccable lineage but uninspiring character, could sometimes be a puzzling one. It had been clear from the start that Chrysanthus wanted him close, where he could be watched and controlled – the inevitable consequence of the whispers that followed Longovicium. Yet the very scale of Marcus's task forced Chrysanthus to give him the mobility and the freedom to operate he needed. That meant cavalry, and cavalry based close enough to the coastal settlements at highest risk of attack to react with a fair chance of success. Nominally, he was also in command of the garrisons of the Saxon Shore forts of south-east Britannia. In reality, most of the static detachments were useless against any raid more than a few miles from their walls.

They arrived at the gates of the palace and Marcus dismounted and handed his mount's reins to Luko. 'Find an inn and get the men something to eat,' he said, handing the standard-bearer a purse of silver. 'But make sure they stay sober. Once they've eaten send Ninian to wait for me here.'

He presented his pass to the soldiers on the gate, where Chrysanthus's chief of staff, and the controller of his network of spies, waited to escort him to the *vicarius*. 'I hope I find you well, Aulus?' Marcus greeted him. If anyone in Britannia had knowledge of his visit from Stilicho's courier it would be Aulus Ostorianus.

'I suppose that would depend on your definition of well.' The other man's expression didn't change. A pair of peacocks crossed their path, the male displaying the rainbow-hued fan of his enormous tail and the female screeching her admiration. 'Bloody pests, they shit everywhere. If it was up to me I'd wring their necks, but his wife dotes on them. Did you ever hear of an ancient form of torture where a man is tethered to four horses all being urged in different directions?'

'No, but it sounds painful.'

'So now you know how you find me. How is life in the wetlands?'

'Damp.'

A bark of laughter escaped the pursed lips. 'When they carry me out of my office in a shroud, as they undoubtedly soon will, your recommendation as my replacement will be on the *vicarius's* desk within the hour.' Ostorianus led the way along a corridor lined with religious paintings. 'These are new,' he said. 'Chrysanthus believes they will help his visitors reflect on the words they are about to utter. I hope you have a good excuse for all that silver you appear to have lost to the Saxons?'

Ostorianus spoke in jest, but Marcus knew his words hid genuine concerns. It was unusual, these days, for a raid to count fewer than three wooden hulls and ninety warriors, and often they amounted to many more. A big raid would sweep a swathe of sparsely defended country clean of cattle, plunder and people. It could last for days while a substantial enough force was gathered to drive the raiders back to their ships. Actual battles were relatively scarce. Most likely the Saxons would withdraw under the watchful eyes of the Roman cavalry, and sail away showing their arses and baring the tits of their female captives. Fortunately, the larger forts of the Saxon Shore – Branodunum, Gariannonum, Othona and the other strongholds north and south of the Tamesa – acted as a deterrent to any larger incursion and provided a place of sanctuary to anyone who could escape the Saxon axes. Nevertheless, it was simple for a few ships to ghost their way up an estuary in the dark, and it was up to Marcus and his cavalry to deal with them. They'd been coming for generations. Sometimes a trickle, sometimes a steady but manageable stream, and sometimes a deluge that brought fire and blood and slaughter to the length and breadth of the province.

'You know the Saxons, Aulus,' Marcus replied with a tight smile. 'Slippery as wetland eels.'

'Here we are.' They had arrived at a pair of ornate double doors guarded by a single soldier. 'We should talk again soon, Marcus. Your dazzling wit always brightens up the darkest corners of my troubled mind. Eels, ha, ha, you'll need to come up with something better than that.'

Marcus nodded to the soldier and the man knocked on the door.

'Enter.'

III

Inside the enormous room a hunched figure sat at a desk next to a large window overlooking the muddy brown waters of the Tamesa. Julius Chrysanthus looked up from between two neat piles of scrolls and waved Marcus to a seat in front of him. The *vicarius* had a long neck and bulging eyes that gave him a permanently surprised expression. His hair was styled in tight raven curls that could only be a wig, and he wore a tunic edged with gold ribbon beneath a thick cloak against the chill draught from the river. At a smaller desk close by, two clerks paused in their labours and flexed their aching, ink-stained fingers. 'If you will excuse us, prefect, I will just finish this letter before you present your report.' Chrysanthus cleared his throat. 'Where was I?'

'The necessities, lord,' the older of the two clerks whispered.

'Ah, yes. *As a result of the recent predations . . .*' The clerks' *styli* flew across the parchment in front of them. Marcus knew from his previous visits that the fastidious Chrysanthus always insisted on having two copies of his words recorded simultaneously, and would check them later for accuracy. If Marcus had been looking for a word to describe him on their first meeting, that word would have been 'ineffectual'. Now, he wasn't so sure. '*. . . we are lacking in all the usual necessities that miti-gate the privations of employment in a province which has so little to offer*

14

in compensation: oil of the olive tree, garum, of course, and wine of the better sort. I am aware of the impact recent events on the Rhenus have had on our naval capabilities, but I would entreat the Augustus to order six shiploads of the aforesaid necessities to proceed with a suitable escort from Gesoriacum to Londinium, at the earliest possible convenience, to provide succour for the residents therein, and ameliorate the effect of the recent, unavoidable rise in taxes . . . No, scratch that final part out, end it at *therein*, and add all the usual salutations.'

Chrysanthus took a sip from a silver cup at his right hand. Small beer, Marcus guessed; he would not allow wine to pass his lips during business, and Marcus knew better than to expect an offer of any.

'Now,' the *vicarius* paused to allow the clerks to position new sheets of parchment and refresh their *styli*, 'I bid welcome to Marcus Flavius Victor, *praefectus alae*, temporarily commanding the forces of the Saxon Shore. Your report please, prefect. The main points will suffice. I have no doubt all the fine detail will be in the written document.'

'Very well, lord.' Marcus winced at the scrape of the *styli* that accompanied his words. 'On the Feast Day of Saint Cornelius it was my privilege to command a force which intercepted one hundred Saxons who sailed on three ships from . . .'

Chrysanthus waited until Marcus concluded with a report of his most recent success a week earlier. 'So,' the *vicarius* said. 'It appears that I must congratulate you, prefect. Five Saxon raids on our coasts in the last four weeks, three successful interventions on your part, upwards of one hundred and sixty-seven raiders captured or killed for the loss of only three of your cavalrymen. Is that correct?'

'By God's grace it is, lord. Fortunately, the other incursions caused only minor damage and the deaths of a few old and sick villagers.'

'And you seized six ships to be sold off for the treasury?'

'I must have expressed myself poorly, lord,' – just how much did the old bastard know? – 'two of the captures were worm-eaten hulks immediately condemned by my shipmaster. We would have been risking lives even trying to sail them to Londinium. They were taken out to sea and burned to the water line.'

'Hulks indeed,' the rheumy eyes narrowed, 'if some of the examples we've seen at the dockside are any guide. It sometimes beggars belief that the Saxons have such a reputation as expert shipbuilders.'

'The Saxons who raid our coast are among the poorest,' Marcus felt bound to point out. 'Driven by hunger and privation to risk everything they have for plunder and slaves. They would come in willow coracles if they thought they could survive the voyage.'

'You wouldn't be selling these *condemned* ships back to the Saxons, would you, prefect?'

All Marcus could manage in reply was an outraged 'On my honour, lord . . .' before he realized the gurgling, choking sound emerging from Chrysanthus was actually laughter.

'I speak in jest, of course.' He waved a hand to tell the clerks to delete what they'd written. 'But if you knew what I do nothing would surprise you. Which brings us to the missing silver.' He picked up a scroll from the pile to his right. 'I have had a complaint from the *curator* of a village six miles inland from Branodunum about a raid just after the feast of the Epiphany. He said he'd had a report from a woman you released that not all the silver the Saxons took was returned to them.' The *vicarius* raised an eyebrow.

'I take a small portion of their silver because they don't pay their taxes and that means you can't afford to pay my men.' Marcus risked the almost-truth.

'Leave us.' Chrysanthus nodded. The clerks gathered up their writing materials and bowed before hurriedly exiting the room. Marcus waited, puzzling over the curious direction the interview had taken and wondering what came next. Chrysanthus seemed to be waiting for something, or perhaps he was just trying to put some thought into words. Eventually, he said: 'You must think me a weak old man, Marcus Flavius Victor?'

'I . . .'

'No,' the thin lips twitched into a smile, 'don't deny it. In many ways I *am* a weak old man, but it wasn't always so. When I was your age I was a soldier. That nonsense you were involved in before Longovicium could have seen your head on a block, but you persevered in any case. The only reason you still retain your head is that you won. Five years later, the Picts continue to mind their own business in their northern fastness beyond the Wall, because of you.'

'That situation may not last,' Marcus pointed out. 'As our weakness becomes ever more apparent, their strength grows. King Janus is unlikely to keep them in check for much longer.'

'And that is the real reason I brought you here, Marcus. At a time when Britannia has never needed more to be united it has never been more divided. Rome will not always be there for us. As far as Honorius is concerned, we are a small island a long, long way from Italia. A nuisance, not worthy of his time or trouble. Britannia will need men like Marcus Flavius Victor. Men who have a connection and a loyalty to the land and its people, and who are prepared to shed blood to defend it. Militarily, we are as divided as we are bureaucratically. What is required is a man who can unite the soldiery and lead them.'

Marcus shook his head with a wry smile. 'With the greatest respect, *vicarius*,' he said, and found he meant it, 'I doubt there is a more unsuitable man on this island.'

'I thought you would say that,' Chrysanthus said evenly. 'But I believe you are wrong. Let me put another premise to you, Marcus. If not you, then who? Oh, there are unscrupulous commanders who will be quick to gather their troops together and persuade some poor unfortunates to hail them Augustus or Caesar, or some other ludicrous title. What this island needs isn't some ambitious fool who will strip Britannia of her troops and leave her defenceless while he makes some crazed bid for the purple. It needs someone hard, even brutal, ruthless enough to do what needs to be done to take control and clever enough to keep it. Someone like you. You already have the loyalty of the Wall garrisons, and victory at Longovicium won you more friends among the fort commanders. Did you know there are men in the Sixth legion at Eboracum who worship your sister as a goddess in the belief that she led them to a bloodless victory over the Picts?'

'And you would trust me with that kind of power?'

'You—' Chrysanthus frowned as he was interrupted by a soft tap on the door frame.

'My apologies, *vicarius*.' The speaker was a tall, handsome man, slightly younger than Marcus, perhaps approaching forty. He had a long nose, intelligent grey eyes, and the easy manner that went with wealth and privilege.

Chrysanthus pursed his lips in evident distaste. 'You know Claudius Constantinus, of course.'

Marcus bowed. Constantinus was Britannia's *magister militum* and nominally his superior, but Chrysanthus had altered the chain of command so Marcus reported directly to the *vicarius*. Marcus knew Constantinus resented the change, as his next words seemed to confirm.

'I was just passing and learned that our defender of the Saxon Shore was here to tender his monthly report. Since the report will eventually come to me, I thought it would save time if I joined you.' Constantinus smiled. 'I hope I haven't spoiled your flow, Marcus?'

'As it happens, *magister militum*,' Chrysanthus said with a tight smile, 'this officer has completed his report to me. Fortunately, I have duties that take me elsewhere, so I will not have to endure it again. You may use this room if it suits your purpose. Marcus, you will think on what I said?'

'Of course, lord.' Marcus managed to hide his confusion. Chrysanthus pushed himself up from his desk. Marcus waited until he'd left the room before he picked up the scroll containing his report.

'Oh, there'll be no need for that.' Constantinus slipped into the *vicarius*'s seat without ceremony. 'Just think yourself fortunate that I've saved you from an hour-long lecture about the state of the province. Lord, he's a dull old dog, Chrysanthus.' He paused, evidently seeking Marcus's agreement, but Marcus stayed silent. 'You know, Marcus,' Marcus found himself the focus of the intense grey eyes, 'Londinium should be the richest city in the Empire. It has fallen before, any number of times, and risen to ever greater heights. It will rise again. Our trade is strangled, our frontiers besieged.' Constantinus was talking about Britannia now, not just Londinium. 'What Chrysanthus was about to tell you is that Rome will soon abandon us to our fate, if she has not already. What are we to do?'

'What can we do?' Marcus knew what Constantinus wanted to hear, but he wasn't in the mood to provide it. Let the man say it himself.

Constantinus didn't hesitate. 'We must show we have the strength to guide our own affairs.' Marcus nodded; there was no denying that, it was more or less the same message he'd had from Chrysanthus. But of course, there had to be more. 'To do that we need a strong man, a warrior who can command the loyalty and respect of all Britannia's troops.'

'As *magister militum* . . .'

'We both know that would not work. Nominally, I have control of the few thousand soldiers of the field army in the south, but in reality their loyalty is split between me and that old fool Chrysanthus. Terentius Cantaber, who commands the Sixth at Eboracum, the most powerful infantry force in the province, has little liking for me. On the other hand, he has the greatest respect for you as a soldier. And who moulded the garrison of the Wall into an army at time of need, and could do it again when the need is even greater? Marcus Flavius Victor.'

Marcus stared at him. Did he mean it? Of course he did. Because it made perfect sense. Everything he'd said was true. All of it was possible, perhaps even necessary, but he sensed there was more to come.

Constantinus waited for a reaction, and when none was forthcoming Marcus noticed a little twitch of irritation at the corner of his lip. 'I will do everything in my power to bring the forces of Britannia together under your command. We will create a single field army powerful enough to suppress any domestic threat. I will try to convince Chrysanthus to join us, but he is an old man with old-fashioned notions.' Marcus wondered if he'd missed the words 'of honour' or whether Constantinus thought they were too sensitive for his ears. The *magister militum*'s next words confirmed his suspicions about who had engineered this meeting. 'In any case, he is not the only bureaucrat capable of keeping a firm grip on the province's finances.' Aulus

Ostorianus's jolly features swam into Marcus's head. *We should talk again soon, Marcus.* Indeed, we should. 'Whoever is in charge, the civilian situation is of secondary importance until we have created stability and we can only achieve that through the military. From a position of strength we will negotiate treaties with your old friends the Picts, the Scotti, and Niall of the Nine Hostages on Mona, which will buy us time . . .'

Marcus wondered at the way the man conjured up a solution to the province's woes that had evaded generations of the Empire's soldiers and diplomats, but he only had one question.

'Buy time for what?'

'However strong we are,' Constantinus said carefully, 'the long-term prosperity of this province and this island can only be achieved against the background of a stable and peaceful Roman Empire. Those who have cast Britannia aside are no longer capable of gaining that outcome. Stilicho and Honorius have twice allowed the barbarians to reach the gates of Italia; it is only a matter of time before they kick in the door. Stilicho is finished and Honorius is weak. Like Britannia, Rome needs a strong leader. You once had ambitions to be Emperor, Marcus, but the time was not right.' It wasn't true, it had all been a ruse to bring Briga and her Picts to a place where she could be defeated. Did Constantinus know about Marcus's blood-father, Magnus Maximus, a great Roman general who had fulfilled that very ambition and set himself up as joint ruler of the West? If he did it would only make him more certain of his man, as his next words confirmed. 'Once we have consolidated what we have in Britannia, I would propose that we take ship to Gaul, where I have already prepared the ground. There I will place the purple on your shoulders and the gold crown upon your brow and proclaim you Augustus.'

He waited for the acknowledgement of his genius.

Marcus laughed. Oh, it was neatly done: the appeals to his vanity and his conscience, the precise placing of each gaming counter – power, strength, stability, peace – and, finally, the hook is set. *I will place you on the same throne on which your father sat.* Suicide. Marcus had a finely honed sense of his talents and abilities, but he had no illusions that even a mix of cunning, ruthlessness and a willingness to steal, cheat, and, yes, kill, would keep a Brigantian bastard alive for long in the circles in which Constantinus mixed. No, the brute would serve his purpose, whatever that may be, and then he would be disposed of. He felt a dangerous glow ignite inside.

He met the other man's eyes with a cold stare which contained an unmistakable message. 'I fear you have mistaken your man, Constantinus,' he said softly. 'I am many things and I have done many things, but I would never play the traitor.'

When he turned away he had to clench his fists to stop his hands shaking.

IV

Venta Icenorum (Caistor St Edmund)

'I was angry,' he told Valeria. 'And I think what Chrysanthus said unnerved me. Yes, we can feel it happening, but to hear it from him . . .'

'So one man hinted he would give you control of every warrior in Britannia, and the kind of power that would effectively make you king of all the Britons, and another pledged to wrap you in the purple, all within the hour? It sometimes amazes me that you've lived so long, Marcus.' She shook her head. 'You really just turned and walked away after everything Constantinus told you?'

He shrugged. 'I was glad to get back to the wetlands. The air here may be damp, but at least it doesn't stink of treason.'

They sat in the main room of the large, fortified villa, within a morning's ride of the coast, that he'd commandeered as his head-quarters. A fire crackled in a brazier near the window, but made little impact on the chill air. The villa was on one of the few slightly raised areas of ground in the wetlands and sat at the centre of a substantial estate, with a village where the people who worked the farms and factories lived in damp, noxious hovels. High walls surrounded the house, an unusual feature that must have provided the owners with an illusion of security as the Saxon raids became ever more frequent.

'It never occurred to you,' Valeria continued, 'that you were putting your neck in a noose, or that by playing Constantinus along and asking for time to consider the offer you might have gathered the information Chrysanthus needed to put a noose around *his*? You'll need to kill him, Marcus. Because if you don't, he'll kill you.'

That thought certainly *had* occurred to him, but it came as a surprise to hear it articulated with such cold ruthlessness by his sister.

'How?'

'You're the one who's well versed in murder, brother, not me. Why don't you talk to Zeno?'

'Poison?' Marcus almost spilled his drink. 'In Christ's name, woman, what do you think I am?'

'Since when did you become so particular?' Valeria said. 'You either want him dead or you don't. If you do, it has to look like an accident or Chrysanthus will feel honour bound to investigate. Of course, there is another option.' She looked him in the eye. 'Perhaps it's time to leave. Time to find Brenus?'

He nodded. It made sense. But . . .

'There's also this.' He handed her the scroll case that had arrived from Stilicho. 'It complicates things even further, if you can believe that.'

She took the scroll from the pouch and unrolled it, picking up an oil lamp to provide more light. He saw her eyes widen as she read the content, but she made no comment until she'd reached the end. 'You're right,' she said, 'it does complicate things. In essence three of the most powerful men in the Empire have made you an offer you can't afford to refuse. At best, you will have to disappoint two of them, perhaps with fatal consequences, and all three options go against your own desire, which is to release Brenus from his captivity. What will you do, Marcus?'

He shook his head. 'I don't know. I feel like a fly trapped in a spider's web. The more I wriggle the more I become enmeshed.'

'Then perhaps I can help you find an answer.'

*

Marcus ran his eyes over the sleek little ship moored in the shadow of a giant willow tree and his heart soared at the import of what he was seeing. The final piece had fallen into place. She was clinker-built as most of the Saxon boats were, with her side planks overlapping each other, and fixed to a light frame that would allow her to ride high in the waves. They'd have used green wood to build her – oak by the looks of it – because newly harvested timber was easier to work and more flexible than seasoned. Her mast was unstepped for ease of concealment, but Leof already had men fitting the oars, and on a windless day like this he wouldn't need her sail even when he reached the open sea.

'Is she as good as she looks?' Marcus called across to the young Saxon.

'As dry as a saint's old bones and well found, maybe six months old,' Leof assured him. 'She'll swim like an otter in open water.'

'When did you capture her?' Marcus asked Valeria.

'We had word of a Saxon raid the day after you left for Londinium,' she said. 'There were twenty of them, the youths of some coastal community sent out to make mischief far away from home. We couldn't save the village, but we ambushed them on the way back to the ship, killed them all, freed their captives and recovered this silver.' She nudged one of the sacks at her feet.

'Good,' Marcus smiled. 'Take what the men are owed in wages and send the rest to Chrysanthus in Londinium. I have a feeling I'm going to need his good will before long.'

'Perhaps you could ask him to free us from our duties for a month while we look for Brenus?'

'If I thought there was any chance of him agreeing, I would,' Marcus said. 'But all it would do is make him keep a closer rein on me. I can hardly break wind without him knowing, as it is. Half the servants at the villa are probably in his pay.'

'Then how will we ever get away?'

'God will provide,' he assured her, with a mock piety he knew would infuriate her.

Leof appeared in the little ship's prow.

'As far as anybody else is concerned,' Marcus told him, 'she's an anti-quated hulk with rotting timbers and a bilge you could take a bath in. We burned her to the water line and sank what was left.'

Leof grinned. 'So I take her to the others?'

'You do. And when our business is done, this one's yours.' The grin grew wider. If he lived to enjoy it, Marcus had just given the young man a fortune and a potential source of income for life.

When they returned to the villa, Marcus pleaded exhaustion after a long day in the saddle and announced he was taking to his cot early.

'Are you sure, Marcus?' Valeria asked. 'Perhaps it would be good to take your mind off all this for a while? There's a travelling circus in the village. Clowns, jugglers, illusionists and acrobats, and exotic beasts. We were planning to give it a visit.'

'I've had enough of illusionists for a lifetime after my little chat with Constantinus,' Marcus smiled. 'But don't let that stop you.' He went to a wooden chest, retrieved a small leather pouch and handed it to Valeria. 'Invite anyone who's off duty and buy them a drink at the tavern. Good night.'

Marcus woke, instantly alert, but uncertain why, and the depth of the darkness confirmed dawn was still a long way off. A few moments told him there was no point in staying in bed, he was never going to get back to sleep. He wrapped himself in a cloak and, with a smile that would have sent a shiver through his sentries, went to inspect the guard.

The two men at the door of the main complex straightened as he emerged into the torchlight, no sleepyheads here. 'Anything to report?'

'No, lord,' said Tosodio, a trooper who'd deserted the Sixth legion to join Marcus. 'It's all been quiet since those lucky bastards rolled back from the tavern. Cold, though.' He brushed droplets of water from his cloak. 'Might even snow tonight.'

Marcus nodded in agreement and walked towards the gateway in the south wall. 'Who goes?' The challenge came from the shadow of a small hut the sentries used.

'Marcus Flavius Victor, prefect Ala Sabiniana.'

'State the watchword and approach and be recognized.'

'The watchword for tonight is Sabinus, Falco. I should know because I set it.'

'Sorry, sir.' The tone was troubled but resolute. '*Draconarius* Luko insisted no one was to pass without the watchword, not even the Emperor himself.'

'All right, Falco.' Marcus walked past him to the bottom of the steps leading to two ostentatious but more or less pointless towers flanking the gate. 'You may tell the *draconarius* that your beer ration is hereby reinstated.'

'Thank you, sir.' He could hear the grin in the young man's voice.

A single guard in the gatehouse overlooking the walkway: Senecio, who never seemed to sleep. 'Lord,' he said, as Marcus reached the top of the stairs.

'How did you know it was me?'

'By the sound of your footsteps and the fuss that fool Falco made of you.'

'I'll just make a circuit of the walls. All quiet?'

'It is here,' the Numidian said. 'But who knows elsewhere. I told Luko we should have a man on each wall . . .'

'But he said I didn't think it was necessary?'

'That's right, lord. Maybe I'm just getting nervous in my old age.' A flash of white teeth accompanied the words.

'No,' Marcus said. 'Maybe I'm just not nervous enough. I'll talk to Luko in the morning.'

The walls stood three times the height of a full-grown man, with the villa at their centre, and encompassed an area perhaps a hundred paces across. Marcus left the shelter of the tower and walked out into the darkness, and immediately wished he'd thought to snatch up a thicker tunic. The icy wind came from the north-east and cut through his cloak like a knife, carrying intermittent squalls of rain and sleet that quickly soaked his hair and ran down his neck. He pulled the cloak closer and hauled the voluminous hood over his head.

A few miles to the east the restless waves of the Mare Germanicum would be pounding the muddy shoreline, but Marcus could see nothing beyond the light of the torches fluttering in their sheltered niches every twenty paces along the wall. He reached the first corner and turned into the wind. Fool, he thought, for coming out into this, but once you started something it was as well to finish it. Not quite the waste of time he'd thought, though. Some quirk of the wind had extinguished the torches on the north wall. He'd send Falco to relight them and ensure they stayed lit.

Marcus hurried on until he reached the next corner, but he'd only gone a few paces along the north parapet when he heard the distinct sound of metal on stone behind him. He turned instinctively, left hand raised to pull back the hood that inhibited his vision and hearing, and the right reaching for the sword that wasn't at his waist. Idiot.

A bigger idiot than he knew, it turned out. With a soft hissing sound something dropped over his head to trap his left hand against his throat with terrible force, tightening with every heartbeat until it was sawing against the flesh of his palm and the soft skin of his neck. Some kind of cord, his mind told him. Not that it mattered. Whatever it was, it was going to kill him if he didn't do something about it. His attacker tried to kick his legs from under him, but his feet were solidly planted as he tried to force his hand away from his throat. He could feel the fists that held the cord working against the back of his neck and he knew that if he fell there'd be a knee in his spine and, hand on the throat or not, he'd be dead in seconds. The assassin growled softly, like a mongrel chewing on a cast-out bone. Marcus clawed backward with his right hand, trying to get his fingers round into the other man's groin to tear at his scrotum, but all he felt for his trouble was a piece of solid thigh muscle. He was choking now, the breath restricted to a tiny passage as his throat was crushed. Soon his strength would ebb away and his killer would be able to finish the job at his leisure. The thought enraged him and he threw his head backwards feeling a satisfying

27

crunch and causing the iron grip on his neck to loosen marginally. The assassin cursed and the cord retightened instantly, accompanied by a raised knee in his back to improve his purchase. Marcus felt his vision begin to fade. Not long now.

A sharp slap, like a leather rein whipped against a horse's flank, and he was falling forward with the killer's weight on his back. Some ploy to make him give in to the inevitable? But the cord loosened and stayed loose and the weight against his spine remained inert. He pulled the cord free from his neck and, with the last of his strength, heaved the weight off. His head spun as he pushed himself to his feet and the breath rasped in his throat. The shadowy figure of his attacker lay hunched against the base of the parapet. As Marcus stood swaying, Senecio, his short, curved bow in one hand and a torch in the other, ran at full pelt along the parapet towards him. The Numidian held the brand over the fallen man and Marcus saw the long shaft jutting from the assassin's left temple. With a muttered curse, Senecio put his foot on the dead man's neck and hauled his arrow free.

Marcus looked from the assassin back to the gate tower. A hundred paces, in the dark, and in a blustery wind. Their heads could only have been two handspans apart. Suddenly he felt sick and his legs threatened to collapse under him. Senecio dropped the torch and put out a hand to steady him. The Numidian grinned.

'It never occurred to me I might miss, lord.'

28

V

By the time they reached the courtyard the villa was in turmoil, with lights everywhere and men spilling from doorways. Valeria appeared, unruly dark hair framing her head like a lion's mane, buckling a sword belt over a linen tunic that reached to mid-thigh and utterly unconscious of the eyes drawn to her long, pale legs.

'What happened?'

'A professional killer, I think.' Marcus massaged his throat. 'He almost had me. God only knows how he managed to scale the walls.'

Two men carried the body from the parapet and dumped it in the centre of the courtyard. Ninian brought a lamp and shone it on the dead man's face. Weathered, bearded features with a prominent hook of a nose and an expression that reflected bewilderment at a death he hadn't seen coming. 'I've seen this man before,' Valeria said. 'Zeno?' she called her husband forward.

'One of the tumblers from the circus,' he confirmed. 'There were four of them, very accomplished acrobats. They'd stand on each other's shoulders and juggle flaming torches between them. That would explain how he was able to climb the wall.'

'Constantinus?' Valeria said quietly.

Marcus bit his lip. 'I don't know . . . Ninian?' he called to the former priest he'd freed from Pictish slavery. 'Take some men and have the members of the circus questioned. Bring his friends here if they've been foolish enough to hang around.'

Zeno was rooting around beneath the man's tunic and came out with a leather pouch. He opened it to reveal some kind of diagram. 'It's a plan of the villa,' he said. 'A very exact plan. Someone knows an awful lot about the Ala Sabiniana.'

'There are many ways this information could be gathered,' Marcus pointed out. 'The village women clean for us. Tradesmen, craftsmen who did the repairs when we took the place over.'

'That's true,' Valeria agreed. 'But not many of them would have known the exact room where you slept.' She showed him where a cross marked his quarters. 'It was just his good fortune, or yours, that he happened to come on you while you were walking the walls.'

Marcus felt a chill run through him. Was it possible one of his own had marked him for death?

A commotion at the gate interrupted his thoughts. Ninian and his men herded three prisoners inside with the points of their spears. They wore dark clothing and might have been the brothers of the dead assassin.

'We found them in the bushes between here and the village with four horses. They must have been waiting for their friend here.'

'Tie their hands and set up a brazier over by the drain.'

While the coals were heating, Marcus studied the three men. Cowed for the moment, but he didn't doubt that given the chance they'd be over the walls and gone before a man could lay a hand on them. Muscular and lithe, they had the spare look of men who made their living on the road.

'Bring that one forward.' He pointed to the tallest of the three. When the man stood before him, he used a poker to stir the coals so they hissed and sparked in the metal bowl, and left the iron rod to heat.

'You know how this works,' he said to the man. 'There's a hard way and an easy way. The hard way involves hooks and knives and you'll end up telling me what I want in the end anyway. You may be brave,

30

and you may even, in some way, think it's honourable to stay silent, but all you'll be doing is extending the pain for no purpose. Let's start with this,' he showed the man the map of the villa. 'Who gave you it?'

The assassin shook his head. He spoke an odd, almost antiquated form of Latin, with an accent so strong that at times Marcus had trouble understanding him.

'Only Bato knew.' He saw the look in Marcus's eyes and winced. 'I know you'll think I'm lying, but however much you torture me it won't change anything. He was told to contact a man in Londinium at a certain place, at a certain time.'

'In the fort or the palace?' Constantinus or his ally Aulus?

'Neither. In a tavern down by the river. He told us to stay outside. We never saw who he met.'

'So you're telling me you have no idea who you were working for?'

'No.' The dark eyes flared with something like defiance. 'We received our orders from the *magister officiorum* in the court of the Emperor Honorius at Ravenna when we arrived there from Metulum.'

A hiss of disbelief from Valeria. Marcus wasn't certain which caused the greater shock, the fact that Honorius had so swiftly confirmed Stilicho's prediction that the Emperor would like to see him dead, or that the killers had arrived at his court from the general's current location. If it was a coincidence it was an unlikely one.

'You know the name Stilicho?'

'Of course. The general arrived in Metulum just before we received word of our mission. But I doubt he has any part in this. At Ravenna we were given warrants to travel to Londinium, under our normal guise of performers. We were not to strike until we had knowledge of your precise location and proof of your guilt.'

'Proof of my guilt?'

'A meeting had been arranged, with a man posing as a fellow conspirator. If you attended, it would be proof of Marcus Flavius Victor's part in a plot to wrest control of Britannia and ultimately topple the Emperor. You were seen with him at the palace.'

Marcus felt the fury building up inside him. Not just at the prisoners, but at those who'd sent them, and set this intricate trap from which there appeared no escape.

'And then you came here to kill me.' The words were a death sentence and both men knew it. 'I should have you all cut to pieces on the off chance that you're lying.'

'But you know I do not lie, and you said . . .'

'I made no promises,' Marcus snarled. 'In any case, what does a backstabbing assassin know of honour?'

'Marcus.' He'd almost forgotten Valeria's presence. 'We need to talk.'

He left the assassin by the brazier to contemplate his short and painful future and walked off to join his sister.

'You shouldn't do this,' she said quietly.

'Why not?' he said. 'It would be simple justice.'

'By killing them aren't you only confirming your guilt to the Emperor?'

A bitter laugh escaped Marcus. 'It doesn't appear my guilt is in any doubt.'

'There is a better way,' she insisted. 'These men were only following their orders, mistaken though those orders are. Whatever they have done they are loyal servants of the Emperor, doing their duty as any soldier would do.'

'Then they must accept their fate as any soldier would do.'

'You are beset on all sides and you believe you are trapped,' Valeria continued as if he hadn't spoken. 'But there is still hope.'

'What would you have me do?'

'First you can send a message to the Emperor.' She told him how.

Marcus returned to the brazier. 'Bring the others forward,' he ordered. 'And keep a tight grip on them.' He put on a glove of thick leather and picked up the poker, which was by now glowing a dull red at the tip.

'No!' the youngest of the assassins cried as he was hustled towards the fire. The man Marcus had been questioning grimaced and began to whisper a prayer.

Marcus approached the first man and raised the glowing poker so the assassin flinched away from the heat. 'Your name?'

The man licked his lips. 'My name is Pinnes.'

'Well, Pinnes, I am reminded that despite the wicked nature of your crime you are servants of the Emperor and were only doing your duty as you saw it.' Pinnes almost buckled at the knees with relief, but Marcus continued relentlessly. 'Nevertheless, there is a price that must be paid.' He raised the poker and Pinnes howled and bucked as the tip seared the flesh of his forehead. Marcus kept his hand steady until he'd drawn the letter C. When he'd completed the brand to his satisfaction, he ordered the others brought forward in turn.

'The pain will remind you that your actions have consequences,' he told them when all three had been branded, their faces now grey with agony. 'This marks you as condemned and ensures you will no longer be able to pursue your murderous profession. The fact that you are alive will provide proof of Marcus Flavius Victor's loyalty to his Emperor. Now, return to whoever sent you and pray he is as merciful as I am.' He nodded to Ninian. 'Take them back where you found them.'

He pulled the glove off and threw it onto the fire. Valeria had watched the men's torment without a change of expression and once again it occurred to him how alike they were. 'And now?' he demanded.

'Now we find Brenus and free him.'

VI

'I'm giving you another opportunity to get yourselves killed, because you're the best of the best.' Most of the troopers from Valeria's squadron grinned at Marcus's description of their prowess, but a few faces were more sombre. 'Most of you were with me at Longovicium, but there'll be precious little glory in this fight, even if we win. And no honour. From the moment we take ship we'll be fugitives from the Empire. Once we land, we'll be in the lair of the Saxon wolves. That is where my son is, and where I must go. If any soldier wishes to stay behind, no one will think the worse of him. But decide quickly. When the man who sent the assassins discovers they've failed, he won't be far behind them.'

Was there another option? Marcus couldn't think of one.

Only Stilicho held out the possibility of a reprieve and reaching Stilicho meant taking to the sea. Once they'd rescued Brenus from his captivity in Saxonia, Marcus and Valeria had worked out a tentative plan to sail south and either make their way through Gaul to Italia, or sail up the Rhenus river. Just names to Marcus, but Zeno had passed that way on his journey from Constantinopolis to Britannia. Stilicho's letter and warrant would hopefully provide passage, fresh horses and accommodation. The general spoke of an Empire in turmoil. With a little diligent planning, the chaos Stilicho described could be used to avoid the type of authority that might have Marcus's name on a list once his departure from Britannia became known.

He'd chosen the thirty men he trusted most, plus Valeria, Zeno and Luko. None of them had taken advantage of his offer to stay behind. They bustled around the courtyard of the villa gathering together the gear and the rations they'd need for the initial part of the journey.

Julius was saddling up his mount when Tosodio, the former legionary, approached him. 'I thought you told me your brother offered you land and wealth if you joined him in the north? Why would you exchange that for what looks like a one-way trip to Hades? Trupios I can understand,' he said, referring to one of the German warriors who had stayed with them after Longovicium, 'he's more or less going home, like Leof. But you have a good reason to stay.'

'It's true that Janus said he'd make me a lord,' Julius admitted cheerfully. 'But the squadron's my home now and Marcus can't recover his boy on his own. Besides, I consulted a druid.'

'Rubbish,' Tosodio scoffed, but his voice held a hint of uncertainty. 'There's no such things as druids any more.'

'You can think what you like,' Julius shrugged. 'But some still follow the old ways. A girl in the village showed me a way through the swamp. An old man lives alone on an island. An ancient, with white hair and beard and a copper torc at his neck he said was a druid's mark. His hut stank of fish.'

'What did he say, this druid?'

'He told me that all that awaited me in the north was pain and death, and I believed him. If Janus gave me land he'd have to take it from somebody, and like as not that somebody would want it back. So I'll stay with Marcus, and the men I trust.' He punched Tosodio on the arm. 'Even you, you miserable bastard.'

They'd discovered very quickly that when you were hunting Saxons it paid to travel light. A man sheathed in chain armour and wearing an iron helmet was as useful as a marble statue when he was up to his knees in swamp mud, and like as not dead if he came off his horse in the dark. Marcus, like his soldiers, wore a jerkin of overlapping strips of hardened leather reinforced at the shoulders and chest with iron plates, and a simple pot helmet of the same material. The boiled leather would turn a sword edge, but not an axe, so the trick, as Luko often pointed out, was to stay well clear of any Saxon swinging an axe.

Leof had berthed his four charges in one of the winding channels off a secluded estuary far from human habitation, and thus less likely to attract any prying Saxon raiders. They would be crewed by Saxon incomers recruited by Leof and lured by the promise of ownership of the transports once Marcus had no further need for them. The river had gently sloping banks where the boats could be safely beached for repairs and the alterations that were required to make them capable of carrying the horses. They lay in a row with the smaller boat closest to the river mouth. The young Saxon had used Marcus's authority to recruit craftsmen and set up workshops and tented living quarters among the trees on the riverside. The three transports would carry fourteen horses apiece in seven stalls in front of the mast and seven behind. Two of the ships were already fitted out with the wooden stalls, and every available craftsman was working on the third. They'd tested two horses on the first completed ship and had quickly discovered that a horse left to its own devices in a wooden stall in heavy seas was as likely to break a leg as not. After some thought and experimentation, Leof had come up with an answer. He fitted the stalls with heavy ringbolts to which padded leather slings were attached to support the animals' bodies. Each animal would consume close to two amphorae of water every day, plus six quarts of oats or barley, and as much hay as Marcus's quartermasters could provide. Almost every inch of cargo space not taken up by the stalls would be needed for water barrels, sacks of feed, wine and supplies for the crew. That was why the swift little sailer Valeria had captured the week before was such a gift from God. Instead of every man jammed into the already overfilled hulls of the transports, twenty would travel in the relative comfort of the new ship. The others would be split among the transport ships, alternating their duties between looking after the horses, sleeping and keeping the

Saxon captains and crews honest. Marcus had no doubt it would be tempting to simply sail the ships to the skippers' former home ports in Saxonia rather than fulfil their contract. To ensure they complied, the only men to sail armed would be Marcus's cavalry troopers, though he'd agreed to have a chest of swords on board against the event of an attack by Frisian pirates.

'I still think we should have cut doors in the side above the water line for the ramps,' Marcus greeted Leof when the squadron had made its way through the maze of fields and marshes to the inlet where the ships lay beached on the muddy bank. 'It would have saved a lot of time and effort in the long run.'

'I told you, lord, no matter how much silver you offered them, none of these men would sail across the Mare Germanicum in a boat with a hole cut in the hull. We Saxons like the gods on our side and it stands to reason the gods wouldn't take kindly to cutting a big hole in a perfectly good ship.'

'No matter,' Marcus conceded. 'It's too late now in any case. How long until the last ship is ready?'

'We'll need another day to complete the work, lord. And half a day to load them. It depends on the horses, and you know how nervous the buggers get about anything new.'

'We need to work faster,' Marcus frowned. 'Our enemies could already be on the way here.'

Marcus had sent word to Chrysanthus that he was taking ship to intercept a new Saxon raid, but he doubted if that would fool Constantinus. The *magister militum* was probably already on the road with a cavalry regiment. Leof had done a good job of concealing the ships, but Marcus was fairly certain that, remote as the location was, nothing would have escaped the sharp eyes of the hunters and fishermen who used the area. Once someone in officialdom started asking questions it wouldn't take long for the curious story of the phantom ships and their shy owners to come out. Then the wolves would be truly loosed.

In preparation for that moment, he ordered Luko and three others to form a screen of lookouts three miles inland. They would watch the most likely routes to the site while the horses and the last of the supplies were loaded.

Time and tide and weather. Everything had to be right. Yet to Marcus's frustrated eye everything appeared to be going wrong. They'd completed the alterations on time, but he could sense a growing menace that was reflected in the tense faces of the men. They could only sail with a high tide and they needed to sail by night. If they missed the next high tide they would be stranded here helpless for another full day. To add to his worries, the wind was strengthening, rippling across the surface of the river and whipping through the reed beds.

And somewhere out there the forces of darkness were gathering.

VII

Marcus called Leof across. 'What do you think?'

Leof blew out his cheeks. 'The wind's brisk, but as long as it stays where it is, we'll be fine. We'll row downriver and then out past the bar. Once we're in the open sea it will carry us where we want to go, unless it changes.'

'And if it does?' Valeria asked. Marcus wasn't the only one who was nervous. What little experience she had of ships had always been within sight of land and the open ocean was unknown territory.

'Then it will carry us where *it* wants to go. Of course,' he looked at the sky and frowned, 'if the wind freshens any further who knows what may happen. It will make for an interesting journey. I would pray to your God, lady, that it doesn't. If Jesus was truly a fisherman he will understand.'

'It was Petrus who was the fisherman, Leof. As you well know.' Valeria glared. The Saxon might be a Christian in name only, but he was no fool. She glanced at Marcus. 'Ninian asked me if you would like him to bless the ships before we sail?'

Marcus looked to Leof, who was clearly sceptical. 'For myself, it would do no harm, but my countrymen who are going to sail the transports would not thank you for it, and I believe it may do more harm than good. They have their own gods and it will be to them they look. They are already unhappy we don't trust them with weapons. May I make a suggestion, lord?'

'Of course,' Marcus said.

'Let Ninian bless *our* ship and give her a suitable name. We are all Christians and it will please the men.'

'It won't trouble the other shipmasters?'

'I don't believe so, lord.'

'Then, if we have time, we will make it so,' Marcus said with appropriate gravity. 'But we must have the last of the horses on board first.'

'When will you bring the scouts in?' Valeria asked.

'I've told three of them to return before dusk so we can board their horses in daylight. Luko has agreed to stay out until dark. There's a risk we won't have time to board his beast, but I think it's one worth taking.'

Later, Marcus knelt beside his men as Ninian stood over them and delivered a prayer calling for God's grace to favour the ship that would carry them to Saxonia to save the soul of Brenus. He completed the service by reciting a parable about a whale, whose significance Marcus didn't understand, casting water over the ship's bow from a pewter cup etched with reminders of other Christian stories. She was to be called *Heart of Petrus*.

Afterwards Marcus asked Ninian about the name. 'Well, Saint Petrus was the father of the church and the first bishop of Rome, lord. He must have been a brave man because when he knew he was about to be crucified he asked to be executed head down, because he was not worthy to die in the manner of our Saviour. It seemed appropriate that our journey should be watched over by a brave man with a great heart. I hope I have done right?'

'Of course,' Marcus assured him. 'But I'm curious. The whale?'

'I only know one other parable involving water, lord,' Ninian grinned. 'And that is about our blessed Lord turning water into wine. Under the circumstances the whale seemed more appropriate.'

When Ninian was gone, Marcus studied the mud below the ships and heaved a sigh of relief at the sight of the rising water trickling into

40

hollows and footprints low on the bank. He filled in time by inspecting the other transports. With the horses and stores aboard there would barely be enough room for the crews to pull their oars, but that couldn't be helped. They would have to manage. He checked the stalls and slings. The animals sensed his tension and pulled at their tethers and shuffled their hooves, but the men had done their work well and the leather straps were just tight enough to carry their weight without causing them any discomfort.

Where were the scouts?

With dusk falling, he told Leof to pay the craftsmen what they were owed, along with a bonus to keep their mouths shut. At last the scouts appeared, including Julius, who came to make his report as Marcus ordered them to board their mounts.

'Luko said to tell you he'd seen signs of activity in the woods up towards the settlement. Deer and wild boar flushed into the open and flocks disturbed. It could be just a patrol, but he thought not. If they come before full dark, he'll try to distract them.'

Marcus looked down at the river in the growing gloom; the glint of water was a few inches higher now. With the craftsmen gone he ordered the huts dismantled and thrown into the marsh. No chance of concealing their presence entirely, of course, but anything that could sow confusion and make his enemies hesitate was worth doing. When the work was completed, he ordered every man but himself, Valeria and Zeno aboard the ships.

'He'll come,' Valeria assured him as they stood looking west while the light ran through its nightly ritual from dusty silver, through iron grey and cobalt to pitch black. It was only then they saw the little pinpricks of light among the reeds in the far distance. If it had been summer Marcus might have mistaken them for fireflies.

'Christus,' Zeno whispered. 'They're searching for someone.'

'Quickly, get to the ship.' Marcus ran with them to the *Heart of Petrus*, where Leof hung over the side staring at the water creeping slowly up the hull. 'Are we ready to sail?' He knew the answer even before he asked the question.

Leof shook his head. 'Another hour, perhaps a little less if we're prepared to take a risk. But I won't answer for us floating any sooner than that. Are you coming aboard?'

Marcus shook his head. He trudged through the mud and back up the bank towards the clearing where the workshops had been.

The last ship in the line still had its ramp down, but he ordered it withdrawn. It wasn't, he told himself, because he didn't believe Luko would be coming back, only that when he did, they'd have no time to board the *draconarius*'s mount. Luko was the ever-present who'd ridden at his side for a dozen years and more. Not quite a friend, and sometimes an irritant, but the thought of losing Luko was suddenly unbearable. A bad omen, though Valeria told him he wasn't meant to believe in such superstitions, and a terrible start to his quest to free his son.

The torches had moved away to the left and he experienced a flare of new hope. Whatever happened now they should have time to get the ships into the estuary. Hopefully, it also meant Luko was still alive and using every ounce of his wits to lure their adversaries away from the river.

He cast a glance at the dark, swirling water. It couldn't be long now. Logic dictated that he should return to the ship, but he kept his feet planted in the muddy sward. He wouldn't abandon his old comrade just yet. He allowed the minutes to pass until the pinpricks of light moved to the right again and he realized they were appreciably closer. All he could hear around him was the whisper of the reeds and the whistle of the wind through the skeletal branches of the trees. A shout somewhere in the distance. He closed his eyes, trying to test the level of threat with the inner senses that had always served him so well. They were closer, much closer. The torches had been a ruse. Leof called a warning. He sprinted towards the ship.

'Cast off. Cast off.' He roared the order as he ran past the moored ships. Immediately they pushed out into the centre of the stream. Marcus reached the *Heart* and leapt aboard. His eyes darted to the shore. Still time. 'Wave them past before you let go,' he called to Leof, ignoring the young Saxon's glance of alarm.

Leof did as he was instructed and the three more cumbersome vessels rowed past the *Heart of Petrus* and out into the estuary. They waited a few more moments before shouts from among the trees along the bank told Marcus it was now or never. 'Cast off,' he ordered. The rowers on the right side of the ship dug their oars into the mud and pushed the slim vessel out into the river.

Marcus was just coming to terms with the fact that Luko was gone when he heard a tremendous crashing amongst the riverside scrub. A horse broke from the trees with its rider low on its back, and plunged directly into the river.

Luko.

The cavalryman swam the animal towards the ship and slipped from the saddle trying to grasp a rope thrown by a crewman. In the darkness, he missed at the first attempt and floundered for a few moments as the *Heart* slid past him. If Luko had been wearing chain armour he'd have gone straight to the bottom. Instead his padded leather tunic trapped enough air to keep him afloat. The vital seconds allowed him to snatch a second rope and his comrades swiftly hauled him aboard. He fell spluttering to the deck at Marcus's feet.

'Sorry, lord.' Luko shook his head as he looked up and sent a spray of water droplets flying from his beard. 'I managed to draw their attention for a while, but they got between me and the ship. There are hundreds of the bastards. A full cohort, I'd reckon.' Marcus helped him to his feet and he looked over the side to where a splash of white foam in the gloom showed where his mount had struggled out of the river and onto the bank. 'A pity. I liked that horse.'

By now the oars were biting the water with real urgency and powering the sleek little ship after her larger consorts. More shouting from the shore as men called to each other in confusion. They may not have known precisely where the vessels had been moored, but, clearly, they expected to find something. Torches flickered among the reeds as the *Heart of Petrus* disappeared around a bend and slipped into the darkness. Ahead, the river widened before it reached the estuary. They continued through the darkness in silence. Leof had tested this route at every stage of the tide and knew every twist and turn, passage and obstacle. As they reached the river mouth they saw a cluster of torches on the southern headland.

'Should we move closer to the north bank?' Marcus suggested.

'Only if you want her bottom ripped out, lord.' The darkness hid Leof's smile. 'Best we stay in the main channel.'

Someone didn't like to see them leaving without sending a message. A single flaming arrow arced out from among the torches and dropped to hiss into the water a few feet from the ship's side.

And then they were gone.

VIII

A day into the voyage and Marcus wished he'd let Bato the assassin do his worst. They sailed due east from the Saxon Shore with a stiff breeze on their left beam. Not that Marcus knew much about it, or cared, huddled in his soaking cloak in the bottom of the boat and retching into the bilge. At sea, the *Heart of Petrus* was a fragile, ever-shifting mass of planks and ropes that creaked, groaned and hissed ominously with every passing wave. The great square sail fluttered and snapped in the wind above him, held taut by ropes as thick in circumference as Marcus's arm, driving the ship through the water at what seemed a terrifying speed. Even at this speed they had pace to spare, for Leof was holding the *Heart* in check to keep station with the transports out there somewhere in the rain. A few feet away the mutter of prayers pinpointed where Valeria lay in Zeno's arms, finding her own way to endure the ordeal as the *Heart*'s bow crunched through another wave and dropped like a stone into the valley beyond, taking their stomachs with it.

Clouds the colour of pewter and ash scudded across the sky. From the brief glimpse Marcus managed before he brought up his breakfast, the sea was of a similar dull hue, only a seething mass tipped with whitecaps of spume and froth. Leof dutifully brought him reports of occasional sightings of fishing craft, but what he was supposed to make of the information he wasn't certain, because he'd never felt so helpless. It was an uncomfortable situation for a man used to command, and one he didn't enjoy. There was no denying that in a crisis he'd be about as useful as the ship's cat, if they had one.

So far, the voyage had been entirely uneventful, though it hardly felt like that to those who'd never sailed in open water, and to whom each crashing wave had the potential to carry them to a watery grave. Marcus knew that when Constantinus returned to Londinium he would have done everything in his power to requisition ships to hunt down the fugitives, but Leof showed little concern they would be discovered. If Marcus was escaping from the authorities in Britannia, it would make more sense to head for the coast of Germania or Gaul than to chance the great northern sea in the depths of winter.

Squalls of rain blew in with the stronger gusts of wind, but most of the water in the bilge was caused by the waves breaking over the bow. Leof monitored the depth, and every few minutes he would shout the order 'Bail!' Seasick or not, everyone aboard who wasn't involved in sailing the *Heart of Petrus* picked up a leather bucket or a bowl and bailed until the master was satisfied. If this was what Leof called a moderate sea, Marcus prayed he'd never witness anything worse. Using his pack as a pillow, he settled down to try to get some sleep, or at least to close his eyes and forget what was going on around him. It might have been minutes or hours later that Leof shook his shoulder.

'Sorry to wake you, lord,' the Saxon said, 'but I think there's something you should see.' Marcus could tell by the change in the light that it wouldn't be long until dark. He forced himself up until he could look over the side. 'In the far distance, a little to the east.' Leof pointed to the position he meant, but it still took a few moments before Marcus could see anything in the misty drizzle and waning light.

'That line of breaking surf?'

'Frisia, lord. The first of the islands that ring the coast. Each one has a slightly different profile and if we can keep them on our right, they will lead us all the way to the Albis.'

'Will we anchor there for the night?' Marcus tried to keep the desperation from his voice.

Leof shook his head. 'It's not possible, lord. There's no holding ground off the islands, only soft sand. If we get too close those breakers you can see will throw us against the beach and pound us into little pieces. Even if we were fortunate and driven between the islands, the combination of current and tide would mean we'd never get out again. It is said that the tribe that inhabits the islands feeds off the bodies and souls of those who are wrecked upon them. Better to drown at sea, I think,' he said solemnly, 'than come to such an end.'

Marcus swallowed. An ancient superstition, no doubt. But when he looked again at the low, brooding landmass with its fringe of white, a shiver of dread ran through him. 'Thank you, Leof, for everything you have done. Without you we would never have come this far alive, perhaps never even contemplated saving Brenus. I will always be in your debt.'

'There is no need to thank me, lord,' Leof replied with a shy smile. 'I owe you, and the lady Valeria, my life. You took me into your confidence and your regiment when no one could have complained if you had cut my throat, even myself.'

'In any case,' Marcus said, 'the pledge that you will have this ship remains, and if by any chance she is lost, you will have another.'

Leof laughed. 'If she is lost, lord, every last one of us will be lost with her, so that's one pledge I doubt you will ever have to honour.'

The next time Marcus woke it was full darkness and shadowy figures were bustling about the hull with conspicuous urgency. Something had changed. The rise and fall of the ship seemed much more pronounced and was accompanied by a kind of twisting jerk that strained every joint and knot of the planking. A much stronger wind now, whistling through the ropes, carrying loose packets of sleety snow that stung Marcus's face. More water in the bilge, too, but no one seemed to worry about that, which was worrying in itself. Men were working on the sail and he watched the bottom of the ghostly pale cloth begin to rise in a series of jerks. He opened his mouth to call to Leof and discover what was happening, but two sailors pushed him aside and manoeuvred a long oar through one of a series of rope loops set into the top rail of the side. 'Here, grab a hold of this.' One of them shoved the thick shaft of the oar into his hands and he tried to get a grip on wood smoothed and blackened by the effort and sweat of long use. It was at an awkward height, but another crewman piled grain sacks so he could at least sit.

'What do I do?' he asked the man.

'Just hold the oar where it is for now. When you hear the order to set, allow the blade to drop into the water, then pull, lift, bring the oar back and try to keep to the rhythm. Long and slow, eh,' the sailor said, 'just like when you're with a woman.' A laugh accompanied the words, but there was no humour in it.

Ahead of him, he could see Zeno, similarly hunched over an oar, and Luko's muttered curses from behind confirmed he was in the same position. Valeria appeared at his side with a wineskin and lifted a cup to his mouth. When he'd gulped down the rough wine, she thrust a chunk of bread into his hand. 'Eat while you can,' she said.

'What's happening?' he asked.

'The storm picked up just after night fell, but the biggest problem is the wind direction. It altered gradually through the evening and is now driving us towards Frisia. That's why Leof's had to take in the sail and deploy the oars. He says he needs the crew free in case of an emergency with the ship, so you can count on rowing for at least one hour, maybe two, before he can spare them to take over.'

Two hours? A wave broke over the side and salty spray slapped him in the face. 'What about the other ships?' he asked. 'They don't have enough passengers to man the oars.'

'Leof says they'll just have to take their chances.' She raised a hand to wipe the spray from his eyes. 'All we can do is pray.'

With that she was gone. Marcus used his last moment of leisure to cram the bread into his mouth. What else was there to do? Oddly the seasickness had left him entirely.

'Set!'

IX

A night to be wiped from memory. Aching shoulders, blistered hands, hunger like a rat gnawing at your innards, and an exhaustion so overpowering that it made strong men weep. And all in a state of heart-pounding terror as the relentless waves threatened to hammer the little ship to pieces. Was this his third or fourth spell at the oars? Did one of the other ships come tearing out of the night still under full sail and almost cut them in half during one of his rest periods, or had he dreamed it?

When dawn finally broke Marcus could barely open his eyes for the salt that caked his face.

Leof came to crouch beside him as he hauled at the heavy oak spar for what seemed like the thousandth time. Marcus had never seen a man so tired: the Saxon looked ten years older, his beard grey with salt and eyes red-rimmed. Valeria said he'd spent the entire night at the steering oar, forcing the *Heart of Petrus* across the waves against the power of the wind.

'Not long now, lord.' Leof's voice was little more than a croak; whatever remained after a night shouting commands in the tumult of wind and wave. 'The wind's been dropping for the last hour, and we'll have the sail up again before the morning's out.' He looked at Marcus's bandaged hands as he worked the oar, blood seeping through the dirty cloth. 'My apologies for making you work your passage, but needs must.'

'Needs must.' Somehow Marcus managed a smile. 'What of the other ships?'

'We have two of them within sight.' The news was better than expected. 'They're a little battered, but we'll find out just how badly when it's safe to come within hailing distance.'

'And the third?'

'That damn fool Godric. I can only think a block jammed and he couldn't get the sail down. If the lookout hadn't been sharp, he'd have pounded us to kindling. Once we know where we are with the others, I'll take the *Heart* inshore and see if we can find her.' Marcus had an image of a ship smashed to pieces on the shore and the bodies of horses floating in the surf, but Leof's next words reassured him. 'He may be an idiot, but Godric's not a bad seaman and he has a good crew. I don't rule out finding him somewhere putting her back together.'

When conditions allowed them to inspect the other ships the damage was much less than Marcus had feared. One had lost a man overboard. Pompeios, one of Marcus's troopers who'd thought it a good idea to take a shit over the side in the middle of the storm and had learned the folly of it. The other had a split sail that Leof assured him the crew would fix within the hour. All of the horses had survived intact. They sent the ships off in the direction of Saxonia and Leof took the *Heart* south towards the coast.

They found the missing vessel riding at anchor a mile off one of the islands. At close range, the isle carried much less menace than it had from out to sea the previous afternoon. A patchwork of green and brown, covered with the humps and hollows that gave each of the islets its distinctive contour, and surrounded by a broad sandy beach.

'Is that people?' Valeria pointed to a small cluster of figures emerging from a fold between the sand dunes.

Leof cursed under his breath. 'Yes,' he agreed. 'Some of the islands are inhabited, some not. I'd rather this one was not. We'll see what happens.' He called to the lookouts to keep a sharp eye to both seaward and landward.

A few minutes later they heard a shout from the lookout in the bow. A tall column of smoke rose from the north end of the island.

'Shit,' Leof said.

'A signal?'

'Most likely. They're letting someone know we're here.'

'And . . . ?' Marcus persisted.

'That all depends who the someone is.'

'Godric is moving,' Valeria called.

'Not before time.' Leof waited until they were in clear water before he closed on the other ship. 'Godric?' he called. The man at the steering oar of the ship waved an acknowledgement. 'I need you to make your best speed.'

'What do you think I'm doing,' Godric spat. 'I'm not blind. I saw the bastard smoke.' He called out something else, but the words were lost in a gust of wind.

'He wants to know if he can open the chest and arm his men?'

'You think there's going to be trouble?'

'Best to be prepared,' the Saxon said.

Marcus saw that Ninian was in charge of the horses on the other ship, and he called out the order. The former priest nodded, and he and Godric disappeared.

'Tell us what to expect,' Marcus said.

Leof frowned. 'The truth is I don't know, lord. I was fifteen when I sailed from Treva on the raid when you captured me. All this, the sailing and seamanship, is in my blood, a mix of experience, memory and instinct. For the rest, I am just guessing.'

'Guess then, Leof,' Valeria insisted.

'Very well,' the young man agreed. 'My guess is that the smoke was a signal to a pirate chieftain – there are any number on the Frisian coast – announcing our presence and location. It will be repeated by other groups up the chain of islands, and as we go further east there will be more signals that confirm our direction of travel. I assume we will be their target, but there is another possibility.'

'Yes?' Something in his voice sent a chill through Marcus.

'Every inhabited island will have its watchers. The signals will alert them to the presence of ships. We are at least two hours' sailing from our friends. If they're seen by watchers further up the chain and the pirate is based further east, it's possible they are in greater danger than we are. That is why I have asked Godric to risk his spars and ropes. Apart, either of us is a juicy morsel for the thieves who haunt this coast; together we may be strong enough to give them pause.'

'How many ships can we expect?'

'I don't know. At least two, possibly three.'

'All we can do is stay alert and prepare as well as we can,' Valeria said. 'And be ready for whatever occurs. All the better if they come for us. If they find the others first . . . how will the shipmasters react, do you think?'

Leof hesitated, taking the measure of the men he'd recruited to sail the transports. 'They both know this coast as well as Godric, so they'll understand the danger. When they first sight the pirates their instinct will be to run, but no fully laden transport can outrun a pirate for long. Pirate ships are built like raiders, to take men to their prey as quickly as the wind or their oars will carry them. Once they're caught,' he shrugged, 'the outcome is not in doubt. With so few crew they will be overwhelmed and slaughtered in moments.'

'If you can get us on board, I am sure we can win a ship back,' Marcus told Leof. The Saxon nodded his agreement, though his expression betrayed his doubts. 'But every man and every blade will count. Is it possible for Ninian and his men to cross to the *Heart*?'

Leof looked across to the other vessel, twice their size and rising and falling among waves that still held much of the waning power of the storm. 'That would depend on how brave they are.' He frowned. 'And how stupid.'

X

'Tell me what you see?'

In the minutes since the masthead lookout's hail Marcus had ordered his men fed; now they were crouched in the bottom of the ship in their leather armour, waiting for his command. Not that it would be any time soon. The distant ship, or ships, still appeared only fleetingly as a dark mass over the wavetops when the *Heart of Petrus* was on the rise. He and Valeria stood in the stern beside Leof, who stared northwards with narrowed eyes.

'I need to get closer to be certain,' the shipmaster frowned. 'Four ships, and two of them are our transports. The pirates are concentrating on the closest vessel. It's doing its best to evade them, but I doubt it can stay clear for long. They are like terriers worrying a bull. A pair of small fast boats similar to us.'

'How long will it take us to reach them?'

'I doubt before they take her.'

Now Marcus could see the individual ships. As he watched, the two pirates closed on the transport's beam. They must have had grappling hooks because soon men were swarming up the transport's side and the vessels visibly slowed.

'God help them now,' Valeria said.

'God's not here,' Marcus growled. 'So it's up to us. Can you bring us to the opposite side from the pirates?' he asked Leof. 'They're going to be busy for the next few minutes. Our best chance is to take them by surprise.'

Leof nodded and hauled on the steering oar to put them on a course that would carry them to the clear side of the transport. Marcus called to the men to get ready. They'd be boarding in two groups from the right-hand side of the ship. Marcus would lead the first, who would attack with armour and swords only. Several of those troopers already held grappling hooks and coiled ropes. The second wave would carry their shields on their backs. Valeria and Zeno had agreed to stay on board with the crew of the *Heart* and be ready to repel any pirate counter-attack using the long cavalry spears.

By now they could hear confused shouting from across the water and the ringing clash of metal that signalled the ship's crew were not going to give up without a fight. Marcus glanced over the side. They were ten ship-lengths clear of the little cluster of vessels, but remained unseen. He could feel his heart pounding against his ribs and the familiar surge of energy that needed to be controlled and focused until it was as deadly a weapon as the sword at his side.

'Show them no mercy,' he called. 'For they will show you none. We'll board in the centre and form two groups. Luko will take the first and second sections and clear the bow. The others will form on me and clear the stern. Kill fast and kill clean.'

Suddenly, the clamour of battle took on a new urgency.

'Christus, what's he doing?'

The cry came from Valeria by the steering oar. From his position in the bilge Marcus could see nothing, but as he strained to look over the side, Leof shouted, 'It's the second transport, lord. The idiots have come back to help their friends. The captain has moored against the pirates and the crew is clearing them of any guards they've left on board.'

Marcus considered the new developments. Did it change anything? 'The plan stays the same,' he called to Leof. 'How far?'

'Three ship-lengths. Get ready.'

The men in the bottom of the boat tensed and those with grappling hooks readied them with the metal hooks in right hand and rope in the left.

'Two lengths . . . One.'

The stern of the ship appeared above them and the rowers raised their oars so that Leof could bring the *Heart* in to gently kiss the side of the other ship.

'Now!'

The hooks landed simultaneously with a solid clunk, but the pirates were entirely focused either on the fight or on the more obvious threat to their boats from the second transport. Marcus hauled himself up onto the side of the *Heart* and with the help of the rope was able to throw a leg over the transport's boards and drop into the centre of the ship onto somebody's head. The owner of the head felt nothing; he was one of the transport's crew and he was already dead. Not too far away someone was very much alive. A man with a pock-marked, bearded face gaped in wide-eyed outrage at being disturbed as he rummaged in the entrails of the first. The thick lips twisted back into a snarl and the bloody knife he was using to delve for valuables amongst the viscera darted at Marcus's throat. But Marcus had dropped into the boat ready to fight and his sword was moving even before the thought had occurred to the pirate. The heavy blade swept up to cleave through his bottom jaw, catapulting his head back with enough force to break his neck and send blood and teeth flying. Even as his victim fell, Marcus was moving along the sloping, wet boards towards the stern where the crew's last survivors still fought for their lives against about twenty pirates. Ninian, Falco and Tosodio dropped over the guard rail to join him. The horse stalls were to their right, their occupants shuffling and kicking in alarm at the noise of fighting and the scent of blood.

Marcus led his men through a space so narrow and cluttered with baggage and supplies they struggled to stay upright in the choppy seas. Fifteen paces now. Someone tapped Marcus on the shoulder and as he half-turned a shield was thrust at him. He took the grip in his fist and hefted it to cover his front. Beside him, Ninian and Tosodio did the same. In such a confined space the three shields filled the entire gap between the stalls and the slope of the hull. A new clash of swords erupted from their rear, but Marcus could only ignore it and trust his comrades to do their job.

At last the men in the stern realized the danger. A cry of warning and the pirates at the rear of the fight turned, eyes widening at the sight of the locked shields and drawn swords. Their hesitation allowed Marcus to advance another two paces and past the last of the horse stalls, allowing his men to spread out across the full breadth of the ship. He roared a challenge designed to strike fear into his enemy and to banish his own. In other fights he'd always had the option to retreat, even if he'd seldom chosen to exercise it. Here, amid the closely packed sacks and water barrels, there was nowhere to turn and nowhere to run. The unfamiliar deck moving beneath his feet affected his balance and the agility so crucial to survival. Given the chance, he was certain the pirates would have run, but the second transport jammed against their boats removed any possibility of retreat. They had to fight.

There were fewer than he'd expected, perhaps fifteen men. He guessed as many as half of the pirate band were attacking the second transport, but the blood spattered across the boards and swilling in the bilges gave testament to how dangerous the remainder could be. Marcus led nine cavalrymen, but the confines of the ship meant only five could face the Frisians at any one time. The pirate leader was a tower of a man with a chest as broad as one of the water barrels – Christus, why were the bastards always so big? – and the great gore-stained sword he wielded in both hands was as massive as the man himself. He wore a sweat-stained leather jerkin and cloth leggings tied in place with twine, and a rusting pot helmet protected his head. Most of the Frisians had light, sandy-coloured hair, but the pirate chief's thick beard and long moustaches were black as pitch. Six or seven of the transport's crew still lived and fought, which meant the giant could only meet Marcus with half his men, but he didn't hesitate. His mouth gaped in a roar that would have stunned an ox and he charged the line of shields.

Marcus had seen men in the grip of battle madness, but never anything like this. The big man frothed at the mouth like a wolf with the death rage and his eyes bulged from his head as he charged up the centre of the boat with that enormous sword raised shoulder high.

'Cover me,' Marcus called to Ninian on his flank. He stepped out of the line screaming a challenge at the big Frisian, and slapping his sword blade against the oak shield. Honour and pride had no place in a pirate's life, but the pirate chief's authority depended on his invincibility and savagery in a fight. A more prudent warrior would have ignored the taunts and concentrated on what was in front of him; instead the pirate half-turned to bring the great blade down on Marcus's head.

Marcus raised his shield to protect himself, knowing he was exposing his flank, but trusting Ninian to cover him. Three layers of seasoned oak made up the shield, but the Frisian sword sliced through the wood like parchment. Marcus saw the oak splinter and tear as the point of the iron blade sliced within a finger's width of his nose, only to be halted by the iron boss at the centre of the shield with an impact that almost broke his left wrist. In the same instant he twisted with all his strength so the oak layers wedged against the broad blade of the sword. He heard a curse of rage and then a cry of agony as Ninian stepped from the Roman formation to plunge his sword into the Frisian's unprotected armpit. The planks beneath their feet shuddered as the giant dropped like a falling tree.

With a roar, the men of the Ala Sabiniana surged past Marcus to take advantage of the pirates' dismay at their leader's death. Four went down in the first rush. Then it was like hunting rats as the survivors, outnumbered and beset on all sides, darted this way and that, ducking beneath the horse stalls in a bid to escape the relentless blades of their tormentors. They were fishermen and traders: happy to murder for profit, but they wouldn't stand up against trained soldiers with the giant gone. The master of the transport ran past Marcus waving an axe, his face contorted in a mindless rage at the near loss of his ship. Soon blood and brains spattered the planking from bow to stern.

Marcus sent Luko and his men over the side to deal with the remaining pirates, who were still attacking the second transport, unaware of their chieftain's defeat. When he had a chance to draw breath, he went to the side rail and called down to Valeria. 'Our sea wolves turned into rats the minute they saw real soldiers,' he said. 'Best you stay where you are until we have the ship cleaned up.'

'And me, lord?' Zeno asked.

'There's dead and dying pirates all over the place and we have a few flesh wounds that could do with seeing to, Zeno. Any of the crew they got hold of . . . well, they do like to see a man squirming with a knife in his guts.' Zeno ran for his medical sack. 'And bring Leof up with you.'

By the time Leof dropped over the transport's side the last of the Frisians had been despatched. 'Christus save us,' he said, when he saw the twisted bodies and smelled the nauseating mix of blood, guts and excrement which is the aftermath of every battle. 'And may God save their souls.'

'Their heathen souls can rot in Hades where they belong. The question is what we do with their ships?'

'Why, keep them, lord,' Leof said, with a glint in his eye that spoke of his desire to command a fleet. 'To do anything else would be a waste.'

'We've lost half the crew of this ship and the shipmasters complained all the boats were undermanned in the first place,' Marcus pointed out. 'Can you teach two scratch crews of cavalrymen how to raise and lower a sail, to row in unison, and to navigate, and all within the next two hours? Because that's what it will take.'

Leof shook his head. 'I think not, lord.'

'Could we tow them?'

'They would only slow us down, lord, and to what end?' Leof said.

'Then we have to sink them. Strip them of anything that might be of use and we'll hole the bottoms.'

Leof winced. He went to the far side of the ship and looked down on the two pirate vessels, two sleek, fast craft very similar to the *Heart of Petrus*. 'If I might venture another suggestion, lord?' Marcus nodded. 'Two perfectly sound ships crewed by dead pirates would cause an almighty stir along this coast. Who knows what the crews will look like by the time they're found? I doubt anyone would want to go cruising in them again.'

'Ghost ships.' Marcus laughed. 'Very well, prepare your ghosts to cast off before they all go over the side.'

XI

It took another twelve hours to reach the mouth of the Albis, a river Leof said would take them into the very heart of Saxonia. When they were in position, the young Saxon kept the ships well out to sea until night fell and the tide was right to carry them towards the shore.

A long wait, with the ship's planks working their way into Marcus's bones, the ghosts of the past working their way into his head, and sleep never coming. A face and a presence haunted his thoughts, but both were ethereal and unformed, more imagined than seen.

Brenus.

Marcus had last seen his son more than six years earlier, when the boy had been eight or so. There was a time when the very sight of Brenus had repelled him. He'd never been able to forgive his son for the death of Julia, the mother who'd died to give him life. Oh, he'd tried, or so he told himself, but Brenus had grown up a sickly child, forever prone to minor illness. A snot-nosed brat happier to hang on to his grandmother's skirts than become involved in the rough play or simulated battles of the other children.

Marcus had been bred to war, trained to battle and had first ridden by his father's side at the age of twelve. He had no time for weaklings, and, as far as he was concerned, Brenus had been weak in mind and body. It was only after Brenus was kidnapped and Marcus had been forced to choose between duty and his son that he'd finally realized the truth. In his desperation for the boy to grow up in the image of his father, he'd alienated Brenus before he was even old enough to understand why the father acted as he did. He imagined himself as Brenus would have seen him then, huge, bearded and red-faced with fury, when the trembling child cried in fear at being placed on a pony's back. At the age of seven, he'd found Brenus watching from the bank while the boys from the estate splashed in the river pool where generations first learned to swim. Marcus had come up behind him and tossed the shrieking child into the centre of the pool, then watched as he'd struggled to the bank looking like a drowned rat, to run off with a terrified glance at his father.

He now understood he'd driven Brenus into his grandmother's arms and had precisely the opposite effect he'd intended. If his son had been weak in body, it was because he was unformed. How could the father know his son was weak in mind if he did not even make the effort to know him? The only time he had a clear memory of his son's face was in his dreams, and when he woke, that memory swiftly faded to be replaced by a shadowy silhouette that could be anyone. He couldn't even remember the colour of Brenus's eyes.

What was he like now, at fourteen? How tall was he? Would Marcus even recognize him? Had he been broken by his captivity and the relentless toil that went with slavery? Had he been abused? Marcus winced at the thought. He was still alive, that was all that mattered, or had been six months earlier when the captured Saxon Leof had questioned sailed from Treva. A Roman boy, a hostage or a prisoner, living in the home of one of the settlement's elders.

Since that day Marcus had used every trick and strained every sinew to put together the expedition that would free his son. But now, with the Saxon coast almost in sight, he felt not excitement and anticipation, but a deep-seated fear greater even than anything he'd experienced in battle. A fear that turned his heart to ice. What right, after all that had gone before, did he have to expect his son's love, or even respect?

Marcus was the son of two fathers: his blood-father and the father who raised him and who gave Brenus his name. He had loved both, but only one had returned that love. If Brenus spat in his face, could he blame him? That chill again, like a knife to the heart. One thing was surely not in doubt. Brenus would be thankful for his release. How could anyone, man or boy, who had endured captivity do otherwise? That would have to be enough.

As they waited for the tide to turn, Marcus asked Leof if there was likely to be any official presence or guard at the entrance to the river but the Saxon only shrugged. 'On any given day, who knows? There is a boat and a man called Dudda who is legendary for his greed and his laziness. Perhaps he will row out to check us over, perhaps not.'

'Then we need a plan, in case he does,' Marcus suggested. 'One of our number has contracted a mysterious disease, maybe it's plague, maybe not. Zeno has the skills to create the illusion. Better he lets us through.'

Leof laughed. 'Dudda has seen every trick that has ever been dreamed up. Even if he believed you, why would he allow four ships to pass unhindered when only one is infected? If we force our way through, he will raise the alarm and every port and every settlement would be closed to us. There are places where the river narrows and can be blocked; what happens then?'

'So what do we do?' Marcus demanded, less than pleased his plan had been dismissed so comprehensively.

Close to nightfall the four ships approached the mouth of the Albis in line astern. Torches flickered at bow and stern because there was no chance of concealment in such a narrow channel. Leof and Marcus stood in the stern of the *Heart of Petrus*, but Valeria, Zeno and the bulk of the cavalrymen who had sailed in her were distributed among the three following vessels. They were under oars, but the incoming tide did most of the work for them.

'It won't be long now, lord. You keep your head down and your mouth shut. We're just a crew of right sailors hired to keep these big lumps behind us from running aground and get them upriver as far as Lupfurdum. Ah, that's nice of them.' Marcus saw the pinpricks of light amid the gloom that told of a settlement a moment before a large pyre flared to mark its position. 'Here he comes now.'

A boat approached from the shore to the right, the oarsmen rowing with quick, purposeful strokes. Before he dropped to take his place among the crew, Marcus noticed an enormously fat man standing in the bows, wearing a jerkin of oiled leather and baggy trews that would have provided a home for a herd of wild boar. Some kind of chain of office hung beneath the multiple folds of his chin. The boat took station off their right side and the man called out to Leof in a guttural Saxon of which Marcus could make out about one word in three.

'Toll inspection. Back oars so we can give you a look over. You're out late?'

Leof shrugged. 'You know how it is when you're escorting these transport tubs. We're four days out of Gaul. Be as well towing a barrel. That and we had a bit of pirate trouble off the islands. Nothing we couldn't handle, but they took a bit of rounding up. Since then we've been out in the channel while they were getting up their nerve to come in.'

'Aye, I heard there were four ships in the offing. Dudda,' the man introduced himself.

'Leof.'

'Do I know you, Leof?' The big man might be fat, but there was nothing wrong with his eyesight.

'I come and go on the river,' Leof said. 'But not for a while. You'll be coming aboard?'

'That I will. Hold her steady.' The other craft closed to kiss the *Heart*'s planking and Dudda sprang aboard with astonishing agility for a man carrying so much weight. He joined Leof by the steering oar and looked the ship over, nodding approvingly. 'So you're just the escort, eh. Not carrying anything to sell upriver. Gaul,' he sniffed. 'Wouldn't be the first time some enterprising lad tried to slip a few amphorae of wine past old Dudda.'

'Not me,' Leof grinned. 'Though I might sell a couple of these lazy bastards off as slaves.' He nudged Marcus with his toe. 'Ain't that right, Cedric?'

Marcus answered with a glare and a grunt and Dudda laughed. He rubbed a pair of meaty hands together. 'Three fat transports out of Gaul,' he said appreciatively. 'Should I be talking to one of their masters?'

Leof shook his head. 'No, they agreed I should speak for them.' He nudged one of a number of leather sacks at his feet and it responded with a satisfying clink that made Dudda smile.

'So what are they carrying?'

'Horses. Fourteen apiece.' The smile grew wider. The right kind of horseflesh was a valuable commodity in any currency. 'Though we lost one to the storm, so forty-one all told.'

'Forty-one?' Dudda licked his lips. 'You'll be telling me they're just ponies, or only fit for the plough?'

'No,' Leof said. 'If you gave them the once over, you'd find they were prime beasts. Roman stock. Mostly mares, but a couple of geldings. There's a *jarl* up in Lupfurdum been wondering where they are for a good two weeks.'

'Roman stock.' Dudda frowned. He was a man who expected to be cheated and this was unusually frank. 'I thought they were very tight with their horses, the Romans.'

'That they are,' Leof agreed. 'You have to know the right people. And the men who own these ships know the right people.'

'And their value?'

'They were bought for a pound of silver apiece, but the *jarl* is paying two pounds. What is the toll on cargoes these days?'

Leof watched as Dudda considered for a moment, thought about inflating the figure, then, with a perplexed grimace, decided against it. Perhaps the spirit of frankness was catching? 'The toll is one fiftieth part of the value, which in this case would be set at the selling price of two pounds of silver.'

Leof bent and picked up one of the bags at his feet. 'This bag contains one pound of hack silver.' He pulled at the drawstring and retrieved a piece so Dudda could see it. Much of the silver in Saxonia was in Roman coins, and a man could never trust just how silver they were, but hack silver was different. He handed the piece to Dudda, who weighed it in his hand and studied it closely. He was looking at the real thing.

'Of course, I'll need to bring the ships in and inspect the cargoes properly.'

Leof picked up a second bag of silver.

'As I said, the new owner has been expecting his horses for a week and more. With what's left of the moon I can get up past Treva tonight and make an early start in the morning. If those big lumps land, we won't get out again until the next rising tide, if we're lucky. That would be wasting your time and mine. Now we can weigh out every piece of silver to make sure the exact toll on these beasts is paid – I reckon it at just over a pound and a half – or I can just give you these two bags and thank you for your time and your patience . . .'

Dudda weighed the first bag in his hand. He was clearly tempted. No doubt part of the toll routinely found its way into his own purse.

'And, of course,' the unmistakable glint of gold twinkled between Leof's fingers: two gold *solidi*, enough to buy and stock a small farm, 'there'll no doubt be some *jarl* back on shore who needs convincing that the ships have been properly inspected.'

Dudda stared; this was too much and he knew it, but greed got the better of him. The two coins disappeared into the folds of his jerkin and he replaced them in Leof's outstretched hand with a wooden disc that would allow them passage upriver. He picked up the two bags of silver and called the toll boat over. A long pause as he stood by the rail, and the look he gave Leof sent a certain message.

Marcus waited until the boat had disappeared towards shore before he joined Leof in the stern. The young Saxon let out a long breath. 'You did well,' Marcus assured him. The words had meant little, but the interplay had told its own story.

'Yes, lord.' Leof signalled to the rowers to take up the rhythm and signalled with a torch to the waiting ships. 'We're in,' he stared at the boat heading to the shore, 'but I doubt it will be as easy to get back out again.'

XII

The four ships crept slowly through the darkness with the *Heart of Petrus* in the lead and Leof relaying instructions to those behind from his position in the stern. High tide on the Albis provided access to creeks and inlets inaccessible at any other time, but progress through the narrow waterways had to take into account the myriad fallen trees that could tear the bottom out of a ship in an instant. A westerly wind carried rain and sleet that soaked everyone in the boats and the only sound, apart from Leof's low voice, was the rustle of the wind through the reeds and trees and the occasional splash that might be a rising fish, or some river animal.

They were still many miles below Treva. Marcus had questioned Leof's decision to make land so early and in this unforgiving swampland, but the Saxon pointed out that they needed to moor somewhere on the north bank, unless they wished to swim to Brenus. They also had to be downstream of Treva, because once they'd snatched the boy from his captors like as not the city would be in uproar and their pursuers' first act would be to block the river.

'The simple answer, lord, is that there is no other suitable landing place before we reach the city. I know these swamps. My brothers and I hunted and fished here when I was young. I will pledge to carry us to a place where we can land men and horses and to guide us to dry land.'

'So your home is close by?'

Leof laughed at the hint of suspicion in Marcus's voice. 'My home is with you, lord, at least until we reach Gaul and you let me loose with the *Heart of Petrus* and the scroll that says she is mine.'

'I shouldn't have doubted you, boy,' Marcus said. 'Now, what awaits us when we finally get out of this stinking mudflat?'

'Very well.' Marcus could see Leof's frown of concentration in the flickering light of the torch. 'If time was not so pressing, I would moor up soon, because this leat narrows until it is barely wide enough to take the transports, but after that it widens into a lagoon where we youngsters used to fish and swim. There is a strand where we can land the horses and I know every trail through the marshes. We will rest at the farthest edge until dusk and then make our way to Treva under cover of darkness.'

'And when we get there?'

'I was only a boy when I last visited the city with my father. Who knows what changes have happened in the years since? Treva is not a city as you would know it, lord, but a township surrounded by scattered farms and estates. The man I spoke to said the Roman boy was being held on a substantial estate belonging to an *ealdorman*. No doubt the *ealdorman* also owns a house in Treva proper, where he can retreat behind the palisade in times of trouble, but he lives on the estate.' Marcus had heard all this before, but it helped to have it repeated. He'd drawn a small map based on the instructions, but the good lord only knew how accurate it would be when the time came.

'How far is it?'

'It will take us three hours, I think. That will give us time to find and recover Brenus and get back to the ships by first light.'

Leof made it sound so simple, but Marcus knew that no operation conducted in darkness and an unforgiving land far from home was likely to proceed according to plan. All it would take was for a horse to go lame or take a wrong turning, a dog barking at some farmstead.

Still . . . 'And we will have to wait for the next high tide to take us out again?'

'There is no helping it, lord.'

'And when we come across Dudda?'

'I doubt he will be so cooperative next time. I fear we will have to force our way past him. Then we will be fugitives in this part of the world.'

'True,' Leof could hear the grim smile in the older man's voice, 'but very dangerous fugitives indeed.'

It took two hours to unload the horses and, despite his misgivings, Marcus was glad they would have a full day's rest before they set out at dusk. After the prolonged sea voyage they were uneasy and skittish and would clearly take time to become reaccustomed to dry land. Rather than go immediately to the edge of the marsh as Leof suggested, he decided to picket the animals on the strand and leave their departure as late as possible. In the meantime they unloaded much of the silver they'd transported and as great a proportion of the supplies as they could comfortably carry.

Valeria argued that they should be riding light to get in and out of Treva as fast as possible.

'I see the point of the silver,' she said, 'because it's possible we may have the opportunity to buy Brenus back without getting involved in any trouble, but why carry the supplies to the city only to bring them back again?'

'That would be sensible if everything goes well, but when was the last time you saw everything go to plan during a military operation? Remember all those times we meant to intercept Saxon raiders among the marshes and ended up clutching at wisps of smoke and up to our backsides in mud. When you rode to Eboracum to invite Dulcitius and the Sixth legion to join us at Longovicium you almost ended up as his prisoner. If things go wrong and we have no supplies we'll be stranded among the enemy and chewing on our sword belts within three days. The supplies buy us time. Time to run and time to think.'

Valeria remained unconvinced, but, when the time came, she

helped distribute the silver among the pack horses as the men saddled up. What the pack animals couldn't carry was divided among the remounts. Each man received one bag of fodder and another of basic supplies: flour; hard *buccellatum* biscuits that could be chewed for hours and gave a belly the illusion of sustenance; smoked fish and salted meat.

Then there was the question of guards for the ships. The shipmasters and their Saxon crews had proved faithful so far, but here in their homeland was there a possibility they'd be tempted to stray? Yet assigning two men for each vessel would require one fourth of his entire force.

Leof persuaded him to trust the sailors. 'For one thing, I believe they *can* be trusted,' he said. 'Of course, there is also the fact they haven't yet been paid, and if the gods favour us we'll return before the tide gives them the opportunity to sail.'

They made their way through the marshes an hour before dusk, and reached dry ground just before darkness fell. The land beyond was a patchwork of barren-looking fields, cleared and ready for the plough, gloomy strips of forest, and bogland cut by sluggish brown streams. Good land, Leof claimed, with a native's pride, but Marcus looked on it and saw nothing but little profit for much effort. At first, progress was painfully slow even with the benefit of a soft yellow moon, but eventually they reached a track the Saxon insisted was a cattle trail that would lead them to Treva. They rode armed and armoured, ready for trouble, and with their senses heightened to a pitch such as only men set down in unfamiliar, hostile country can experience. The settlements they passed were little more than dark shadows seen when the moon appeared between clouds. Once or twice farm dogs caught their scent and set up a row, but Leof never went close enough for the occupants to trouble them. Yet the nearer they came to Treva the little groups of houses became more frequent and their progress slowed again as Leof pondered the best way to proceed. Eventually they reached a wide river and Marcus sensed their guide's unease.

'What's wrong?' he whispered.

'I could swear there was a bridge here the last time I came this way.' Leof dropped from his horse and slipped down the bank. Marcus waited with the others, their horses shuffling impatiently until Leof returned a few minutes later, wiping his hands. 'I was right, some of the timbers are still there, but it's been burned.'

'Is there another bridge close by?'

'I don't know; this is the only way we ever came to Treva.'

'Then we try elsewhere,' Marcus said. 'North or south? Upstream or down? Where would they have built the new bridge?'

Leof thought for a moment. 'The most logical place would be upstream where the river narrows, but Treva was always a thriving place and maybe it would make more sense to cross lower down, perhaps directly into the city itself. There is a central market.'

Marcus hesitated. Downstream would take them closer to their destination, but if the new bridge had been built close to the city they might be forced to ride through the streets. The chances of thirty-odd horsemen passing unnoticed were minimal. There was also the possibility that the bridge itself might be guarded at night.

'Marcus?' Valeria hissed. 'You must make a decision or we'll never be back in the marshes by dawn.'

'North then,' he said through gritted teeth. 'Upstream.'

'I'm sorry, lord,' Leof whispered. But there was nothing to say.

No bridge for a mile. One mile turned to three. Marcus was beginning to think they would have to hide the bags of silver and swim the horses when Valeria called him forward to where she'd been leading with Leof. The road ahead curved towards the river and a sturdy bridge. There was only one problem, as Valeria pointed out.

'The guardhouse on the far side.'

Marcus peered into the gloom, but it was a moment before he detected it. A wooden hut, substantial enough to hold four or five guards. Even if they were asleep there was no chance of walking the horses across the wooden timbers without waking them.

'We could kill them,' Luko suggested. 'They won't know what's hit them, and over the rail they go into the river.'

'Where they'll float down to Treva and the hunt will be up by morning,' Valeria pointed out. 'And we need to come back this way. What if someone comes to relieve them?'

'There's only one possibility.' Marcus addressed Leof, 'You'll have to try and talk our way through again. But there'll be no killing,' he told Luko. 'If we need to force our way across we'll tie them up and put them somewhere safe.'

Leof nodded. He unstrapped his sword and handed it to Luko, and unhooked the two bags of silver he carried. 'They might search me,' he explained as Marcus accepted the bags.

They watched as he rode forward until he reached the bridge, where he dismounted and led his horse across with a rattle of hooves that would have woken the dead. A shadowy figure emerged from the hut and grumpily ordered Leof to halt. They listened, barely daring to breathe, to a muffled conversation. Seconds passed, then minutes, before Leof led his horse back across the bridge and remounted.

'Get ready,' Marcus ordered. 'We'll have to move quickly.'

But when the Saxon approached close enough for them to see his face in the moonlight he was smiling.

'It's a toll bridge, lord. He doesn't care who we are, but if we want to cross the bridge we have to pay the toll.'

'How much is it?' Valeria reached for a bag of silver.

'A damned sight less than Dudda would have charged,' Leof laughed.

XIII

'Can this be it?' Marcus struggled to make sense of what he could see in the moonlight beyond the edge of the clump of trees where they'd concealed themselves.

'It is where the prisoner described it, lord,' Leof replied. 'Though it's a lot larger than I'd expected.'

'You said an estate.' Valeria crouched close by among the bushes. Two hundred paces away across the fields the houses and outbuildings of a sprawling township were scattered among muddy fields. Despite the hour they could hear the sound of raucous laughter and singing from somewhere in the centre. The outline of a building more substantial than the others could just be discerned in the gloom. 'This is more like a small town' – a new burst of song echoed through the still night – 'and that sounds like a small army.'

'Tell me what I'm seeing,' Marcus urged Leof. 'I am blind in this.'

The young Saxon considered for a moment. 'It appears to me that the man who is holding your son is not just a lord, but an *edilhingui*, a leader of lords. He is rich enough to finance and retain a permanent retinue of warriors. In time of peace there is little enough for them to do but practise arms or fight amongst themselves, drink his ale in the feasting hall and sing long into the night about their great exploits, as you can hear.

These men are housed among the farmers, who bear the cost of feeding them. The *edilhingui* will likely live with his family in the largest building, the one on the far side of the estate. If the prisoner was correct and the situation remains unaltered, that is where your son is being held.'

'Christus,' Marcus whispered. This changed everything. 'How many will there be?'

Again, Leof hesitated, studying the settlement and counting the buildings. 'Somewhere between twenty and thirty, I think, but I cannot be certain.'

Marcus nodded. Not so bad. The numbers were even, but the odds favoured trained Roman soldiers against barbarian warriors, however brave. That was until you remembered the Roman soldiers were all alone in a hostile land surrounded by enemies and with their only avenue of escape four frail wooden ships twenty miles away.

'This . . . *edilhingui*?' Valeria struggled with the unfamiliar title as she put Marcus's thoughts into words. 'He is a man who needs silver. Do you think he will be open to negotiation in the matter of Brenus?'

'No, lady,' Leof said eventually. 'The *edilhingui* will be a proud man, and cunning. He will agree to consider your request, ask for a sight of your silver, and from that glance calculate your worth. You will no doubt earn his respect, then he will have you killed.'

Marcus nodded and studied the settlement again, cursing himself for a fool for imagining this might be straightforward. The only consolation was that the settlement didn't appear to be surrounded by a palisade, nor even a ditch. He'd thought to surprise Brenus's captor by night and either dazzle him with silver or frighten him with the glint of swords, but he knew this *edilhingui* would be neither dazzled nor frightened. If force or greed wouldn't work, there was only one other way to rescue Brenus. By stealth.

They smeared their hands and faces with mud from the fields.

'Shit.'

'What is it?' Marcus hissed.

'This isn't mud,' Luko said. 'It's shit from the manure heaps. They must have been spreading it today. Christus, I stink.'

'How can you tell the difference?' Julius laughed.

'Quiet.' Marcus rubbed the reeking filth on his cheeks and under his tunic reckoning it would help disguise the scent of their bodies from any dogs. He split his force into two. Eight men would accompany him to the *edilhingui*'s house, while the others, bar three to stay with the horses, would watch the feasting hall and be ready to counter any reaction if anyone raised the alarm.

'You'll command them,' Marcus told Valeria. 'If anything goes wrong and you think all is lost, get them back to the boats before dawn.'

'No.' Valeria didn't even look at him. 'Brenus is my kin as well as yours and I'll be with you when you rescue him.'

'Luko then.' Marcus knew there was no point in arguing. Luko gave him a wry look and moved among his men whispering instructions and encouragement.

A chill breeze blew from the east, and they moved to the right until it was in their faces. Flat, muddy fields cut by a stream guarded the approach to the settlement and it wasn't long before their boots were heavy with the damp, clinging earth. There was no helping it, but every man knew the extra weight would hamper him in a fight and might mean the difference between life and death.

Marcus tried to picture Brenus's face, but it could have been any child's face, bland and uninteresting, with an expression that was wary, sullen and obstinate. It came to him that he'd never seen his son smile and he almost froze on the spot at the shock of the realization.

Valeria's shove in the back kept him moving forward. He could hear the whisper of her repeated prayers and he knew Zeno would be trailing close behind her like a devoted hound. It occurred to him now that the reason she'd insisted on accompanying him was unease – perhaps fear was the proper word – at the reception he would get from his son. Brenus had every reason to resent, if not hate, the father he had not seen for six years. How would a fourteen-year-old boy sold into a life of slavery and believing himself to have been abandoned feel?

As they approached the first of the buildings Marcus raised his hand for the column to halt. The waning moon provided a sort of light, but one that gave little definition. His eyes searched the shadows for evidence of another human presence. Somewhere not too far away a dog whined in its sleep. He tensed at the sound, waiting for it to catch their scent, but the whine wasn't repeated. The only other noise was singing from the feasting hall that reverberated through the thatch-roofed wooden houses and barns. It came from their left, and he signalled to Luko to take his men that way. Marcus moved to the right, followed by Valeria and the others. Small fields or gardens and fruit trees surrounded each house, with pig pens, hen hutches and storehouses scattered around. It was a relatively simple matter for men trained to move silently at night to slip from one piece of cover to the next. There should be more dogs to see off foxes, wolves and perhaps even bears in this savage land, but if the cacophony from the hall was a regular occurrence, they'd never be silent. Best to keep them indoors on nights like this.

Valeria nudged him, and he saw that they were approaching the largest house, set back from the rest amid a large orchard and gardens. He heard the sound of murmuring voices, but from without or within? Who could move the most silently among them? Senecio? But he was with Luko. Julius then. He waved the Pict forward, pointed to the house, and made a circling motion with his finger. Julius recognized the gesture and nodded. He dropped to his stomach and slithered snake-like across the open space between the farm and the apple or pear trees that flanked the house. Within three heartbeats he'd disappeared from sight.

While he was gone, Marcus studied the house. A big square building, two storeys high and with various additions to the side and perhaps to the rear. Servants' quarters? If so, that was likely where he'd find Brenus. Not much in Roman terms, but a veritable palace compared to the hovels he'd seen occupied by Pictish kings.

Julius reappeared from the darkness and Marcus drew him aside and put his mouth to the other man's ear. 'What did you see?'

'Windows on all sides, but shuttered as far as I could tell,' this in a voice as soft as an angel's wing. 'A single entrance to the front, but there are two guards, one to each side. They talk to each other now and again to keep themselves awake. Big buggers, armoured beneath their cloaks, and with fancy axes.'

Marcus nodded. The guards were a nuisance, but he hoped nothing more. A pity, but it couldn't be helped. He signalled his companions to gather round. 'Julius, you've seen the ground. Take the guard to the right of the door. Ninian, the nearer.' The former priest drew a curved dagger from the sheath at his belt and held it where Marcus could see it. Marcus nodded. They had to be certain. 'I'll distract them while . . .'

Valeria touched his shoulder. 'If they see you blundering around, they won't be distracted; they'll be alerted.'

'What then?'

'A woman.'

'A woman in armour?'

'Of course not.' She began working at the straps of her leather chest armour.

'No,' Zeno said.

'Can you think of a better distraction?' She drew her cloak around her and hunched her back in imitation of an elderly woman. 'Leof?' she hissed. 'I need something to say.'

The Saxon frowned. 'You could try: *Yfel holian mîn cû. Tilian êower sîene ðæge pro?*'

'*Yfel holian mîn cû. Tilian êower sîene ðæge pro?*' She mouthed the words twice to ensure she had them, and he nodded.

Julius and Ninian slipped into the darkness, and Valeria followed. A few moments later she appeared in a shaft of moonlight between two buildings and limped towards the guards calling out the Saxon words Leof had given her in a querulous voice worthy of an aged crone. One of the men laughed and said something to the other.

'What does it mean?' Marcus asked.

'She's telling them she's lost her cow and wonders if they've seen it passing.' Leof grimaced. 'It was the best I could do.'

'Christ,' Marcus hissed.

The silhouettes of the two guards slowly emerged from the gloom, but an instant later there were four shadowy forms, not two, a struggling mass and a few muffled grunts, and then stillness. Valeria straightened and waved them forward.

Marcus handed his sister her weapons and armour. 'That was perfect,' he congratulated her.

'Then let's go and get Brenus.'

They dragged the two bodies around the corner of the house, leaving only wet smears to mark their passing. Marcus had wanted to avoid killing, but this was the price of recovering his son and he wouldn't be here if he wasn't willing to pay it. Valeria took her place with the men crouched by the door.

XIV

Marcus inspected the door and gave it a gentle push. The lack of play immediately told him it was barred on the inside. His first instinct was to put his shoulder against it, but he recalled Valeria's reminder that brute force couldn't solve everything, and crouched to study the problem more closely. A deeper shadow caught his eye that on closer inspection proved to be a small hole in the wooden panels, at just above waist height.

'Did you search the guards?' he called softly into the darkness.

Not a keyhole, as might be found in a Roman door, but his mother had something very similar at her house at Grabant, on the estate in Brigantia. Valeria appeared at his shoulder and placed something in his hand. Two narrow strips of metal, perhaps a handspan long, but hinged at the centre. Yes, that was it. He pushed one of the metal strips through the hole at an angle until it dropped perpendicular to the other. The result was a solid clunk that made him wince, but told him he was right. A simple slide lock – a bar with three or four pegs attached. He twisted the metal in his hand till the tension increased. He had to use all the strength of his wrist to turn it until he was rewarded by the soft rumble of the bar sliding through its cleats.

Marcus nudged the door open and slipped inside into total

78

darkness. His sword was clutched in his right fist, though he had no memory of drawing it. He moved forward cautiously, one hand raised in front of him, and his feet searching their way across the rush-strewn floor. The others moved silently behind him and he heard the slight squeak of the door being closed. He froze, every sense seeking out what was around him, eyes gradually becoming accustomed to the deeper darkness. A large space filled with shadows, the sound of gentle snoring from somewhere above. His nostrils twitched and he tensed. A host of scents, but foremost among them the acrid smell of a recently doused torch. Very recently. The soft, muted growl of a dog being kept in check. Christus, they knew. He held his sword a little tighter and took a single step forward.

Only the faintest glint of the axe blade saved him. Marcus ducked to his right in a low crouch and felt the iron head brush his left shoulder as it plunged to smash some piece of unseen furniture. In the same instant he stepped forward and spun left bringing the sword blade up to gut his unseen attacker. But the man was too close and for a moment they struggled body to body, close enough for Marcus to smell the beer on his opponent's breath, each wrestling to manoeuvre his weapon into position for a killing strike. Chaos all around. A huge dog, some kind of mastiff, loosed at last, flew past with its white fangs bared, only to yelp piteously as someone plunged a sword into its breast. Women shrieked from the sleeping platform overhead, and were doing more than shrieking judging by the piss pots that began to rain on the warriors by the door.

'For Christ's sake will someone shut them up?'

At least two or more Saxons had joined the fight – more guards or the man's sons or servants? He thought he heard Valeria shout the name 'Brenus', but it was lost in the clamour. Marcus's cavalrymen still outnumbered the defenders, but he had his own problems. The man he fought was almost as big as the Saxon pirate leader, and enormously strong. Marcus had a firm grip of the arm holding the axe, but he could feel the Saxon clawing at his belt for the wicked little *seax* these people wore even in their sleep. At the same time yellow teeth that would have done credit to the guard dog snapped at his face hoping to clamp on his nose or an ear. Too close to use his sword to stab or slash, but he sawed the edge across the back of the man's knee, trying to slice through the vulnerable tendons there. Whether he was in the correct place, he didn't know, but it provoked a reaction. The Saxon threw himself backwards, tearing his axe hand from Marcus's grasp and trying to find space for a full-blown swing that would have brought the edge down to split Marcus's skull, reinforced leather helm and all. His enemy was quick, but Marcus was quicker.

As the Saxon gave way, Marcus moved forward, belly to belly, close enough to neutralize the danger from the axe. Consternation and confusion in glaring eyes only inches away. The Saxon's left hand clamped on Marcus's right wrist, but now it was Marcus whose free hand was working at his belt. He pulled his dagger free and plunged it again and again into the soft flesh of his adversary's lower belly. At first the only reaction was a rumble of complaint from deep in the massive chest, but quickly the agony built and the rumble was replaced first by a mew of pain and then by a cry of torment. The terrible wounds would have defeated a lesser man, but the Saxon wasn't finished. He dropped the axe and released Marcus's sword arm and two massive hands closed on Marcus's throat. For a moment Marcus was transported back to the walls of the villa in the wetlands and his life ebbing away. But this time he was not helpless.

He ignored the hands that were killing him and allowed his left hand to drop. When it was level with the Saxon's groin, he dug the dagger point deep into the flesh. Sawing and tearing, he ripped the blade upwards, slicing through the Saxon's abdomen. The big man shuddered and froze; Marcus became aware of a warm flood across his knife hand and the deadly grip of the great hands loosened.

Above him, someone lit a torch and for a moment he was blinded. When his vision cleared the Saxon's wide eyes were staring from a face as white as old bones. Marcus stepped back and the man toppled forward into a great pool of his own lifeblood.

'Lord!'

The warning gave Marcus just enough time to meet the new attack and the clash of the two swords rang through the room like a bell. Before he could think, the blade was back, probing and testing, flickering right and left, down and up, now at his eyes now at his groin, wielded by a snarling blur of whirling fury. A young man, dark-haired and tall, eyes filled with a burning hatred. One of the *edilhingui*'s sons determined to avenge his father? The point sought out Marcus's throat and he only just managed to force it away. Christ he was quick. That deadly blade flickered like a streak of lightning so it seemed everywhere at once. Marcus had met enough enemy champions to understand that there were two kinds of true killers, those who were skilled and those who were fast. Here, he faced a man who was as fast as any he'd encountered. He knew then there could be no chance of forcing the boy to yield. Brave or not, he would have to be killed.

Marcus had one great advantage. His opponent might be deadly in all other respects, but he was slight, with the slim figure of one not quite fully formed. Strength. Strength was what would win him his fight. Unless his enemy killed him first. He had to fight off three more attacks, vaguely aware that the clamour surrounding him had ebbed, before the chance came. He managed to trap his opponent's blade with his own and forced it against the young man's chest so he couldn't free it. At the same time he used all his strength to propel him back against the wall of the room. The fiery eyes glared at him with a kind of demonic fury he'd never witnessed before. His left hand still held the dagger that had killed the father and he brought it up and placed the point against the young man's throat. Neither the expression on his pale features nor the pressure on Marcus's blade faltered. In the name of Christ did the boy have no fear? He felt a pang of regret as he gathered his strength to push the point home.

'No, Marcus!' The sharp cry, filled with a kind of terror, came from Valeria, and he hesitated. 'It's your son. It's Brenus.'

Marcus gaped at the boy. He stepped back, his legs ready to give way beneath him. As the pressure on his sword lifted, the boy smiled and swung his blade at Marcus's neck – only to drop like a stone as Ninian hit him on the back of the head with his sword pommel.

'Sorry, lord,' the former priest said. 'But son or not, the bastard was going to kill you. He was quick as a Pict's temper,' he added admiringly.

Brenus had fallen face first, and Valeria bent to turn him over and check he was still breathing. She looked up and nodded. Marcus stared at his son with something like awe. *His son*. It was difficult to equate this tall, lithe youth with the sickly child he remembered. Free from the twisted savagery of hatred, his face in repose had more of his mother's fine-boned features than his father's craggy jaw and heavy forehead. Only the long nose was evidence of Marcus Flavius Victor's part in his bloodline.

'We don't have much time,' Valeria reminded her brother. 'We need to get him back to the horses.' Marcus's men were already dragging bodies to the back of the building and throwing fresh rushes over the bloodied patches on the floor. Servants and retainers for the most part, but one was certainly the son of the man Marcus had killed. A board game lay on the floor where two men had been playing it when they must have heard something that alarmed them. Should he feel guilt at their deaths? They had taken his son and this was the consequence.

'Lord.' Julius was crouched over a prostrate body. Marcus grimaced. Falco, whose beer he'd stopped less than a month ago and hardly much older than Brenus. An axe had opened his chest, leather armour and all, so it was a cauldron of viscera and blood and splinters of bone. Falco's face was ash grey, his eyes wide, and his whole body shuddered.

Marcus went to kneel beside him and cradled his head. 'Be still, boy,' he choked out the words.

'I'm sorry, lord . . .'

'What?'

Falco's hand closed on his like a vice and his eyes bulged from his head.

'They made me do it . . . the map . . .'

'It's of no matter,' Marcus assured him. And it wasn't. Because as he said the words he forced the point of his knife up into the soft flesh below Falco's ear and into his brain.

Valeria shook her head. They didn't have time for this.

'Lady?' Leof appeared at her side and the look on his face sent a shiver through her. She acknowledged the Saxon's slight twist of the head and accompanied him.

Marcus returned to where Brenus lay and touched his son's face. The first gesture of affection between them. Did the flesh of the cheek flinch away from his fingers or did he imagine it? It was of no consequence. All that mattered now was the future. Whatever pain he had caused Brenus, he would make amends for it a hundred times over. The boy had the makings of a warrior and Marcus Flavius Victor knew how to forge true warriors.

'Marcus, you have to see this.' Valeria's voice came from above and contained an edge of despair that made Marcus immediately leave Brenus and run to the ladder. When he reached the level of the sleeping platform, he saw her standing head down over four prone figures. It was only when he came closer that he noticed the unnatural angle of the heads, the staring eyes and gaping throats. 'In Christ's name, no,' he whispered.

'You said to shut them up, lord,' Tosodio grumbled. 'They just wouldn't shut up.'

Marcus had to restrain himself from lashing out at the former legionary. They'd come here to recover Brenus, and he'd known from the start there would be a price to pay in one form or another, but this was just wanton butchery. He'd never wanted this. He looked to Valeria and shook his head, but she just stared at him with tears running unchecked down her cheeks.

'No, Marcus,' her voice had the jagged edge of a rusty saw. 'This is what you must see.'

He joined her and looked down at the victim she indicated. An old woman, frail and shrunken, lying on her back with her pure white hair fanned around her head and stained with her own blood. She had her eyes closed and if it hadn't been for the gash in her throat, she would have looked quite peaceful. It only took him a single heartbeat to see beyond the wrinkles to the woman she'd once been.

'May God forgive me,' he whispered, in a voice that shook with sheer horror.

He had murdered his own mother.

XV

'Mother.' Marcus shuddered at the sight of the still, slight figure on the cot. 'Venutia. I killed her . . .'

'No,' Valeria hissed. 'It was an accident. An accident of war.'

'How did she come to be here?' His mind spun with the bewilderment of it all. They had believed her dead these six long years. Venutia had already been ill when she was taken in the Saxon raid along with her grandson, and no one believed she could survive even the long sea voyage in an open boat. Memories flooded back of the beautiful Brigantian princess she had been, and the love she had shared with Brenus, the man Marcus had called father. His earliest memory was of holding her hand as they'd walked in the shade of the apple trees on the estate, during some endless warm summer. He must have been four or five years old. A tear ran down his cheek into his beard at the long-forgotten recollection of that soft hand in his, the feeling of unconditional love, and the comforting presence looming over him. Yet there had been a strength to her that had steered the family through the turmoil of the Pictish years and the time of the usurper, a time, Marcus now understood, that might have torn them apart. Now she was gone, and he must bear the burden of her violent passing for the rest of his life.

'Do not blame yourself, Marcus.' It was as if Valeria could read his mind. 'That is the last thing she would want. She was our mother, a kind and loving mother, and we should be thankful for everything she gave us, and more so for the resilience that allowed her to stay with Brenus all these years. But we both know she should have been dead long since. No,' she shook her head, 'I am not being heartless. A woman knows these things. Our beautiful Venutia believed she was dying even before they were taken. I think the only thing that kept her alive was the need to be close to Brenus and to help him survive. You saw what he's become. Perhaps she knew she was no longer needed. The woman on the bed is only a husk of the Venutia we knew. We must remember her as she was, a strong, capable mother who guided us through our lives and was always there for us. Come, we must leave her now. These people will treat her as one of their own.'

Marcus hesitated, but he knew she was right. He closed his eyes and tried to quell the nausea building up inside him. He barely registered the silent rush back through the buildings of the settlement, hustled by the arms between Zeno and Valeria, or that nearby two of the troopers half-carried, half-dragged Brenus across the muddy fields to the horses. He would vaguely recall a moment of consternation when the door of a hut flew back to trap them, frozen, in a pool of light, while a Saxon warrior or farmer vomited up the results of a night's drinking into his midden before staggering back into his home. Someone must have helped him into the saddle because he only truly became aware that they'd left the slaughterhouse stench of the Saxon *edilhingui*'s home when his mount's hooves rattled on the wooden boards of the toll bridge. Brenus was somewhere behind, too dazed to know where he was and supported between Ninian and Luko.

'When will you tell him?' Valeria asked the question he didn't want to hear.

'I don't know,' he faltered. 'Not soon. He has enough reasons to hate me without that. Are we on time for the ships?'

Valeria didn't answer, and that was an answer in itself. As they rode on in the darkness, he tried to remember his mother's face as she had been. The mother who had loved her son without reservation and found him a true father when the man who sired him had all but abandoned them. Magnus Maximus, the man Marcus called his blood-father, had been a young Roman officer serving in Britannia, an aristocrat of impeccable pedigree, and a man destined for either eternal fame or an early grave. In the end he achieved both. His mother would never say how they met, but whatever happened Marcus had been the result. Maximus had left Britannia by the time Venutia gave birth, driven, his mother had said, by duty and his loyalty to the Emperor. It had seemed a plausible excuse when he was young. An older, more cynical Marcus could see that in a world where a bloodline was as important as ability, if not more so, a Brigantian wife, however high-ranking and beautiful, and a half-Brigantian son might be a social impediment to an ambitious man, and his blood-father was ambitious beyond measure. Yet Maximus had never forgotten his son, even after Venutia married another. Exotic gifts would arrive for the boy from far-off lands, suggestions for his learning and education and the money to pay for it. Marcus now suspected that his blood-father had been in direct contact with his father Brenus, an auxiliary cavalry officer, to prepare him for what was to come. It was from Brenus he'd learned his soldiering and skill at arms; the ruthlessness it required came naturally. One sunny day, when he was twelve years old, Venutia had presented him to a god-like figure in golden armour mounted on a great black horse. It was the first time he'd met his blood-father.

The escapers' route took them across fields, pasture and bog, away from the main tracks and drove roads, but occasionally they needed to cross one or the other. They were approaching a road when Leof signalled a halt and drew the column into a stand of trees. From their place in the shadows beneath the skeletal branches they first heard the rumble of hooves, then watched as a band of horsemen carrying torches rode by at the gallop.

Marcus exchanged a glance with Valeria. 'They've —'

Whatever he was going to say, the words were stifled by a scuffle behind them, and a thud as someone came off their horse. Leof cursed at them to be quiet, and Marcus turned, furious at the indiscipline, to find Brenus on the ground with Luko astride his chest, one hand over Brenus's mouth. 'He tried to cry out to those Saxons, lord,' Luko said. 'I had a feeling he was making out to be groggier than he was. He would have betrayed us in an instant. The little bastard bit my hand.'

Marcus dropped to the ground beside his son. He was about to order Brenus's release when he saw the look of savage hatred in the dark eyes visible above Luko's hand, and he knew there was no point. 'Gag him and make sure you keep a tight hold of him from now on.'

When he was back in the saddle, he felt Valeria's eyes on him. 'He'll feel better when we're on the ship,' he assured her.

By now it was clear they wouldn't reach the ships before daybreak, but Leof thought there was still a chance of gaining the concealment of the marshes, which was much the same thing. Yet their unease grew as the sky in the east lightened and the flat, barren features of the brown and grey fields around them began to take shape.

'There!' Leof's voice betrayed his relief as the endless reed beds came into sight. 'Jesus, no!'

Marcus followed his eyes and his heart stopped as they found the point where a plume of smoke billowed over the horizon a few miles ahead and grew into a slim pillar of dirty black that drifted away on the breeze. His mind told him the fools at the landing place must have set a fire, but the colour of the smoke suggested a different story. Only pitch burned like that. A ship was on fire. Every last one of them knew the truth of it and a rumble of unease ran through the men.

'What now?' Valeria whispered.

'We have to be sure.' Marcus tried to keep his voice steady. His people needed to know he remained in control. 'Leof, take Senecio and see what's happening at the ships.'

They waited, hidden among the outer reeds, until the two men returned. Marcus took Leof aside with Valeria. 'He burned the *Heart*,' Leof gave them the bad news through gritted teeth. 'He must have done it out of sheer spite. And the crews of the other ships in her. We could hear them screaming from two hundred paces.'

'He?'

'Dudda and about fifty men.' Leof spoke with the weary resignation of defeat. 'It was a mistake to show him all that silver. He couldn't keep his eyes off it. The local fishermen would know the marshes as well as I do and it was the first place they'd look. We can't stay here, lord. They're searching the river banks and they'll have sent to the city for more men as soon as they found the ships.'

Marcus looked to where the others stood with the horses. No panic or fear in those faces, only expectation. They'd followed him here not for silver or glory, but because they knew he depended on them for their skills and their loyalty. All had a friend or a family or a lover waiting for their return. They'd already lost comrades, yet they trusted him to get them back. But without the ships he had no idea how. The only certainty was that Leof was right. They couldn't stay here.

'What will they expect us to do?' he asked the Saxon.

'The crews will have been questioned before they died, so they'll know exactly who we are,' Leof replied with a frown. 'They'll soon hear you've taken the boy. The first thing they'll think is that we'll try to find more ships, so they'll alert the settlements along the river and the coast.'

Marcus bit his lip as his favoured option burned as fiercely as the ship. 'South of the river then,' he said with a confidence he didn't feel. 'Where's the nearest place we can cross? The Rhenus and safety can't be more than four or five days' ride away.'

'At this time of the year, with the snow melt and the rains, I doubt there's a ford within a hundred miles,' Leof dashed another hope. 'And west of here, towards the Rhenus, all you have is people who are taught to hate the Romans in the womb. They'd have your head on a pole in front of Irminsul before you were halfway to the river.'

'What then?' Marcus struggled to hide his frustration. 'We have to find a way back to Imperial territory.'

Zeno had joined Valeria and had been listening to the conversation. 'Stilicho,' he said.

Marcus looked at the *medicus* as if he'd gone mad. 'Stilicho's letter said he was in Illyricum, which might as well be the other side of the world.'

'You'll never find a seagoing ship with the whole country roused against you,' Zeno persisted. 'You can't cross the river. To the north are savage lands occupied by people whose cruelty men only whisper of, people who eat their own children.' He crouched over a patch of mud and broke a twig from the nearest bush. 'While we were waiting for dark yesterday, I spoke to one of the shipmasters. He knows this river well. From here,' he scratched a circle in the mud to show their position, 'the river flows first east, then turns directly south, then east again.'

'So?'

Zeno drew a line leading from the river to the south. 'After ten days, this tributary will lead us to within four or five days' ride of the Danuvius, the frontier of the Empire in those parts. If we can reach the Danuvius I pledge upon my life, lord, that I can take us to Metulum.'

Marcus looked to Valeria. 'Do you support him in this madness?'

She shrugged. 'What other choice do we have?'

And to Leof. 'But you say the river craft are lost to us?'

The Saxon frowned and studied Zeno's crude map. 'Here, lord, yes, but fifty miles upstream, who knows. This is a trading river. Barges and transports carry amber, leather, timber and slaves, cattle too, from the east to Treva, where merchants send their wares to the markets of Germania and Gaul and sell them for enormous profit. Those ships then return, loaded with whatever they can get. For enough silver I believe we can find a shipmaster who will carry us upriver at least as far as Lupfurdum.'

Marcus took a deep breath and walked away to the edge of the reeds. Despite the pressure to make a swift decision, he needed time to think. Stilicho. Was it really feasible? He conjured up an image of that stern, aristocratic face. If he could reach Stilicho anything was possible.

He turned and strode to the map. 'Where is the nearest settlement where we are likely to be able to get a ship?'

Leof crouched again and picked up Zeno's twig. 'About here, lord, a place called Leuphana. It is as far east as I have sailed on the river.'

Marcus took the twig and etched a wide curve in the mud from the circle that marked Treva to Leuphana. The route was calculated to take them in a direction that would deceive their hunters and be well out of the way of any pursuit. 'Then today, and for as long as it takes, you will guide us along this path,' he told the Saxon.

They would go east. To Stilicho. But first they must brave the north, and the lands of the people who ate their own children.

XVI

Marcus ordered food to be distributed before they set out. Likely enough there wouldn't be another opportunity for a while. He noticed Brenus sitting with his back against the trunk of a stunted alder, his mouth still gagged with a piece of cloth tied in place with a strip of leather. The latent savagery in the dark eyes had faded now to be replaced with something much more difficult to read. A cold calculation, perhaps? Certainly a knowingness beyond his years. Marcus felt he was being measured, and found he desperately wanted his son to be impressed.

'Has he been fed yet?' he asked Luko, who was guarding the boy.

'I'm afraid the little bastard will eat me if I let him loose,' Luko grinned. 'Begging your pardon, of course, lord.'

'Ungag him and leave us.'

Luko did as he was ordered. Brenus worked his mouth and spat. Marcus offered his son a water flask, but Brenus didn't even look at him. Exasperated, he laid the flask on the turf beside the boy along with a crust of stale bread.

'If you're sensible, I'll have Luko leave the gag out,' he said. Still the boy didn't respond, and Marcus wondered if he'd forgotten the Latin that was his mother tongue. He tried again. 'You have nothing to fear, Brenus. You are safe now.'

At last the boy looked up. 'My name is not Brenus.' His dry mouth slurred the words, but there was a force to them that sent a shiver through Marcus. 'I am Wulf, son of Wigga. You killed my father and I swear on Donar's hammer I will avenge him. You are all going to die.' The last words were loud enough for most to hear and accompanied by a cold smile. A dozen heads turned towards them. 'You are trapped. My father was the lord of a hundred sworn warriors. Wherever you run in this land, they will hunt you down.'

A murmur of unease ran through the men and Marcus crouched beside his son. 'Do you want me to have you gagged permanently?' he rasped. 'Son or not, I will not have you endanger my soldiers. Do you understand, *Brenus*?'

The boy's nostrils flared at the sound of the name and he glared at Marcus. But eventually he nodded.

Marcus untied his bonds and shouted for Luko. Brenus picked up the water flask and drank deeply. 'Is my grandmother here?' he asked.

Marcus hesitated long enough to still his racing mind. 'Venutia knew she was too old and frail to accompany us.' He almost choked on the lie. 'She said she would slow us down and didn't want to place you in danger. She begged your forgiveness.'

Brenus said nothing, but the eyes, already so familiar, bored into Marcus. Eventually he turned away.

'Aye, he's your boy right enough, Marcus Flavius Victor,' Luko said as they passed.

'Keep him close and keep him safe, Luko,' Marcus said quietly. 'But whatever you do don't ever make the mistake of trusting him.'

North, over a country so flat it made the wetlands of eastern Britannia seem positively mountainous. They tried to stay away from the main tracks, but often the terrain made it impossible. Endless forests of oak and beech, so dense as to be near impenetrable, with the occasional relief of patches of farmland cut by sluggish streams and stinking ditches; meagre pasture, brown and frost-parched; sinister dark lakes surrounded by mud-slick marsh studded with alder and willow. Whenever they came across habitation, be it the small cluster of houses of a settlement or a single farmstead, they avoided it by as much as the ground nearby allowed. Low clouds of murky pewter wept a soft, all-enveloping drizzle that provided the illusion of concealment, but Marcus didn't deceive himself they passed unseen.

Valeria rode beside Brenus a few horse lengths back in the column. He'd said nothing since his outburst in the marshes, and, at first, she could tell his thoughts were focused only on escape. More than once when he thought the vigilance of the men around him had relaxed, he tensed, ready to make a break for the surrounding trees, only to be dissuaded by Luko's predatory chuckle from behind.

'Do you remember me from Grabant, Brenus?' she asked the boy. 'I used to watch over you while you played by the stream. I was your mother's friend and I would like to be your friend too.'

The attempt to breach the carapace of silence with which Brenus surrounded himself amounted to nothing, but Valeria remained undeterred. She could understand his bewilderment, and, to a certain extent, his animosity towards Marcus. At some point he would realize his father would never allow him to escape, and recognize the need to make friends among his companions.

'You called the Saxon chieftain your father, yet you were his prisoner. He must have been a remarkable man?' Her question was met with another long gap and she smiled. 'Sulking doesn't suit you. When you purse your lips like that you look like your . . . my brother. We will be spending many hours together, I fear. What else is there to do but talk?'

'My name is Wulf.' She hadn't expected him to surrender quite so quickly. 'If you wish to talk to me, remember that. And I was not his prisoner.'

'But you were taken as a slave,' she frowned. 'An eight-year-old child. It must have been terrifying.'

'It would have been, but for Grandmother.'

'She was ill, I remember.'

'But she was strong.' The Latin he spoke was hesitant, as it would be in one who hadn't used the language for so many years. 'When they came, everyone was screaming and running around. Grandmother filled a leather sack with food and clothes and wrapped a cloak around me. Then she prayed.' He shook his head at the memory. 'She prayed until this big warrior burst into the room and then she stood up and faced him, holding my hand. He had a sword, and she was old and old people are just vermin to the slavers, but he must have seen something in her eyes, because he just nodded and waved us out into the courtyard. They roped us to the others and marched us to the boat.'

Another long pause, but she understood not to break it. The young mind was searching his memory and arranging his thoughts to turn them into words.

'I remember the damp and the cold, and the stink of the bilgewater and the sick, the constant movement of the planks and the whistling sound of the wind through the ropes, but I wasn't afraid, because Grandmother kept me close.' Valeria felt a twinge of anguish pierce her heart at the reminder of her mother's comforting presence. For six years they'd believed Venutia dead, and, for all her urgings to Marcus about letting go, to hear her spoken of with such love tore something inside her. 'She warmed me with her body,' the boy continued, 'and nourished me from the bag. Others died of despair or when the chill ate through their flesh and reached their heart; but for her I might have been the same. When we reached Treva they placed us in a pen, and we huddled together like animals against the cold. At dawn the following day a man appeared, a giant, who almost ripped the gates of the pen from their hinges in his eagerness. Our guards showed no alarm at this disturbance. Apparently, it was his practice to inspect every cargo of slaves when they landed. He stood among us, a chest broad as an ox cart, and a great pale beard and I remember his eyes darting from one captive to the next. Until they fell on me. "The boy is mine," he cried, though I did not know it then. "This boy belongs to Wigga, *edilhingui* of the Angrivarii." The guards came for me, but my grandmother stood with her hand on my shoulder and glared at them. I know now that another great Saxon lord would have cut her down without a thought, but Wigga was different. A truly good man, who treated even his slaves fairly, and a lord who commanded great respect from all who knew him. The guards looked to him, and Wigga laughed with that great roar of his and said: "Why not, two for the price of one is a great bargain, especially if she can cook." It turned out that Wigga had lost his youngest son to the black rot after he'd been gored by a boar. And that is how I became Wulf, son of Wigga.'

Valeria snatched a glance at her companion. His jaw clenched, the dark eyes brooding now and locked on the horizon. He looked so much like his father that she thought, *No, Brenus, I may someday call you Wulf, but that will never make you the son of Wigga*. Yet his affection for the man he called father was genuine and powerful, and her heart emptied for a beat as she understood that it might all have been for nothing. Could a man like Marcus and someone as filled with hatred as Brenus ever be reconciled?

'Wigga took us in and we were accepted,' Brenus continued his story as Marcus called a halt beside a stream, 'but only after a fashion and because of his authority. At first his wife, Berta, resented my presence, though she took to Grandmother well enough; and his other sons would have drowned me in the well if they'd dared. But it was Wigga who mattered, and Wigga who was proud when he discovered his new son could not only speak as a Roman, but read and write as well. The *edilhingui* of Treva controlled trade in and out of the Albis. Quite often those involved in the most lucrative trade were from beyond the Rhenus and spoke Latin as their first language. I could be useful to him. But he also wanted me to be a warrior, so from that moment on I was brought up as a Saxon. I played and swam in the river with Saxon boys, fought with them, suffered alongside them when we stole from the kitchens, and wielded a sword from the moment I had the strength to hold it.' He dismounted and scooped a mouthful of water from the stream. 'Grandmother's dead, isn't she?'

Valeria felt as if she'd been drenched in ice water. Her first instinct was to deny it, but she knew that if she was discovered in the lie, she would never earn his trust. 'How did you know?'

'She would never have willingly left me,' he said, quite controlled. 'Even if she was dying.'

'And was she?'

He nodded. 'Yes. I think knowing I needed her gave her a reason to live, but once she saw me making my own way and my own mark, she began to fade. Berta thought she had only a few days left, at most. Did he kill her?'

'No, it was an accident.'

'She never gave up hope, you know.' His eyes bored into her. 'She always said he would come, even after she knew I didn't want him to. Why didn't he come earlier?'

Valeria hesitated, but it was time. 'When you were taken, Marcus was on the Wall with the Picts massing in the north. He had a plan to force them into battle, and he did, at a place called Longovicium.'

'My father the hero.' The acknowledgement of his true paternity made her blink, but the tone dripped contempt and his stare never wavered.

'To draw the Picts out, Marcus had to give the impression he was prepared to play the traitor,' she continued. 'After the victory, evil men in Britannia wanted that to be the truth. There had to be an inquiry, which took many months. Then more complications: he was summoned south to fight the Saxons. He was trapped. He could not come any earlier.'

'And yet here you are now.' It was almost a sneer and the curled lip reminded her he was little more than a child. She had to restrain herself from slapping him.

'You should be more grateful,' she said. 'Soon you will live among your own people again.'

'You don't understand.' That ghost of a smile again, but this time calculated to infuriate her still further. He stood to his full height and she rose with him, their eyes level. 'I am a Saxon, and my brothers are out there in the forest hunting me even now. They will never give up.

You will never leave this land alive and it will be my pleasure to avenge my father by killing Marcus Flavius Victor.' He turned and led his horse away.

'Brenus?' The boy swivelled, his young face a mask of fury, and it pleased Valeria to know she still had claws. 'You will find your father is a hard man to kill.'

XVII

That night they wrapped themselves in their blankets among the trees, close to a small pond covered with a lurid green scum that turned even the horses away. The next day, at Valeria's suggestion, Leof took position beside Brenus, with Luko, who'd spent the night with his arm tied to the boy's wrist, grinning behind them.

'Can't I even take a piss without you watching?' Brenus snarled over his shoulder. Luko only laughed, but he dropped back when Leof waved him away.

'The lady Valeria said I should call you Wulf, if that is acceptable to you?'

The words were in the Saxon tongue and Brenus gave his companion an appraising look. He was aware Leof had been a Saxon prisoner before being accepted into Marcus's cavalry regiment. That fact alone made him worthy of respect. Leof was also the member of the company closest to his own age, though he guessed five or six years separated them.

'Why do you stay with them?' he demanded with the abruptness of youth. 'This is your land and there is nothing to stop you returning to your people.'

'Nothing but my oath,' Leof agreed. 'And the fact that your father – Marcus – promised me the *Heart of Petrus* which you saw burning back there, and which was the sweetest little sailer on the ocean. Still, I think he would release me from my oath, if I wished it, but I do not wish it.'

'You sound as if you admire him? He is a murderer and a liar.'

Leof laughed. 'That he is, Wulf. That he is. But he's also a warrior and a leader any man could follow. Even perhaps you.' Brenus spat, but Leof only carried on cheerfully. 'Did you know I was captured on the raid that took you and your grandmother? No? I was fifteen, about a year older than you are now. Full of youthful arrogance and spite and desperate to stick a spear in someone's guts just to hear them howl. He could have had my throat cut, probably should have. He had a reputation for ruthlessness and cruelty that men feared. But he didn't.' A memory stirred Leof and he frowned. 'Though the bastard let me think he was going to do it for almost a month. No matter, he realized I could be useful to him and when I'd been of service, he rewarded me. Remember that, Wulf, a great man must always be free with his thanks and his silver. You cannot buy loyalty, but you can earn it. Wigga was like that.'

'You knew my father?' Brenus gaped.

'I knew of him,' Leof corrected. 'I saw him perhaps two or three times. A giant of a man and a great hero to a young boy.'

'And yet you came here prepared to kill him.'

'Wigga let his men get drunk every night and if there was a guard, he was asleep. Marcus would never have allowed that to happen. If you are not strong enough to hold what you have, someone will take it from you. That is the Saxon way.' He could see Brenus's jaw working and he smiled. 'Don't be angry with me, Wulf. It is just fate, and a man can't escape his fate. If Wigga had managed to kill your father I'd be your prisoner now. Though I doubt my countrymen would be quite as kind to a Saxon fighting beside the Romans.'

'But they're not Romans, are they?' Brenus blurted. 'Wigga explained it to me. "The Britons are paid by the Romans to be their own jailers," he said. "They are a weak people. Cows to be milked." A Saxon knows no master. No true Saxon would ever fight for the Romans.'

100

'You see what you want to see.' Leof laughed. 'There are Saxon settlements all over southern Britannia, full of Saxon warriors paid in silver to help protect Roman towns and villas from their own countrymen. A Saxon is no braver or more honourable than any other man. We are a bastard race of many tribes: the Chatti and the Cherusci, the Chauci and the Angrivarii. They banded together because none was strong enough alone to defend themselves against the enemy from the east. That is another thing a Saxon learns young. There is always another enemy in the east who wants your land, or your women, or your silver. Who is this year's enemy? The Longobardi, Vandals, or the Goths?'

'No.' All the bluster seemed to have faded from Brenus. 'My father said the old enemies of the east are no more. They have been replaced by a terror. A nation of cruel merciless beasts who drink the blood of their enemies and who, where they pass, leave no living thing alive, man, woman or child, not even the cows in the field. They call themselves Huns.'

Next evening they made camp among the trees by a large lake. Marcus used the interval to bathe for the first time in many days and his tired bones felt all the better for it. They could see the lamps of a large village a mile away on the far side of the water, but Leof assured Marcus it was unlikely any of the locals would venture out after dark.

'Tomorrow we turn south,' the Saxon said, 'and I have been thinking, lord, about what we should do when we reach Leuphana.'

'You said the shipmasters would carry anyone if they saw enough silver?'

'That is true, more or less,' Leof assured him. 'But I may have made it appear simpler than it may well be.'

Marcus wasn't surprised; it was the way of things that a plan required adjustments when it met reality. 'Valeria should hear this,' he decided. 'And Zeno and Luko.'

He called them over and Leof scratched his chin as he sought the correct words. 'I think that when we approach the river again, we cannot do so as what we appear to be. If a war band approaches the settlement, they're more likely to close the gates than offer us passage.'

'Then we'll be traders,' Marcus said. 'We'll load the remounts with all our supplies; four of us will pose as merchants and the rest as guards for our valuable wares.'

'That still doesn't solve the problem that only one of us speaks Saxon,' Valeria pointed out. 'Two if you count Brenus, which I doubt would be wise.'

'Exactly, lady.' Leof ignored Marcus's snort of irritation. 'But I think there is a solution. Every man in the squadron, apart from me, speaks the Pictish tongue.'

'So?' Marcus shrugged. 'Every soldier on the Wall must be fluent in Pictish before they are allowed on their first patrol.'

'Then my suggestion is that you pose as an emissary from the king of Pictland to one of the great tribes of the east, the Vandals, the Goths or the Suevi. That would account for the heavily armed escort and the way you are so free with your silver. It would deter any avaricious tribal leader from blocking your progress or trying to rob you. Dressed in all your martial finery, I have no doubt—'

'What martial finery?' Marcus interrupted. 'Like everyone else all I have is what I stand up in.'

Leof exchanged a glance with Valeria.

'We carried your helmet and chain armour on one of the remounts,' Valeria said. The helmet was a thing of magnificence: sheathed with silver and studded with garnets, it had a long nose guard, hinged cheekpieces that strapped together beneath his chin, and a broad neck protector. Bands of iron ran from brow to nape and ear to ear to reinforce the dome. Yet, if Marcus was being honest, he hated the helmet. In battle it marked him out as a target for any ambitious warrior seeking plunder and fame. But his blood-father had taught him that a commander had to be more than a leader. He must also be a symbol. 'I thought you'd rather I brought them along than leave them for whoever took over the villa when we left. Every man also has his iron helmet and his cloak.'

'It could work,' Marcus agreed. An embassy, from whatever land or ruler, would always be given a certain precedence. Would he have stood in the way of a small, richly endowed Pictish lord and his escort who said they were on their way to Londinium? Yes, he'd have had his suspicions. But so few men? They were hardly a threat to the Empire. No, on balance he'd have regarded them as a nuisance and a puzzle, provided a small escort to the next fort and been glad to see the back of them.

'Stilicho's letter, with its fine, official-looking seals, might also be an asset, lord,' Zeno suggested. 'Not that I'd advise letting anyone have sight of the contents, but a quick princely wave of the document would do us no harm.'

'And what do you think, decurion?' Marcus asked his sister. 'It seems you have the gift of foresight.'

'Not foresight, brother.' Valeria didn't rise to the jibe. 'Only the gift of planning ahead, which you have so often reminded me should be the first instinct of every good officer. We are strangers, trapped in a hostile land. Our first priority is survival, which means supplies. The second is to reach safety. Anything we can do to achieve that end is worthwhile. I believe Leof's plan gives us the greatest prospect of success, and that you have sufficient guile and experience,' she smiled, 'not to say arrogance, to play the imperious potentate. It is the one way to put our treasure to good use without raising suspicions.' She reached into a bag at her feet and brought out the silver helmet. 'But it does not matter what I think, does it, brother?' She handed him the splendid helm.

Marcus weighed the helmet in his hands and shook his head with a wry smile. 'Then let us say farewell to Marcus Flavius Victor,' he pulled the helm over his head, 'and welcome to our company Cinead, prince of the Picti.'

XVIII

Leuphana (Wittenberge)

'Authority is all,' Marcus muttered to himself. 'If you look like a Pictish emissary and act like an emissary and have thirty swords that say you're an emissary, no man will be able to deny you're an emissary.'

Julius and Ninian had polished his chain armour to a brilliant lustre using sand and gravel from the lakeside beach, and Valeria had done as much as their limited resources allowed to make his travel-stained clothes presentable. The once-green cloak every man wore would cover many a tear and blemish, but on Marcus it could not be allowed to disguise too much. The shine on that fine chain armour, in tandem with the magnificence of his helmet and the gilt eagle on his sword pommel, must be allowed to impress. It helped that he rode tall in the saddle on a horse that had been chosen to carry his bulk and the iron that encased it, and that the rugged contours of his face would have looked perfectly at home in a Saxon feasting hall. For all that his father had been a Roman aristocrat, and an Emperor at that, Marcus had been formed by his Brigantian forebears and by his service on the northern frontier. It was a face that, even in repose, appeared naturally stern. A face with which no man would readily argue.

Leof took station at his shoulder to act as his interpreter. Behind them, in a tight column of twos, rode the finest the Ala Sabiniana could produce, every soldier a veteran and their mounts sleek and well groomed even after four days on the move.

'If anybody is still wearing a cross,' Marcus called over his shoulder, 'make sure it's hidden. There are no Christians here. From now on we are Pictish pagans.'

They approached Leuphana by a track from the north. Much of the area around the settlement had been cleared to create farmland, and when they emerged from the trees a broad swathe of fertile country stretched as far as the river. Scattered, thatch-roofed farmsteads and small estates dotted the fields and woodland, and beyond them a larger settlement lay behind a rough, poorly maintained palisade.

Whoever was watching them from the town, and Marcus sensed they were the subject of more than one pair of suspicious eyes, would certainly be impressed by what they saw. The Saxons marched to war in any old fashion, their pace dictated by the whim of the leaders of the individual war bands. Few though they were, a full squadron of seasoned cavalrymen in perfect column of two, led by a great lord in all his finery, would be a sight few of the townsfolk had witnessed.

The settlement gates hung open and they saw a group of men waiting in the shadow of the gateway. Marcus's right hand strayed towards his sword hilt, but a closer study showed him this was a welcoming party, unarmed and on a scale judged to reflect his perceived status. He halted the column thirty paces from the gates and rode forward with Leof. Following his lead, two elders stepped clear of the group and advanced to meet the approaching riders. The dignitary on the right wore some kind of chain of office at his neck, the other a white robe which presumably marked him as a priest or holy man.

Marcus gave the elders an opportunity to admire his gilded helmet before removing it. Then he waited patiently while Leof greeted the two men with a long monologue punctuated by occasional gestures towards Marcus, who inclined his head with suitable gravity at what he considered the appropriate moments. The official – presumably the town's patriarch – reciprocated in kind, but the priest only stared, stony-faced.

When Leof completed his address, the elder replied at similar length, and Leof translated as he spoke. 'His name is Oswin and he is the head of the council. I told him we are an embassy from Pictland on the way to meet with the King of the Longobardi, with whom the Saxons are on friendly terms, and that we seek to hire suitable vessels to carry ourselves and our animals upriver. He seemed happy enough with the story, especially when I said we were prepared to pay generously. We are most welcome in Leuphana and he is sure they will be able to find suitable vessels for us. The river is not long thawed, and still tricky with melt ice, so he's had several ships wintering here who'll be keen to take on any cargo that will give them a profit. Now he's offering to provide us with food and drink, and perhaps a bed for the night after our tiring journey.'

'Thank him for his offer,' Marcus bowed his head again, 'but we don't intend to trouble him for long. If he could show us to the dockside and introduce us to the shipmasters, that is all we ask of him.'

Leof translated. Oswin frowned at the abrupt refusal of his hospitality and exchanged a glance with his companion. The priest nodded, but was clearly not best pleased, and Marcus wondered why. He turned and waved Julius forward. 'Perhaps you and your people will accept this small gift for your trouble.'

The young Pict reached into a leather sack and pulled out a large silver torc taken from one of the Pictish dead at Longovicium. He dismounted and presented it to Oswin with a bow and a flood of Pictish words that Marcus suspected were actually a mortal insult. Oswin looked puzzled rather than pleased at being presented with a gift that would probably pay for the hire of one of the ships on its own. Marcus looked to the priest, but the man's expression hadn't altered, which was also odd. A reaction or acknowledgement of some kind would only have been human. Julius remounted and Oswin waved them forward, calling out to the men waiting inside the gate.

'What's he saying?' Marcus asked Leof as they followed Oswin, the priest and the elders into the settlement.

'He's telling them we're going to the ships. It's strange, though,' the Saxon frowned. 'He's emphasized the ships two or three times, as if he's talking to someone who's deaf, or if they'd been expecting us to go somewhere else.'

'Where were they going to feed us?'

Leof cast an eye warily at the houses and storage huts they passed. 'The feasting house most likely. I'll be honest, lord, I think the sooner we're out of here the better. That holy man had a hungry look I didn't much like.'

Marcus took in the little groups who gathered at the doors of their homes to watch the column pass. Women and old men mainly, but very few children, which surprised him. Normally a spectacle like this would attract curious children like wasps to rotting fruit. No men working in the gardens, empty workshops, a blacksmith's forge with glowing coals but no one tending it. He turned his mount and rode back along the column. 'You feel it?' he said quietly as he passed Valeria.

'They had word about what happened at Treva.'

Marcus nodded grimly and returned to his place at the head of the column. By now they were deep in the centre of Leuphana, passing through a broad market place with a feasting hall nearby. Still no men in sight, which confirmed his suspicions. A small face appeared in a doorway only to be pulled instantly back inside.

'We'll stay in the saddle,' he told Leof quietly. 'When we reach the quayside, tell the old man he'll be the first to die if anything happens. But do it quietly, with no fuss. I don't want a fight if we can avoid it.'

The buildings close to the river were mainly warehouses and stores, big buildings that would conceal a hundred men apiece, and Marcus was relieved when they emerged from the shadows into the open. Ahead, the river flowed sulkily in swirling eddies from left to right. It was perhaps a hundred and fifty paces across, and small ice floes pocked the surface of its dull grey waters. Four ships were tied up at a wooden wharf and a short pier that stretched into the river. Two of them – broad, deep-bodied river barges perhaps forty paces in length and built to carry livestock and other substantial cargo – lay broadside on to the wharf on either side of the pier, while the others sat next to the pier itself. They all floated high in the water, which suggested they were empty, although piles of cloth bales and baulks of raw timber were evidence that at least one of them was ready to be loaded. Wide ramps had been placed against the sides of the closest two ships.

Not the slightest movement showed on any of them, which was unusual. In Marcus's experience, no sailor or fisherman was ever content if he wasn't making and mending while he was ashore, whether it was replacing caulk in the seams or repairing a net or a sail. About fifty paces of flattened earth separated the warehouses from the wharf, an area that would double as a market or a holding place for livestock.

An awkward pause greeted their arrival at the river. Somehow most of the elders had managed to disappear during the journey through the streets, and only Oswin, the priest and two others remained. Oswin looked up at Marcus with a fixed smile, and would have edged away if Leof hadn't moved his horse in behind him. The old man froze as Leof whispered something and Marcus noted the glint of a blade in the small of the elder's back. The priest called out to Oswin, sharp and urgent, but Leof snarled at him to shut his mouth.

'Tell him all we want is to get on the ships,' Marcus said. 'We can worry about the supplies further upriver. Nobody will get hurt if they stand back and allow us to load the horses.'

'What about the shipmasters and crews? We won't get far without them.'

'They can either stay here and watch us sail away in their boats, or they can come aboard and be well paid for their services. Say it loud, I have a feeling they won't be far away.'

Leof did as he was asked. The priest snarled something back at him, but his furtive glance at the ships told Marcus what he wanted to know. He was just about to give the order to board when Leof shouted a warning.

'Lord!'

XIX

With a confused roar about fifty men broke in a great disorganized mass from the streets opposite the pier.

'Christ save us,' Valeria called. 'What do we do now?'

'We came for the ships, so we'll take them.' Marcus could feel the familiar elixir of battle coursing through his veins, but his mind was already calculating their response to the charge. 'You take Julius and his men and fight your way on board.'

His sister darted a glance at the seemingly empty barges. 'Fight?'

'You'll see. But for God's sake don't kill the crews if you can help it. We need as many prisoners as we can get.' He studied the men advancing across the open ground. 'I'll deal with this rabble.'

He knew Valeria wanted to contest the order – why should she need nearly half the squadron to capture the apparently harmless ships – but she darted away shouting for her troop.

'What should I do with him?' Leof still had Oswin by the scruff of the neck. The priest and the two other elders had used the noise of the attack as cover to scurry back towards the town.

'Throw him in the river. If he can swim, we'll come back for him later. Form up!' Leof did as he was ordered, accompanied by a cry of terror and an almighty splash. Marcus replaced his helmet and drew his sword, turning his mount towards the enemy and taking his place at the centre of the rank of horsemen.

A mere twenty men arrayed in a single line. The Saxons outnumbered them by more than two to one, but they'd made a mistake. Everything that had happened since Marcus and his men entered the settlement had the hallmarks of a hastily prepared plan. Clearly, the community had some kind of warning about the war band that had attacked Wigga's estate, but they couldn't have been aware of the nature of the men they faced. When the townsfolk heard of their approach, Oswin and his elders had come up with a scheme to lure Marcus and his men to the feasting hall. There they'd be fed and given ale, perhaps drugged or poisoned, then, in the close confines of the hall, overwhelmed and slaughtered.

It was a decent plan, with a good chance of success, but when Marcus turned down the offer of sustenance, they'd been forced to quickly replace it. They should have closed the gates behind the intruders and blocked off the streets. In the cramped confines between the houses Marcus and his soldiers would have been under attack from all sides, their horsemanship useless. Instead, the elders had hatched a plot where the marauders would be trapped between the houses and warehouses and the river. Yet here on this broad patch of earth with the howls of the attackers muffled by the leather lining of his helmet Marcus had seldom felt more confident.

'Squadron will advance on me,' he roared.

He led them forward at the walk, but within a few strides he'd increased the tempo to a fast trot, causing consternation among the ranks of the attackers. Two or three of the leaders stumbled and fell to their knees, transfixed by Senecio's arrows. In seconds the headlong charge slowed to a stuttering halt. Even the most seasoned warrior would quail as a line of cavalry horses thundered towards them, and these men were not warriors. They were traders and craftsmen, storekeepers and warehouse workers. One or two carried swords, but these were the men targeted by Senecio; most of the others had spears at best, or reaping hooks, and Marcus saw the blacksmith carrying his big hammer. But Marcus's troopers didn't fear a civilian with a hammer or a spear. They had honed their fighting skills day after day for ten or fifteen years and this was what they lived for.

Twenty paces separated them now. Some of the attackers were already running away, pushing past the priest as he exhorted them to advance. Marcus looked upon them now and he didn't see the enemy. Only victims.

Valeria had little time to think as her little group formed up around her. They lined up opposite the ramp of the upstream ship. Marcus had planted a seed of suspicion in her mind and that seed quickly grew to certainty. Julius and the second section were similarly positioned by the downstream vessel and she signalled him to advance. This was no time for hesitation or doubt. She nudged her mount into motion and with Ninian at her side trotted up the plank and leapt the animal into the bottom of the boat. As it cleared the side, she looked down to see the terrified faces of a dozen men crouched behind the planking where they'd been waiting to attack Marcus's men from the rear. *Bastard*, she smiled. *You knew.* Even as her horse landed her sword was already sweeping down to carve the startled features of the closest enemy. These were cavalry horses, trained to fight, and in the narrow confines of the boat the animal's yellowing teeth snapped at the next man and its hooves lashed out to splinter the planking. Ninian was laughing and behind her she could hear the others, attacking on foot, dropping into the bottom of the ship, and the terrified screams of their victims.

'Prisoners,' belatedly, she remembered Marcus's final words. 'We need the crew alive if you don't want to do all the rowing.' Already the boat's defenders were casting aside their weapons and kneeling to clasp their hands in supplication. Valeria calmed her horse and dismounted. The bilge slopped red with bloody water, but only three Saxons lay slumped on the boards, and the attackers had suffered no casualties.

Ninian and Tosodio herded the prisoners into the stern, including an older man with a ruddy, dour face, who she guessed must be the shipmaster. She saw him staring at her and lifted the pot helmet from

111

her head, ruffled her dark hair and let it flop over her shoulders. The sailor gasped and made the sign against evil and Valeria smiled.

Marcus's cavalrymen had charged in a tight, disciplined line, opening their ranks at the last moment to choose individual victims. The few Saxons who continued to attack had been cut down like stalks of wheat and those who remained either clustered together in defensive huddles or milled around looking for some kind of leadership. He saw the white-clad priest continuing to exhort men to attack and he arced round to where he could come at him from the rear. The priest turned at the sound of approaching hooves, but it was already too late. Marcus's blade swung in an instinctive cut that would have carved the man's skull open. At the last moment he twisted the sword so it struck the priest's head with the flat of the heavy blade and he collapsed like a pole-axed ox.

'Round up the rest,' Marcus shouted. The squadron circled and began to herd the surviving groups towards the ships. 'Leof, tell them to drop their weapons and they won't come to any harm.'

The majority did as they were ordered, and those who continued to carry spears or knives were swiftly persuaded to abandon them by pricks of a sword point.

Marcus walked his mount to where Valeria was waiting by the ramp of the captured ship. She gestured to the cowed prisoners. 'What are we supposed to do with them?'

'Find something to bind their hands,' he said as he dismounted and removed his helmet. 'We'll decide who goes and who stays once the horses have been loaded. Where's the elder – what was his name? – Oswin?' Marcus called to Leof.

The Saxon peered down into the river between the ship and the wharf with a thoughtful look on his face. 'It appears he couldn't swim after all, lord, at least not with that big silver torc around his neck.'

'Damn,' Marcus grimaced. 'Then fetch that priest and anyone else who looks prosperous and bring them to the boats.'

'Marcus?' Valeria called.

'What now?' he snarled.

'It's the ships. Only the two by the wharf are big enough to accommodate the horses, and they'll only take a dozen or so each. The others will have to be left behind.'

Marcus winced at this latest body blow. It meant losing a quarter of the horses. The seven packhorses would be first on the list, but at least six or seven more would have to go and a cavalryman was nothing without his mount. Who knew how far they'd have to ride once they left the river. If they had to move at the pace of men on foot it could double the journey time. Every extra day in barbarian territory increased the danger to them all. He cursed, but no amount of thought or calculation would change the reality.

'You're sure about the other ships?'

'You might fit in a horse and a couple of men, lord,' it was Leof who answered, 'but the guards would be outnumbered by the crew. Most likely we'd wake up one morning and they'd be gone and our people would be feeding the fishes. More trouble than it's worth.'

'All right. The men won't like it, but we've no choice. Tell whoever loses out that we'll find them remounts further upriver. Is that possible, do you think?'

'We'll find something,' Leof assured him. 'They may not be pretty and they won't be cavalry-trained, but our lads can ride anything on four legs.'

Marcus's mind was still whirling from the fight. What next? What had he forgotten?

'We need supplies,' Valeria answered the question for him. 'We're down to three days' food a man and four of fodder for the animals. Should we search the warehouses?'

'It would take hours to find what we need and we don't want to be still here at nightfall. No, you finish loading the horses and getting our prisoners settled. I'll deal with the supplies.'

Marcus replaced his helmet and remounted. He walked his horse through the carelessly scattered dead towards the watchers among the buildings and waved Leof to his side. They halted twenty paces from the crowd of staring faces. 'Tell them they can tend to their dead and injured once we have left. Make sure everyone can hear. I wanted none of this; whoever persuaded them to carry out this foolish attack is responsible.'

He waited until Leof had relayed the message, watching the faces change from fear to puzzlement and in some cases anger.

'I did not want this,' he continued. 'But that shouldn't make them think I am reluctant to shed more blood. They have angered me and that was very foolish. I need supplies, enough to feed fifty men for one week, and the same for thirty horses. To this end I have taken hostages, men, some of them prominent men, who not so long ago were trying to kill me and my warriors. If these people deliver the supplies to the wharf by the two barges, I will pledge to release the hostages on the bank a little way upriver.' A murmur of unease ran through the townsfolk as Leof translated the words. 'Does any man have the authority to speak for them?'

A greybeard stepped out of the crowd. 'I am the last of the elder council.' His voice shook, but not with fear. Marcus could see his jaw working with suppressed fury. 'All the rest lie there,' he flung out a hand towards the dead, 'or in the ships you plan to steal.'

'The shipmasters will be paid, and the barges will be back with their owners soon enough,' Marcus assured him. 'And I will leave twelve of my horses in payment for the supplies, though any two of them would cover the purchase price of the boats. You have two hours to deliver the supplies to the wharf.'

'And if we do not?' the man challenged.

Marcus slowly removed the helmet so all could see his face, the features so grim and unyielding they might have been carved from stone. 'If I have to leave without my supplies, or any part of them, we will discover how many of your friends can swim with their legs tied to a rock,' he said. A new clamour erupted as Leof translated. 'And if as much as a single apple is deliberately tainted I will burn five of the hostages on the nearest accessible strand upstream of here. Do you understand?'

The colour drained from the elder's face, but he nodded. Marcus left Leof to complete the arrangements and returned to the barges. He was surprised to find Brenus, freed from his bonds, among the men helping to board the last of the horses.

'Is he safe to be loose on shore?' he asked Luko.

Brenus answered with a bitter laugh. 'Oh, I have nowhere to run after what you've done here,' the boy said. 'The people would tear me limb from limb before I could give them any sort of explanation. You carry death with you everywhere you go as a hedgepig carries fleas.'

'Careful with that horse.' Marcus handed Brenus the reins of his mount. Oddly, he was heartened by the insult. 'As a hedgepig carries fleas' had been one of his father's sayings. Brenus must have learned it from Venutia.

XX

The faint glow in the leaden clouds told Marcus they were no longer travelling east, but that the barge was now carrying them directly south. A small ice floe, one of the many that dotted the river's surface, hit the bow with a resounding *smack*, but did nothing to check the mesmeric rhythm of the oarsmen who powered the vessel upstream against the slow current. The creak of the oars in their worn leather straps and the swish of the blades in the dark water had a mind-numbing quality. Allied to the unchanging nature of the river and the never-ending fringe of scrubby trees lining the reed-choked banks, it sometimes felt as if time itself stood still.

Once they'd seen the colour of Marcus's silver the bargemasters had been perfectly amenable to carrying men and horses as far upstream as they wanted to travel. As they said, business was business, and one load of cargo as good as another, especially if a man had a purse of silver at his belt and the promise of another when the passengers disembarked. They'd been persuaded to take part in the ambush by tales of the great treasure Marcus and his men carried, but they were Albis bargemen not warriors, and happy to be back on the river. Ten oarsmen to a side propelled each barge, perched on raised rowing benches set at intervals along the flanks. The Saxons were docile enough now, and apparently entirely focused on keeping rhythm, but Marcus had stationed Senecio by the stern post with his bow to ensure they stayed that way. The hostages had been untied and put over the side in the shallows a few miles upstream of Leuphana, and they'd continued on their way with the curses of the priest ringing in their ears.

Theirs was the first vessel; the second, under Valeria's command, kept station fifty paces behind. The horses – twenty-eight of them now – were securely tethered shoulder to shoulder in a line in the centre of the barges, hooded except when they were being fed or watered, and with their troopers a constant reassuring presence at their heads.

Marcus wondered if one of the smaller, lighter ships from Leuphana might overtake them at some point during the night, and carry word of their coming to the settlements ahead, but the shipmaster, a man named Gutrum, assured him it wasn't possible.

'Even if anyone was brave enough to risk your honour's displeasure,' Leof translated the boatman's words, 'he doubts it would happen. Though they're faster than this great tub over a short distance, they carry fewer oarsmen, and in a long haul they'd never catch us. Nor will they travel at night. They're fragile little creatures, those boats. One bump from a big branch and you're food for the eels.'

If their situation had been less perilous it would have been a pleasant way to travel, though a man would be a fool to allow his hand to stray far from his sword. Everything had gone remarkably well so far, but Leof predicted greater challenges ahead.

'It's not just the river that changes with every season,' he told Marcus as they stared out to the tree-lined banks. 'Sometimes the people do too. We're still in Saxon territory and will be for at least another day, but after that who knows? The last time I was here our neighbours were Longobardians, but maybe some tribe of Sarmatians have driven them away east, or the earth has lost its vigour and they've decided to move over the river to find somewhere where the land is richer and more fertile. Even Gutrum can't be sure. He spent the winter in Leuphana after delivering a cargo of timber there, and hasn't been this way for many months. At some point there will no doubt be a toll to pay. It could be that whoever seeks the toll will also take a fancy to the horses, but I believe we carry enough swords to put off any enterprising thieves. I know Lupfurdum only by reputation. Beyond that I am blind. We must trust in Gutrum now.'

Brenus huddled in a cloak close to Senecio, and Marcus went to where the African bowman perched comfortably in the stern. 'You can stand down, trooper,' he said. 'I doubt they'll give us any trouble now.'

'If they do, the bargemaster is the first one who'll pay the price.' Senecio grinned. 'That fat gut of his makes a tempting target. I'll help the others water the horses, lord.'

Marcus took a seat beside his son, but the boy moved away and refused to meet his eyes.

'You can hate me as much as you want, but it doesn't change the fact that I am your father. I regret Wigga's death, I think I might have liked him, but I can't change that.'

'Do you regret my grandmother's death?' Brenus spat.

'Yes,' Marcus sighed. 'I should have told you about her earlier, but would it have made any difference?'

'Nothing you can say will make any difference.' His eyes lifted and he gave Marcus that cold, unsettling stare of his. 'One day I will avenge Wigga, you will no longer be my father and then I'll be free of you.'

'All right,' Marcus nodded. 'If that's the way it is going to be, it appears now is all the time we're going to have. I'm not a patient man, Brenus, you'll have noticed that. But I'm going to try to explain why we are here and what has made me the man I am. It's up to you whether you listen or not, but if you do maybe you'll learn a bit about yourself.'

Brenus stayed silent, but he made no attempt to move further away, and Marcus interpreted it as leave to continue.

'We were born to war, you and I. My first memories are of my mother – your grandmother – showing me the best places to hide if we were attacked by Pictish raiders. Before I was five years old, the Picts swarmed over the frontier, in concert with the Scotti from the west and the Saxons from the east, and brought fire and sword to our land. We were forced to flee to Eboracum while my father, Brenus, fought them until the great general Theodosius rushed to Britannia's aid with an army from Gaul. The Picts are like a plague that returns every few years no matter how often you think you've destroyed them. I joined my father in the saddle when I was younger than you are now, and learned the art of war and the ways of command from him. He was a hard man, because only by being hard could he defend what he loved. Nothing was ever good enough for him. Yet I endured, and when they came again, I was an officer of the Roman cavalry. I fought beside Magnus Maximus and Flavius Stilicho to keep Britannia free.'

'Free?' Brenus spat. 'My grandmother told me our tribe, the Brigantes, were free before the Romans came with their army and their forts and their tax collectors, and that if the Brigantes had combined with the other tribes of Britannia they would still be free. Yet you boast of fighting for our oppressors?'

'You can only fit the skin you are given.' Marcus felt an odd mix of irritation at the accusation he might be a traitor and relief that his son still cared enough to answer. 'I was brought up as a Roman, and your grandmother played her part in that. I know the history of my tribe as well as you do, but a man can't change the past. All I could do was try to live up to the reputation and ideals of Brenus, the man for whom you are named. We were Romans now, he said, though he insisted on wearing the symbols of his tribe, and we would fight and die as Romans to protect what we had. He died protecting Britannia.'

'And you could not even protect your mother and your son and all the others at Grabant who depended on you.'

Marcus winced at the contempt in the boy's voice. 'Yes, you could tell me I should have left a squadron at Grabant,' he admitted. 'But I needed every man in the saddle to do what I had to do. And I was right,' his voice hardened more than he intended and he saw Brenus's eyes narrow, 'because those troopers saved Britannia and broke the power of the Picts.'

'In essence, you sacrificed us.'

119

For a moment Marcus was rendered speechless. Where had this come from? This grown-up Brenus was more like his mother than made him comfortable. He felt a presence at his shoulder and turned to snarl at whoever it was to leave them alone, but it was only Senecio with two cups of bitter Saxon ale, one of which he handed to Brenus.

'No,' Marcus shook his head. How could he have known? The Saxon raiders had never penetrated so far inland before.

'And then you left us for six years.' Brenus looked as if he wanted to throw the ale in Marcus's face. 'Left us to rot as far as you knew.'

'My duty was to the province.' Marcus struggled with the words. 'I did what I had to do.'

'Your own mother. She lived in hope every day that Marcus Flavius Victor would come for us. I was eight years old and I believed her. I did not always hate you. It was only when Wigga placed his arm around me and told me he would be a true father to me that I realized I'd never had a father. The man who spoke to me gently and reassured me that I had nothing to fear was entirely different from the tyrant I'd feared and avoided, and who had never shown me a moment's love.'

'You were a weak child. You—'

'Killed my mother?' Brenus's eyes blazed. 'Yes, that is why you despised me at first. But weak or not, I was your son. You couldn't find it in your heart to forgive me something for which I was blameless? Instead you used my weakness as an excuse to continue blaming me long after it was justified. The truth is you never wanted to be a father.'

Could it be true? Marcus tried to search his memory. He'd been on campaign beyond the Wall when Julia had come to her birthing. Julia. Even the name made his eyes twinge. She'd been so young when his mother brought them together. A cousin's daughter, high in rank and a good match. Tall and poised, with silky black hair, she'd been wise beyond her years and tolerant of the awkward, sometimes uncouth soldier he'd become. The odd thing was that she'd worshipped him from the very start, and he'd been besotted with her. Brenus, whatever had happened since, had been the result of a union blessed with genuine love. When he'd had word of what happened he'd felt like falling on his sword. All that had stopped him was the knowledge that he had a son. But, from the moment he set eyes on Brenus, all he'd seen was the thing responsible for Julia's death. Why was he left with this puny infant? How could the child replace what he'd taken from his father? He'd visited Julia's grave and left the same night, returning only when he had no other option, or when guilt dragged him back to Grabant. It wasn't logical or sensible, but, at the time, it had seemed the only way he could cope with his grief.

'Perhaps,' he acknowledged at last. 'I had no experience of that kind of loss, so . . .' he bit his tongue on the word 'futile' that would have reduced Brenus's survival to a mere inconvenience, 'so . . . needless. I resented you, and I regret it greatly. I am sorry, Brenus, sorry for everything. But if I cannot change the past, at least I can help guide your future. When we return to Britannia you will take your place with me among the defenders of the Wall. You are a fine young man, a young man any father would be proud of. Eventually you will command a cohort, and perhaps one day you will wear the title Lord of the Wall with pride as your father and your grandfather before you.'

'Why would I fight for the Romans?' Brenus seemed genuinely perplexed.

'Because Britannia is your home and Rome *is* Britannia. If you don't want to fight for Rome, then at least fight for your people, the Brigantes. Without Rome we would all have been barbarians speaking Pictish long since.'

'You call the Saxons barbarian,' Brenus pointed out. 'But they are not naturally cruel and brutish. Most of them treated me well, even before Wigga adopted me. Wigga said Rome is no longer interested in Britannia. He laughed and said the sea wolves are already gathering, and that when Rome goes the people of Britannia are as lambs to be shorn or slaughtered at the pleasure of the Saxons. Look at the way Saxon ships sail unmolested in inshore waters and our people are able to raid and kill with impunity.'

'Not if I have anything to do with it,' Marcus growled. 'I see you are not convinced. In that case I will make you a pledge. If you do not wish to return to Britannia and your people, I will find you a place at Stilicho's side. With your skills and intelligence you could do very well. Otherwise I will pay for your passage back to Treva. Does that satisfy you?'

He waited for an answer, but Brenus just stared at him with his impenetrable dark eyes.

XXI

The chill left the air as they travelled further south and smudges of blue broke the monotony of the low, grey cloud, but if anything the atmosphere on board the barges became more frigid. Partly, it was to do with the surroundings. The river itself remained unchanging, but here the forest encroached close to the bank and the trees had an ominous, brooding quality, a hunger that waited to devour any living thing unwary enough to venture on shore. Further downstream they had sometimes seen deer or other animals on the bank lapping at the water, but here there was nothing. Occasionally the wall of forest would be broken by a clearing where some enterprising farmer or settler had removed enough trees to build a house and provide pasture for a few animals. Yet this only served to add to the feeling of loneliness and desolation, because in every case the fields were overgrown with scrub and weeds and the buildings mere ruins, with caved-in roofs and collapsed walls.

Gutrum studied the trees with narrowed eyes and touched an iron nail, the head rubbed to a bright shine by constant requests for reassurance. He was plainly nervous and the crew took their mood from him.

'He can't make up his mind whether to moor for the night or take a chance and stay on the river with a torch up front,' Leof reported.

'Everything has changed since the last time he was this far south and there's too little river traffic for his liking, even for the time of year. This is pirate territory, they come tearing out of a side-stream before you even know they're there, and he hoped they'd been wiped out or at least chased off. Now that he's seen the rotting buildings, he reckons they'll have had time to get back.'

'Tell him we can handle any pirates.' Marcus nodded to the cavalrymen perched along the sides of the barge.

Gutrum nodded at Leof's words and his meaty features took on a momentary expression of resolve. He called out something to the crew and the oarsmen laughed, but there was little humour in the sound.

'What did he say?'

'What if the pirates are the least of our worries?'

Leof saw Brenus by the ship's side and went to join him.

'If you're thinking of swimming for the bank, I wouldn't bother. If the wolves don't eat you the locals probably will.'

The boy shook his head. 'There's nothing out there for me. I hardly know what to think. I don't really know who I am any more. A few days ago I was Wulf, a Saxon, with a family, even though I knew I wasn't truly one of them. Now everyone calls me Brenus and a man I hate, who always despised me, is my father.'

'He doesn't despise you now, does he?' Leof laughed. 'And if you don't know what to think, how do you think he feels? After Longovicium he spent years planning and preparing and conspiring a way to get you back. That's right, years. He couldn't move until he had the ships. Once he had the ships, he needed crews to sail them. How does a great man charged with defending Britannia's shores escape the clutches of his duty and his honour? I've never had much in the way of honour so I don't know, but Marcus does. He had to wait for the right moment. It just so happened that, when it came, someone high up in Britannia, maybe even Rome, tried to have him killed, but he would have done it anyway, because he owed it to you.'

'He owes me nothing.'

'You can say that, Wulf, or Brenus, or whoever you are now,' Leof said, 'but you know it's not true. He suffers for every day he ignored you as a child and every day he missed you growing into a man. You're good, young Brenus, but there's so much more he could have taught you. He's the trickiest bastard I've ever seen in a fight and he can ride anything born in a stable. You can still learn from him. Do you want to be a farmer, on that estate in Brigantian country? Of course not, I've seen you use a sword. You were born to be a warrior. You are the son of Marcus Flavius Victor. And let me tell you this, Brenus, this is a time for warriors. A time for young men like us, who can fight and who are prepared to kill. A time of chaos. I heard you speaking to Marcus about Rome, and you're right, the Empire is all but finished with Britannia. It has been for years. Only the efforts of a few strong men like your father, who were prepared to cheat and steal and murder, if necessary, to keep the soldiers with swords in their hands and horses between their legs, have allowed Londinium to maintain that last fragile link. Rome is fighting enemies on every frontier, but, more important, it's decaying from the inside. Zeno, the *medicus*, reckons there'll never be a single Empire again. Arcadius, who rules the east, has abandoned his brother Honorius, who's terrified of the barbarians and hiding in some Italian swamp. Now I don't know much about ruling, but I do know about fighting. Honorius should be out there leading his troops, not sitting on his arse in some palace and leaving all the sweating and bleeding to the likes of this Stilicho your father admires so much.'

'Wigga would have said the same,' Brenus agreed. 'A leader's place is at the front, taking the same risks as the men. He was proud of being bigger, better and faster than any of his *frilingi*.'

'Your father would never send any trooper to do a job he couldn't do himself,' Leof nodded. 'But he also knows that sometimes it makes more sense to talk than fight. Every man's hand was against him in the month before Longovicium, but he somehow convinced every garrison commander along the Wall to give him troops, and then managed to make common cause with two of the Pictish kings while everyone was looking the other way.' The Saxon laughed. 'By Donar's mighty prick, you should have seen the look on the Picts' faces when Corvus and his Selgovae stabbed them in the back and old King Coel about turned and marched his Votadini straight back to Caer Eidinn.'

'He betrayed them?'

'They were the enemy,' Leof scoffed. 'You can't betray your enemy. He lied and he cheated and he connived and he won. And that's the most important thing you can learn from your father. How to win. That's why we need to get back to Britannia. When Honorius is done with the province, he'll pull out the Sixth legion, which is the single most effective fighting force on the island. Like as not he'll try to do the same with the auxiliary garrisons along the Wall and the Saxon Shore. But the majority of them are Britons, born and bred, and he'll be fortunate if most don't desert and join their families. Those men will be looking for leadership and your father's the man who can give them it – if he gets there in time.'

'Because there'll be other men also seeking to take advantage of the chaos?'

'That's right, Brenus,' Leof smiled. 'Men like Constantinus, the *magister militum*, who we reckon set up Marcus for the assassins. Mark my words, when the Empire abandons Britannia it will leave a void that can only be filled by kings and warlords, or bastards prepared to fight and kill to become them. Your father would very much like it to be a single king, but he's clever enough to know that's not going to happen, not at the start.'

'Why not?' Brenus demanded. 'Surely it makes sense.'

'Of course it makes sense, but since when has sense had anything to do with what happens? If you asked your grandmother what she was, what would she say? And I don't mean a woman.'

'She would say she was a princess of the Brigantes.' Brenus couldn't keep the pride from his voice.

'That's right. A Brigantian. Not a Roman, or a Briton. A Brigantian. And if you asked someone from a farm around Colonia the same question, they'd call themselves a Trinovantian. No matter how long Britannia has been a province of the Empire, the people have never forgotten who they were. Your father is a Brigantian. He holds lands and estates in the north and has the allegiance of the people. More important, he knows and has the respect of the commanders and soldiers of every auxiliary garrison along the Wall. With a little good fortune he could command the most powerful military force in Britannia, enough men at least to carve out a kingdom for himself in the north.'

Brenus chewed his lip and nodded. 'It is something to think on.'

'Yes,' Leof said. 'Something to think on.'

The next day they reached what appeared to be a fork in the river and Gutrum steered towards the east bank where the channel narrowed appreciably. Marcus demanded to know what was going on. Leof was asleep in the bow and Marcus was surprised when Brenus answered.

'Gutrum says this is known as The Island, a sandbank that appears and disappears at the river gods' whim. The word on the river is that the left channel is the most navigable, but he will proceed with care. He also says we will be within spear throw of the land, so he suggests that we be ready in case of an assault. This has always been disputed territory and the haunt of true savages.'

Marcus issued the instructions. 'Tell him to slow for a moment,' he told his son. He climbed into the stern and called to Valeria's barge to close. He explained the situation to her and she waved that she understood.

'How are your supplies?' he shouted.

'We have enough food for the men for another day, perhaps two if we're careful, less for the horses. We need to resupply soon.'

Marcus nodded his agreement. 'Gutrum says we're still four days short of Lupfurdum, but there must be somewhere closer we can call in for food and water. Take care.'

'You too,' she said. 'How is Brenus?'

'I should have sent him with you,' he said, but the words were accompanied by a smile and Valeria laughed.

The island itself was little more than a low mound clothed in grass that wouldn't hide a mouse, so as they proceeded down the narrow channel every eye scanned the trees to the left seeking out signs of potential trouble. Marcus had seldom felt more exposed, and sweat dripped from Gutrum's nose as he rubbed the iron nail on the side. Sometimes the channel closed to the point where the branches reached out to almost touch the barge, but for the most part they had room to spare and the water here was dark and inky, with a hint of limitless depths.

A faint, formless sound in the distance and every man on board tensed. Not a sound, but a song, which became clearer with each stroke of the oars. A deep melodic air that echoed through the trees and out across the water. They were on a bend now, and without warning the trees on the bank thinned to open out into one of the familiar clearings.

Gutrum had gone deathly pale. 'What's he singing about?' Marcus asked. The bargemaster only shook his head.

A ruined hut came into view and a man, wild-haired and massively powerful, hewing rhythmically with an axe at something on the ground. The axe man looked up from his toil, but the song never faltered and he greeted the sight of the barge with a broad toothless smile.

'Father, look.' The front of the ruin was visible now and they could see some kind of rack hung with joints of meat.

'Oh, Christ,' someone muttered.

Legs, arms, torsos, nameless lumps of flesh, and strings of viscera waving in the breeze like obscene ribbons.

The axe man's song ended and he gave whatever was on the ground one final blow with all his strength and bent to pick up the fruit of his labours. A head, hanging from his fist by a hank of long blond hair. A woman or perhaps a youth, it was hard to tell. From somewhere close by a loud wail broke the silence. This time it was Senecio who pointed. A stockade filled with small children, half hidden by the ruined house.

'Take us in to the bank.' Marcus unsheathed his sword. There was no response and he turned to Gutrum with a look of savagery. 'Take us in.'

Gutrum shook his head and gabbled something to Brenus. 'He says though you kill him he will not allow a man from the barge to set foot on that ground. Any who does so without his consent is cursed and will be left behind.'

Marcus glanced at the smiling axe man and went to the side. Five paces to the bank, but the water looked deep. Still, the children . . .

'Look at them, Father,' Brenus nodded to the oarsmen.

Marcus turned. To a man they were glaring at him with a mix of fury and terror and intent. In that instant he knew that, swords or no, if he left the ship they would leave him behind. Even if his men filled the barge with blood, nothing they did would stop these men from doing what their instinct dictated. They would rather die than be tainted by whatever possessed the man in the clearing. He slammed the sword back into the scabbard as the barge picked up speed.

'I can still take him, lord,' Senecio called from his perch in the stern, curved bow drawn back to his ear and the arrow ready to fly.

'Best leave well alone, lord,' Leof said quietly.

A moment later the clearing slipped from sight.

XXII

Lupfurdum (Meissen)

The sun shone and the trees receded as they approached Lupfurdum; men and women toiled in open fields and fishing nets lined the river banks, and people waved and called greetings from the little communities they passed. Settled country, a world away from the dreadful clearing whose sights and memories and frustrations would linger long in Marcus's mind. According to Gutrum this was the territory of the Gromaci, a numerous tribe whose position on, and control of, this section of the river provided opportunities for trade which the major clans had been swift to grasp. The Gromaci revered merchants and traders in the way great generals were lauded elsewhere, and they prided themselves on their bargaining skills.

'It is said that when a man negotiates with the Gromaci,' Leof translated, 'he should count his fingers to make sure he hasn't sold them one or two by mistake.'

Everyone on board the two barges anticipated their arrival at Lupfurdum with a relish intensified by the gnawing hunger in their bellies. After what they'd seen in the clearing no one had been eager to make a landfall, even if it meant the little food that remained must be rationed for man and beast.

When they finally approached the settlement it became clear Lupfurdum was on a much grander scale than anything they'd encountered since Treva, and much more substantial than Leuphana. Barges and ships of every shape and size lay alongside a long wooden wharf on the left bank of the river. Above them loomed a sizeable fort on a rocky outcrop, ringed by a stout wooden palisade, and beyond it a township that stretched far into the distance. A relay of small boats ferried people and goods from the right bank, while other fully laden vessels arrived from upstream. A broad flat area between the river and the fort outcrop teemed with people moving among what looked like temporary structures. From his perch in the bow with Gutrum, Marcus could see enclosures filled with livestock and stalls piled high with food. Gutrum barked an order and two crewmen dropped a great flat stone tied with a rope through a hole in its centre to anchor them in the current.

'Gutrum believes this is the first market of the year, which is marked by a great gathering to give thanks to the gods for surviving another winter,' Brenus translated the bargemaster's words. Leof was among the men, chivvying them into their polished leather armour to impress any authority that challenged their arrival. Marcus had already dressed in his mail, ready to take the leading role in the performance, with the glittering silver helmet couched in his elbow. He'd noticed his son's creeping inclusion in the company's affairs and it pleased him greatly, but he was wise enough not to show it, other than with a grunt of acknowledgement.

A little knot of horses left the fort and wound their way down through the settlement on the hillside to the river bank. A few minutes later a small craft decorated with a great deer's skull on a pole left the wharf and rowed its way towards the two barges, to take station by the side of Gutrum's barge. Eight or ten men occupied the vessel, but the undoubted leader was a tall, lean-faced elder in a long white tunic. Snow-white hair fell to his shoulders and he wore a silver ornament in

131

the shape of a half-moon on a chain at his throat. Gutrum, Leof and Marcus stood on rowing benches so they could see down into the smaller boat.

The elder looked up at the three men and made a long speech punctuated by gestures of his arm upstream and to the fort behind him. When he'd finished, Leof translated for Marcus, while Gutrum thanked the man.

'He likes using ten words where there is only need of one, lord,' the Saxon said. 'The short version is that he bids us welcome, but his king has decreed that every boat which passes his gate must pay a toll in return for his protection through his territory. Regrettably, in the event of the toll not being forthcoming he would be forced to confiscate our ships and all their contents.'

Marcus blessed the occupants of the smaller boat with a benevolent smile. 'I am Cinead, prince of the Picti, and I have journeyed here from the island of Britannia,' he addressed the elder, pausing to allow Leof to relay his words. 'I welcome his king's protection and am happy to pay for it, but rather than continuing our journey today, we would seek his leave to attend the fine market I see there and purchase provisions to see us through the days ahead and horses to replace those we lost upriver.'

The elder frowned and consulted with one of the warriors at his side before replying. 'He says King Hermeric will undoubtedly wish to meet a great lord of the Picti – he appears to be well versed in the name, lord – and he will no doubt be curious as to why such an illustrious figure bestows his presence among us. I think that's a question, lord, but he's too polite to ask.'

Marcus smiled. 'Tell him that I am commanded by King Janus of the northern Picts to seek an audience with the king of the Goths with the purpose of making an alliance between our two peoples against the Romans. And I would be delighted to attend King Hermeric, if only his representative would give me time to access a gift suitable for a man whose fame has spread far beyond his kingdom's borders.'

Another muttered discussion, followed by an invitation for the barges to follow the messenger to the royal moorings.

On the way to the shore Marcus called to Valeria. 'We'll disembark the horses first and give them some time ashore. I need to put on a show worthy of a prince, so we'll take a bodyguard of a dozen troopers on the best mounts. Do we have anything amongst the silver that's fit for a king?'

'Most of it is hardly fit for a dinner table,' Valeria laughed. 'But you still have that long silver chain you took from Briga. Do you trust them?'

The question had been on Marcus's mind since the messenger's boat set out from the shore. 'What other option do I have? We can't fight them, that's certain. I'm depending on this Hermeric's respect for a fellow royal. I don't know what kind of relationship he has with the Goths, maybe none at all, but I doubt their king would be very pleased if he heard the Gromaci had obstructed an embassy to him. Kings know the importance of maintaining contacts with their neighbours, especially in places like this where frontiers seem to be so fluid. On balance, it's in his interests to milk us for as much as he can get and send us on our way.'

When they reached the bank, Marcus's men fixed ramps and immediately began to disembark the horses. The animals danced uncertainly on the unfamiliar solid ground, but they soon calmed down. What Marcus hadn't expected was the large admiring crowd they drew.

'They've never seen anything like them.' Valeria drew his attention to a group of native horses tethered nearby. The Roman mounts had been bred for battle and were half as tall again at the shoulder and broader in the chest than the small, shaggy local animals.

A richly dressed Gromaci nobleman approached and slapped Marcus's mount on the shoulder. Leof's hand strayed towards his dagger, but Marcus motioned him to leave it where it was. The noble opened the horse's mouth and studied its teeth, clearly liking what he saw.

'You are selling?'

It took Marcus a moment to understand the words were spoken in Latin. 'No,' he said, slightly shaken. He'd forgotten that a place like Lupfurdum, a crossroads between east and west, north and south, would likely attract traders from the Roman provinces as well as elsewhere. 'But we are buying. I'm looking for six remounts and four or five packhorses.'

'A pity.' The man rubbed the horse's head affectionately. 'But I can supply what you require. Not like these,' he laughed, 'but adequate for your needs. When you have seen the king just come to the market and ask for Miro.'

'You know we have been summoned to the king?'

'Of course,' Miro smiled. He looked at the helmet beneath Marcus's arm. 'He will measure you for wealth, with which he will certainly be satisfied, and power, which by the quality of these animals is considerable. Then strength. He likes to hear of battles, and I would guess you have considerable experience in that area. Is there anything else you need other than horses?'

'I need supplies for men and horses for at least a week.'

'I will arrange it, and see you are charged a reasonable price.' He saw the look of doubt on Marcus's face. 'Do not worry, my friend,' he laughed. 'We Gromaci drive a hard bargain, but we pride ourselves on our reputation for honesty, and we expect the same from others,' he shook his head, 'which is our greatest weakness, if you like.'

Marcus directed him towards Luko, who'd taken on quartermaster duties.

'What was that all about?' Valeria asked.

'I seem to have made a new friend.' He told her about the horses and supplies.

'According to the bargemen we still have at least another day on the Albis before we reach the river that will take us south. Why buy the horses now?'

'Where will we have another opportunity like this?' Marcus said. 'Every spare horse for fifty miles has probably been brought to this market. Look at all the barges moored on the river. It should be simple enough to hire one to transport the spare horses. I'd planned to change barges here, anyway, but Gutrum has agreed to take us the rest of the way.'

The messenger reappeared, eyes widening as he saw the horses, but he made no complaint. Leof and the other troops assigned to the escort fell in behind them.

XXIII

Of all the barbarian kings Marcus had encountered, Hermeric was the most impressive. A silver diadem encircled his brow above dark, hooded eyes and features that would have been absurdly handsome, but for the pockmarks left by some childhood illness. His hair was long and black and a beard of the same hue framed a mouth that was almost feminine. He sat on an intricately carved wooden throne and wore a white tunic of finespun wool with a cloak of deep blue arranged artlessly over his shoulders, pinned by an enormous amber brooch on his right breast. The whole image the pose conveyed was so serious and *noble* Marcus knew Valeria would be stifling a smile. To the king's right a wooden mount framed a silver-tipped spear. On the left of the throne stood a long bronze panel inscribed with sheaves of wheat, the head of a cow and a pile of metal ingots. On the wall above Hermeric's head hung a great bronze disc so polished that Marcus at first mistook it for a mirror until he noticed that it was engraved with the movements of the sun and the moon across the skies. He guessed the display was intended to convey Hermeric's dominion over his warriors, trade and the seasons, and it was difficult not to be impressed.

Marcus stood back and did his best to emulate Hermeric's look of benevolent nobility while Leof introduced him as Prince Cinead and repeated the story about an embassy to the Goths. Hermeric nodded gravely at the appropriate moments and gave no sign such an audience was anything unusual. Leof finished his introduction and Marcus stepped forward. 'King Janus sends greetings to his royal cousin and hopes he will accept this gift in thanks for facilitating our embassy's passage through his territory.' He motioned Valeria forward and she placed a modest-sized walnut chest in the king's hands, enjoying his surprise as he felt the weight of it.

Hermeric's eyes narrowed as he lifted the hinged lid of the box, only to widen as he recognized what it contained. He reached inside with his right hand and pulled out a heavy silver chain, each link the thickness of a man's little finger. Gasps of appreciation from the king's followers turned to cries of delight as coil after coil emerged to reveal a length that would girdle a man's waist at least twice.

Hermeric clapped his hands with pleasure. He motioned forward another of his retinue and spoke to him with obvious enthusiasm. The man smiled. 'My king thanks you for this gift,' he said in a fluent Pictish that made Marcus's heart stutter and brought out a soft hiss of surprise from Valeria, 'which is certainly not modest. He has called for a feast to celebrate his honoured and most welcome guests and your men will be entertained in like fashion. King Hermeric also cannot allow such a gift to go without responding in kind. Tomorrow you will have the pick of the market to choose a present that will give the ruler of the Goths as much pleasure as he has just enjoyed. He particularly recommends the amber which is unmatched in quality in all the world.'

Marcus rose next morning with head numbed and tongue parched from Hermeric's hospitality. They'd eaten and drunk till long after dark and he'd struggled to satisfy the Gromaci monarch's apparently insatiable appetite for news and gossip from elsewhere. Hermeric had the look of a warrior, but Marcus guessed he owed his kingship to what was in his head rather than his scabbard. He had a shrewd intelligence and a quick mind and he laughed as he told how he'd used his interpreter to test whether his guests were truly Picts 'because it was noticed some of your horse-trappings were in the Roman style'.

Valeria met him at Gutrum's barge where she was supervising the reloading of the horses, including ten unfamiliar animals onto a new vessel.

'Your friend Miro knows his horseflesh,' she said with a hearty cheerfulness that reminded him she'd left the feast early to check the guard on the ships. 'They're not Roman cavalry mounts, but they're all sound enough and I don't think he cheated us too badly. And we have all the supplies we can carry. You look as if you had a long night?'

'One cannot refuse the hospitality of kings.' Marcus winced. 'He demanded to hear the story of the battle of Longovicium three times.'

'Did the Picts win this time?'

He laughed. 'No, but we emerged covered in glory, naturally.'

'Are you coming aboard?'

'Not yet, and neither are you. King Hermeric has kindly offered us the pick of Lupfurdum's treasures as a gift for the king of the Goths, and we can hardly refuse.'

They walked across the turf to where the market was being held. Miro met them before they reached the first stall. 'I am here to ensure everything is to your satisfaction,' he said. 'You may choose any single item in the market without payment, unless it pleases you to reward the stallholder for his good taste. The king, of course, will recompense the seller.' The easy smile of yesterday remained in place, but there was something awkward and uncomfortable about the way his words emerged.

The reason became clear as they were able to examine the wares on the stalls. 'If this is the best they have then Lupfurdum is far from the treasure house we've been led to believe.' Valeria examined an amber necklace, the finest the stallholder had to offer, which, though pretty, was hardly a gift fit for a king. Elsewhere the story was the same. Goldsmiths, silversmiths, amber merchants all extolling the virtues of pieces that were ordinary at best.

'I think the king made his offer in good faith,' Marcus said, with one eye on Miro a discreet distance away. 'But then he, or more likely his advisers, decided it was a little too generous. Still, we cannot leave without accepting something. Let us look a little further.'

They walked past a pen where slaves were being held before auction. Marcus glanced at them without interest and walked on, only to stop in his tracks a few moments later.

'What's wrong?' Valeria whispered.

'Nothing. I don't . . .' He retraced his steps to the pen, wondering why his heart was pounding like this. A picture of huddled, ragged, shivering misery, perhaps twenty of them, male and female, with one or two children, all equally devoid of hope. Except one.

His gaze had drifted over her as he'd passed and their eyes met for a single heartbeat. Not enough time to register her physical form, or even her features. Just a pair of blue eyes gazing dejectedly from behind a lush curtain of tousled auburn. Yet that one glance set emotions in train that were beyond his understanding.

A second look and his breath caught in his throat. Her head was turned away from him now and all he could see was her hair and the pale flesh of her shoulders showing through the tears in her dark blue dress. As if she could feel his eyes on her, she looked over her shoulder directly at him. Nothing had prepared him for the shock of that moment. A face from his dreams, familiar as any of his company, and yet not. Almond-shaped eyes set in an elongated oval, a delicate nose turned up slightly at the tip, and full lips set in a thin line. Yet the mere physical detail could not do justice to the whole. Dark circles encompassed the eyes, the result of either exhaustion or tears, and dirt stained her cheeks.

'That slave. She is the gift I claim for the king of the Goths.'

Miro gaped, but not as widely as Valeria. 'A slave? Which one?' the trader demanded. 'The mousy-haired waif? Surely we can find you a more appropriate gift? I know the stallholders have been hiding their wares, but you will have something fitting if I have to beat it out of them.'

'The slave is all I want, on King Hermeric's honour.'

'Marcus?' Valeria laid a hand on his arm.

'No, Valeria,' he hissed. 'I will have her. If I have to fight every man here.'

'If that is what pleases you.' Miro shrugged and called the slave trader to bring the girl to them.

'I'm surprised Hermeric didn't take her for himself,' Marcus said.

Miro stared at him and shook his head with an almost pitying smile. 'King Hermeric has all the women he needs, and to his credit he keeps his wives blessed with heirs. But lately his tastes have turned to other passions.' His voice dropped to a whisper. 'You are fortunate you haven't let him set eyes on that pale youth in your company. There might well have been a different outcome to your visit.'

Before Marcus had the chance to absorb what he'd just been told, the slavemaster appeared with his captive. Hands bound before her, she was smaller and more slender than he'd appreciated, but, though her lip trembled, she held her head high and the fire in her eyes remained undimmed. Older than he'd first thought, probably close to thirty. Hunger had stripped her features of excess flesh and the bones of her cheeks were sharply defined. The ankle-length blue dress she wore was tattered and mud-stained at the hem and ripped at the throat to show the slightest curve of a small breast.

'Ask him where she was taken,' he told Miro, noting the slight widening of her eyes as she recognized the Latin tongue.

Miro put the question and the man spread his hands in a shrug accompanied by a laugh. 'He doesn't know,' Miro translated. 'He purchased her from an Alan war band on their way west. They assured him she was well born, but who knows, and hadn't been badly used. Be warned, she is a Christian and fussy with it. She won't touch the slops the others are happy with, even though he threatened to force them down her throat. She hasn't eaten for three days.'

'Will he release her to me?'

'Of course. I've told him the king will be generous in compensating him. Could I suggest that a small gift might speed up the transfer.'

Marcus reached into the pouch at his belt and brought out a small link from a silver chain. 'Tell him to untie her.' He looked into the girl's eyes. 'You will be safe now,' he said. 'What is your name?'

She closed her eyes for a moment and swayed on her feet. Valeria stepped forward to steady her and she bit her lips to disguise her emotion at the comforting presence. She had to swallow two or three times before she was able to reply.

'My name is Anastasia.'

XXIV

Marcus was keen to discover more about the newcomer's background, but Zeno shook his head. 'Look at her bones sticking out, she's like a skinned rabbit, and she can hardly stand for exhaustion.' He insisted Anastasia be allowed to satisfy her hunger and become accustomed to the barge and its occupants before anyone questioned her.

'Can you not see the poor creature is terrified,' Valeria admonished her brother. 'She heard what you said about presenting her as a gift to the Goth king. I've assured her that was just a ruse to set her free, but she's spent weeks not knowing what her fate will be and no amount of reassurance from a bearded savage like you will change that. Give her time, Marcus.'

Anastasia ate with the voracious concentration of one who seldom encountered food and was worried she would never encounter it again. She swiftly devoured a platter of smoked meats and another of smoked fish, accompanied by hard-boiled eggs and fresh bread and vegetables from Lupfurdum's market. Yet for all her attention to the welcome fare there was an animal wariness that never left her. The blue eyes flickered constantly to left and right as if she feared someone was about to snatch her plate away. When she was satisfied, she wrapped herself without a word in the cloak Valeria had provided, closed her eyes and fell asleep for eight solid hours.

They moored at dusk and slept on board. At some point during the night Marcus became aware of soft voices. He looked up to see the huddled shapes of Valeria and Anastasia in the dim light of the moon, their heads close together in the stern. Nothing they said was audible but there was something comforting about the faint murmur. It was a few moments before he realized he wasn't the only person on board listening to the two women. By the position of the glint of light he could tell that the owner of the staring eyes was Brenus.

The next day the landscape changed entirely. Gone were the drab flatlands to be replaced by soaring tree-covered crags that dominated the river to left and right. The heights made Gutrum, who'd plied his trade entirely beneath the familiar great skies further north, nervous, but the master of the third barge assured them they were in no danger of ambush as long as they were in the country of King Hermeric. Still, the river was much narrower now, a simple bowshot across for a man like Senecio. From his position in the bow Marcus stared up at the cliffs and imagined the damage a company of spearmen, or worse, archers, could do from that elevated position.

'The lady Valeria says I must thank you for my deliverance and my freedom, my lord.' Anastasia had a soft, almost melodious voice and an accent difficult to place.

'No thanks are required,' he assured her gravely. 'It would be a poor sort of man who would ignore a lady in distress.'

'But you did not know I was a lady,' she replied. 'I certainly do not look like one. And my poor companions were equally distressed. Nevertheless, my thanks stand, and now I must ask you what is to become of me?'

Marcus exchanged a glance with Valeria who stood near the stern watching the encounter with obvious interest. 'That depends on your own needs and the requirements of my mission.' He cringed inwardly at how pompous he sounded. 'If it were up to me alone ...' he shrugged, 'but I'm sure you understand I have a duty to get the people under my command, and who have followed me loyally, back to their families. You will know by now that we are not the Pictish embassy we claimed to be, but Roman soldiers stranded far from home?'

'Yes, the lady Valeria explained your situation to me. Like you, my only wish is to return home, though I no longer know if I have a family and I do not know what my circumstances will be when I reach there.'

Marcus arranged a meal sack beside him and invited Anastasia to sit. 'Perhaps if you could tell me how you came to be here, I might be able to reassure you?'

She took her place, spreading the folds of her dress around her as if she was at a banquet. He had to force himself not to smile.

'I was taken from my home outside Salona, on the coast of Dalmatia, by a mixed war band of Goths and Alans. We have lived in peace beside the Goths for three generations, but these were different, pagans not long from the east. They swept through the rich estates surrounding the city, killing and pillaging.' The words caught in her throat. 'My . . . my husband died trying to protect me from them. I was fortunate they chose to take the most comely women and the fittest men to sell as slaves. They dragged us behind their horses for mile after mile. I wonder I was able to endure it, my flesh,' she gestured to her feet and he saw that they were scarred and scratched, 'fell away in tatters. If they had not allowed us a fire at night I believe we would all have died of the cold. We crossed the Danuvius and they began to sell us off one by one at farms and settlements, until, at last, only I was left.' Her eyes dropped. 'They did not ill-use me, apart from the occasional cuff or push. I believe there was talk of offering me as a concubine to a prince or a king. Somewhere around the headwaters of the Fuldaha river they met a slaver who was gathering stock for the spring market at Lupfurdum. He gave them news of some great movement of their fellow tribesfolk and made them an offer for me which they accepted. And that is how I came to be here.'

The place names meant nothing to Marcus and he summoned Zeno to join them. 'Oh, yes, lord, Salona is a very famous place. It is to Dalmatia what Londinium is to Britannia. A truly Christian city with many fine churches, baths and a famous theatre. Is that not so, girl?'

Anastasia took a deep breath, as if the memory of home caused her pain. 'It is.'

'Salona cannot be so far from Metulum, lord.' The *medicus* gave the words significant weight, and Marcus nodded his understanding. If Stilicho was still there . . .

'Then perhaps we can be of greater service to you than I thought possible,' Marcus said. 'For Zeno tells me our ways converge, more or less, though how we will get there I do not know.'

'Why, it is simple.' Anastasia frowned. 'The Fuldaha joins this river not four days from Lupfurdum. I doubt you will find boats large enough to transport your horses upstream, but Loki the slavemaster said that when the water is low in the summer he uses a trail east of the river.'

'Did he describe this trail?'

'He said it is like all trails. Sometimes you go up, sometimes down, but much of it is easy going, passable even with a heavy cart. If we are going south you must always keep the river to your right and carry on until you reach the true mountains. Beyond the mountains is the Danuvius.'

'And the Danuvius means civilization, lord,' Zeno interjected with enthusiasm. 'Once you're on the Danuvius and you know where you are, you can't fail to find Metulum. We could hire someone to take the girl to Salona,' he suggested.

'We have a long way to go before we get to that point,' Marcus said. 'If we reach Metulum and Stilicho has moved on, which I believe is likely, then we will follow him. But,' he turned to Anastasia, 'whatever I decide at Metulum I will ensure you have passage to Salona either by land or by sea.'

'Then I can ask for nothing more,' Anastasia inclined her head, 'and again I owe you thanks.'

Marcus noticed Brenus standing by the head of one of the horses, watching with his usual burning intensity. Did his hatred for his father really run so deep? 'Come here, boy,' he called. 'You have not been introduced to our guest. Lady Anastasia, this is my son, Brenus.' He waited for the explosion, but Brenus chose not to deny his parenthood. Instead, he bowed deeply.

'It is my honour to welcome you to our company.'

Marcus blinked. It had never occurred to him that Brenus might be possessed of this combination of manners and charm.

Anastasia smiled. 'When I woke on my patch of mud yesterday morning in the slave pen, I would have thought I was dreaming if anyone had told me I would be free by nightfall and the recipient of such gallantry soon after. My thanks, young man.'

Marcus saw his son's cheeks redden in a deep blush. 'You have something in common,' he said quickly. 'Brenus was a prisoner of the Saxons not two weeks ago.'

'Then perhaps we can compare our captivity at some point,' Anastasia said. 'There are times, even after so brief a period of freedom, that I wonder if I dreamed it. Yet I know it changed me, and it still astonishes me that I was able to adapt so quickly to such a dramatic change of circumstance.'

Brenus went even redder if that were possible, and mumbled something unintelligible before heading back to tend the horses.

'He is a very handsome young man.' Anastasia watched Brenus go. 'And his time in bondage doesn't seem to have touched him. You must be very proud.'

'Of course.' Marcus managed a smile. Handsome? Was that how you would describe his son? He remembered Miro's offhand comment at the slave market and frowned. Brenus, for all his attributes as a fighter, was little more than a boy. He needed protection from a world he barely knew. Marcus suddenly realized there was more to fatherhood than manly chats and reassurance. He was still pondering how to achieve this when he realized Anastasia had continued the conversation.

'I'm sorry,' she said. 'I know you have much to think about, but I have not bathed for a week and my hair is full of creatures I hesitate to identify. Valeria said it might be possible to set up some kind of curtain so I could wash in privacy, and she would help with my hair. She even has a dress that might replace these rags.'

'Of course,' Marcus said. 'I'll arrange it immediately.'

While Anastasia washed herself inside a cocoon of sailcloth, Marcus took Valeria aside.

'What do you think of her?' he asked.

'I like her,' Valeria didn't hesitate. 'But it's difficult to make a real judgement because she's still disorientated. When she wakes up tomorrow, she won't know for certain whether her freedom is a dream or she's still in captivity.' Her expression changed. 'I believe she has suffered much more than she has revealed. She needs our help and our patience. She's certainly of noble birth, as she says, and she's intelligent; she speaks at least three languages, which I think helped her survive her time with the slavers. Fortunate, don't you think, that we happen to be travelling in the same direction she wants to go?'

'What do you mean? She can hardly have known.'

'No,' Valeria laughed. 'Just the opposite. I just wondered what you would have done if she'd been taken from Constantinopolis or somewhere else you have no intention of going?'

Marcus frowned. The thought had never occurred to him. 'I suppose I would have put her on a boat when we reached the Danuvius and given her enough silver to get herself home.'

'Really?' Valeria said. 'Have you even considered why you decided to become her saviour?'

'She was a Christian in distress. It was my duty to help her.'

Valeria sighed. 'This is your sister, Marcus. You're not explaining yourself to some petty bureaucrat on the border. There were two or three other women in that pen who may or may not have been Christians, and who might well have been just as beautiful. You didn't even notice them, did you? You only had eyes for one person.'

'And if I did?'

Valeria's eyes narrowed. 'You acted without thought and your lust for Anastasia could have endangered us all. It was only your good fortune that Hermeric had no interest in female slaves.'

'Not lust . . .'

'What then?'

'If you're concerned about lust,' Marcus snapped, 'you should talk to Brenus. The boy is like a puppy, his eyes never leave her.'

'And why do you think that is?'

'I just said . . .'

'Oh Marcus, how can you be so blind? Brenus is besotted with her because she is the reincarnation of the mother he never knew. All the stories he ever heard about Julia are mirrored in that woman. Her beauty, her modesty, the way she carries herself, even that air of ethereal, wistful helplessness. When he looks at Anastasia, it is Julia he sees. And in some ways so do you.'

XXV

Marcus turned in the saddle to check the line of riders who followed, stifling a groan at the chafing of his thighs against the saddle and a dull ache at the base of his spine. The barges had carried them for another four days upriver from Lupfurdum until they'd reached a trading settlement. Here they were able to resupply again and a trader assured them that the major tributary entering the river on the far bank was the Fuldaha, the stream they would follow south. Marcus paid off Gutrum and the other bargemasters and they unloaded the horses on the east bank of the tributary.

A noticeable trail followed the line of the Fuldaha, more or less, and soon they were amidst the pattern of field, swamp and forest that had become so familiar in the north. Anastasia proved a proficient rider, which was as well given the length and trials of their journey. There were times when the forests closed in and they lost sight of the river entirely, but always the ground rose again and soon they would reach some rocky height overlooking the dark waters.

On and on. Four more days in the saddle through an unforgiving landscape of endless forests of oak and beech, cut by hidden streams and deep gullies. Ceaseless lurching descents followed by lung-bursting, scrabbling climbs till even as seasoned a cavalryman as

Marcus might admit to being sick of the sight of his horse's ears. For a time wolves dogged their footsteps, lithe grey shadows on the fringes of vision that whined and threatened, but none ever dared come close. In the forest they seemed entirely alone, but Marcus understood how vulnerable they were and insisted they sleep in their armour with their swords at hand. Had it not been for a sudden turn in the weather that showed blue skies and a glorious golden sun through the branches above they might have become entirely lost. As it was, they were able to continue more or less south, though the relative warmth brought with it a plague of stinging black flies that feasted on their sweat.

Less accustomed to long hours in the saddle, Anastasia was only kept upright by sheer power of will and some inner strength belied by her slim figure. Marcus suggested they halt for a while to allow her to rest, but she refused with a pained smile.

'Every hour I endure is another hour closer to Salona,' she replied through gritted teeth. 'And besides, if I dismount, I doubt I will ever be able to get back on this beast again. You will have to carry me over your saddle like a sack of grain.'

Marcus laughed at the image the words conveyed. 'Salona means a great deal to you?'

'Of course, it is my home, the only place I can feel safe, even after all this.'

'Zeno says your province has suffered greatly these past few years?'

She frowned, and stifled a yawn. 'In truth, the Goths have largely left us alone. There are many different tribes and bands, and when they were granted lands on our borders, their king, Alaric, who holds sway over Illyricum, gave assurances they came as settlers, not warriors. All they wanted was peace, he said, and he kept his word. All my life there have been tales of Alans and Sarmatians and Visigoths waiting to cross the river with fire and sword, but until the day I was taken none had dared during Alaric's time. The Goths are Christians, after their fashion, and we were able to worship and live together, even to prosper. But they are a restless people. Those with the most fertile soil and the best pasture were happy to work the land, but the less fortunate wanted the same benefits. Alaric does not have the power to provide for all. If he cannot give them what they desire, many of his warriors will desert him and he will be a king no more, and then what will the future bring?'

They dropped in single file from a hillside into a low-lying swamp that flanked a rocky stream. Tall trees rose like pillars from murky waters that lapped the horses' knees. Halfway across Marcus sensed movement at the periphery of his vision and raised a hand to his lips. Beyond Anastasia's left shoulder an enormous, pitch-black bull appeared like a ghost from a stand of alders fifty paces away. Broad in the chest as a two-wheel cart, it stood as high at the shoulder as the horse Marcus rode, and his outstretched arms would barely have spanned the curved, wickedly pointed horns. The majestic animal ambled to a halt and sniffed the air, nostrils flaring.

Marcus had once seen the yellowed skull and horns of such a beast above the gateway to King Corvus's capital at Mairos, but he had never thought to witness the reality: an *urus*, the great beast of legend. Small obsidian eyes glinted myopically in the gloomy light beneath the tree canopy and he wondered what they saw. If the bull charged, those wicked horns could gut a horse or a man with the slightest movement of the enormous muscled shoulders and no amount of Senecio's arrows would stop him. Marcus could almost feel the Numidian's fingers twitching on the bowstring and he willed him not to move. They would all have seen the bull by now, but not a man stirred or called out, each waiting for their commander's lead. They stayed motionless for what seemed an age as the great beast pawed the waters beneath its hooves into a churning froth before giving an enormous snort of what might almost have been disdain and swivelling in a single smooth movement to return the way it had come.

Marcus sensed the collective relief at the bull's departure and dared to breathe again.

'An impressive animal.' A slight tremor belied the lightness of Anastasia's tone. 'We were fortunate, I think, that he was only curious.'

Marcus reached out to touch her arm in a gesture of reassurance, but his mind was too full of questions to register the flinch it caused.

'Are creatures like that common in this land?'

'I have never seen the like, but this is not my land.' The tremor was gone, replaced by a coldness, but perhaps that was understandable after such a confrontation. 'The slavers kept their torches lit every night and left a gift of food and drink to appease the spirits of those who occupy these hills and valleys. I am a Christian, but there is something about this place that inspires awe and dread.'

'I don't doubt it,' Marcus said. 'There was something of the spirit-animal about that beast. The people of this place will have their own gods and their own ways. Better that we don't interfere with them. I take it as a good omen that the beast allowed us to pass unmolested.'

XXVI

They bedded down for the night in what appeared to be a hollow on a pinnacle of high ground overlooking the Fuldaha. It was only when they were settled that Marcus realized their refuge was similar to the ancient abandoned settlements that peppered the hills north of the Wall, with the remains of a turf bank and a distinct gap where the entrance had been. Once Julius and Tosodio had watered and fed the horses and tethered them between trees on each flank, Leof lit a small fire in the centre of the dell to cook their evening meal.

Anastasia could barely keep her eyes open, but Brenus offered her a plate of barley porridge and urged her to eat. Marcus watched them. Was what Valeria said true? Was he in competition with his own son for the shade of his dead wife? Anastasia treated Brenus with the artless grace of a beautiful older woman to any young man of his age, appearing not to notice his over-attentive deference. Brenus in his turn didn't appear to be aware of how awkward and boyish he looked, but was happy to bask in the glow of her presence. In a close company it was impossible for such an intriguing drama to go unnoticed. Marcus saw Julius nudge Leof and whisper something to the Saxon with a nod towards Brenus, but Leof only shook his head with a wry smile that said it was none of their business.

And what of the third player in the drama? Marcus wasn't a man to analyse his feelings, perhaps because to do so would force him to recognize his own shortcomings. Yet Valeria's words had awakened a wriggling worm inside his head. What *did* he feel for Anastasia? And, perhaps more importantly, what prompted those emotions? The first sight of her had knocked the breath from him as if he'd been hit in the chest by a shield boss. There had been nothing artful about the way she'd looked at him. He'd been just another potential buyer who'd glanced into the slave pen and turned away. A barbarian, as far as she knew, tall, bearded and battle-scarred. Perhaps she'd noticed an air of authority, of command, but probably not. For Marcus it had been a moment of what he might call purity, for want of a better word. There had never been the slightest doubt in his mind that he must free her. He'd given little thought to what would follow. After all the hours they'd spent together in the saddle, how much of what he saw as regard, or perhaps something stronger, was nothing more than the camaraderie of shared hardship? Was he a fool to believe he meant more to her than any of the others? Valeria talked with her more than any and he had a feeling she would be able to tell him the truth of it. But to ask would mean revealing his true feelings and, for the moment, he preferred not to do that. He watched as Valeria laid her blanket among the leaf mould beside Anastasia, and turned away. Whatever the reality, they still had a long way to go. Time would provide an answer.

He dreamed of the aurochs. It stood on the far side of a forest clearing, hooves pawing great scars in the earth and eyes glowing like coals. When it charged, he felt a pang of regret that he must kill it, but when he tried to draw his sword it was frozen in the scabbard. No matter how hard he tugged it wouldn't budge, and the great black bull grew larger and larger until it filled his vision and he could feel its breath on his face. Terror filled his mind and he found he couldn't even scream.

'Lord,' someone shook his shoulder and he opened his eyes. Ninian crouched over him silhouetted against the moonlit sky. 'Movement,' the former priest whispered. 'Between us and the trail. I thought it might be more wolves, but . . .'

Mind racing, Marcus rolled to his feet and hooked his sword to his belt. He tested the draw and was relieved when it slipped easily from the scabbard. Valeria hustled Anastasia into the centre of the hollow beside the doused fire and hissed at Brenus to look after her. Someone had given the boy a sword and Marcus felt a pang of regret, because it should have been he who returned his son's blade. To left and right, where the horses were tethered, the sides of the hill were so steep and rocky as to make an attack unlikely, but Marcus signalled to Senecio and Zeno to guard the beasts as a precaution. Six men, anonymous in the darkness, scurried past him to cover the rear of the position. Was it enough? That depended on how many they faced and they wouldn't know that until the enemy attacked. His place was at the entrance to the ancient sanctuary, the most likely point of attack, where Valeria had gathered the main strength of their little force.

As he moved past Anastasia, she put out a hand to catch his wrist.

'Lord,' she said urgently. 'A sword, or any kind of blade. I will not be taken again.' Marcus looked to Brenus but his son's entire concentration was on the darkness to the north. Anastasia's eyes glistened, not with fear, but with determination. He drew the dagger from his belt and handed it to her.

'It will not come to that,' he said, but before he could move again something zipped past his ear, followed a heartbeat later by a shrill cry of agony.

'There!' Brenus pointed towards a huddle of shadows within the perimeter and behind Valeria's defensive line.

'In Christ's name how did they get inside? Are they ghosts?' A second arrow from Senecio elicited a new shriek from somewhere close to the horses. They were human enough to bleed. There seemed to be only ten or so in the dell at the moment, but who knew how many more were swarming up the bank?

'Stay with Anastasia.' Marcus launched himself towards the attackers twenty paces away. The majority had formed up for an assault on Valeria's defenders, but two or three shadows dashed towards the horse line. Marcus changed the angle of his run to take them in the flank.

The closest sensed his presence and cried out a warning. A dulled spear point, seen only as a blur of movement, stabbed towards Marcus's throat, but his blade had already been poised to sweep it aside. His hand automatically went for the knife at his belt and he cursed as his fingers closed on air. Instead, he dropped his shoulder to ram into his enemy's chest. The impact smashed the shadowy figure backward and he hacked at the falling body as he passed. He hesitated, seeking out the next threat, and that wasted heartbeat almost cost him his life. A spear rammed into his side and he grunted. A glancing blow, God be thanked, painful, but deflected by the iron rings of his chain armour, and the thrust left the perpetrator defenceless against the blade that ran him through the middle. Marcus wrenched his sword clear as the dying warrior fell back clutching at his torn stomach. He ran to the horses seeking the final infiltrator who'd been sent to loose them, but Zeno called from the darkness. 'Dead, lord. You should see this, though.'

But Marcus was diverted by a clash of iron from the centre of the dell. Somehow more attackers had crept or fought their way onto the hilltop. The only weapons that stood between them and the rear of Valeria's defensive line were Brenus's sword and Anastasia's dagger.

He hauled himself onto the back of the closest mount, hacked at the tether holding it to the horse line and urged it towards the shadowy scuffle in the dip. No time to build momentum, but this was Marcus's element, on a willing horse with a blade in his hand. Anastasia cried out and he winced as he realized Brenus was down, surrounded by a huddle of black-clad warriors jostling to deal the killer blow. Within three strides he was among them, the horse snapping at heads and shouldering attackers aside. Marcus swung his sword to right and left, guided by pure instinct and rewarded by the cries of the maimed. Then he was falling, conscious of his mount's shoulder dropping and with just enough warning to throw himself clear to avoid being crushed.

Stunned by the impact and weighed down by his armour he'd never felt so helpless. The edge of a spear point ripped his cheek in a lightning flash of agony and he flailed blindly with the sword, bringing his assailant down on top of him. A face from the depths of Hades, bright iron seeking his throat. A cry of agony and a dead weight on his chest. Anastasia's pale features appeared above him and she struggled to pull the dead attacker away, Marcus's dagger embedded deep in the man's spine.

Anastasia helped him to his feet, but as he opened his mouth to thank her, she turned quickly away. Marcus's head spun and blood dripped from his cheek onto his chain armour as Luko and his men arrived to drive the last of the infiltrators from the dell.

Brenus lay a few feet away, his body partly covered by the corpses of two enemy dead. Marcus went to his son, sick at heart at what he might find. But when he moved the first attacker clear, he was relieved to see the rise and fall of his son's chest. He studied the grimacing features until Brenus's eyes opened and he blinked at the sight of his father. The boy's hands frantically searched his body and he shook his head in wonder.

'How . . . ?'

'Amateurs.' Marcus reached down and pulled Brenus to his feet. 'They were so desperate to kill you they got in each other's way.'

The clash of metal and cries of injured warriors continued from the northern edge of the dell, but Marcus could tell the struggle was confined to the outer perimeter, which presumably meant Valeria had contained the main attack. He patted his son on the shoulder and they ran to join her. Valeria grimaced at the sight of his wound.

'How do we fare?' he asked.

'One dead. Felix,' she answered his unspoken question. Felix, who could talk the birds from the trees, but who'd never lose at dice again. 'Five wounded, but none of them too badly. Our friends move like ghosts in the dark and they're brave enough, but put them up against trained soldiers and they're like mice under a stooping hawk. The ones on the front slope have run out of ideas, but they aren't going anywhere. What do you want to do? Attack? I doubt they'd stand.'

Marcus considered for a moment. 'Let's have a look at these mice of yours.'

The bodies of the dead lay scattered across the dell. Marcus suppressed a shudder as Leof's sputtering torch illuminated what should have been the face of the closest. Instead, the features were hidden behind an outlandish cloth mask with crudely drawn, red-rimmed eyes, flaring nostrils and dripping fangs. The mask was topped by a kind of tangled wig from which sprang a pair of curved horns from a cow. Marcus crouched over the body and drew back the mask.

'In Christ's name,' Valeria whispered. 'What is this?'

Marcus had expected to see the features of a seasoned warrior. Instead, he was presented with the pale, almost serene countenance of a young woman. Wide staring eyes and lips drawn back to show a row of white teeth filed to needle points to mimic those of the mask.

'They're all the same, lord.' Zeno approached from the horse lines. 'Just girls.'

'Those horns,' Marcus frowned. 'And the *urus* we saw today. It can't be a coincidence. Any movement?' he called to Ninian.

'They've drawn back, lord,' the former priest said. 'But I don't think they've gone far.'

Marcus considered for a moment. Yes, they could attack, as Valeria suggested, but perhaps there was a better way.

'We'll return their dead,' he said. 'Have Luko form a defensive screen with ten men and the rest can carry the bodies down to the base of the hill. Treat them with respect and lay them out as if for a Christian funeral. We'll do it by torchlight so they can see what's happening.' It was a risk, one that could invite a shower of spears from the darkness, but some instinct told him it was the correct thing to do.

When the task was complete, Marcus crouched at the rim of the dell and waited while Zeno worked to stitch up his wounded cheek. At some point he thought he heard whispers and rustling, but he could see nothing. An hour or so later they watched the night sky turn orange as a great blaze flared upon a hilltop about a mile away.

'It looks like they'll be busy for a while,' Marcus said. 'Time to move on.'

XXVII

The stench of rotting flesh surrounded the small township like a solid wall, accompanied by a familiar incessant drone that confirmed what Marcus knew even before he set eyes on the first corpse. They'd emerged from the forest on to a plain of lush, cultivated pastureland that offered the hope, now dashed, of an opportunity to replenish their dwindling supplies. Some of the townsfolk hung from nooses on make-shift gallows or lay, shrunken, twisted and blackened, amid the ashes of their funeral pyres. Most, though, rested in a great heap in what must have been the market place, at least a score of them, men, women and children, hacked about this way or that, the air above shimmering with the stink of their putrefaction and darkened by clouds of fat, black flies.

A cursory search of the stout, thick-walled, timber houses revealed that nothing of any value had been left. Worse, not a cow or a pig remained in their enclosures. The raised granaries and storehouses among the buildings lay empty apart from a few mouldering husks that wouldn't have tempted a starving goat.

Marcus called the searchers back, but Valeria slipped from her horse and dropped to her knees beside the great charnel pile, bowing her head and whispering a prayer.

'They're pagans,' her brother reminded her. 'You're wasting your breath.'

'They are people, Marcus,' she replied. 'And they deserved better than this.'

She rejoined him in the saddle and they returned to where the remainder of the company waited amid recently planted fields that would never be harvested.

'What happened here, Father?' Brenus asked.

Marcus turned in the saddle and looked back towards the houses. 'A raid, maybe. Zeno reckons this is a volatile region where the tribes are constantly squabbling over the richest land, but,' he frowned as the thought occurred to him, 'the killing and the manner of it was excessive. They went to great lengths to make sure none was left alive.'

'More than a raid, lord,' Leof interrupted. 'Look at the tracks all around us. Warriors, yes, and a few horsemen, but accompanied by scores, perhaps hundreds of others, men, women and children, and with wheeled carts or wagons. They arrived from the east and when they'd done what they came to do, they continued west, the wagons more heavily laden than before. Not a raid. More likely a whole tribe on the move. By killing everyone here they sent a message to the whole area. This is no longer your land. We are here now.'

'Do the tracks give any indication of who they are?'

Leof shook his head. 'Not Huns, I think. From what I've heard they're never more than a bow's length from their horses. Otherwise, who knows in this part of the world? Goths, Vandals, Suevi, Alans. Whoever it is, best to stay away from them unless we want to end up like those poor bastards in the town.'

It was a likely enough explanation for what they'd seen and it satisfied most, but over the next two days it became clear it was too inadequate to encompass the reality of what was happening in the countryside around them.

Mile after mile of emptiness.

Oh, the birds sang and foxes barked, but the land had been wiped clean of every domestic beast. An emptiness whose monotony was

160

broken only by death. There was no shortage of death. Bloated bodies lay scattered in the fields in ones and twos, cut down as they ran and their eyes pecked out by ravens and crows. Every dwelling they encountered had either been burned or was cloaked in that familiar, sweet, sickly scent they came to know so well.

'Not a tribe on the move,' Valeria said quietly. 'An army on the march.'

'Or a nation,' Marcus said. 'I doubt an army would cut a swathe this wide, nor pick it so clean. Gutrum hinted at a great movement of tribes and Stilicho spoke of pressure from the east. Perhaps this is what he feared.'

'We should turn due south, now,' she insisted. 'The sooner we get across the Danuvius and into what passes for civilization in these parts, the better. There is no chance of replenishing our supplies. The men can survive on hard biscuits, but we're running low on fodder for the horses.'

'We should,' Marcus agreed. 'But look what awaits us there.' He pointed to where lines of drifting smoke hung above the far horizon. 'We've been fortunate so far, we're either in their rear or in a pocket between two elements of invaders. To turn south would take us dangerously close to whoever is causing this. Better that we keep east for as long as we can. How far does Zeno think we are from the Danuvius?'

'Anywhere between one day and two is what he *thinks*, but the truth is that he knows as much as you or I.'

'What about Anastasia? She must have passed through these lands.'

Valeria glanced back to where Anastasia rode in the centre of the column beside Brenus. 'I'll ask her.' She turned her mount and rode back, sending Brenus away with a look and taking his place.

'You seem to be doing your best to avoid my brother,' she said after a moment's consideration.

Anastasia blinked, momentarily perplexed by the suggestion. 'No, it's . . . He has much on his mind and I try not to get in his way.'

'I think it's more than that,' Valeria persisted. 'I've seen the way you look at him when you believe he can't see you. He is not as fierce or as frightening as he looks, Anastasia. Either give him a chance to show that, or at least be honest with him, and tell him how you really feel.'

'And risk being abandoned in this wilderness?' In her agitation Anastasia struggled to keep her voice low. 'All I want is to get back to Salona and resume my life.'

'I don't understand.' Valeria stared at her. 'Marcus has shown you nothing but kindness.'

'You mean he wants me to warm his bed . . .'

'No. He has feelings for you. Genuine feelings.'

'On your honour, Valeria,' Anastasia reached across to grip her wrist; her voice had a harsh quality now, 'no one else must know. I lied when I spoke about my capture. My husband didn't die trying to defend me. He sacrificed me in a vain attempt to save his own life. Instead, the barbarians pulled me from my sanctuary and his reward was a cut throat. That moment of betrayal haunts my every waking hour. Don't you see? I can never trust another man.'

Valeria shook her head. She could see that nothing she said would alter Anastasia's position. 'Very well. You have my word. And believe me, Marcus *will* find a way to return you to Salona. How far are we from the Danuvius, do you think?'

Anastasia frowned at the unexpected change of subject. 'I recognize those hills on the horizon,' she pointed south. 'The river lies just beyond. Two days' ride at most.'

Valeria passed on the information to Marcus, fighting the urge to reveal what she'd learned. Better he discovered for himself. She struggled to keep her voice neutral, but he must have sensed something. 'Are you feeling all right?' he asked.

'Just a little tired, Marcus.' She managed a smile. 'We all are. This journey seems to have gone on for ever, and no end in sight.'

'You still agree we should continue east?'

'Two more days,' she nodded. 'After that we have no choice. We must turn south or the horses will break down and we're no longer the first squadron of the Ala Sabiniana, just easy prey for any passing bandits.'

Another long ride across a vast swathe of desolation that dulled the senses and chilled the heart. By now the fires away to their right had long since burned out. Marcus again pondered the merits of an immediate turn south, but his scouts reported an endless barrier of hills filled with deep gullies and broken ground. Next morning all signs of the rampaging army gradually disappeared. Here, the farms and settlements remained untouched by war, but the occupants certainly knew of the terror wrought just beyond the horizon. Julius reported that every last soul vanished like summer mist at the first sighting of his armed band of mounted warriors.

As the sun reached its highest point a line of stunted trees appeared directly across their path. 'We need to make a decision soon, Marcus,' Valeria prompted. 'The horses can't take much more of this.'

'We'll water them at the stream,' Marcus pointed to the trees. 'Then we'll make a decision.'

Not a stream, as it turned out, but something that made the decision for them.

'This is no barbarian trackway.' Valeria stared at the raised causeway running from north to south. Weeds and grass grew between the larger stones, but the line was clear as far as they could see and it was flanked by two part-filled drainage ditches. A road, long unused, but a road built by the legions. Marcus felt a surge of relief rush through him. A Roman road. And if you followed it for long enough any Roman road would eventually lead you to Rome. 'But how?' Valeria continued. 'We're at least a day's ride beyond the frontier.'

'Frontiers change,' Marcus said. 'For a time, however short, the turf wall was the frontier of Britannia. We were still using the roads leading to it two hundred years after it was abandoned. No doubt Zeno will have an answer.'

Zeno proved as bewildered as any of them, but Luko, seeking a place where he could take his ease, discovered that the moss-covered stepping stone he used to cross the ditch was more than just a rock. 'You should see this, lord,' he called.

A Roman milestone had toppled from its position into the ditch.

Luko scraped the moss away with his foot and Marcus and Valeria pondered over the worn Latin lettering. 'It looks like this says we're eleven miles from somewhere called Eburum,' Valeria called over her shoulder to Zeno.

'I've never heard of it.'

'And thirty from Vindobona.'

'Christ save us,' the Greek laughed. 'Vindobona is a city on the Danuvius. We could be there by morning.'

XXVIII

The news they were within reach of civilization brought smiles to the faces of even the surliest of troopers after so many days on constant alert crossing the death zone. Marcus allowed his men their moment of triumph, but reminded them there must be no loss of vigilance. Roman road or not, they were still inside enemy territory and he posted flank guards to left and right and a pair of riders to front and rear. The flankers, negotiating rough ground and patches of forest beyond the roadside ditches, naturally slowed the column, but better to lose a few miles than invite an ambush. His caution proved justified when they spotted fresh tracks on the roadway for the first time.

'I'd noticed,' Valeria said, when he pointed them out. 'They're heavily laden and travelling in pairs. A merchant caravan? Zeno believes this is what they once called the Amber Road, a trade route between Italia and the tribes of the northern seas.'

Marcus shook his head. 'Not traders. Traders would have followed the road all the way south, for convenience. These are warriors of some sort who've been patrolling to the west. Bandits or a patrol sent by whoever holds sway over these lands. Whoever they are we'll let them get well on their way and stay on our guard.'

When they camped for the night, Marcus doubled the sentries and before they bedded down he sought out Anastasia. 'Tomorrow we will reach the river. The company must necessarily continue south, but Zeno believes it would be possible to purchase passage for you on a transport ship which would carry you closer to your home. You don't have to make your decision now, but it is something to think on. Of course,' he smiled, 'I think I speak for us all when I say we would be just as happy if you stayed with us until we reach the coast.'

She turned away so he couldn't see her eyes. 'I will consider it,' she said. 'My only wish is to reach home as soon as I can.'

They set out the next day with a sense of anticipation that affected every man and woman. The river might not mean home, but it did mean the Empire, and the Empire meant sanctuary. But they'd only travelled a mile when Leof, the lead scout, cantered back to the main column. 'Riders ahead,' he called. 'I left Ninian watching them.'

'Bandits?' Marcus demanded. 'Soldiers? An ambush?'

'Not an ambush, lord, or at least it didn't look like it. They were soldiers, in fish-scale armour, and armed with lance, sword and shield, but whose soldiers I couldn't say. Around fifty of them in line across the road and among the trees on either side. They were happy to let us see them. They're just out of sight over the rise.'

Marcus looked to his right and left. It was possible the visible riders were a ruse to draw attention away from the real attack about to fall on his flanks or rear. 'Luko? Tell the flank guards to move out another twenty paces. Lady Anastasia, you will move to the centre of the column. Brenus,' he saw his son's eyes narrow, 'to me.' Anger turned to puzzlement as the boy nudged his horse to Marcus's side. They waited until Luko returned.

'Nothing, lord.'

'All right.' Marcus nodded thoughtfully. 'Brenus, bring me my helmet and Stilicho's warrant. Zeno, Leof, Julius and Senecio, you'll be with us, and for Christ's sake and mine, try to look like soldiers.'

Valeria moved close. 'Are you sure about Brenus?'

Marcus automatically checked the straps of his armour. 'The boy might learn something and it's about time I showed some trust in him.

166

He did well on the hill and he'll be as safe with me as he would be staying here with you.' He studied the terrain around them. 'We can't fight them, there are too many, and I doubt we can run, even if we had anywhere to run to. If I was leading them I'd have sent men to cut the road behind us. If I don't come back get Anastasia home if you can.'

'I will.' She tried to hide the heartache she felt.

Brenus brought the ornate helmet and Marcus gave the nose protector a polish with his sleeve. 'Will they be impressed, do you think, Leof?'

'They'd better be, lord.'

They walked their mounts slowly up the road with Brenus carrying a branch cut from a stunted spruce tree. The green foliage was the universal symbol of a desire to talk in Britannia, and Marcus prayed it would be recognized here. Ninian was waiting on his horse among the trees at the top of the rise.

'Any change?' Marcus called.

'None, lord,' Ninian said. 'They just sit there. They must have known we were coming.'

Everything depended on who – or what – they were, and his first view of the line of riders left Marcus little the wiser. They sat their horses with the composure of men who knew they outnumbered their opponents better than two to one. Tall in the saddle, and uniformly bearded with sandy pelts that reached their breastbones; their scale armour sparkled in the sun. For the moment, their swords remained in leather scabbards attached to their saddles, but that meant nothing when a man understood the deadly potency of the long spear each warrior carried. They wore pot helmets of a simple design, apart from a single warrior in the centre whose helm was topped with a plume of red horsehair. It was the round shields they carried that gave Marcus hope. In his eyes they were too large and unwieldy for a proper cavalryman, but each bore the image of a pair of stylized, wide-eyed fish, which at least hinted that the owners were Christians.

The plumed warrior in the centre raised a hand as they approached, but there was nothing welcoming about the gesture. 'You will dismount from your horses,' he called in a heavily accented Latin. 'And lay your weapons on the roadway.'

Marcus ignored the order, drew his helmet over his head and passed it to Brenus, who handed him the scroll containing Stilicho's travel warrant. He sniffed and inspected the line of riders, allowing his eyes to drift from left to right, then back again until they settled on the man who'd spoken.

'Who stands in the way of a peaceful embassy to General Stilicho?' he demanded.

'Not many come down this road, these days, and none of them peacefully.' The commander chose not to be impressed. 'The last to come this way were the Marcomanni and we're still finding the bones of the families they burned alive among the ashes of their homes in Vindobona. Come to think of it, you don't look much different from Marcomanni bandits and you speak Latin like a dog barking. Still, that's a nice helmet your bum boy is holding.' Brenus growled and his hand went to his sword hilt. Marcus reached out to grip his son's arm and the cavalry officer laughed. 'And I like the look of your horse. Maybe I'll take all three of them away from you?'

'That would be a pity.' Marcus saw the other man's eyes narrow at a clatter of hooves on the roadway. He looked over his shoulder to see Valeria approaching at the head of her squadron deployed in a compact Boar's Snout wedge that bristled with swords. 'Because it would mean you'd have to kill us all, and I can guarantee we'd take an awful lot of these fine-looking soldiers of yours with us. Besides, it would be a pity for friends and allies to fall out because of a misunderstanding.'

'What do you mean, friends?' the commander demanded, but his tone held more puzzlement than threat.

'You say you come from Vindobona,' Marcus accompanied his words with a smile, 'which I take to mean that you have the honour to serve the Emperor Honorius. I also have that honour. Marcus Flavius Victor, prefect of the First Ala Sabiniana, greets you.'

'I've never heard of Marcus Flavius Victor or the Ala Sabiniana, but yes, we serve Honorius, may the Lord protect him. What in God's name brings you slinking down the old Amber Road at a time when the country is crawling with barbarians of every form known to man?'

'That's a long story,' Marcus assured him, 'and an even longer journey. We began our travels in Britannia, and have come by way of Saxonia and lands unknown. I need to reach General Stilicho.' Marcus held out the dispatch case containing Stilicho's letter. The other man recognized the twin seals and nodded. 'By his authority, I would ask you to show us a way to cross the Danuvius and point us in the direction of a supply depot, for we are near weak with hunger. Then we'll take the quickest route south. Whom do I have the honour of addressing?'

'I doubt you'd count it much of an honour, prefect,' the officer grinned. 'Gunderic, decurion of the second squadron, Ala Thracum Victrix.' He nudged his horse forward and offered his hand. 'Though victories have been hard to come by of late. I reckon we can escort you over the river – we've been out for five days searching for a big band of Alans who were reported to be sniffing around, but they seem to have drifted west – and supplies shouldn't be a problem. As for putting you on the quickest road south . . . well, why don't we discuss that once you're across?'

Marcus nodded. 'Talking of your Alans, I fear you and your superiors may be underestimating the threat from the east. For the last five days we've seen nothing but devastation and death. It could never have been caused by a single band or a single tribe. We're talking about tens of thousands of warriors and their followers.'

'That would fit with what my commander has been hearing from up and down the river.' Gunderic frowned. 'It looks like the entire Goth nation is on the move and looking for trouble.'

'I don't understand.' Marcus stole a glance at Anastasia. 'From what I've been told Alaric and his Goths are settled already south of the river, in Dalmatia.'

Gunderic shook his head. 'Alaric and his Tervingi aren't the problem. They're what we call tame Goths, more or less. This is the Greuthungi, of the Great Plain, or they were before the Huns forced them west. Their king, Radagaisus, and his priests have convinced them their salvation lies beyond the river and the mountains. That means Gaul, or maybe Italia itself. They say he's been joined by Alans and Suevi, but every bandit north of the river will want his slice of the plunder. Stilicho will need to stop them before they get to the mountains or Honorius might not have an empire to rule.'

XXIX

Vindobona (Vienna)

'Welcome to Pannonia Prima,' Gunderic proclaimed.

Marcus had always believed that a posting to the Wall provided a unique challenge to a Roman officer, but as they approached the southern bank of the Danuvius on a Libernian galley of the Classis Histrica, he realized he was mistaken. Vindobona occupied a strong position on high ground at the meeting of the river and one of its feeder streams. Yet not quite strong enough, as was proved by the blackened ruins that surrounded it. Someone had put the city to the torch, and not so long ago either. By the landing place, he could see a rocky slope where the original river wall of the fort had collapsed into the stream, presumably a result of flood or earthquake rather than war. The garrison had constructed a new wall set back from the bank and along a shorter frontage. In fact, on closer inspection, it was clear the entire fort had been rebuilt on a much smaller scale within the perimeter of the original walls. The city's public buildings – the basilica, forum and baths – were mere blackened ruins, showing little or no attempt to repair them.

'Five years ago, when the Marcomanni came down the Amber Road in their thousands,' Gunderic explained as they made their landing, 'only a cohort of legionaries and two regiments of auxiliaries garrisoned Vindobona. You can't hold a fort built to be defended by five thousand men with fewer than a thousand. We had to abandon the city until General Stilicho put together an army and we were able to drive the bastards back over the river where they belong. It has taken until now to rebuild what you see.'

'Five years, yet it still seems almost deserted?'

Gunderic nodded. 'Most of the people who returned fled again a few months ago when we heard of the great movement of the Goths. Fortunately it looks as if most of the tribes have moved far upstream, but there is no telling what they will do once they get over the river. It's possible they'll turn east towards Pannonia or Illyricum. That's why I'd advise you to continue east for a few days until you reach Gerulata. The fort at Gerulata is long abandoned, but there's a decent road south through the mountains to Iadera and the coast where you can take ship to Ravenna. That's where you'll find Stilicho if he's not already on campaign.'

'I was told to seek General Stilicho in Metulum,' Marcus frowned.

Gunderic shook his head. 'He's long gone from these parts. Italia is where he will be, laying out his plans and gathering his forces. They say Honorius has moved his court to Ravenna, and Stilicho won't stray far from the Emperor.'

'Then your advice sounds good, and I thank you for it,' Marcus said. 'One of our company was hoping to find passage on a transport downstream to a port within easy reach of Salona. Where can I organize that?'

'The truth is,' Gunderic shook his head, 'you can't, unless your friend is prepared to wait for a month. All river traffic apart from military vessels has been suspended because of the threat from the Goths. Now, if you'll follow me I'll introduce you to the legate of the Tenth Legion Gemina, who commands here. He must authorize the supplies you need, but the pouch you carry bearing Stilicho's seal will ease your way. It's unlikely he'll keep you long. As you can tell, the rebuilding of the fortress and the defence of the river take up every minute he has.'

Gunderic proved to be correct and the overworked legionary commander was happy to see the new, exotic arrivals on their way before they complicated his life still further. Marcus arranged with the quartermaster for the rations and fodder to be delivered to the camp the squadron had set up among the ruins.

When he returned, Anastasia was seated with Valeria and Zeno by the fire, with Brenus hovering nearby, and he went to sit with them. He told them about Gunderic's advice.

'So not Salona then?' Zeno said.

Valeria noticed the look of dismay on Anastasia's face. 'We'll find a ship when we reach the coast,' she assured her. 'And Marcus will provide you with an escort.'

'What happens when we reach Italia?' Brenus asked.

The tone was brusque, bordering on the insolent, but Marcus ignored any implied disrespect. 'Judging by what we've heard, I'd say we'll receive a warm welcome,' he answered his son evenly. 'Stilicho will need every fighting man he can lay hands on if he's to stop this Radagaisus. He's promised me a command, and I trust him to keep to his word if he can.'

'If he can?' Valeria frowned.

'The legate also told me fear of Radagaisus has hardened the attitude against barbarians across Italia, even in Emperor Honorius's court. A man in Stilicho's position will always have enemies. It doesn't help his cause that he's been forced to ally himself to certain Goths and Franks in order to hold the Empire's borders. There are whispers that he has lost the Emperor's trust. Who knows what he can or cannot do?'

'Whatever General Stilicho's circumstances,' Valeria said, 'we have long since cast the die and Italia is the next step on our journey home.' She glanced at Anastasia. 'Or wherever else we choose to go. Marcus is right, the Empire needs soldiers and we are soldiers. Not barbarians, but Roman soldiers. My sense – or at least my hope – is that we will be honoured, or at the very least accepted. We can ask no more.'

'They call this road the Via Istrum.' Zeno, who, as was his habit, had taken the opportunity to question anyone at Vindobona who would give him the time, about the place and its people. 'If we followed it to the very end we could bathe in the waters of the Pontus Euxinus.'

The road ran more or less parallel to the river and within a mile or two of the main stream, depending on the various twists and turns of the waterway. Here there was more than one Danuvius hidden amongst the willows and oaks to their left. Marcus's outriders had returned with reports of multiple streams carving their way through the fertile dark soil, each teeming with fish, large and small, waterbirds of every hue, and with sign of otters, beaver and deer imprinted in the thick mud of the banks. To their right the land was flat as a table top and chequered with fields that would once have held neat rows of emerging crops. Now they lay neglected and long untended, empty, like the small farmsteads that dotted them, with their crumbling walls and collapsed roofs.

If Anastasia felt dismayed at Marcus's failure to find a ship, she hid it well, and, despite the neglected landscape, the very air seemed more breathable south of the river.

On the morning of the second day they reached the ruined fort at Gerulata and turned south.

XXX

It had once been a Roman signal tower, perched upon a hill overlooking the small fort that guarded the road between Gerulata and Andautonia. Now both tower and fort were in ruins, their garrisons long gone, but that didn't mean the fort wasn't occupied. And if Marcus was any judge, the occupiers were about to receive an unwelcome surprise.

From his lofty perch he could see a circle of eight wagons on what had once been the fort's parade ground, with men moving among them. They'd placed a sentry in one of the crumbling gate towers, but appeared to have done nothing to block the gate, the doors of which must have been removed when the fort was slighted. What the sentry couldn't see, but the watchers on the hill could, was the band of horsemen, perhaps forty strong, hidden in the trees two hundred paces from the gate, and the scouts they'd placed to survey every wall of the fort.

'A trader's caravan?' Valeria suggested. 'There must be something very valuable in those wagons to attract so many bandits.'

'Maybe,' Marcus accepted the possibility. 'They're not soldiers. I haven't seen sign of a sword or a spear.'

'What do we do?'

'I don't know,' he admitted. His instinct was to move on and leave events to take their course. 'Get Zeno to bring Anastasia up here. She knows these lands and their people, perhaps she will see something that will enlighten us a little more.'

Anastasia arrived a few moments later and joined them behind the earth parapet that surrounded the remains of the tower. Marcus asked her what she could see.

Her gaze was naturally drawn to the wagons in the fort. 'The men are Goths or Alans, I think, traders, or perhaps an extended family seeking new lands to farm. Yes, see, there is a woman with a child in the shadow of the largest of the wagons.' She looked to Marcus for confirmation that she was right and he nodded.

'The woods to the left, at the edge of the clearing.'

Her head turned a little and she released an audible gasp.

'What is it?' Valeria hissed.

'The men in the forest. They're Huns.'

'You're certain?'

'Those fur-trimmed caps they wear mark them, and the fact that every man carries a bow across his back. Yes, I'm sure.'

Marcus stifled a curse. 'We should go now. There's nothing for us here but trouble and death.' He turned to leave, but neither woman moved. 'What is it?'

'The Huns will leave none alive, Marcus,' Anastasia said. 'That is their way.'

'They outnumber us almost two to one.'

'At Longovicium we were outnumbered ten to one,' Valeria pointed out.

'That was different,' Marcus growled. 'These people are nothing to us. Why should we risk our lives for them?'

'The Goths and Alans are fellow Christians,' Anastasia said quietly. 'We cannot leave innocent Christians to be slaughtered by pagan savages.'

Marcus opened his mouth to continue the argument, but the look in Valeria's eyes silenced him. If a soldier lived long enough he learned there was no dishonour in making a dignified retreat.

'What do you suggest?' he challenged his sister. 'This is not Longovicium.'

'Perhaps not, but in one way it is very similar,' she said. 'We will have the element of surprise.'

They waited until nightfall to begin taking up position, leading their horses down a steep forest track with infinite care, testing every individual tread in the knowledge that a stumble might be the death of them all. Anastasia stayed on the hill with Brenus, who accepted he had no place in an attack by highly trained horse soldiers who'd been fighting together for years. Before they left, Marcus passed him a heavy pouch of silver.

'If things go wrong,' Marcus nodded towards Anastasia, 'get her home as best you can.'

Marcus and Valeria had spent what was left of the daylight studying the Huns. Clearly these were warriors who knew the value of both concealment and silence. Likewise, their preparations showed a troubling familiarity with what lay ahead. Each man fed his horse a handful of grain or fodder before he ate his own sparse meal, then placed his blanket on the ground and lay down with the animal tethered at his side. As they waited for darkness they unstrung their bows and sorted their arrows, discarding any that were warped or had damaged flights. Their scouts returned to the camp at dusk and Valeria breathed a sigh of relief that none would be in a position to interfere with her plan.

'They will attack at dawn,' she predicted, 'when the people in the wagons are breaking their fast. That is when we will hit them.'

Marcus didn't know how she could be so certain, but he didn't object. It made sense for the attackers to wait for the waking hour when men's fuzzy-minded thoughts were focused on the day ahead or the task in hand. If he were the Hun chieftain he would form up in darkness not too far from the gate, then make one quick dash to turn the parade area into a killing ground. Forty Huns against half as many farmers, and some of them helpless women and children. It would be over in moments. There'd be no need to unsling their bows, which Marcus counted as a blessing. He knew the value of a good archer and he suspected that warriors who lavished as much attention on their weapons as they did on their horses would be very good indeed.

Now he and Valeria carefully positioned the men of the Ala Sabiniana among the trees at the bottom of the slope, about a hundred and fifty paces from the road leading to the fort. The Huns would come from the woods to their left. Valeria had placed Senecio in the branches of a tree closer to the well-beaten track where he could provide warning of the attack and pick off any leaders he could identify. The trees that provided the enemy with concealment would also screen the cavalrymen until the last moment.

'They won't know we're there until they feel the edge of our swords,' Valeria had assured the squadron. 'We'll hit the rear of their attack in wedge formation, empty as many saddles as possible, then wheel to take the van. Remember, God is on our side. These are pagans, show them no mercy.'

Marcus noted approvingly that Valeria's plan, in the event that the Huns didn't prove quite so cooperative, left the Ala Sabiniana close to the fort's gateway after they wheeled for the second attack. If the ambush went badly they'd have the option of retreating into the fort. The enemy would then have the choice of assaulting a position defended by more or less equal numbers or laying siege to the position. Neither of which was likely to be favoured by an opportunistic murder band.

A sky as black as the inside of a grave, broken only by the firefly gleam of the ever-shifting stars. Then, through the trees to the east, minute by minute, moment by moment the great void altered hue by increments the eye could barely register until a faint glow announced the advent of the new day.

Marcus checked the strap on his ornamental helmet and tested the draw of his sword. Almost without realizing it he was staring at Senecio in the branches of an oak tree on his flank. Senecio's eyes were fixed on whatever was happening to his left, but as Marcus watched he turned and waved his arms to signal that the Huns were in the saddle.

The Ala Sabiniana was already in formation with Marcus and Valeria at the head of the wedge and there was no need for a command. As the squadron lurched into motion the scrub to their left parted without warning and an almost childlike figure on a pony appeared from the bushes like an apparition in a dream. Marcus had a glimpse of a fur cap and a cloth tunic, startled dark eyes and a gaping mouth. The warrior drew breath to shout a warning only for Senecio's arrow to transfix his throat with a sound like a snapping twig.

'I thought it was they who were supposed to be surprised?' he hissed at Valeria.

'Just ride,' she snarled.

XXXI

The first Huns who came into view were already at the canter and their entire focus was on the gateway ahead. They rode four abreast, more or less, in a straggling column with the rear horsemen forty paces behind the leader. Small men on small horses, dressed in strange padded jackets and with exotic curved swords already to hand. Every warrior carried a short bow slung over his back and had a pouch of arrows attached to his saddle. Marcus knew their reputation belied what his eyes were telling him, but, inside, his heart soared.

Valeria had chosen the perfect tactic to turn the charge into chaos and ruin.

A cry of warning. They'd been seen at last. A stutter of confusion ran through the little column before Valeria's whooping riders smashed like a thunderbolt into the rear section of the attack, scattering men and animals. In a moment six or seven of the Huns tumbled into the dust, their horses sent reeling by the big Roman mounts. Unhorsed, the stunned warriors were at the mercy of those who followed. Marcus hacked at a passing blur beneath a fur-trimmed cap and was rewarded by a shriek as the blade sliced through bone and sinew. Crimson blood misted the air in the wake of the charge. Then they were through and clear and wheeling right, though not all because at least one riderless Roman horse ran loose among them.

The wheel brought the still compact formation on a line to intercept the lead element of the Hun charge in the shadow of the fort's gatehouse. Here all was milling confusion. It should have been a repeat of the first attack, a hammer blow of death and destruction. But the dozen heartbeats they took to perform the wheel had given the Huns the breathing space they needed.

A squat warrior on a pale horse screamed out orders, but each Hun reacted to the attack in his own fashion. Now it was the nimble little ponies which came into their own, with riders born to the saddle orchestrating their movements. They spun, darted and twisted to stay clear of the charging Roman horses. A few went down, and more of their riders fell victim to the Ala Sabiniana's swords. But not enough.

Marcus targeted the squat leader's pony in a thundering charge. The impact alone would have broken the smaller horse's back, but its rider twitched the reins and they jinked clear. Frustrated, Marcus took a passing swing at the Hun that should have spilled his guts, only to watch in disbelief as the warrior threw himself horizontal across the pony's back and allowed the blade to pass harmlessly over his prone body. Before he could blink, the Hun was upright again and Marcus flailed wildly at the wickedly curved sword that hacked at his right flank. The blades met with a ringing clash and the Hun was past, only to pirouette to resume the attack. What in the name of Christ was this? Narrow eyes glittered above sharp cheekbones, a flat nose and a mouth that gaped wide in a gap-toothed grin.

The bastard was laughing at him.

Two riders exchanging blows blocked them for a moment. Something slapped Marcus's shoulder and his ears rang as the deflected Hun arrow clattered off the cheekpiece of his helmet. He risked a glance around him. Valeria was busy chasing a Hun who twisted and turned and whose only thought was for survival. Leof leaned low in the saddle hacking at a dismounted warrior. Julius the Pict and Luko had combined in an endlessly circling combat that would have been

181

almost comical but for the fact that Luko suddenly reeled in the saddle and clutched his arm.

The Hun archers.

Those with the time and space had unhitched their bows and sought out the Roman troopers with deadly barbed shafts from the back of their galloping ponies. The cavalrymen were largely protected by their chain armour, which only a perfectly aimed arrow could penetrate, but they were vulnerable elsewhere. Marcus knew that unless they could find a way to stop the archers they would quickly be forced to retire into the fort.

'Kill their horses,' he roared. 'Forget the riders. Kill the horses.'

The cry was aimed at Senecio, but Marcus would never know whether it reached him. For the squat Hun was back looking for blood and now it was Marcus on the defensive. The agile little pony circled, dancing and whirling to keep its rider just out of reach of Marcus's long sword as he manoeuvred for a position to strike at the Roman's unprotected back or flank. The probes became increasingly more difficult to defend and sweat blurred Marcus's vision as he fought to keep the Hun within the eye pieces of the helmet. He dragged his reins to keep his enemy in sight, but he knew it couldn't last. Sooner or later the larger horse was going to stumble or misstep and the look in the Hun's eye told him his opponent knew it too.

Kill the horses.

Senecio may not have heard, but someone had.

Suddenly the air was filled with the unmistakable butcher's block thud of missiles penetrating meat and muscle. Horses whinnied in fear and agony. Desperate cries of alarm in an unfamiliar language. Marcus sensed it all, but his only thought now was for his own survival.

Christ, the Hun almost had him.

Two consecutive impacts closer to hand and the grinning warrior disappeared from view. For a moment Marcus believed he was doomed, but in that same instant the Hun's pony crashed into his flank. He made a desperate grab for a saddle pommel as his horse almost foundered, simultaneously flailing with his blade in the direction of the Hun. A moment later powerful arms seized him round the waist. Already off balance, the weight of his assailant hauled him from the saddle. He had a glimpse of the Hun pony, nostrils frothing blood and two arrows projecting from its throat, before they hit the hard-packed earth with a jolt that knocked the wind from him and the sword from his hand.

Marcus struggled to his feet searching for his blade. It lay two paces away but by the time he'd taken half a step his legs were kicked from beneath him and he was rolling in the dust once more. He just had time to twist onto his back before the Hun fell on him with a curved blade in his right hand. Somehow, Marcus managed to get a grip on the warrior's wrist, but there was a terrible strength in the lean body and an even more terrible certainty in those dark, almond eyes. For a few moments they tested each other's power, but Marcus felt his forearm begin to shake and little by little the point closed remorselessly on his defenceless throat. His right hand had been scrabbling for his sword, which couldn't be more than a few maddening inches away, but that hope had gone. Now he brought the hand round and ground the handful of grit he'd grasped in desperation into his enemy's eyes. The Hun cried out, his left hand went to his blinded eyes and the power in the right momentarily waned. Waned enough for Marcus to push the knife hand to one side and in the same movement bring his helmeted head up into the Hun's face with bone-breaking force. For all the helmet's decorative appearance, it was a formidable weapon in its own right. Iron bands riveted to the crown formed a protective crosspiece that shattered the delicate bones of the Hun's nose. He fell back and Marcus leapt to his feet tearing at his helmet straps and hauling it from his head. He was aware that the sound of fighting had receded, but he only had eyes for the man who had been so desperate to kill him. He took the helmet in his right hand and raised it full length to bring the heavy iron down on his helpless enemy's skull.

'Bastard. Bastard. Bastard.'

Each breathless expletive was accompanied by a new blow until the Hun's features were all but obliterated.

'Marcus,' Valeria's voice penetrated the red haze that filled his mind. 'It's over.'

He looked up to find the Ala Sabiniana, battered but more or less intact, in a half-circle on their horses around him. Zeno was working on Luko's injured shoulder. The surviving Huns had withdrawn beyond bow range and were lined up in front of the trees where they'd camped. For the moment they looked harmless enough, but that might change.

Marcus bent to pick up his sword and, with three savage blows, hacked off the dead leader's head. He picked up the blood-spattered skull by its long, black hair and raised it towards the Huns.

'Hear this,' he called. 'I am Marcus Flavius Victor, and this is what happens to the enemies of Rome.' He threw the head with all his strength so it bounced along the packed earth of the road for twenty or thirty paces. 'Take what remains of your leader and never return.'

'A pretty speech.' The voice came from behind him. 'But one I fear you may live to regret.'

Marcus turned and looked up. A tall man stood on the ruined parapet above the fort's gateway, a long bow held casually in his right hand. To his right and left fifteen or so other archers gripped their bows in a manner that was anything but casual. They held them raised and drawn, with the arrows nocked and very clearly covering the horsemen of the Ala Sabiniana.

'Is this the way you greet your rescuers in these parts?' Marcus called.

'Rescuers?' The tall man laughed and shook his head. 'All I see is a few fools who blundered in and spoiled a perfect ambush.'

Marcus took a step forward, but Valeria pushed her mount between her brother and the gate.

'It is an odd kind of ambush that allows the wolf into the sheepfold.' She removed her helmet, allowing her russet hair to spill over her shoulders.

'A woman?' The man's tone matched the perplexed look on his handsome features. 'What kind of Roman unit has women in its ranks? And you can fight.'

'Yes, I can fight, man with no name, and if your archers don't put up their bows you will see just how well. Valeria Victor, decurion, first squadron Ala Sabiniana. This is Marcus Flavius Victor, who commands.'

'I am Fritigern,' the tall man announced. 'The head of this little band of sheep.' He clicked his fingers and the bowmen put up their weapons and disappeared from the parapet. 'You'd better come inside,' he called. 'We were hoping to be on our way by now, but it would be bad manners not to share what little we have with our . . . saviours.' The word was accompanied by a self-mocking smile.

'What about them?' Marcus nodded towards the horsemen by the trees.

'We'll let the Huns collect their dead. They're harmless enough now that Octar is gone. You did the world a service there, my friend.' Fritigern vanished from view and appeared a moment later in front of the gate. Valeria dismounted and led her horse towards the fort and Marcus joined her. 'Keep to the sides of the entrance if you don't want to experience the nasty surprise we'd prepared for the Huns.' Fritigern kicked aside some of the straw that had been spread across the entrance to reveal a deep pit with a pair of sharpened stakes in the bottom. 'This is one sheepfold the wolves would have regretted raiding.'

Now he was closer Marcus could see the slight dips in the straw marking other pits that pock-marked the entrance and the area inside the gate. He knew from experience the damage the traps would have done to the charging Huns and their ponies. Beyond the pits, Fritigern's wagons were now drawn up in a solid defensive line and he guessed the archers had been posted there to pour arrows into the few Huns who might have escaped the chaos unscathed. His respect for their new acquaintance grew.

Fritigern was as tall as Marcus, of more slender stature, but with a farmer's heft to the shoulders and arms that warned against mistaking lack of bulk for weakness. He had sandy, shoulder-length hair and a neatly trimmed beard framed lips set in a sardonic half-smile which suggested he found the world perpetually amusing. Yet it was the eyes that made the man, ash-grey as the sky of a winter's morn, with shadowy depths that testified to a keen intelligence. Dressed in a knee-length tunic edged with blue cloth, he spoke a Latin that sounded odd to Marcus's ears, but with a fluency and ease that made it his first, or at least most accustomed, tongue. A cultured man, if Marcus was any judge of manners.

'At least one of your number is a soldier,' he complimented Fritigern.

'The Romans call us Goths, or Visigoths if they are being particular, but we say we are Tervingi, and I am of the line called Balti. As such we are farmers by inclination, and sometimes by choice, but soldiers at need, as those Huns would have learned had you not intervened.'

Fritigern led them to the former parade ground where his horses were tethered. The remainder of the Ala Sabiniana filed in after them and Julius and Ninian set up a new line for their mounts.

'There is water in the well,' Fritigern said, as the cavalrymen unsaddled their animals and led them to the rope. 'You know your horses,' he said to Marcus and Valeria.

The compliment contained a hint of a question, but Marcus chose not to answer it for now.

'You said I might have cause to regret what you called my *pretty speech*. What did you mean?'

The Goth laughed. 'You called out your name loud enough to have it heard in Andautonia. I have no doubt more than one of the Huns understood what you said; they are not as stupid as they look. In time that name will reach their king. Octar, the man you killed, is his brother.' He saw Valeria wince and his smile broadened. 'Yes, Uldin is the most merciless and vengeful of a people famed for those traits. Your good deed today may have made you a truly worthy enemy, Marcus Flavius Victor.'

XXXII

'I was surprised that a man wearing such fine regalia should be a mere prefect.' Fritigern eyed the gilded helm as he, Marcus and Valeria sat on the veranda of a crumbling barrack block sharing a plate of smoked meats and fish. 'I have seen kings beyond the frontier less finely attired. Surely a general at the very least must have ridden to our aid? Not that we required it, of course. And,' he turned to Valeria, 'though your shared name provides a clue, I am much too polite to enquire how such a fine lady became involved with an uncouth band of cavalrymen.'

Valeria opened her mouth to give this impertinence the response it deserved, but Fritigern raised a hand in a manner that struck her as almost imperious, and she bit her tongue. 'What I will ask,' he continued, 'because I am by nature a curious man, is how such an exotic band of adventurers comes to be in these lands? It is plain you are not native to Pannonia or Illyricum, and I know enough of what lies beyond the river to believe you did not begin your journey there?'

Marcus exchanged a glance with his sister and she shrugged. What difference did it make? 'We are a delegation from Britannia, seeking out General Stilicho.' Did he detect a hint of recognition at the name? 'When last we heard of him he was said to be in this area.'

'If he was ever here, he certainly will not be now,' Fritigern said with some force. 'Any problems he has in the east are but a pinprick compared to the spear thrust that now threatens the Empire's vitals from the north. Our brethren in the east, the Greuthungi, are on the march, and only await the great thaw for passage through the mountains. They say their king, Radagaisus, has a hundred thousand followers and fifty thousand of them warriors. And where the wolf hunts, the carrion birds are never far away. Every variety of eastern brigand, bandit, thief and murderer will travel in his wake. But wait – Britannia, you say?'

Marcus nodded.

'Then you certainly came from across the river. You must have been very fortunate indeed not to encounter some element of Radagaisus's horde. Yet I ask myself why. My knowledge of the Empire's geography is necessarily limited, but it is certain there are much easier, more direct, and far less hazardous routes you might have chosen. And then there is the composition of your following. Soldiers, yes, well trained and equipped. But so few? I am well enough acquainted with the Roman military to know that a prefect would normally command a regiment, perhaps three hundred men. Yet you count fewer than thirty. I confess, it is a puzzle. What brought you by this route and this chance meeting of ours?'

'We could ask the same of you.' Valeria worked a fishbone from between her teeth. 'From a distance you give the impression of settlers seeking a new land, but I only see one woman among you and she never strays far from a wagon driver who looks like a sparrow among hawks in this company. And what is so attractive about the presence of a few *farmers, but soldiers at need*, that draws a prince of the Huns and a squadron of his warriors to slaughter them?'

'Did I say Octar was a prince?' The Goth feigned surprise.

'The brother of a king. How could he be anything less?'

'Yes, we are soldiers,' Fritigern admitted. 'And in the past we have given the Huns no reason to love us.' He cast a sideways glance at Marcus. 'Perhaps, like you, we will offer our services to General Stilicho against Radagaisus.'

'Radagaisus is a Goth; isn't it more likely you'd be travelling to join him?' Marcus said.

Fritigern laughed. 'Radagaisus is an Ostrogoth, a pagan, and a very different animal from us civilized Tervingi. Why, I'll vow that this is the first time he has crossed the river other than to cut a few throats, while we have been part of the Empire for more years than I care to remember. I was seven years old when my family and my tribe migrated south over the Danuvius to take up the lands in Thrace offered to us in return for our service to Rome.'

'Then you will also remember a battle called Adrianopolis.' The interruption came from Zeno, who was working on Claudius, a trooper who'd suffered an ugly face wound from the edge of a Hun sword.

'How is he?' Marcus called.

The *medicus* shrugged. 'I'll sew him up as best as I can, but those bastards chopped him up pretty badly. Adrianopolis was when the Goths turned on their new friends, annihilated a Roman army and killed the Emperor Valens.'

'I was brought up on tales of Adrianopolis,' Fritigern said. 'And if you know of the battle you will also know that I take my name from the man who led our people in that great victory.' He nodded slowly and his tone turned sombre. 'Adrianopolis was the result of a misunderstanding and a betrayal, like so many of the differences between Rome and the Goths. The lands in Thrace were not what was promised. My people were better off than most, but the earth seemed to grow only more stones, and we came close to starving. It is different now. We have farmlands worthy of the name and most of us are well settled. Why, I have been accused of being more Roman than the Romans.' His mood changed again and he laughed at the thought. 'No, my friends, I would not join Radagaisus. He is a fool and no general, or he would have crossed the Danuvius at Vindobona, taken the most direct route to Italia and likely none of us would now be alive. So now you know our story, what about yours?'

Marcus turned his head to search the compound. 'One of the reasons we are here concerns my son. Brenus!' he called. 'Where is the boy?'

'He must still be on the hill,' Valeria said. 'We should have sent someone before this. Those Huns may still be around.'

Marcus called for Julius. 'Take four men and escort Bren and the lady Anastasia from the signal tower.'

Yet it was only a few moments before they reappeared in the gateway. Julius had dismounted and he and Brenus carried a limp body between them. Anastasia led their horses and Marcus could see she was weeping. His heart sank at the sight.

'No,' Valeria whispered.

They laid Senecio on the dusty parade ground. A single Hun arrow had pierced the Numidian's left eye, but otherwise his expression retained its same unruffled calm. As the men of the Ala Sabiniana gathered round, Zeno gave Senecio a cursory glance and shook his head.

'He literally wouldn't have known what hit him. Dead before he hit the ground.' He turned back to the trooper he'd been tending.

'One of your men?' Fritigern said quietly.

'One of our best.' Marcus bowed his head over Senecio's corpse. 'A good comrade and a better friend.'

'Then I am sorry our salvation has come at such a high price.'

The words were evidently heartfelt and Marcus's regard for the Goth rose still further.

'It is my fault,' he said. 'I brought him to this place. He has marched every step of the way with us. This is Brenus, my son.' Brenus brushed his hand across his nose and took a deep breath before making a bow. 'He was taken by the Saxons in a raid on Britannia.' They watched as Senecio's comrades took the body away to prepare it for burial. Nobody could be sure what the rites of his people were, but he'd nominally been a Christian and he would be buried as one. 'We discovered where he was imprisoned,' Marcus continued. 'And these men volunteered to help me rescue him. Unfortunately, the Saxons burned our ships, but we had the resources to make our escape and have travelled by river and mountain and across broad plains to reach this country.'

Marcus looked around for Anastasia, but she was crouched beside Zeno, helping him arrange the bandages on the injured man.

'Then your mission to General Stilicho is only a stratagem.' Fritigern didn't seem surprised or offended that he might have been misled.

'No,' Marcus assured him. 'It is but another part of the story. The general and I are old comrades from his time in Britannia. He wrote to me before I left the island suggesting I might be of more use at his side than in my home province, where my status was subject to certain misunderstandings.' Fritigern grunted as if he had an intimate knowledge of the type of *misunderstandings* Marcus referred to. 'I do not know whether he was aware then of this Radagaisus's movements, but he spoke of growing problems in the east.'

Fritigern considered the new information for a few moments. 'If you are intent on joining General Stilicho I believe we can be of use to each other, at least for a few days,' he said. 'My wagons would be more secure with a mounted escort against the possible return of the Huns. I don't count it likely,' he assured Marcus, 'but a man can never be too careful. Yes, we would slow you down, but not too much, I think. We know these lands, the ways of its people and especially those of the officious Imperial clerks who might stand in our way. I understand what it is like to feel your way through a strange land never knowing what danger lies beyond the next corner. Travel with us and you need no longer concern yourself with such matters.'

Marcus frowned. It wasn't a possibility he'd considered, but it made a certain sense. 'I'll have to consult with Valeria, and we won't be able to travel until we've given Senecio the respect he deserves, but I don't see why not.'

'Then we will stay the night here and leave at dawn.' Fritigern smiled. 'Another day will make little difference.'

The Goth walked away to where one of his men had been watching the conversation. 'We'll travel together, Sigaric.' He explained the arrangements he'd just made.

'Is this wise?' the other man asked.

'I think it will profit us,' Fritigern said in a low voice. 'But be wary, Sigaric. It seems to me that this our new friend could be a very dangerous man.'

Marcus went to where Anastasia was still helping Zeno. She stood and walked to meet him, rubbing a hand across her brow that left a bloody smear on the white flesh.

'Who is that man you were speaking to?' she said before he could greet her.

'Fritigern, the Goth who leads these people. He is very grateful for our help.'

Anastasia stared to where Fritigern stood with one of his men. 'It is a long time and he has changed much since the only time I saw him.'

'You know Fritigern?'

She turned and looked up into his eyes. 'The last time I saw him was in Salona,' she said quietly, 'where men knelt before him and called him King Alaric.'

XXXIII

'So you are acquainted with General Stilicho?' Fritigern and Marcus walked their horses beside the lead wagon. 'Naturally I know of him, but I would be interested in your impression of his character. He divides opinion among the Goths.'

Marcus and Valeria had agreed there was no harm, and potentially some profit, in allowing Alaric to continue with his deception for now. Alaric was a king, and for all their knowledge of this land it could be that his king's remit ran to these hills and valleys. Marcus was all too aware of the ebb and flow of fragile alliances that kept the Empire together. Only a fool would risk upsetting that balance before he knew more.

'I can understand that,' Marcus replied eventually. 'You mentioned that you had been accused of being more Roman than the Romans? Well I would venture Stilicho is more Roman still. Ever since he was a young man he has been branded part-barbarian. The only way he could refute the charge was to be more loyal to the Emperor, more effective as a soldier, and more valuable to his superiors than any other of his class. I would say he is a fair man, but that fairness is always tempered by the need to adhere to these values. I know he is a brave man, because I have stood beside him in battle. Is he a *good* man? Only God can decide that.'

His companion nodded slowly and they continued in silence for a while. In one sense Fritigern had been correct: it was much more pleasurable to travel with companions who knew the country and its people. Not that they saw much of the people. The Goth avoided settlements when he could and sent others to bargain for supplies in those places where they seemed likely to be plentiful. The wagons advanced at a leisurely pace and Marcus and Valeria and their troopers alternated between the saddle and travelling on foot, allowing their mounts a proper rest for the first time in weeks. The people they did encounter were either peasants, who kept their distance and weren't inclined to talk, or military units on their way north to reinforce garrisons on the Danuvius frontier. The soldiers were perfectly accustomed to roving bands of Tervingi traders and gave them no trouble. To a certain extent, Marcus felt quite at home, because the land here reminded him of the country south of the Wall, with waves of gently undulating hills carpeted with wood and meadow, lush fields filled with budding crops and swift-flowing rivers to irrigate them. It became warmer with each passing day and the heat from the sun on an April morning surpassed any summer in Britannia Marcus had ever experienced.

'There is a river not far from here where we can water the horses and allow our people to rest out of the sun,' Fritigern said.

'You're very solicitous of your men,' Marcus ventured. 'That is the sign of a good commander.'

Fritigern stared at him, conscious of the unvoiced question in the statement. 'A commander's greatest asset is the men who follow him,' he said. 'It pays him to look after them until someone with more power decides they are but coins to be spent. The currency of war.'

'Yes.' Marcus understood the currency of war, none better. 'You sound as if you have experience of spending these coins of yours.'

'I'm a Goth.' The other man laughed, but there was no humour in it. 'Just over ten years ago I fought under the Emperor Theodosius when he made battle against his old comrade Eugenius at the Frigidus river. I know not what forced them apart – religion or politics, no doubt – but I remember every detail of that fight. Theodosius kept his Roman troops in reserve and threw the Goths against Eugenius's line. Again and again and again. You have heard tell of rivers of blood? A fine metaphor. Well I saw a river run bright with the blood of the Goths. Sixteen thousand of us had rallied to Theodosius's banner. By the end, only six thousand remained whole. Theodosius could count the casualties among his own troops in the hundreds. I vowed then that if I ever fought beside a Roman again, I would do it on my own terms, not his. My people would never again be sacrificed on the altar of Roman ambition.'

By now they'd reached the river and they crossed by a small bridge before the wagons parked in a defensive circle. The drivers and cavalrymen watered their horses nearby and then tethered them in the shade before lying down beside them. They dined on bread and olives washed down with surprisingly good local wine and water from the stream. Marcus sat with Valeria, Zeno, Brenus and Anastasia. Fritigern spoke with his men before joining them.

'You were talking about your people . . .' Marcus said with a significance that could not be denied.

Fritigern gave him an appraising look. 'How much do you really know, Marcus Flavius Victor?'

'I know your men watch mine and my men watch yours. I know that if I wake up to pass water at night I'll like as not be sharing the same patch of forest with a Goth.' Marcus looked to his sister and grinned. 'Though I think the ladies resent it more than the others.'

Valeria snorted. 'He thinks he can patronize us because we are mere females, Anastasia, but he will do it once too often and that's when a woman grinds a certain kind of mushroom in his stew.'

'In some species it is said the female is deadlier than the male,' Fritigern laughed along with the rest. 'But I ask again. How much do you know?'

'I recognized you from Salona, majesty.' It was Anastasia who answered. 'Perhaps six years ago.'

'I am not your majesty. I am Alaric, a Balti of the Tervingi tribe, and a member of the nation called Goths.' Zeno, who'd been unaware of the subterfuge, winced at the infamous name and crossed himself, but Alaric ignored him. 'Some call me king, others have less polite names for me. Tell me,' he turned to Marcus, 'what did you think when you first discovered who I was?'

'I wondered how Stilicho would react if I brought him your head.'

Alaric laughed aloud, a great growling roar that had everyone in the clearing craning their neck to see what was happening. 'If you believed he would appreciate my death you don't know Stilicho as well as you think. Alaric is not his enemy and he understands that. There are certain matters on which we differ, yes, but what are a few details among friends?'

'I too count Stilicho as a friend,' Marcus said.

'Then no doubt we will do very well together,' Alaric smiled and his eyes met each of the small circle in turn. 'All of us. And you, Marcus, will do Stilicho a service by keeping me alive.'

'So our two missions combine and you will accompany us to Ravenna?'

Alaric shook his head. 'You misunderstand me, and my relationship with the general. He does not command me as I do not command him. As I said, I deal with Rome on my own terms. After Frigidus, the Goths south of the Danuvius looked to me for leadership. Perhaps this was out of respect for my abilities, but more likely it was because I was the most senior commander to survive the battle. We Goths didn't fight at Frigidus for the Romans out of friendship, we had been promised silver, good land and above all citizenship. In effect, we would become Romans. But, in the years after the battle, Theodosius delayed and prevaricated. When he died, his debts remained unpaid, and the Senate were not going to be beholden to a band of heretic barbarians. Oh, we were offered a few talents of silver, and the possibility of land in Gaul, but it was always honey tomorrow, and there was no longer any mention of citizenship.'

'Never put your faith in the gratitude of kings,' Marcus said with an intensity that made Alaric stare. 'In effect you were robbed of the fruits of your victory.'

'As barbarians we had no recourse to the law.' The other man shrugged at what had always been a reality. 'Stilicho was an ambitious man on the rise then, but not quite at the peak of his powers. He too had been at Frigidus, but he was in no position to help, and it would have done his prospects harm if he did. We were too few after the battle to use force to take what was rightfully ours. That was when I turned east, where I might get a hearing from the Emperor's elder son, Arcadius, and when men began to use the word king. Nowadays they say Arcadius trembled in fear at my approach, but that was not the case. A certain Rufinus, in whom the real power of Constantinopolis lay, contacted me with a new offer. I should scour Arcadius's enemies from Macedonia and Thrace and great rewards would be mine, and if General Stilicho sought to interfere, as Rufinus believed he might, they would send an army to help me defeat him. Naturally, like all Roman promises the support was never forthcoming and the rewards were as easy to grasp as a wisp of mist on an autumn morning. While I pacified Macedonia, Rufinus was blackening my name as a looter and a murderer. Fortunately, he died, and I found a new sponsor, Eutropius, and that is how I became a Roman general.'

Marcus laughed. 'Should I salute you?'

'You mock me in front of our friends,' Alaric waved a hand that appealed for their support. 'But it is true. Eutropius appointed me *magister militum* of Illyricum, and as far as I know that rank has not been rescinded. It is true you are only a prefect, despite your glittering helm?'

'That is my rank,' Marcus admitted. 'But I had responsibility for the northern frontier, as Lord of the Wall, appointed by General Magnus Maximus, who became joint Emperor with Valentinian for a time. I suppose you could say that position carried the responsibility of a general.'

'I know of Magnus Maximus,' Alaric cried. 'It was the first time I met Stilicho. I was just twenty with command of my first war band when he asked me to fight for Theodosius against the usurper Maximus at a place not far south of here. Maybe it was my arrogance, or just that I was young and foolish. I saw no profit in becoming involved in Rome's civil wars. In the end, it cost me, because others rose and I was forgotten, but I still believe I was right.'

'Magnus Maximus was my father.' In the silence that followed Marcus wondered what deep-seated urge had inspired the confession.

'Your father was Emperor?' Brenus didn't hide his astonishment. 'I am the grandson of an Emperor?'

'He shared the purple with Valentinian.' For a moment it felt as if they were the only people in the clearing. 'But men called him usurper. He was defeated and killed.'

'And you didn't think to tell me?' The words emerged as a challenge.

'Would it have made a difference if I had?'

'Yes.' Brenus pushed himself to his feet. 'It would.'

They watched him walk away towards the river. 'A fine boy.' To Marcus's spinning mind Alaric's voice seemed to come from far away. 'With a strong will and a good heart. One day he will make you proud, my friend.'

XXXIV

Brenus kept his distance for the remainder of the halt, but Marcus determined to seek him out once they resumed their journey.

To try to explain the unexplainable.

He'd convinced himself his reluctance to share his lineage with Brenus was to protect the boy from the legacy of a blood-father with a name so toxic it had been wiped from history. Maximus had never acknowledged Marcus as his son, though he'd ensured he'd been brought up as the offspring of a Roman noble. The boy took his name from the man Marcus thought of as his true father. Brenus had been a Brigantian nobleman who married Marcus's mother Venutia, even in the knowledge she carried another man's child. Now Marcus felt sick to his stomach that he'd denied young Bren even a single father, when he had been gifted with two, no matter how tainted one of them turned out to be.

He looked back to where Brenus rode at the rear of the column and steeled himself to confront his son. When he was part way Valeria, who was riding beside Zeno, moved to intercept him. 'You should hear this, Marcus.'

'What is it?' Marcus demanded as Valeria ushered the two men towards the trees, where they would be out of earshot of the wagons.

Once clear, Zeno said, 'You shouldn't trust King Alaric, lord.'

Marcus frowned. 'Why? He's given me no reason to doubt him.'

'What if I were to tell you that what I listened to was a litany of lies, half-truths and evasion the like of which I've never heard before?'

'You'd think he hadn't ridden with us on the road to Longovicium,' Valeria laughed.

Marcus ignored the jibe. 'For a start, I'd ask you how you know this,' he said to Zeno.

'I only know Alaric by reputation,' the Greek admitted. 'But I know the Goths and I know what happened in Arcadius's court during that time. What *they* believed of him, and the consequences of his intrigues with Rufinus. Perhaps,' he said with a sour glance at Valeria, 'if you'd trusted me enough to tell me who he was at the start I could have given you warning of the kind of character you were dealing with.'

Marcus glanced at Valeria, but she was staring towards the front of the convoy, where Anastasia seemed to be deep in conversation with Alaric. 'All right,' Marcus said. 'Tell me.'

Zeno took a breath. 'For all I know, what he said about his dealings before he met Rufinus is true, and it's certain the pair made some kind of pact that distracted Alaric away from Constantinopolis and Arcadius. But his talk of pacifying Macedonia for Arcadius is a lie. The reality is that he turned to banditry on an enormous scale. His soldiers plundered, murdered and extorted their way from one end of the province to the other and back again.' Marcus noticed the *medicus*'s fingernails were stained with dried blood, presumably from poor mutilated Claudius struggling for life in one of the nearby wagons. 'What is certain,' Zeno continued, 'is that he left Macedonia and Thrace populated only by grieving widows, and orphans scratching around in the fields for the few morsels of grain his foragers missed.'

'All that could be explained by his need to keep a great host fed and watered. No king will be a king for long unless he is able to reward his subjects.'

'He passes himself off as a reasonable man,' Valeria said. 'Would a reasonable man leave in his wake a nation of starving widows and orphans?'

'Exaggeration,' Marcus shrugged. 'Time and distance distort. How many times have we been told a garrison or a village had been annihilated only to discover nine tenths still lived and a few roof tiles were scorched?'

Now it was Valeria and Zeno who exchanged a glance. 'I'm not saying I doubt your memory, Zeno,' Marcus assured him. 'Is there more?'

'There is more, lord. For one thing, he portrays himself as a great military commander, but Stilicho defeated him twice and chased him from Italia with his tail between his legs. But let us come to the unfortunate Rufinus with whom Alaric made his bargain to avoid Constantinopolis. He was right that Rufinus, at that time, was the true power in the east, but what he did not tell you was that he was also a deadly rival of Flavius Stilicho.'

'Alaric said he died.'

'Yes. "Fortunately, he died." Those were his very words,' Zeno said. 'Fortunate indeed for his rivals Stilicho and Eutropius, to whom Alaric owes his rank of general, and presumably the honours which accompany such an elevated status. What he didn't say was that Rufinus was murdered by a man called Gainas. Gainas is somewhat coincidentally a Goth, and a kinsman and former tutor of the very same King Alaric. At the time there were whispers that Stilicho and Alaric had conspired to bring about Rufinus's end. With Rufinus gone, Gainas manoeuvred himself into a position where he was the sole conduit to Arcadius, but he overstepped himself and was accused of treason. Gainas fled, but before he could reach safety he was hunted down by Hun mercenaries under the command of a warrior named Uldin – I'm told you are familiar with him, lord – who tortured and executed Gainas and personally handed his head to Arcadius, now Emperor once more.'

'Uldin killed Alaric's kinsman?'

'In the most barbaric fashion. I'm told the look on the dead man's face made Arcadius flinch. When word reached Alaric he took a blood oath to kill Uldin in the same way.'

'So that's why Uldin wants him dead.'

'And you killed Uldin's brother,' Valeria reminded him. 'Which makes you Uldin's enemy, and Alaric's ally, whether you like it or not.'

'And makes this,' Marcus sighed, 'revealing as it is, of little value.'

'Better that you know the manner of the man you ride with, lord,' Zeno said. 'Alaric is clever, ruthless, manipulative and utterly devoid of scruples.'

'Let me see,' Valeria smiled. 'Who else do we know who combines those worthy qualities?'

'What will you do, lord?' Zeno asked.

'Do? What can I do? Nothing.' He blinked at a sickening crunch as one of the wagons nearby lurched over a rock and crashed down with enough force to break an axle. 'In any case we'll part from these barbarians in two days at the most, and hopefully I'll never set eyes on Alaric again. Now, if you'll excuse me, I have other matters to deal with.'

Brenus didn't acknowledge his presence when he rode up, but neither did he object when his father took station beside him. They rode side by side in a strained silence before Marcus spoke.

'I am not a man who has much experience of making apologies,' he said. 'But I always seem to be apologizing to you. I'm sorry you were hurt and that I didn't tell you about your grandfather.'

'I'm not hurt,' Brenus said. 'If anything I'm confused. I was brought up to believe I was the grandson of Brenus, a great British hero; now I discover I'm someone completely different.' His tone softened. 'If I blame anyone it's Grandmother. We were together in Saxonia for six years. Why wouldn't she tell me the truth then, when she knew she was dying?'

'I suppose she didn't want to trouble you.' Marcus accompanied the words with a wry smile. 'I liked to think it was because I was protecting you, but I was deluding myself. The truth is that I was ashamed.'

'Valeria says you have no shame,' Brenus laughed.

'You shouldn't take your aunt too seriously,' Marcus said with mock severity. 'She is cursed with a strange sense of humour. Do you want to know about your grandfather or not?'

'Yes, lord.'

Marcus studied him. A handsome boy, who would grow tall and strong, with a quick intelligence and a genuine sense of duty illustrated by his care for Anastasia. Alaric was wrong, Brenus wouldn't make him proud. He was already proud of this son of his.

'In some ways Magnus Maximus was a great man,' he began. 'Only a great man could have persuaded the legions of Britannia to hail him Emperor and inspire the loyalty that convinced them to follow him to Gaul, where he set himself up as a rival to Valentinian and Theodosius. He was certainly a brave man, or perhaps it's more truthful to say that he was a man who knew no fear.'

'A man like you, then, Father?'

Marcus laughed. 'I've known fear, Brenus, more often than I care to remember. I have known abject terror on the battlefield. I suppose one definition of bravery is the ability to overcome that terror and stand and fight when others run. I think Maximus genuinely did not know the meaning of fear, but don't be deceived into thinking that's an admirable quality. His rise was driven by a combination of ambition, arrogance and selfishness. If he thought about others at all, it was as weapons at his disposal, to be dispensed with when they were no longer required.' He paused. Was that entirely true? His mind drifted back to his childhood and Maximus's infrequent appearances in his life. Perhaps his memory deceived him, but he had a sense there had been a genuine, deep and shared love between Maximus and his mother. The social strictures of the day, his class and his calling had contrived to keep them apart, but certainly Venutia had retained that love until her dying day. Perhaps Maximus had been the same?

'Father?' Brenus's voice cut through his thoughts.

'What?'

'I asked if Maximus – Grandfather – used you as he did other people.'

Marcus had to consider the question before he answered. 'In a way, he tried to mould me into the tool he wanted me to be. He certainly used me as his spy as he prepared his bid for power, but I fear I didn't live up to his expectations. At one point I think he planned for me to rule Britannia while he was off creating an Empire in his own image: a single, unified entity, pitiless, Christian and authoritarian. But it never happened. By then Brenus, who I thought of as my true father, had too great an influence over me. Perhaps that was part of the reason Maximus had him killed.'

'Your father killed your stepfather?'

Marcus nodded. 'Brenus sensed his lust for power and opposed any plans to weaken the defences of Britannia. Maximus sent him into a carefully prepared ambush.'

'I don't think I would have liked my real grandfather much,' the boy said with a frown. 'I prefer Brenus, the British hero.'

'So do I,' Marcus smiled. 'So let us forget Maximus and create a few legends of our own.'

Together.

XXXV

'What were you talking to Alaric about?'

Anastasia blinked at Valeria's abrupt enquiry. They'd halted in the late afternoon and most of the men had gone off into the woods searching for signs of game with which to supplement their supplies.

'Salona and Dalmatia,' she shrugged. 'When he heard of my abduction he apologized for failing to stop the raiders. He is an impressive man, with great plans for the province.'

'Perhaps,' Valeria admitted. 'But take care. Zeno does not trust him.'

'And Zeno is correct about everything?' Anastasia met her stare with unflinching eyes. 'In many ways Alaric reminds me of Marcus.'

'Yes. And that is why my advice stands.'

'I see you have been reconciled with your son,' the Goth said as he and Marcus returned from the hunt. 'That is good. I have no sons of my own, at least none that I know of. I am envious of you.'

'And yet you are a king,' Marcus said evenly. 'But I have never asked you why a king should be travelling with a mere twenty companions. Or why some of the wagons are oddly heavily laden, while others, like the one where my injured man is being cared for, are not. Perhaps there is another reason rather than blood feud that attracted Uldin's Huns to you?'

Alaric stared at him. 'You must not believe everything you hear about me, Marcus. In the east I am considered, unfairly I think, as some kind of demon.'

'What do you mean?'

'Your pretty little dark-haired girl isn't the only one with a good memory for faces,' Alaric said. 'My man Sigaric there served in the court of Arcadius, before the Emperor decided he didn't like the smell of Goth. He believes he recognized that shifty little Greek who calls himself your *medicus* and is never out of arm's length of your sister. It was rumoured he was Arcadius's spy and perhaps even his personal poisoner. I'd be wary of eating anything he cooks. What did he tell you about me?'

'That you may not have been entirely candid.' Marcus looked across to where Zeno sat with Valeria, remembering his passion for collecting plants and mushrooms, and the hare stew he'd prepared the previous evening.

'Pfft.' Alaric shrugged as if it meant nothing. 'Sometimes there is more than one truth. I may have been guilty of the sin of omission, but everything I told you is broadly as I described it.'

'You failed to mention that you invaded Italia and Stilicho beat you hollow.'

'That hardly reflects credit on me,' the Goth said. 'And it is nothing to do with why I am here.'

'Then why are you here?'

Alaric considered for a moment before he answered. 'First let me tell you about Radagaisus.'

'You said he was a fool and that Stilicho will defeat him.'

'I said that, yes,' Alaric agreed. 'But Stilicho will need all the help he can get to achieve a victory. Radagaisus's great horde is made up of Goths of every variety, and others the Romans regard as barbarians: Alans, Suevi, Vandals, even a few Huns. These in turn are divided by tribe and clan, some of them hereditary enemies, and all of them rivals for whatever resources and prizes they come across on the march. I have led an army through the Alps, I know what it takes to keep them under control and I know what it takes to keep them alive. Every grain of wheat and barley and every cow will be as precious to Radagaisus as any ingot of gold. You understand?'

'I understand. Radagaisus's first priority if he reaches Italia will be to secure enough supplies to feed his people. I also understand that if he succeeds there will be only one king of the Goths and it won't be you.'

'Yes,' Alaric smiled. 'You are evidently cleverer than you look. It is in my interests as well as Stilicho's that Radagaisus should fail. There are chieftains and warriors among his host I know well, men who have fought at my side . . .'

Now Marcus saw it. 'You've placed some of your own people among them.'

'How else would I know what he does and what he plans and where he will go next? He also has other followers with whom I have a certain influence. What if twenty persuasive men were to walk among Radagaisus's army replete with compelling arguments against the king for those prepared to listen, and silver to entice those less so. What could they not achieve?'

'What indeed?' Marcus was impressed and didn't hide it. 'And Stilicho knows all this?'

'No,' Alaric admitted. 'He believes I am in Epirus ready to deal with any threat that develops from the east while he gathers his forces in Italia. But I have an army and officers who are capable enough of achieving that without me. I can do more for him as a thorn in Radagaisus's meaty paw—'

'I don't understand,' Marcus halted the Goth. 'If you own the loyalty of a force large enough to defend the eastern frontier, why not offer you an alliance and bring you to Italia to fight at his side? You said yourself he needs all the help he can get.'

'Firstly, because Honorius has no grounds to love me – that is the reason Stilicho gave – and secondly because he already counts among his allies certain others who would not welcome Alaric the Goth as their comrade, which he would prefer me not to know about.'

'Who?'

'Uldin, for one.'

'Stilicho treats with pagans?'

'Uldin is a Hun chieftain and a pagan, it is true. But he is also a mercenary whose spear and bow are for hire to anyone willing and able to pay him. He is also a great warrior and a man worthy of respect. Oh yes,' he saw Marcus's surprise. 'You can still respect someone you have vowed to kill.'

'And who has vowed to kill you,' Marcus pointed out. *And I killed his brother and in my vanity called out my name to his followers.* If word of Octar's death reached Uldin it would complicate matters when they reached Stilicho. Yet he couldn't allow that to deter him. Likely enough Uldin would be in the field against Radagaisus by the time they arrived in Ravenna. He noticed that Alaric had gone silent. 'There is more?'

'Why should I help save Honorius from Radagaisus for no reward?'

'Because it suits your purposes for Radagaisus to fail.'

'Yes, but what happens after Radagaisus is defeated? Stilicho can't sell a hundred thousand captives into slavery, the markets would be overwhelmed. Neither will he kill them all, he's not that kind of man. Just to keep them from starving would stretch his logistics to the limit and beyond. It would take months, and every soldier in his legions, to herd them back across the mountains and when they get there they'll just break up and become a hundred different problems. In any case, Stilicho will only win if enough of Radagaisus's warriors can be persuaded he is leading them to destruction. When they abandon him, they become my responsibility.'

Marcus choked on a laugh. 'So all that would have been achieved is that Radagaisus the fool would be replaced by Alaric, who is anything but. What makes you think Stilicho would be naive enough to enter into an agreement that would make you king of all the Goths and hand you the power to be an even greater threat to Rome than the man he has just defeated?'

'I *don't* believe he would be so naive,' Alaric said carefully. 'And that is why he and I must agree an outcome that is to the benefit and profit of both our peoples. An outcome that will see Italia's lands free of Radagaisus and his folk and Alaric the Goth safely occupied elsewhere.' He hesitated a moment. 'And why I need the help of Marcus Flavius Victor to achieve that end.'

'You want me to be your envoy to Stilicho?'

'In a way,' Alaric agreed. 'You are joining him in any case and you would be doing him a great service.'

'But . . . ?'

Alaric stepped close so his mouth was next to Marcus's ear.

'This is how it would be.'

XXXVI

When they woke the next morning the Goths were gone.

'Did you say something to annoy him?' Valeria kicked the ashes of one of the Gothic campfires from the previous night. 'I heard movement, but I thought they were just shifting the wagons. I'm surprised the guards didn't alert us.'

'Julius warned me.' Marcus saw his sister's puzzlement. 'It's not as if they hid their departure. They made so much noise I doubt if there's anyone in camp who didn't hear them. If Alaric wanted to leave without any awkward farewells there was nothing I could do to stop him.'

'But why, after everything that's happened?'

'It's just his way, I think,' Marcus said. 'Always trying to stay one step ahead. I suppose that's what's kept him alive all these years. Part of me thinks we're well rid of them. I liked the man, but those Goths were uncomfortable travelling companions.'

'At least he left us the wagon to carry poor Claudius and our supplies.'

'They had wagons to spare. From what he said yesterday the beds of about half of them are filled with silver.' A thought struck him. 'That's why they left. He knew he'd said too much and was worried we'd steal it from them.'

'Bren will miss him.'

'What?'

'You didn't notice that they were as thick as thieves last night. Alaric wanted to know about the Saxons and the other northern tribes we'd encountered, and he entertained Bren with stories about growing up in the east. They got on so well Alaric told him if he ever got tired of being ordered around by you, he could join him and be a Goth lord.'

Marcus wondered what else had passed between the Goth and his son, but that could wait until they were on the road. From his discussions with Alaric, assuming he could be trusted, he knew they were perhaps five or six days from the coast. The Goths would most likely have departed their company at some point in the day anyway. Providing he could secure passage for men and horses on a suitable ship they would be in Ravenna within two weeks. After that everything depended on Stilicho's whereabouts. If he was with Honorius's court, Marcus would seek him out at the first opportunity. If not they'd have to track him down, presumably somewhere in the north. But he hadn't forgotten the potential complications that lay along the way.

And then there was Anastasia.

By now, despite their unusual clothes and armour and strange accents, they were well used to dealing with the authorities and passed through Andautonia, a prosperous place nestling at the foot of beech-clad mountains, without delay. From there they turned west across a great flat plain with skies that seemed to stretch for ever. To Marcus's surprise the next milestone beckoned them to Metulum, where the message from Stilicho that had prompted this entire odyssey had originated. They bypassed Metulum and their route brought them once more to the mountains, but the road followed a river valley and the going was relatively easy. From time to time Marcus would update his comrades on the condition of Claudius, the injured trooper who had somehow survived the heat and his often jolting transport.

'Zeno thought he was like to die, but the fever has lessened and there's no sign of mortification,' Marcus announced. 'He needs complete quiet and as much immobility as we can give him, so the *medicus* keeps him stupefied with some potion or other. There's no point in his friends visiting him until he recovers.'

Each day the sun rose and the morning haze lifted to reveal a cloudless sky of pristine blue, and by the time they'd broken fast it was warm enough that a man no longer needed his cloak. By noon the sun would be beating down from its highest point and they'd stop for at least an hour to allow the horses to rest and the troopers to take their ease in the shade.

At the little town of Arupium the road took a sharp turn east of south and followed the course of a river along the flank of a range of craggy mountains topped with peaks of fractured stone. This was a lush landscape of luxuriant greens and beautiful clear streams that ran almost blue, their depths shadowed with the outlines of giant trout whose rich, white flesh brightened their meals of an evening.

This was Anastasia's country now, but he could tell she was increasingly troubled. She would know Salona must be less than a week's ride along the coast. The time for a decision was coming. Marcus's heart stuttered when she sought him out at one of their regular halts.

'I have to apologize for seeming distant in recent days, lord,' she said. 'But it is as if my mind has been split in two. I sense the feelings you have for me, but I cannot rid myself of the fear of another unknown future in a strange land after what I have suffered. Salona is dear to me as Britannia must be dear to you.'

'I can understand that.' Marcus heard the catch in his voice.

'Nevertheless, if you are willing, I would like to accompany you at least as far as Ravenna, where I can make a final decision.' She laid a hand on his arm. 'Give me time, Marcus.'

'Of course.'

Marcus's mind was still spinning when they resumed their journey and he remembered he had meant to talk to Brenus.

'Valeria tells me you spoke to Alaric before he left,' he said. 'Did he give you any indication why he was considering such an abrupt departure?'

'No, mainly he just wanted to know about the Saxons. Where did their lands begin and end? Who were their kings? What were their customs? He was also interested in our journey here. The rivers we travelled and the terrain we crossed. Why would that be?'

Marcus smiled at his son. 'For a man like Alaric all knowledge has value. Who knows if he might wish, or be forced, to seek lands beyond the Danuvius? So he thinks ahead. And he's right. One day he might need that information.'

'But why seek it from me, a fourteen-year-old boy, when he could have asked you or Valeria?'

'Firstly because he likes you and he wanted to get to know you better.' He saw Brenus's look of disbelief. 'It's true. He told me he has no sons of his own, and I doubt he could speak so freely with any of the children of his own people. And you may be young, but he has seen your qualities on the journey. You have a good memory for detail, and during the journey you probably had more time to take in our surroundings than anyone else.'

'That makes sense,' the boy agreed.

'Valeria said he offered you a place with him.'

'It was a joke,' Brenus grinned. 'If I ever tired of your bad temper and tall tales, I was to seek him out. But he said I should stay close to you until you had taught me everything you knew. He said you were not just a great warrior, but a clever soldier – I think he meant cunning – he said the ambush on the Huns was something Stilicho would have done.'

Marcus let out a guffaw of disbelief. 'That was Valeria's idea and she almost got us all killed. I would have ridden away and left the conniving villain to his fate, and so would Sti—'

The road had breasted the summit of a mountain ridge.

'What is it, Father?'

But Marcus's eyes were fixed on the vista that had opened out before them. They'd reached the sea. But what a sea it was. The seas of northern Britannia and the Mare Germanicum they'd crossed to reach Saxonia were mostly grey, with white-capped waves, or the estuarine, muddy brown of churned-up silt. Just occasionally, if the sky was clear and the sun was in the right place, they might be a sort of dirty, dark blue. But he'd never seen a blue like this. Not *a* blue, now that he looked again through eyes narrowed against the sun. Many blues. Closest to the land a blue that was almost a translucent green that reminded him of Anastasia's eyes. Slightly further out different shades he'd only experienced previously in a pouch of gemstones a trader had once tried to sell him in Eboracum. Sapphire, aquamarine and topaz the man had called them. And finally, where the shallows dropped away, the deepest, darkest blue he'd ever seen. All shimmering with tiny diamonds of reflected sunlight. What lay before him was a bay scattered with islands of every size and shape, dusted with green and outlined in gold, that stretched into the distance until they disappeared into the haze.

'Iadera, lord.' Zeno appeared at his shoulder and pointed to his left, where a flat plain ran from the foot of the mountains out to the sea. White villas and isolated farms dotted the cultivated fields and meadows, and, in the distance, at the very edge of the land, Marcus could just make out the city and port. His eyes strayed once again to the sea beyond.

'What sea is this?' he asked Zeno.

'They call it the Mare Adriaticum, lord.'

The Mare Adriaticum, and beyond it, not three days away, Italia, the distant homeland that existed only in his imagination, but had ruled his life and dominated his existence from the day he was born. After all this time on the sea and the road and the river, the thought took his breath away. He realized now what he hadn't dared admit to himself on the journey. There had been times when he believed they would never make it.

But now they were here, and somewhere out there lay Italia and salvation.

XXXVII

From a mile out to sea Italia was still only a thin dark line on the dawn horizon, the outline unbroken by hill or mountain. In the gloom, Marcus could just make out the white streak away to their right that the captain of the *corbita* assured him was Ravenna. They'd been fortunate that the huge merchant ship had docked in Iadera to pick up a cargo of the delicate, exquisite glassware for which the city was famous. Fortunate, too, that the captain had been warned of a revival of the pirate trade for which the Mare Adriaticum had once been famous. It meant he was only too glad to welcome a score and more of experienced fighting men to supplement his small crew, though he balked at the horses being stowed beside his precious glass. He charged an exorbitant sum to transport the wagon, which, as well as the unfortunate Claudius, now carried all their equipment.

Valeria appeared at Marcus's side from where she'd been asleep in the broad stern. A light breeze rippled the surface and drove them along at a steady pace and when she looked over the side she exclaimed with pleasure at a pair of dolphins that raced and danced and dipped in the bow wave. By now they could see a tiny pinprick of light gleaming from the white strip that identified the city, presumably some kind of beacon to guide mariners and fishermen to harbour.

'What will happen when we land, Marcus?'

It was a question without an answer, and she knew it, but one that had to be asked because it focused their minds on the possibilities and how they should react to them.

'I don't know,' he admitted. 'I've had this day in mind since the moment I read his letter. In my head it was simple. We disembark. We find Stilicho. He welcomes us as old friends. In a way we're home. Back in the Roman army where we belong. Then who knows? I hadn't counted on an invasion of Italia.'

She shook her head. 'So we hope for the best . . .'

He smiled. 'Yes . . .'

'But we plan for the worst?'

'As always.'

She frowned. 'What is the worst?'

'Oh, I'd say the worst is that Stilicho's somewhere in the north, but Uldin the Hun isn't. I doubt the Emperor Honorius will be very welcoming if we leave dead Huns lying all over the streets of his capital.'

Valeria considered for a moment. 'We'll need to replace the horses quickly then?'

'Yes,' he agreed. 'We'll split up when we reach shore. You find horses and I'll seek out Stilicho.'

A gust of wind blew a skein of dark hair over her eyes and she brushed it away with her hand. 'It may not be so easy,' she said, 'finding the horses, I mean. We got a decent price for our animals in Iadera, but they'll be at a premium in a country that's about to be at war.'

'Take the last of the silver and pay what you must,' Marcus told her. 'Hopefully, Stilicho will reimburse me when we find him. If we have horses at least we always have the option of running, if it comes to it.'

'You make it sound simple.'

Marcus stared at the fast approaching land. 'From Italia, they tell me, if you keep going north you'll eventually reach the sea. We'd be journeying through a country ravaged by war. War means chaos. And nobody's better equipped to take advantage of chaos than we are.'

*

216

Stilicho's seal was enough to see them through the port and into the city, with a modest customs charge for the wagon and a less modest bribe for not searching it. Day labourers sat in small groups waiting for work and Marcus doled out a few silver coins to have the wagon wheeled into a shady spot outside the port gates. Once they were through, he split the party into three. Valeria would take two sections of troopers and search for a horse dealer, while Marcus made enquiries about Stilicho's whereabouts. There was no point in hiding their presence. Honorius would have spies checking everybody who came and went through the port, probably Stilicho too, and only God knew who else. Better then to be a man of consequence and authority. Which meant he would march into the city escorted by a bodyguard made up of the rest of the squadron. Zeno, Brenus and Anastasia would stay with the wagon until Valeria returned with suitable animals to harness to it.

Valeria set off to search for a market and Marcus inspected his troopers before tucking his gilded helmet under his arm and marching up the street at their head in proper military style.

He'd never experienced anything like Ravenna. Somehow ordinary things like stone, stucco and tile combined to create something entirely *beyond* the ordinary. Mansions and churches shone like silver and gold, so bright they hurt the eyes. Scented trees lined broad avenues and every house was surrounded by gardens filled with bushes swathed in pink and white blossom, and exotic flowers bordering the paths. These were clearly the homes of the city's elite and Honorius's advisers. Hopefully, it meant Stilicho was not too far away.

They turned the next corner and Marcus sucked in a breath as he found himself faced by a line of grim-faced soldiers. Now he had a choice: advance and bluff it out or retreat and try elsewhere. If they'd let him. Before he could make up his mind, a second company appeared from a side street to his rear, and the decision was made for him. The Ala Sabiniana's natural inclination was to resist, but Marcus knew it wouldn't do. 'Be still,' he ordered. 'Keep your hands away from your swords.'

Their captors had the polished look of elite soldiers and he guessed they belonged to some kind of Imperial guard. They were dressed uniformly in knee-length tunics of emerald green and they held shields of a similar hue decorated with the Chi-rho, the Christ symbol. Each man carried a spear in two hands and the gleaming iron tips were pointed at Marcus and his men.

'Who commands here?' Marcus tried to take the initiative.

'That is not your affair.' The moment he heard the voice Marcus knew they were in deeper trouble than he'd imagined. It came from a young man in the centre of the rank ahead and it carried the natural authority of genuine power. 'All you need to know is that you are under arrest and you will accompany me.'

'Arrest?' Marcus feigned shock. 'We arrived in this city less than an hour since. On what grounds?'

'You will discover that when you appear before the magistrate.'

'Please,' Marcus persisted, though by now he knew he was wasting his time. 'There has been some mistake. See,' he withdrew the leather scroll case with Stilicho's seal from his tunic, 'I am here at the invitation of General Stilicho. Send for him and he will vouch for us.'

The young man put up his spear and walked forward to inspect the seal. He held out his hand and, after a momentary hesitation, Marcus handed the scroll case over. 'Now I understand,' the officer said in a tone Marcus didn't appreciate. 'You betray yourself with every word you speak.' Marcus opened his mouth to protest, but the officer didn't give him the opportunity. 'Silence! Take these men away.'

A moment of anticipation, when anything might have happened, but it passed in a heartbeat. Marcus handed over his sword and the others reluctantly followed his lead. 'We will go with these people,' he assured them. 'All will be well. I will explain everything.'

But as they marched along the street in front of the inquisitive eyes of the people of Ravenna, he knew it was a lie. Whatever had happened here wouldn't be solved by explanation. Either Stilicho had abandoned him, or Honorius believed what he'd been told by his informants in Britannia. Marcus Flavius Victor was a traitor and an enemy of Rome. A usurper whose only fate would be death, like his father before him.

The guards ushered them through the streets and across a bridge spanning a broad canal or sluggish river, where they reached a large walled compound. A ramp led to a double door in the base of the wall, which opened without fanfare. Inside, their captors herded Marcus and his men along a cramped corridor that led deeper into the earth, where the air was cool and damp. Passages and doorways appeared to either side, but the guards pushed them directly ahead, where a door that looked like the entrance to Hades creaked open and they were bundled through. A single torch set high on the wall flickered weakly to illuminate the dank, unwelcoming interior of a windowless room. Green mould coated the walls and water dripped from the ceiling to form shallow puddles on the stone floor. Not a cell, but a storeroom of some sort, possibly left unused because of the damp. The one thing it had in its favour was its size, which would have accommodated two or three times their number. Less welcome was the large bucket placed in a corner that Marcus guessed was the sole latrine facility.

'The first sign of trouble and we remove the torch,' said their jailer. 'You won't much like sitting in the dark when the swamp rats come to visit. Then again, you'll notice there are air holes in this door. Anybody lays a hand on the guard who comes to feed you – not that I would if it was up to me – and we close them off. Maybe you'll survive the night, maybe you won't.'

With that he slammed the door shut with a bang that echoed along the corridor.

Luko reacted first. 'Might as well make the best of it,' he said, and chose a relatively dry spot where he could sit with his back to the wall. The others followed his lead, tentmates sticking together as they always did. Marcus waited until all were seated before finding a place close to the door. 'What's this all about, lord?' the *draconarius* continued. 'I thought General Stilicho was going to welcome us like long-lost cousins, with a hero's *phalerae* and a fistful of gold.'

'You didn't really believe that, did you?' Marcus said. 'Since when have you had anything from me but hard rations, deadly peril and crotch-rot from too many days in the saddle?' That raised a laugh and a few cries of 'aye' and 'but the plunder we took along the way' and 'you forgot about the women'. 'The main thing is that they haven't treated us too badly and the lady Valeria and her people are still out there. She'll reach Stilicho and get this sorted out. Just think of the pleasure she'll get walking in here to our rescue. We'll never hear the end of it.'

The laughter that accompanied his words sounded hollow less than an hour later, when the door swung open and a new batch of captives were marched in under guard. Valeria was clearly only just managing to contain her fury. Marcus pushed himself to his feet and went to meet her before she said something they might all regret.

'What happened?' he asked, as the door closed behind her.

'We were in the market place to the south of the city. I'd come to an agreement for a price for our horses and remounts when we were suddenly surrounded by a flock of preening peacocks hiding behind shields . . .'

'We could have taken them, lord,' Leof said. 'They were just a pack of garrison rats.'

'But we knew it could have compromised you with Stilicho,' Valeria continued. 'I demanded to know why we were being detained, but all they'd say was that I'd find out when I appeared before the magistrate. In the end we handed over our weapons and they brought us here.' She lowered her voice. 'What about Zeno and the others?'

'Still free for now,' he whispered. 'But who knows for how long.'

'Could this be to do with what was in Stilicho's letter?'

'It may be,' he admitted. 'I can't think of any other reason the Emperor would have us arrested. I'm fairly sure those men were from his personal guard. If I can only talk to him I'm confident I can convince him of my loyalty. One thing is certain, though. This is nothing to do with you and the others. It's about me, and I'll make sure whoever is in charge knows it.'

'You don't know me very well, do you, brother?' Valeria smiled. 'Or these other fools. We haven't travelled halfway across the world to abandon you just when you need us most.'

Marcus swallowed the lump that had formed in his throat, but when he spoke his voice sounded unintentionally gruff.

'In that case we can only hope our judge is open to reason,' he said.

Later their captors delivered a sack of loaves and enough olives to allow them a handful each. 'At least they aren't going to starve us to death,' Valeria said between mouthfuls. 'But we should ration this for the morning. Who knows when they'll feed us again.'

Morning? Who could tell morning from night in this windowless crypt? They'd been arrested two hours after dawn, which made this just beyond noon, more or less. As the hours passed the air grew appreciably staler, until it was like trying to draw in something solid. Where there had been chill their bodies created a stifling, almost liquid warmth that soon had the clothes sticking to their flesh. Marcus tried to keep track of the time, but eventually he succumbed to a restless twitching doze. When he woke he had no idea whether it was day or night. Valeria lay beside him, hair plastered to her forehead by sweat and muttering fitfully to herself. A glance around his surroundings showed the others in much the same condition.

They were roused at last when the door was thrown back to allow in a gust of chill air. The men raised their heads hoping for signs of more food, but Marcus only had eyes for the stooped figure who walked in behind the green-clad guards.

'No,' Valeria whispered.

'Lord, how it stinks in here,' the familiar shrill voice complained. 'But what can one expect from a band of unwashed Brigantian barbarians.'

A lizard's bulbous dark eyes surveyed his surroundings from below heavy brows and the fleshy pink dome of a hairless skull.

Julius Postumus Dulcitius.

XXXVIII

The guards pushed the cavalrymen back at sword point and Marcus watched as soldiers carried a table and two chairs into the room and set them up to the right of the doorway. Dulcitius was just as Marcus remembered him as *dux Britanniarum*, the military commander of northern Britannia. An angry old man with a fixed expression that combined arrogance, spite and cynicism. He'd earned Dulcitius's hatred for the manner in which he'd engineered the victory over the Picts at Longovicium, even though Dulcitius had concocted a report giving himself all the credit. He was dressed in an ankle-length surplice of white cloth pinned at the right shoulder with a golden brooch, the thick diagonal slash of Imperial purple from his upper arm to his left hip identifying him as a member of Honorius's court. Dulcitius took a seat in one chair, and a clerk the other, fastidiously placing his stylus and wax tablets just so, ignoring the prisoners.

'You are the magistrate?' Marcus couldn't hide his disbelief.

'It surprises you that I have risen so high?'

'Nothing about you will ever surprise me, Dulcitius. What surprises me is that an emissary from Britannia bearing the seal of General Stilicho is subject to this indignity. Surely the Emperor cannot have been informed of my arrival?'

222

'Oh, the Emperor is perfectly aware of your existence, Marcus Flavius Victor, and your purpose.' The statement was bland enough, but the last three words contained all the venom of a scorpion's sting and Marcus felt a shiver of unease. The clerk's stylus darted across the wax like a chicken pecking at seed on the farmyard floor.

'My purpose, as you put it, is to pledge my services and those of my men to the Emperor. To that end I demand that we are taken before him so that I can make the offer in person.'

Dulcitius leaned forward with his arms on the table. 'Oh, that would suit you perfectly, I'm sure, and that is why the Emperor has ordered that your trial take place here and not in the basilica, where your presence might further alarm the citizenry.'

'Trial?' Valeria cried. 'No citizen of Rome can be tried without first knowing the charges against them. Of what crime are we accused?'

'Ah, the lady Valeria,' a cold smile accompanied the words. 'You should know that the Emperor has strongly held opinions about the place of a woman in the household. However, I shall indulge you just this once. You, specifically Marcus Flavius Victor and his followers, are charged with conspiring to bring about the death of the Emperor Honorius, may God bless his rule, desertion from your post, unlawful entry into Italia, and, of course, treason. In short, I have before me a troop of paid assassins.'

A growl went up from the soldiers at the dread word, but Marcus raised a hand. 'This is all nonsense, Dulcitius, and you know it. A complete fabrication. We are here at the invitation of General Stilicho to offer whatever military skills we have in aid of the Emperor's cause.'

'We will talk of fabrications later,' Dulcitius said dismissively. 'First there is the question of who sent you. I have not quite made up my mind. Was it Radagaisus and his Goths? A certain Constantinus, who has been causing trouble in Britannia and who we have just learned murdered our *vicarius* in the most base manner? Or are you acting on your own behalf? Perhaps you would care to enlighten me?'

'I know neither Radagaisus nor this Constantinus, except by reputation.' A lie in Constantinus's case, but one which Dulcitius was unlikely to be able to rebut. 'There is no plot. You have Stilicho's seal; take it to him and he will confirm he summoned me here to join him.'

'General Stilicho is a busy man,' Dulcitius sniffed. 'He would not thank me for approaching him over such a trivial matter.' He held out his hand and the clerk passed him the leather scroll case the guard officer had confiscated earlier. 'In any case, it is perfectly obvious this seal is a forgery. A skilful one, admittedly, but to the knowing eye patently false.' He opened the case and peered inside. 'If, by some chance, it was not, it would contain the letter you say the general wrote inviting you here.' He fixed Marcus with his beady lizard's eyes. 'Would it not?'

'The letter was of a personal nature. I saw no need to bring it from Britannia.' The truth was that Stilicho's letter was hidden beneath the seat of the wagon. Marcus had decided to leave it there precisely because there were sections that could be misconstrued by someone like Dulcitius and used against his rival. 'You should find a travel warrant with the general's signature, surely that will suffice to prove our innocence. The general would never place such a document in the hands of someone he believed untrustworthy.'

'Another forgery, no doubt.' The dark eyes gleamed. 'If you were in possession of a travel warrant why would you come to Italia by such an indirect route? One might even call it sneaking in like a thief in the night. You could have come through Gaul or Germania with much less inconvenience. The deposition from the captain of the transport that brought you says you mentioned crossing the Danuvius at Vindobona. How did you come to be there?'

Marcus sensed Valeria stiffen. Of course he couldn't mention that he'd been drawn to Saxonia to rescue his son. Dulcitius would instantly wonder where the boy was and start a search for him. The only consolation in this dreadful situation was that Brenus, Zeno and Anastasia were still free, though only God knew how long that would continue.

'Our ship was blown off course by a storm and we were stranded in Saxonia. Events and circumstances forced us to journey here by the route we took.'

'Events and circumstances.' Dulcitius's lip curled in a sneer. 'Lies and evasion more like. What we have here is a man whose name is already synonymous in Britannia with the word treason, who appears unannounced with a gang of cut-throats and falsified documents designed to allow him access to the Emperor. And this at a time when the Empire has never been in greater peril. The Emperor had word some months ago that a potential usurper was conspiring against him in Britannia, and your presence here on a mission to assassinate him only proves the truth of it.'

'You know my loyalty to the Emperor has never been in doubt.' Marcus pushed his way forward, only to be halted by the guards. For all his anger he knew the case Dulcitius had made against him, driven by spite, envy and hatred though it was, was all the stronger for being entirely circumstantial. How could you disprove or refute evidence that didn't exist? With a chill in his heart he saw all too clearly how this would end, and Dulcitius confirmed it with his next words, as a new set of guards filed through the door to surround the accused with spear points.

'You are all found guilty of treason. The sentence of this court is death, to be confirmed by the Emperor and carried out at his convenience.'

A roar went up from Marcus's men, but he raised his arms for quiet. To fight would only mean slaughter, and perhaps there was a way to avoid at least that.

'The guilt, if guilt there is, is mine and mine alone,' he addressed Dulcitius directly. 'These men fought for Rome, and for their *dux Britanniarum*, at Longovicium where you won your great triumph.' Dulcitius smiled, knowing what it took to drag those words from Marcus. 'I beg for the mercy of the court and the Emperor on their behalf.'

'Very well,' Dulcitius nodded slowly. 'I am not devoid of pity, and it is true they fought bravely. To them, I give the choice of slavery or serving in the Emperor's armies . . .'

'They will serve.' Marcus stifled any protest.

'For the lady Valeria, the choice is between sharing your fate or joining my household as a slave.'

225

Marcus felt a surge of fury, but Valeria laid a hand on his arm.

'I would rather die than spend another moment in your company,' she said.

'So be it.' Dulcitius looked almost regretful now their fate had been decided. 'You will be held here until the Emperor confirms my sentences.' He frowned. 'The axe, I believe. I am not a vengeful man, whatever you may think.'

With that, he pushed himself to his feet and walked from the room, followed by his guards and the clerk.

Marcus turned towards his men, but when it came to it he couldn't find the right words, and it was Luko who spoke.

'I don't like this, and neither do the lads. If it came to it we would have fought and died beside you.'

'Your loyalty to me has never been in doubt,' Marcus said. 'If you want to honour me, then live the rest of your lives as men, decent men who continue to value loyalty, courage and integrity. Just promise me General Stilicho will eventually hear what happened here. He'll settle with Dulcitius one way or the other. If nothing else that will give me some comfort when the axe swings.'

'If he doesn't, be assured we will,' Luko growled. 'You can bet your soul on that.'

Valeria sat with her back to the wall and Marcus went to join her. 'I'm sorry,' he said. 'I never thought it would come to this.'

She looked up at him, eyes steady, her face framed by the lank tresses of her long, russet hair.

'Truly, Marcus? Is it any different from Longovicium where we charged to what looked like certain death? It certainly was for poor old Caradoc, and it could have happened to any one of us.'

'Maybe Honorius will refuse to confirm the execution of a woman?'

'It's possible,' she'd obviously considered the prospect, 'but I won't whore myself to that slug Dulcitius whether it means my life or not. One way or the other I wouldn't want to be Dulcitius when Zeno hears of it, because his passing will be infinitely worse than ours. My beloved knows ways to make dying last an eternity. Dulcitius will spend his last years in screaming agony, watching his body putrefy a little more with every passing day.' She smiled at the thought.

'With Zeno still free there is always hope,' Marcus said.

'You don't believe that any more than I do, Marcus. When will it be?'

'They'll come for us at dawn. They'll kill us here, I think. Maybe in a courtyard, but somewhere away from the public eye.'

'Good.' She closed her eyes. 'I would like to see the sun again, one more time.'

Marcus lapsed into a dream of a long, hot summer with his son, riding through endless lush meadows, splashing through streams and crossing sun-dappled forest floors. He knew the dream wasn't real, but that didn't dull the pleasure of it. Brenus would be ten, and growing into the fine young man he now was, face creased in a broad grin at the feel of the breeze on his face. Their eyes met and each mirrored the pride the other felt and the joy they experienced from their shared company. A door creaked and when he opened his eyes he thought it must be an extension of the dream, because there in the flickering torchlight stood Brenus, and he was wearing that same expression. A jolt ran through Marcus: they'd been captured. But if that was the case, why was the boy smiling?

Brenus stepped aside and a tall man filled the frame of the door. A commanding figure, who needed no guards to ensure his safety in a room full of the condemned, only the long sword that hung at his left hip. His eyes searched the room until he found Marcus and he lifted an object he'd been holding in his hands, so it glittered in the flickering light of the torch. The sight of it took Marcus's breath away. His gilded helmet.

'I have a feeling you may be needing this,' Flavius Stilicho said.

XXXIX

'You were fortunate your son reached me when he did,' Stilicho said when they left the prison, escorted by men of his personal bodyguard. 'I was able to intervene with the right people and explain that a mistake had been made.'

'And you have our thanks for it,' Marcus assured him. 'But what happens now?'

The general considered for a moment. 'Best I take you to my home, I think. My wife must know what has happened. But there can be no delay in presenting you to the Emperor. If Honorius hears that I have freed you there will be no shortage of willing tongues whispering words like treason and conspiracy in his ears.'

Marcus frowned. This was a different Stilicho from the general he remembered, worn thinner by whatever he'd experienced in the last nine years, the neatly trimmed beard whiter. Bone weary, with none of the natural warmth their friendship had once warranted. He even appeared irritated that he'd been forced to intervene to save their lives.

'Theodosius was a great man.' Stilicho's eyes took on a distant look and he might as well be talking to himself as to Marcus. 'Strong, clever and with the ruthless streak required of any Emperor. Sadly, Honorius has been gifted with none of his father's attributes. He prefers to hunt, attend the theatre, or feed his collection of fowl, rather than sit in council and be forced to listen, or think, or make decisions. The Emperor's lack of interest and enthusiasm for his responsibilities has given me an unprecedented amount of influence, but such power brings with it a jealousy verging on hatred among those closest to the throne. You know I have always thought of myself as a true Roman, Marcus, but the Emperor increasingly refers to my Germanic roots. Someone somewhere is using my Vandal father as a weapon against me, poisoning Honorius's mind, and perhaps worse.'

'Then we have brought you nothing but trouble,' Marcus said.

'No, old friend,' Stilicho at last managed a smile, 'you have brought me hope.'

Eventually they reached a large, walled enclosure that could only be accessed from the main thoroughfare by a bridge across a wide canal. The escort turned away and Stilicho ushered Marcus and his companions through a great iron-bound gate guarded by more soldiers of the *magister militum*'s personal guard. A cobbled roadway led through carefully tended gardens to a sprawling two-storey mansion. The great house took up three sides of a courtyard that could have doubled as a legionary parade ground, and stretched far into the distance beyond.

'You and the ladies will stay with us, of course,' Stilicho said. 'And I will find suitable accommodation nearby for your soldiers.'

'We also have a wounded man,' Marcus pointed out. 'If I could beg the indulgence of your hospitality . . .'

'I will make sure a room is prepared for the *medicus* and his patient.'

'What is going on here, Flavius? Who are these ragamuffins?'

A tall woman emerged from the house accompanied by a servant girl who held the voluminous folds of her elegant dress from the dust. She had the imperious air of the genuine aristocrat and a perfumed haze surrounded her that made Marcus immediately conscious of his sweat-stained tunic and the prison stink of his unwashed body.

'My wife, Serena,' Stilicho said. 'May I introduce Marcus Flavius Victor, of whom I have spoken.' The final words contained a certain edge that might have held a warning.

'My lady.' Marcus dropped to one knee and his soldiers followed suit.

Stilicho's wife bowed her head in acknowledgement, but the stern expression didn't alter.

'If you will excuse us?' Stilicho drew Serena aside, and they waited while he explained their presence.

Eventually, Stilicho gestured Marcus forward.

'I apologize for the lack of cordiality in my welcome, prefect,' Serena's voice betrayed her tension, though her words sounded heartfelt, 'but you must understand how dangerous this could be for us. The last thing my husband needs is to be associated with more barbarians, especially those tainted with the scent of treason, however unjustifiably.'

Marcus stiffened at the word barbarian. 'If you do not want us . . .'

'No,' she shook her head. 'I mean you no insult. Stilicho speaks well of you and there is no undoing what has been done. The Emperor alone can decide your fate. Fortunately, the only voice he hears is that of the last man who spoke to him. If you assure him of your loyalty and pledge your sword to him in the matter of Radagaisus, I have no doubt he will accept you into his service. But I advise you not to think that this will be the end of the affair. It will not be long till other voices begin whispering in his ear. As a soldier you will know that the most dangerous enemy is not always the one directly to your front.'

Stilicho had sent horses to bring Zeno's medical wagon to the house. As it now trundled into the courtyard, Serena – and her servant – returned within, announcing she would select a room for the wounded man.

'Come,' Stilicho said to Marcus as an ornate carriage appeared from the side of the house. 'My aides will see to the billeting of your men while we seek an audience with Honorius.' When they were in the carriage Stilicho was pensive for a while, then his nose wrinkled. 'Perhaps we should have delayed long enough to allow you a change of tunic,' he smiled. 'Still, you look what you are, Marcus Flavius Victor. A soldier. Honorius will appreciate that. You must make allowances for my wife,' he continued. 'She is as much an adviser to me as

230

a companion these days, but she has become abrupt of late. You know that my daughter is married to the Emperor?'

Marcus nodded.

'That fact gives us direct access to power, but it comes at a price. There are those close to Honorius who see Maria as a barrier to their own ambitions. They are men without principle and they would not hesitate to use her to bring me down. When Maria and her mother are together they have to guard their every word. Any indiscretion, however innocent, could be fatal in the hands of our enemies.'

'I'm beginning to think I should have stayed in Britannia,' Marcus said.

Honorius's palace lay in the centre of Ravenna and took up an entire city section bounded by four major streets. Marcus experienced a shiver of unease when he recognized the uniform of the guards as the same worn by the men who'd arrested him on behalf of Dulcitius. He mentioned the fact to Stilicho.

'Dulcitius overstepped himself,' Stilicho said. 'He will do it once too often. He allowed his enmity for you to cloud his judgement. Even so my intervention might not have saved you had he not omitted to pass certain information to the authorities concerning the situation in Britannia. There was indeed a potential usurper in the province. An auxiliary commander from the south-west who also went by the name of Marcus, but who died or was killed around the same time you left the island. Therefore you could not be him and had no motive to murder the Emperor.'

A palace official accompanied them through a succession of broad corridors until they reached an enormous set of double doors guarded by four soldiers. Even Stilicho had to wait until Honorius personally sanctioned their entry. As the minutes passed, Marcus steeled himself for his encounter with the Emperor who would decide whether he lived or died. Eventually the doors opened and they were led forward into a great marble-floored auditorium lit by large windows set high in the extravagantly painted walls.

Marcus struggled to conceal his astonishment at the first sight of the

Emperor. Honorius sat on a gilded throne, holding a dove in the crook of his arm, with other birds pecking at seed scattered on the floor below. 'Stilicho, is it you?' The young man had a high forehead encircled by a gold diadem and narrow, mismatched features. Marcus had a sudden thought that the long nose and jutting chin didn't belong on the same face. 'Shouldn't my most famous general be in the north bringing death and destruction to this Radagaisus and his pagan horde you say threatens us all? And who is this? Another of your pet barbarians, like the Hun savage Uldin, or that clod of a Goth Sarus in whom you set so much store?'

Uldin. Marcus blinked at the familiar name, but it was the word barbarian that seared his brain like a lightning bolt. He took a breath and opened his mouth to say words he knew he'd regret, only for Stilicho to reply a heartbeat before his tongue condemned him.

'Uldin is a mercenary who leads some of the finest warriors ever to take to the saddle,' the general said evenly. 'And if I had not recruited Sarus, like as not he would have joined his fellow Goths in the north. I have the pleasure to present Marcus Flavius Victor, prefect of the First Ala Sabiniana. The prefect is a proven commander who has fought at my side on behalf of the Emperor in the past, and has journeyed from Britannia, at great cost and some peril, to do so again.'

'So this is Dulcitius's usurper?' Honorius studied Marcus with new interest. 'He certainly looks the part.'

'A misunderstanding, Augustus, as I explained in my note to you.' The words were spoken with an authority that declared the matter closed, evidence that, at least for the moment, Stilicho still retained some power over the young Emperor. 'As for Radagaisus, the latest intelligence is that he has just crossed the Danuvius somewhere north of Lentia. He is advancing with little urgency, which gives us time, but it is now beyond doubt he is moving on Italia. We must not make the mistake of underestimating him. This is no raid. An entire nation is on the march, uprooted by fear, driven by hunger, and fuelled by hope. It will take every man and every sword we have to stop them. That is why I propose to offer Marcus Flavius Victor a command in the Imperial service, if you will agree.' The general stepped forward. 'He may also be of some use in solving that other matter we spoke of,' he said in a voice so low that only the Emperor and Marcus would hear.

Honorius stared at Marcus, stroking the dove's head. 'Very well,' he nodded. 'But as a barbarian he will only command barbarians. Is that clear?'

'Of course, Augustus,' Stilicho bowed his head.

'You say we can't buy the Goths off, as we have done in the past?'

A moment of hesitation before Stilicho answered. 'I do not believe we can afford to accede to Radagaisus's demands, no matter how reasonable they may seem. I suspect he will seek a modest homeland for his own people and promise to disperse the other tribes, with suitable recompense for their troubles, of course. First, they want land. Once they have it, they will contrive to be such a nuisance that we will feel the need to pay them off with bribes or subsidies.'

Marcus saw the young man grimace. 'We will stop them in the mountain passes, then.' The voice had turned plaintive. 'There are places in the Alps where five hundred men could be as a stopper in a wineskin.'

Stilicho nodded. From a tactical point of view it was a perfectly sensible suggestion. 'There is merit in delaying Radagaisus,' he acknowledged. 'It would give us more time. Better, I think, though, to draw him on and meet him with whatever strength I can gather.'

For a moment Honorius seemed almost bored with the conversation. 'This is my new acquisition.' He showed off the glossy, blue and grey dove on his arm. 'I call him Rome, isn't he a beauty?' Honorius stroked the pigeon's head with obvious affection. The bird's small black eyes blinked as though in puzzlement at Stilicho and Marcus and it emitted a soft purring sound that made its chest tremble. 'I find their company quite soothing and much prefer their call to the chatter of my so-called advisers.'

'Am I included in these *so-called* advisers?' Stilicho demanded.

'Of course not.' Honorius smiled as if the jibe hadn't been the provocation it patently was. 'But,' he lowered his voice, 'you should hear what they say about you, Stilicho.'

'I have only done what I promised your father I would do.' Marcus could tell Stilicho was struggling to maintain his composure. 'I kept you and your brother close and free from harm, tried to teach you the rudiments of power and, when the time was right, placed you on the throne with such support as I was able to provide.'

'All very laudable,' Honorius said, 'though I dislike your use of the word *placed*. Let us say I *took* my rightful place when I came of age.' Stilicho bowed his head in acknowledgement. 'Now, I understand that you have sent orders to Gaul calling on the field army to march on Italia without delay. Won't that leave the province at the mercy of the Franks?'

'As I have said repeatedly, Augustus, if we are to defeat Radagaisus, it will take every spear we have. The Gauls must find the strength to hold what they have for the moment, or they will lose it.'

'*I* will lose it, Stilicho. Gaul will go the way of most of Hispania. I won't have it.'

'And once we have defeated Radagaisus we will recover it,' Stilicho insisted patiently. 'Though I am not convinced it will be lost.'

'And the Gaulish field army is to combine with the Italian legions and your barbarians at Ticinum?' Stilicho struggled to conceal his surprise. This was another degree of detail entirely. Detail he'd deliberately planned to conceal until the deed was done. Clearly his staff required an overhaul. 'Surely if you're going to stop Radagaisus before he leaves the mountains it would be more sensible to combine at Mediolanum?'

'It would be if that was our strategy, yes.'

'But you said . . .'

'That was before we knew the scale of the enemy threat,' Stilicho said. 'If we stop them in one pass, Radagaisus will simply attempt another. It is an inconvenient truth that the mountains are full of them and we cannot guard every one. Worse, it is possible, or even likely, that if they are balked his army will disintegrate into its many components: Goths, Alans, Suevi, Vandals and the rest, and they into their tribes. We will have not one invasion of Italia, but a hundred. Warrior bands who will plague the homeland for years to come.'

'Then what will you do?' Honorius demanded.

'We will draw them deep into Italia and we will destroy them.'

'How?'

'I have not yet decided that.'

Honorius stared at him. 'You understand that by combining at Ticinum you will be leaving the rest of the country at the mercy of these barbarians, including Ravenna.'

'I understand, majesty.'

The pigeon must have sensed the growing tension because it struggled free from Honorius's hands and fluttered away to seek sanctuary on a window ledge. Honorius watched it go with a look of dismay, before turning to face Stilicho.

'Then also understand that if you lose,' the young man said with quiet menace, 'it will not just be Italia you have gambled away, but yourself.'

XL

'Christus, lord,' Marcus hissed when they climbed into Stilicho's carriage. 'I don't know how . . .'

Stilicho put a finger to his lips. 'My driver is a trusted retainer, but sometimes it is best to keep one's opinions to oneself,' he smiled. 'Diplomacy is the language of the court and when one feels driven from that path it is better to bite one's tongue. I should be congratulating you on your restraint, Marcus. It can't have been easy for a man whose family has served Rome for generations to accept such insults. But let there be no more talk of barbarians. In truth, you witnessed our young Emperor at something like his best. He was engaged, he listened to my arguments and put forward some suggestions of his own. It is not always this way. Even that final threat was at least evidence he realized something of the enormity that faces us.'

'So what now?'

'Now? Now, I suppose we must find you a command commensurate with your experience. Not any Hun or Goth war band, whatever the Emperor believes. I doubt he will think of you again, although Dulcitius may have other ideas. By then we will be on campaign out of his sight, and, hopefully, his mind.'

236

Marcus nodded. It was all he could hope for. He hesitated. 'I noticed you mentioned that I could be helpful in another matter?'

Stilicho nodded. 'Does the name Constantinus mean anything to you?'

'Dulcitius mentioned someone called Constantinus,' Marcus said carefully. 'We know of a soldier of that name, but he didn't make it clear whether it was the same man.'

'Yes,' Stilicho nodded. 'Claudius Constantinus, appointed *magister militum* against my advice by Chrysanthus, who acted as governor. Now he has killed Chrysanthus and styles himself Duke of All the Britons, though he does not yet have military support to make it so.'

'But with Chrysanthus dead he has political control of the south, where it matters.'

'A very dangerous man,' Stilicho agreed. 'He cannot yet make a direct challenge to the Emperor, but who knows what the future holds? Constantinus is a problem which will have to be dealt with. As a means of strengthening your position with the Emperor, I have suggested to Honorius that you and your men will have their parts to play, but that is for the future. For the moment the greatest threat we face is from Radagaisus who will all too soon reach northern Italia. His army is composed of many different tribes and peoples, but it boasts numbers I cannot match. The Emperor, with the encouragement of men like Dulcitius, suggests I stop him in the passes, but all that does is delay the inevitable and potentially exacerbates the problem. I don't need to stop Radagaisus, I need to destroy his power before *he* destroys everything we hold dear. In truth,' his voice softened, 'your coming is more than welcome, but what difference can thirty even of the very bravest warriors make against a horde like that of Radagaisus?'

The driver turned through the gates of Stilicho's estate. 'We have seen what Radagaisus is capable of,' Marcus said quietly. 'They tell me his army consists of not just Ostrogoths, but Alans, Suevi, and also Visigoths, men of the tribes of the Tervingi?'

Stilicho went still. 'You are very well informed for someone so recently arrived.'

The statement contained a question, but Marcus chose not to answer it yet. Zeno was waiting inside the doorway. Marcus gave him a look that sent a certain message.

'On our journey,' Marcus continued when they were at last in the privacy of the *magister militum*'s office, 'we fell into the company of a group of Goth warriors led by an interesting character. He tried to conceal his identity, but the lady Anastasia recognized him from her time in Salona. When I confronted him he did not deny he was King Alaric.'

'Alaric?' Stilicho exploded. 'Alaric should be with his warriors in the mountains of Epirus protecting my flank against our *friends* in the east, not wandering about Pannonia like some goggle-eyed philosopher.'

'Nevertheless,' Marcus interrupted. 'The man impressed me. He said that he too was concerned about the implications of Radagaisus's invasion of Italia—'

'He did? Well, no one knows better than that double-dealing barbarian about the *implications* of invading Italia. I taught him that, if nothing else, and he still bears the scars.'

'—and he asked me to convey certain proposals that might be of mutual interest in bringing about an outcome that would benefit all parties, apart, of course, from Radagaisus.'

A bitter laugh escaped Stilicho. 'If anything were certain to convince me you'd been speaking to the Goth, it would be that weasel-worded concoction that sounds like an offer of free advice from some country lawyer with pretensions above his station.' He shook his head. 'But even if I was interested in the slightest in his *proposals*, which I'm not, why in God's name would I trust someone like Alaric?'

They were interrupted by a knock at the wooden door.

'With respect, lord,' Marcus said, 'only one man can answer that question.'

'Enter.' Stilicho didn't hide his irritation.

Zeno walked into the room guiding a man with a heavily bandaged face, and Stilicho watched in astonishment as the *medicus* unwound the cloth bandages until the invalid's features were visible, lined and blotched pink by the tight wrappings, but instantly recognizable.

'You!'

Alaric blinked against the unaccustomed light. 'If I ever again suggest being wrapped up like a corpse and transported over half the Empire in bucketing wagons and rocking boats you have permission to cut my throat, my friends.'

'I should cut it now.' Stilicho too was on his feet, barely able to articulate the words, lost somewhere between bemusement and fury. 'Or invite the Emperor to come and do it. And you, Marcus Flavius Victor, brought this viper, this enemy of Rome, into my house? I should have let Dulcitius do what he wished with you. This is treason without the slightest doubt, and you have implicated me and my family . . .'

Marcus allowed Stilicho to work out his anger as Alaric looked on, entirely unperturbed by his lack of welcome. Poor Claudius had succumbed to his wounds on the day the Goths and Britons parted and was now the lonely inhabitant of an unmarked roadside grave in southern Pannonia.

'He convinced me that he could help you in the matter of Radagaisus, which is your most immediate problem,' Marcus explained. 'What he said seemed to make sense. I would ask you to hear him out, lord. If you don't like what he says you must do with him as you will, and me, but let the others go, this is none of their doing.' Stilicho shot a poisonous glance at Zeno, who sat by the window trying to be invisible. 'Even my *medicus* was forced to cooperate against his will.'

Stilicho hesitated for a moment, before subsiding back into his chair with a growl of frustration. 'Very well, Goth,' he glared. 'You once tried to sell me your army.' The words produced a look of warning from Alaric. Clearly much had been left unsaid about the relationship between the man who was king and the one who wielded a power any king would envy. 'Now sell me this proposal of yours, but remember your head depends on it, crowned or not.'

Alaric bowed, but before he could speak Marcus said: 'Perhaps this would best be discussed between you in private?'

'No,' Stilicho shook his head. 'This man's presence cannot be known beyond the walls of this room, and you are all implicated, innocent or not. You will stay and listen, and when he is done you will hear my judgement.'

The final words were spoken with the solemnity of a tolling bell, and left no doubt as to their potential consequences.

'You say you wish to destroy Radagaisus,' Alaric began. 'I too wish to destroy Radagaisus.' He ignored Stilicho's snort of disbelief. 'He is a brave warrior, or the Goths would not have gathered to his banner, but not a great thinker, or he would never have contemplated invading Italia in the blundering manner that he has. I believe he will bring great suffering to my people whether he succeeds or not. That is why he must be stopped and rendered powerless.'

'I will not defeat Radagaisus only to hand over what power he has to you.'

'No,' Alaric said. 'But we have agreed in the past that the Goths can be of great benefit to Rome, even if the Emperor is not yet disposed to give them citizenship. If I grow stronger at Radagaisus's expense, and that strength is placed at your disposal at a time, place, and for a purpose that you decide, surely that can only be for the good?'

'Spare me your honeyed tongue,' Stilicho said. 'And tell me what you propose.'

'You cannot defeat Radagaisus alone,' Alaric spoke with a commander's authority, and now Stilicho chose not to interrupt him, 'or you would not have turned for support to Uldin the Hun, who will fight for any man who pays him, or my beloved brother-in-law Sarus and his pitiful band of renegades. And even then, Radagaisus's strength is such that you cannot be certain of victory in a straight fight.' He paused for a heartbeat. 'But just how dependable is that strength? There are chiefs and princes and warlords among Radagaisus's horde who, not six months past, owed their loyalty to me; and others who, by now, are far from certain that he is the leader they should be following. What has he brought them and their families but hardship and hunger? If only someone they trusted could offer them a better future.'

'You would undermine his army? How?' Stilicho demanded.

'Not undermine, so much as divide them,' Alaric corrected. 'I already have very persuasive people among them making certain suggestions. It would help if they had the authority to make certain promises. All it would take is for a few chieftains to defect, others to show their dissent or doubt at Radagaisus's councils, and who knows what could be achieved?'

Stilicho's expression hadn't changed, but Marcus noticed his left thumb stroking his right palm in a gesture he recognized. 'What indeed?' he said.

'It would help,' Alaric suggested, 'if you could make me aware of the broad outline of your strategy.'

This was the moment of truth. If Stilicho harboured any genuine doubts about Alaric's suggestions, he would never reveal the slightest hint of his innermost thoughts. His answer would signify, at least in some form, his approval or otherwise, and perhaps even resolve the question that must be uppermost in the Goth's mind. Was he going to live or die? Stilicho allowed the silence to draw out until the air seemed to tremble like an overstretched bowstring.

'In the broadest terms,' he said eventually, 'my aim is to draw Radagaisus's army and its followers onto the soil of Italia, and manoeuvre or lure him to a place where I can attack him at my greatest advantage.'

Alaric appeared to consider the possibility for a moment, but Marcus knew that something close to Stilicho's strategy had been at the heart of the Goth's own plans. 'Then might I humbly suggest,' the Goth said, 'that, in this case, hunger is as much a weapon in your favour as the swords of your soldiers.'

'You would not know the meaning of humble,' Stilicho snorted. 'But yes, you may suggest that.'

'Radagaisus will emerge from the mountains with enough food for a week, at most.'

'And how would you be aware of this?'

'You forget, general,' Alaric said with a tight smile, 'I have brought

241

an army through those mountains, albeit a smaller one, and I did not hamper my progress by trailing fifty thousand hungry camp followers in my wake. What if I could ensure that by the time he reaches Italia his supplies are much lower than he'd hoped?'

'That would certainly be helpful,' Stilicho agreed.

'To lure Radagaisus to a place of your choosing you would need a tasty piece of bait,' Alaric's tone turned thoughtful. 'Yet even so, for that bait to work it would have to be singularly attractive, which means there must be no alternative sources of supply.' His face broke into a broad smile. 'I see it now. You will strip the country bare so the only possibility of resupplying his starving army is where you decide it should be. There will be cities that you can hold, even against Radagaisus, but many more you cannot. What will happen to their people, and the farmers and villa owners from the countryside? You have never sought popularity, general,' he laughed, 'but this is brave even for you. I wonder what the Emperor thinks?'

Stilicho stiffened in his chair. 'The Emperor knows sacrifices must be made for the sake of the Empire.'

'My spies suggest that Radagaisus's line of march will bring him to Italia proper east of Lake Benacus. You cannot hold Verona, as I know to my cost, so you will evacuate the city. Mediolanum would attract him, but, like Ravenna, it is much too hard a nut for Radagaisus to crack, even if he was equipped with siege engines, which he is not. He will blunder about seeking sustenance where he can, while his people face starvation. So where? Will you really allow him as far as Bononia?'

'That is none of your concern,' Stilicho snapped. 'All that matters is that you can do what you say you can. Cause dissent among his chieftains, if possible to the point of desertion or mutiny.'

'I can do that.'

'Then all that remains is your terms.' The words were innocent enough, but there was something in the sentiment that made the room go still.

Alaric didn't hesitate. 'Including what the Empire already owes me for the matter of Epirus, I believe sixty talents of gold would be suitable recompense for my help in these matters, given their importance to the Emperor – and to you.'

Marcus heard Zeno gasp at the enormous sum – entire kingdoms had been bought and sold for less. Stilicho didn't even blink.

'I will give you forty talents of gold, agreed?'

'Agreed. And one fourth of the plunder you collect from Radagaisus . . .'

'One eighth.'

'And every man in Radagaisus's horde who is willing to make his oath to me will be given free passage to join my forces in Illyricum . . .'

'There to await my decision as to their, and your, deployment at a place, time and against whom it is my pleasure.'

'And the matter of citizenship for my people?'

Stilicho sighed and suddenly looked very tired. 'Is, as always, at the discretion of the Emperor Honorius, may God keep him safe.'

No handshakes or flourishes of the pen to mark the momentous agreement that could decide the fate of Rome. Just two men staring into the distance as if they couldn't quite believe what they'd done. Marcus realized that what he'd just witnessed was more ritual than negotiation. Each man had the measure of the other long before this day. Stilicho knew what Alaric would ask, but more important, what he would be prepared to accept. The rest was just theatre.

Eventually, Stilicho pushed himself to his feet and went to the door. 'You will stay here.'

He returned a few minutes later. 'Accommodation has been arranged for you in the guest rooms. *Medicus*?' Zeno bowed. 'You will restore the injured gentleman's bandages. He will keep them on at all times until he is escorted beyond the environs of this city. Until that happens you will not let him out of your sight . . . on pain of death.'

Zeno swallowed. 'Yes, lord.' He moved towards Alaric.

'Wait,' Stilicho snapped. 'There is one more thing. I cannot tell you yet where I will gather my forces, but we will need a reliable messenger when everything is in place and you send for me. Do you have such a man?'

Alaric considered for a moment. 'It would need to be someone able to come and go without being noticed, but,' his tired features broke into a smile, 'I believe I have the ideal choice. One who can pose as a servant and whose absence will be taken for granted. I have watched him these past days, and particularly these last hours, and I would stake my life on his reliability, his qualities and his composure if things become difficult.'

Stilicho's face creased in a frown. 'Who is this paragon?'

Alaric's head swivelled and his eyes fixed on Marcus.

'Brenus.'

244

XLI

'No,' Marcus said for the fourth time.

'It must be for Brenus to decide,' Stilicho said. After Marcus's first furious reaction the general had sent Alaric and Zeno away. 'King Alaric is correct that he will be able to move without suspicion where others could not.'

'He has other motives for choosing my son, you must be aware of that.'

Stilicho sighed. 'Knowing Alaric as I do, I have no doubt he sees profit in keeping your son close.'

'Then forbid it,' Marcus rasped. 'You cannot do this to my family after all we have been through together.' Marcus knew he'd gone too far the moment the words were out of his mouth.

The other man's face turned an ashen grey. 'Do you believe I would allow it if I did not think it might make the difference between victory and defeat?' Stilicho said. 'I have given my oath to the Emperor, as have you, Marcus Flavius Victor. I would die for Rome. I would sacrifice my own son, if it came to it.' His long sword hung from a frame and he took the hilt and drew it part way from its scabbard so the wave pattern of the blue-tinged iron glittered in the lamplight. It was a magnificent blade, the length of a man's arm, with a gilded hilt and a pommel inlaid with a gold oath-ring. 'There is no weapon I would not use to stop Radagaisus.' Stilicho shook his head. 'Talk to Brenus. I suspect he will be proud Alaric has shown such faith in him, and used such words. A good boy, and clever: it was he and the lady Anastasia who talked their way past the guards to reach me. Brave, like his father. If you convince him not to go, then so be it, but it must be his decision.'

Marcus bowed his head.

'What did you think of what you heard here today?'

Marcus considered for a moment. 'Your strategy and Alaric's plan complement each other like the weevil and the jay under a walnut tree. The weevil burrows away inside the nut, weakening the whole, while the jay waits to break the shell once the first cracks appear.'

'A decent analogy,' Stilicho managed a smile. 'But still it may not be enough.'

'Then why did you agree? Alaric is no friend of Rome, despite what he told me. And why did you consent to his terms so easily? Forty talents of gold? I cannot even imagine such a sum.'

'I agreed, because, as I told you not a moment ago, I will use any weapon in the furtherance of Rome's defence, even an unreliable, untrustworthy one like Alaric the Goth. As for the treasure, he knows I will be true to my word if I can, but is well aware of the limitations of my power. You're right, it is a huge sum. Where will it come from? I cannot raise it without the Emperor's permission, and how likely is that? In any case, circumstances change. In two or three months Radagaisus could be calling himself Emperor of Rome and have his standard-bearer carrying my head on a pole. I could defeat Radagaisus and poor, brave Alaric may die in the decisive battle. Perhaps,' a wistful smile, 'that is the most favourable scenario. But perhaps not. Forty talents of gold *is* a huge sum, but when balanced against saving the Empire it counts as very little. In my letter I told you about the pressures on the Rhenus as well as the Danuvius. Well, they have only worsened. A new wave of Alamanni, Burgundian, Vandal and Suevi tribes is ready to take advantage of Radagaisus's invasion to cross the Rhenus. I have already withdrawn most of the Imperial troops from Gaul; who do I use to stop them? And if I can't stop them now, I must evict them later. Who better than King Alaric, who will fight all the better with the promise of land and citizenship for his people. And if a few thousand semi-civilized Goths settle Gaul and pledge allegiance to the Emperor, is that any worse than the Franks, who will not?'

'I am sorry,' Marcus said. 'You bear a burden I cannot imagine.'

'Speak to Brenus,' Stilicho said again. 'If he is as stubborn as his father tell him that General Stilicho will pray to God for his salvation.' They talked for a few minutes more, about possible scenarios and how Stilicho might react to them. 'Now,' Stilicho said with weary resignation, 'I have other business to attend to – the days could be twice as long and it still wouldn't be enough – but I will see you out.'

They went to the door and Stilicho opened it. Two men stood on the other side of the hallway, well apart. One was tall and blond and might have been kin to Alaric, the other bandy-legged, narrow-eyed and stocky, wearing an exotic style of clothing Marcus instantly recognized.

'Lord Sarus,' Stilicho said. 'Lord Uldin. My auxiliary cavalry commanders. May I introduce Marcus Flavius Victor.'

Marcus saw Uldin's nostrils flare and the dark eyes glitter with malevolent hatred, but Stilicho appeared not to notice. He ushered the two men into the room leaving Marcus in the corridor with his heart thundering. Another enemy made. One more complication he didn't need. Maybe Brenus would be safer with Alaric after all?

Marcus walked through the marble-lined corridors deep in thought, his mind focused on what he would say to Brenus, but, before he reached the room they were to share, someone gripped his arm with ferocious strength.

'What have you done, Marcus?' Valeria spoke through gritted teeth.

'Zeno told you?'

'Of course he told me.' She released her grip at last. 'Zeno, at least, knew that it would have broken us if he'd left it to you to tell me how he'd betrayed my trust on your behalf a second time. You brought

247

Alaric here under my very nose and you didn't think to tell me? It's Longovicium all over again. Lies, deceit and evasion. Do you never consider how your shameless double-dealing will affect those around you? Do you not understand that it comes at a cost?'

Marcus winced at the barbed savagery in her voice. He'd never seen her so angry, and the truth was that she was correct. 'I did what I thought was right.' He spoke quietly, trying to alleviate her fury. 'The fewer people who knew, the better for all. Zeno had to know. Alaric's life was at stake. If he insisted that it should be kept within the three of us, how could I deny him?'

'Brenus didn't know, even though he shared their wagon?'

Marcus shook his head, and she groaned. 'Christus, Marcus, your own son. What happened to poor Claudius?'

'We buried him by the roadside, Alaric, Zeno and I.' He didn't tell her that Alaric had persuaded Zeno to keep Claudius's death a secret even before he'd approached Marcus with his plan. That would be a conspiracy too far. 'I'm sorry, Valeria.'

'Sorry doesn't mend anything this time, Marcus.'

'No, it doesn't,' he admitted. They stood for a while until he felt the tension ease. Perhaps there was a way to restore her trust. 'What if we went hunting together?' he suggested, 'Stilicho says there is good duck hunting from a little promontory in the marshes not far from here. It's reserved for members of Honorius's court, but seldom used. We could take a couple of bows. It will be like old times when we were children down by the river . . .'

Valeria stared at him for a moment. 'I will think on it.'

'I won't tell you what to do,' Marcus assured his son after informing him of Alaric's proposal. 'General Stilicho says the decision must be yours and he is right. When Alaric spoke your name I was angry. Sometimes it's not easy being a father. My only thought was for your safety and I forgot how often you have shown on this journey that you have a mind and a will of your own.'

They were walking in the mansion's pine-scented gardens with the sun on their backs. A soft breeze from the east ruffled Brenus's dark hair and carried with it the slightest tang of salt from the sea a mile away.

'I only want to make you proud, Father, that's all I ever wanted.'

'I should always have been proud of you.' Marcus tried to keep the gruffness from his voice. 'But I was blinded by love and the tragedy that took your mother. I hope you never have to experience that kind of loss. It leaves a gaping hole at the very centre of you. I should have filled that void with my love for my son, but I allowed my anger to control me.' He turned to Brenus. 'You don't need to do this to make me proud of you. I've been proud since I set eyes on you again at Treva.'

'I know that,' Brenus said. 'But I still want to go. I've spent the last hour learning what to do and how to act when I am among the Goths. Alaric says when Radagaisus is defeated I will be a hero.' Marcus responded with a tight smile. He had seen more dead heroes after battle than live ones, but Brenus would need to learn that for himself. 'General Stilicho would reward me and be for ever grateful. He says a man can prosper on the gratitude of kings and generals. Is that true?'

'It is,' Marcus agreed, but he also remembered his father telling him that the gratitude of kings was always short-lived and could never be depended upon. 'Come,' he took a seat on a stone bench in the shade of an oleander tree, 'sit with me. If you are set on this I have things to tell you. Alaric knows better than I what will happen when you join Radagaisus's host, but you can be certain that it will be shadowed at all times by cavalry loyal to Stilicho. The general will be in the west and will only close on Radagaisus as soon as he is certain of his line of march. That means, when the time comes for you to leave, you must head due west. Alaric will know this and will no doubt have positioned himself on that side of the column to make it easier on you. Once you are clear of Radagaisus, you will have to ride until you encounter one of Stilicho's squadrons. They will have been told to expect you. When you're certain you've found the right people, the watchword is "Theodosius".'

'Theodosius,' Brenus repeated, running the word over his tongue to try it for size.

249

'Yes, he was Stilicho's friend, Alaric's commander and Honorius's father, so you will not forget.'

'No, Father.' Brenus paused, chewing his lip. 'What will happen afterwards?'

'Afterwards?' Marcus tried to sound careless, as if it was something he hadn't considered. 'Afterwards you will be a hero.'

'No, when peace returns. Anastasia thinks we will stay in Italia. She says you will be a general as great as Stilicho and I will be a prince of Rome.'

Marcus stared at his son, knowing the question had to be asked, but not wishing to know the answer. 'What do you want to happen, Brenus?' The boy's head dropped to stare at the ground and Marcus steeled himself for the dread news that his son desired more than anything to return to Saxonia.

'I would like to go home,' Brenus said. 'Home to Britannia, with you.'

'He said that?' Valeria took aim at a mallard and followed its flight across the sky, but decided it was out of range and relaxed her grip on the bow. The heat from the mid-afternoon sun was intense, but the trees lining the marsh provided plenty of shade.

'His exact words.'

'And what did you tell him?'

'What could I tell him?'

'That once he's defeated Radagaisus, Stilicho will send us back to Britannia to settle with Constantinus.'

'You can't be certain of that.'

'No? What was it you said he told you? *Constantinus is a problem which will have to be dealt with, and I have told the Emperor you and your men will have their parts to play.* He means to use you to destroy Constantinus. Perhaps he will appoint you governor of Britannia. He needs a man he can trust.'

'Just words,' Marcus grunted. He drew his bow and fired in the same movement and the arrow sped out to pierce a flighting duck through the breast, dropping it like a stone.

'Good shot.'

'Before we can even think about Britannia, Stilicho must defeat Radagaisus.' Marcus forced his way through the bushes and cursed as he saw the duck floating in a pool a dozen paces from the bank. He sat down to remove his sandals. 'I've insisted we must be close to Brenus, and Stilicho has agreed we will have freedom of movement to patrol the right flank of the Goths' advance. Alaric will send a signal each morning to let us know where he is camped amongst the Gothic host.'

'How is that possible among so many thousands?' she frowned.

'Difficult.' Marcus put his right foot tentatively into the water and frowned as he felt a layer of soft mud. If he'd been hunting in Britannia he'd have had a dog to do this. Still, if he wanted the duck . . . He took another step. 'But not impossible. When he lights his fire at dawn each morning he will add a substance that will turn the smoke blue for a few minutes. As long as we keep watch at dawn we will know approximately where he is camped, and more importantly where Brenus is likely to appear.'

Valeria watched her brother lurch through the pond and pick up the mallard by the arrow through its breast. The water was deeper than he'd calculated and it soaked the bottom of his tunic. 'If only Stilicho could see you now,' she grinned. Behind her one of the horses, tethered to a tree about twenty paces away, snickered and pawed the ground. 'Even the horses are laughing at you.'

She held out a hand to help Marcus up the muddy bank and they walked back to their mounts. Marcus added his catch to the bulging net hanging from his saddle. 'Enough for today, I think.' He wiped sweat from his brow. 'Lord, I'm thirsty. Throw me the waterskin.'

Valeria unhooked the goatskin bag and tossed it towards her brother. Marcus caught the skin, but in the same instant his ears registered a familiar *zzzziiiippp* and it was torn from his hands by a heavy impact. He dropped to the ground from pure instinct as a sharp smack announced the arrival of a second arrow. The horses whinnied and pulled against their tethers. Valeria took shelter behind them and searched the trees with her drawn bow for their attacker.

'Where is the bastard?' Marcus cursed. His bow lay in the open beside his sandals.

'The arrows came from the bushes to our left.' She sensed movement among the foliage and sent an arrow in that direction. 'If you crawl round to take him in the flank I think I can keep his head down.'

Marcus studied the ground between their position and the bushes. His only cover would be a few blades of grass. 'Maybe we should just wait?'

'We can't wait. What if he's sent for his friends?'

Marcus took a deep breath and began crawling to his right, eyes fixed on the bushes and tensed for the arrow that was about to pierce his flesh. Where would it be? His entire left flank was open. A decent marksman could put a shaft in his ear at this range. He tried to make himself smaller, but knew it was an illusion. The sound of an arrow whizzing across the clearing made him flinch, but it was only Valeria providing the cover she'd promised. Enough. Even a duck knew better than to give his hunter an easy shot. He pushed himself to his feet and hurled himself towards the bushes, drawing his dagger as he ran.

Marcus burst through the foliage ready for battle only to discover there was no one to fight. Trampled grass showed someone had been here, but whoever tried to kill him had made a hasty retreat. Valeria came up on his left, an arrow at the ready. He signalled she should cover him as he moved forward through the undergrowth. Not far back, in a stand of trees, he found hoofprints and a pile of dung where a horse had been tethered.

When they returned to their horses he picked up the waterskin. It had been pierced through by the first arrow. Valeria stared at him, her face suddenly pale. 'That arrow would have been in your throat if you hadn't asked me to throw you the skin.' The second arrow was sunk deep in one of his saddle pommels. If he hadn't dropped when he did . . . the thought made him feel weak. With a struggle he pulled the arrow free and hung the waterskin across the pommel.

'Who could have done this? Dulcitius?'

'Not Dulcitius,' Marcus shook his head. 'Remember the arrow Zeno took from Senecio's eye? This is identical.'

Uldin.

'We have to tell Stilicho.'

Stilicho studied the two arrows.

'Yes, this is Hun work. Uldin has a bodyguard, Bleda, who does his killing for him. You would recognize him by the scar that runs from his right eye to his chin. A squat, ugly creature who looks like a toad, but he can kill just as well with a bow or a sword, lance or knife. But why would Uldin want to have you killed?'

Marcus explained about the skirmish that had led to their encounter with Alaric, and the unfortunate demise of the Hun's brother.

'This complicates things,' the general said. 'Uldin is not the kind of man to forget or forgive. Yet I cannot afford to alienate an ally who leads a thousand of the finest cavalry ever to take the saddle. Neither,' Stilicho gave Marcus a wry smile, 'can I allow him to kill my old friend Marcus. We have to get you away from here.'

'Where?' Valeria demanded. 'No matter where you post Marcus in Italia, Uldin will find out and send his assassins.'

'Perhaps.' Stilicho's left thumb stroked his right palm. 'But I believe I have a solution that suits all our purposes.'

XLII

Marcus turned over in his sleep and smiled as his arm fell on Anastasia's warm body. It was only after it had lain there for a time that he realized that where there should be supple, pliant flesh, his wandering fingers encountered only bone and hard muscle.

'If you do not move your hand, my friend,' a soft voice informed him, 'you will be my friend no longer.'

Realization dawned in an instant. It was the morning of the fifth day and last night they'd camped east of Bononia by the narrow river he could hear burbling nearby. The uncomfortable elbow in his back belonged to Brenus and the sleeping companion who resented his attentions was King Alaric the Goth. It was still difficult to believe that Stilicho's solution to Uldin's lust for vengeance had been for Marcus to accompany his son and Alaric into the heart of Radagaisus's army.

'It is the one place he would never expect you to be,' the general had explained. 'You will be able to keep your son safe and at the same time be a constant reminder of Rome's and my interests in this matter. Alaric is a man who sees opportunity everywhere. It may be that at some point during your expedition he will find it more convenient to side with Radagaisus. If that day comes you will have a choice of reminding him of the error of his ways, or killing him. I recommend the second option.'

But, for now, Radagaisus was still hundreds of miles to the north, and would be for many days yet. They'd been smuggled out of Ravenna by the north gate and collected their horses in a field beyond the marshes. Stilicho, and anyone else who took an interest in their journey, would naturally assume that their initial destination was Forum Alieni, a two-day ride and halfway to Lake Benacus, where Alaric predicted Radagaisus would emerge from the Alps. Instead, Alaric insisted they abandon their first camp in the middle of the night and they found themselves with the sun at their backs when it rose the next morning.

He explained his reasoning as they rode. 'A few more days will make no difference. Stilicho expects and hopes Radagaisus will be drawn south to Bononia. If we go by way of Bononia, and then turn north, when next we come this way we will already have travelled this road and that will be to our advantage.'

They stayed in Bononia long enough to ride the city boundary, a circuit that took in the terrain where Alaric believed Stilicho would force his confrontation with the Goths. Next morning they set off north, posing as a pair of down-at-heel merchants and their servant. Brenus led a horse that ostensibly held their wares, but actually carried sufficient rations for two weeks. Fodder for their mounts shouldn't be a problem as spring waned and summer beckoned, or so they hoped. The land here reminded Marcus of the country east of Lindum in Britannia, flat as a gaming board, only appreciably drier. Prosperous villas and farms dotted the landscape, their crops healthy and lush under the ever reliable sun.

'Is it any wonder we Goths covet this land?' Alaric said. 'It reminds us of those from which we were driven, beside the Pontus Euxinus. Fine fertile earth that will yield two crops a year if a man knows his business. We never lacked water in the homeland, but look how the very ground here has been shaped to irrigate every field and meadow.'

'If Stilicho is right those fields will soon be stripped bare and flames will consume the fine homes of those who tend them,' Marcus pointed out. 'Yet I see no sign that the people here fear the threat from the north.'

'This is Stilicho's genius,' Alaric assured him. 'There's no point in creating an unnecessary panic. He will bide his time if there is any possibility that these crops can be harvested and carried off to be used as bait for Radagaisus and his empty bellies. Stilicho will use every moment he has before he forces them from their farms and destroys their crops.'

'But surely it is the general's duty to protect these people and their homes,' Brenus's voice, which had taken to fluctuating between the high pitch of childhood and the bass of youth, came from behind Marcus's left shoulder. 'Why would he give up half his country to this barbarian horde and possibly even place the Emperor in peril?'

'Careful with your *barbarian horde*, boy,' Alaric laughed. 'Those barbarians are my Ostrogoth cousins, and some of them closer than that. Why, I believe the Emperor Honorius would consider you just as much of a barbarian as I am.'

'I am a Roman citizen,' Brenus bristled, his earlier bond to his Saxon captors a distant memory. 'As was my father and his father before him, the Emperor Maximus.'

Alaric exchanged a wry look with Marcus.

'Best not to boast about your Imperial ancestor if you know what's good for you. The fact is that, citizen or not, you don't labour on the soil of Italia or polish a marble seat in the Senate with your fat arse, so you're really no better than Germans. Oh, there are a few in Gaul Honorius would grace with the word Roman, though he's handed most of that province to the Franks. Britannia is a small place far from Ravenna. More of an irritation than an asset. It pleases the Emperor to think of you as barbarians because it's easier to ignore you that way.' A lizard scuttled across the road beneath his mount's hooves and the horse jumped nervously. 'Behave, you old coward,' he said, running a hand over the animal's neck to calm it. 'But to get back to your original question, young Brenus, the general is forced to abandon most of Italia out of necessity. Yes, he could deploy his army where he thinks Radagaisus will emerge from the mountains, but the mountains are like those sponges the divers pick up from the sea bottom.' He saw Marcus's look of incomprehension. 'They're full of holes,' he explained. 'And like as not Radagaisus would send ten thousand of his warriors to find those holes and they'd pour out to take Stilicho in the flank. Stilicho's army is routed and scattered and Radagaisus has his boot on Italia's neck and the Emperor's balls in the palm of his hand.' Brenus choked on a laugh and Alaric smiled. 'You have to understand that Stilicho is outnumbered by at least two to one, possibly much more. But, though Radagaisus's numbers are his greatest strength, they're also his greatest weakness.'

'How can that be?' the boy demanded. 'You talk in riddles.'

'Because he has to feed them,' the Goth looked over his shoulder, 'and not just his army, but the thousands and tens of thousands of followers who depend on his warriors. A warrior with a full belly will always find the will to fight, unless the odds against him are truly overwhelming, but a hungry warrior will blame his chief or his commander. Hunger erodes a man's will as well as his strength. Stilicho knows this, which is why he will turn this land into a desert rather than give Radagaisus the resources that will sustain him.' He turned to Marcus. 'But it takes a brave man to do that.'

'Stilicho's enemies are not just the invaders Radagaisus leads,' Marcus picked up Alaric's theme. 'Those in the Emperor's court like Dulcitius will use his destruction of Roman crops and property to undermine him, even though they're likely to be the eventual beneficiaries.'

'It doesn't seem fair,' Brenus said.

'You've been away from home for six years, Brenus, you should know by now that fair doesn't come into it.'

'How much longer will it take?'

Marcus wasn't sure what 'it' was, but Alaric chose to answer the most immediate question. 'Likely enough we will be with Radagaisus for weeks, perhaps a month and more, and we will have to be on our guard every moment.'

*

Verona. A ghost city inhabited only by stray cats and hungry dogs.

Alaric had suspected what they'd find – for the last two days they'd travelled against a river of humanity carrying every morsel of food and object of value they could fit onto their ox-drawn carts and wagons – but the disappointment still cut deep.

'To carry out my plan we need a wagon, and goods to trade. I had thought to purchase them here with the silver Stilicho provided.' He shook his head. 'It didn't occur to me that the place would be wiped quite so clean, or that a wagon would be so precious that no man in his right mind would part with it for even ten times its value.'

Marcus studied their surroundings. The troops Stilicho had sent to oversee the evacuation would have commandeered wagons to make sure those with no transport were able to save their families from the advancing Goths. Then again, in times of trouble people became very adept at hiding things. 'If we look hard enough maybe we'll find something,' he suggested.

They searched the city first, focusing only on outbuildings large enough to conceal a four-wheeled cart. They found nothing of interest except a number of patches of earth of a slightly different shade from their surroundings. 'They think to hide their treasure,' Alaric laughed. 'But they forget that a Goth can smell silver and gold from a hundred paces.'

Empty-handed, they widened their endeavours to take in the surrounding farms. Apart from one that provided a welcome cache of forage for their horses, they found the barns mostly empty and even Marcus became discouraged. Riding back to the city they decided to try one more farm, a large, prosperous-looking place to the north-west of Verona where the house and barn sat in the shadow of the mountains. 'It's been picked even cleaner than the rest,' Alaric said as he pushed open the main door. 'Look, you can see they've carried off their furniture. There's nothing for us here.'

But as they rode off, Brenus shouted: 'Wait.'

'What is it?' Marcus asked.

Brenus pointed towards the hillside. 'You can't see it clearly, but there's a track that winds through those trees. Someone's tried to disguise the start of it, but it's there.'

'All right,' Alaric said. 'We still have a couple of hours left before dark. Let's take a look.'

Once they knew where the track began it was simple enough to follow it up the hillside, but it ended at a terrace clogged with vines. 'This isn't right,' Marcus frowned. 'Nobody expends this much energy building a trail for no reason.'

They backtracked a little until they came to a wall of foliage at the base of a steep slope cut by a stream. 'Look,' Brenus couldn't hide his excitement. 'See how the leaves in the centre are a slightly different shade of green. The way the branches intertwine isn't natural, they should be growing up towards the sun. These have been dragged or pushed into place.'

Marcus studied the tangle more closely and saw that Brenus was right. He looked to Alaric. 'What are we waiting for?' the Goth said. They pulled the branches apart to reveal a leather curtain stained to resemble the stone of the slope above. It had been artfully done: the combination of curtain and foliage was almost impossible to distinguish from the natural surroundings.

'Well, you found it for us, boy,' Alaric smiled. 'See what *it* is.'

Brenus dug his way through the remaining branches and squirmed into the gap behind until he could grip the edge of the curtain. At first, he struggled with the heavy leather because lead weights had been attached to keep it from moving in the wind. Eventually, he managed to grip the edge and pull it part way across to reveal what lay behind, a deep cave as large as a decent-sized room. Alaric grunted in disappointment. 'We'll need a torch to search it properly, but all I see is furniture and statues stacked almost to the ceiling. This must be an ancient refuge in times of trouble. The farmer couldn't carry away all his treasures so he decided to store them here.'

Marcus fetched a torch from his horse and set flint to iron. 'He's packed it tight. I can see nothing but the same.'

'I'll do it, Father.' Brenus snatched the torch from Marcus's hands and scuttled over the furniture like a squirrel until he disappeared from sight.

'What do you see?' Marcus called.

'There is fine linen here,' the boy called back, his voice muffled. 'And I see sacks and amphorae. Silver, I think, at least some kind of plate and . . .'

'. . . And?'

'I think I see a wheel.'

Two hours later they'd moved enough of the cave's contents to show the outline of a four-wheeled cart.

'A little fine for our purposes.' Alaric wiped sweat from his brow. 'But it will do if nothing else appears.' He went to the cave's entrance and looked out through a tangle of branches to the plain and the farm below. 'In fact this whole place will do very well. Who knows how long we will have to wait for Radagaisus and what perils we may face when his horde passes this way?'

Over the next two days they dragged or carried pieces of ornate furniture back to the farm and placed them in the barn, half-covered by straw as if someone had tried to conceal them. Then they carefully removed every trace of their movements at the base of the hill and used boulders to conceal the start of the track, changing their positions until Alaric was satisfied.

'You've done this before,' Marcus suggested.

Alaric shrugged. 'It is natural that at some point in his life a Goth will need to become invisible.'

They walked back to the cave, where Brenus had cleared space for their blankets and tethered the horses along one wall.

'We'll water them at the stream every day, and exercise them when we can.' Alaric ran a critical eye over their accommodation. 'Whoever created this refuge has left enough supplies to feed a small army. This will be our base, secret and well provided for, until we are able to join my people with Radagaisus.'

'But what do we do until then?' Brenus asked.

'We wait.'

XLIII

It was two long weeks before they came. Naturally Brenus saw them first. Brenus whose growing brain and body needed activity the way a fish needed water, and who was driven almost mad by the enforced inertia. He spent his days exploring the hillside but late one afternoon he came hurtling down through the vines to disturb preparations for the evening meal.

'Riders,' he said. 'Many riders. You can see them from the hill.'

Marcus and Alaric followed the boy up the hillside until they reached a clearing among the vines where they had a clear view across the plain. Alaric's head came up like a hunting dog at the sight of the barely discernible dust plumes moving across the fields in the distance. Closer to the mountain they were able to identify the little black dots of individual horsemen.

'Scouts,' the Goth said. 'Radagaisus is coming down the pass that emerges between the city and the lake, but he wants to be certain Stilicho isn't here to meet him. He'll have been watching for days. Now he's making his move.'

Marcus nodded. 'Those scouts aren't just looking for Stilicho, they're looking for food. See how the patrols split up to check individual farms. They're going to be disappointed.'

As if to prove his point a pillar of dark smoke rose from the plain, followed by another, then a third.

'Why are they burning the farms, Father, when they can use them for shelter?'

It was Alaric who answered. 'Radagaisus is a nomad and he and his people have been wandering the plain north of the Danuvius for five years. They wouldn't thank you for a soft bed and a roof over their heads. They're happy with their tents.'

After the scouts came the warrior bands and their followers, and the columns of smoke multiplied until they filled the horizon. Over the next few hours they watched as scores became hundreds and hundreds became thousands, entire tribes pouring out of the valley to set up camp on the plain. As night fell the landscape was filled with tiny pin-pricks of light from their campfires, and the larger conflagrations of yet more farms and buildings being set alight. Away to their right, the city of Verona burned.

'I must find out where my people are.' Alaric donned the war gear of a Goth spearman and dirtied his face with mud from the stream. 'Prepare the wagon and horses and wait for my return.'

He disappeared into the darkness and Marcus stood beside Brenus staring out across the vast field of flickering lights, wondering how it had come to this. His heart was pounding as if it was he, not Alaric, who was about to walk into the giant maw of Radagaisus's horde.

'Father, I'm frightened,' Brenus whispered.

What could he say? That he was frightened too, and more so for his son than himself? That they were in a situation that was beyond his control? 'You'll be safe with me, Bren.' He choked out the words and put his arm round his son's shoulder. 'Now let's get to work.'

Dawn came with no sign of Alaric. On the plain below, tented encampments stretched away into the distance and the smoke from thousands of cooking fires stained the morning sky. Now they were free of the mountains it appeared Radagaisus's followers were in no hurry to move. More worryingly, the fires made Marcus wonder about Alaric's prediction that the invaders would be short of supplies.

Throughout the day they stayed hidden in the cave, apart from a single foray to the stream for water. Occasionally bands of barbarian warriors appeared on the farm road at the bottom of the slope, but none came close. As the hours passed, Marcus became increasingly concerned that Alaric had been taken or killed. The Goth's disguise had been flimsy at best, and such a great man must surely be known to at least a few in this vast host. If he was to be believed, Alaric had enemies and to spare among the different clans and tribes that made up Radagaisus's army. All it would take was for one of them to recognize him.

Nightfall returned and Marcus stayed by the inner curtain while Brenus slept. He intended to remain awake till dawn, but after an hour he allowed himself to rest his eyes. He woke to find a shadowy figure looming over him and the tang of unwashed body in his nostrils. Not Brenus. Alaric? No, he knew Alaric's scent by now, and this intruder was bulkier by far. The stranger turned his head and his features were illuminated in a shaft of moonlight.

A Hun.

Uldin? No, not Uldin, but someone who might have been his son. Marcus's hand flew to his belt, but before the knife was freed from its sheath he froze at the prick of a point beneath his chin. He stared into the flat, emotionless features of his executioner and saw only death.

'Enough,' a voice whispered. 'Erman is with me.' Alaric strode across the chamber and nudged Brenus awake. 'We have little time. Get the horses in their traces.' He returned to Marcus. 'We must reach my people's encampment before dawn, and it is on the far side of the army. We've cleared the obstacles from the trackway. Come.'

Brenus led the horses down the slope, with Marcus, Alaric and Erman using their weight on the wheels to keep the wagon steady. 'I thought I was dead,' Marcus said. 'Is he a . . .'

'A Hun, yes and no,' Alaric whispered. 'His mother encountered his father only once, when he was on a raid south of the Danuvius. Erman was the result. When they saw what he was, her chieftain told her to drown him, but she refused. He was raised a Goth, but his face was an impediment to his future, so his mother asked me to find him a position. He is devoted to me and Radagaisus counts among his followers a number of Hun war bands, so he is doubly useful.'

They reached the base of the slope where a dozen riders had created a perimeter. Alaric took his place on the seat of the cart. 'Well, what are you waiting for? Get in. If anyone questions us, leave the talking to Erman. We have spent the entire day searching for supplies, and, the gods be thanked, we have been among the successful.'

Erman took his place at the head of the escort and led them west. Marcus and Brenus perched as best they could among the amphorae and sacks in the back of the wagon. Their progress through the darkness was necessarily ponderous, but the campfires on either side of the road provided a path to follow. Few of the inhabitants paid them any notice and those who did took one look at the mounted escort and were inclined to mind their own business.

'People come and go all the time,' Alaric explained. 'This is not like a Roman army. We could be Visigoths, Alans, Suevi, Huns or Vandals. They follow Radagaisus because he offers them hope, though not many of them are truly certain what hope means. They seek land and food in their bellies, but mostly they want the security of being part of a great empire, which will protect them and allow them to raise their children in peace.'

'Don't they understand that by invading Italia they have made themselves that same empire's enemies?' Marcus said.

'They are no more the Empire's enemies than I am,' Alaric snorted. 'They are simple folk. If they think anything, it is that Honorius has been misled by his advisers, men like Stilicho.' He laughed at Marcus's expression. 'Oh, yes, you may believe Stilicho is a saint, but these people know him better. If things had gone as he planned, Stilicho would have had his own Empire in the east and I would have been his supreme commander of an army composed of Goths and Vandals. But he failed and I was forced to return to Italia to seek the recognition of the Emperor of the West, only to be betrayed in my turn by Stilicho.'

'Yet here you are risking your neck for him,' Marcus pointed out.

'And for myself,' Alaric grinned.

Their route took them past the southern shores of Lake Benacus and an encampment more massive than any they'd encountered. It had been fortified with a palisade of pointed stakes and massive bonfires lit a great open space in the centre. As they approached, they could hear shouts and shrieks of merriment and see drunken revellers, male and female, cavorting among the fires. A platform and a great tented pavilion dominated one end of the arena.

'Radagaisus's nightly entertainment,' Alaric said dryly.

Brenus stood up in the back of the cart and peered towards the light. 'I see him,' the boy cried. 'A bear of a man seated on a throne.' Marcus followed his son's pointing finger and found the enormous figure slumped in a carved chair on the rostrum. The great, shaggy head lifted as if he could feel their eyes upon him, and Marcus had an impression of immense weariness that reminded him of Stilicho.

'Yes, that is Radagaisus,' Alaric confirmed. 'He keeps his most loyal followers close and well rewarded. There is drink for all and the warriors compete in contests of courage and skill. Radagaisus has silver aplenty to dispense to the victors, but I wonder if they will be so grateful when he can no longer supply them with food to put in their bellies?'

'How can you be sure they'll go hungry any time soon?' Marcus demanded. 'They don't act as if they're running out of food.'

'It is easy to advise a man to conserve food,' Alaric said. 'Much more difficult to make him do it. Your army is different. Here every warrior makes his own decisions. It is all about trust. Radagaisus promised them he would lead them to Italia, and he has. He has promised them he will provide for them, so they trust him to do that. They live for each day and worry about tomorrow when it comes. Beyond the pavilion, if you look carefully, you will see a great wagon park, all in darkness and heavily guarded. One person who will not go hungry, for now, is Radagaisus. But those wagons won't feed fifty thousand people, never mind a hundred thousand.'

Marcus held that thought as they traversed the breadth of the army, which must have been some three or four miles across. Occasionally, a voice would ring out from the darkness and Erman would reply, presumably with the story Alaric had outlined when they set off. Whether these were guards set by Radagaisus to prevent movement after dark, or individual tribes securing their own territory Marcus never discovered, but none made any move to hinder their progress.

Eventually they reached a compound much more orderly than most they'd passed, with wagons parked in a defensive circle and guards at the only opening. A wooden pole barred the entrance, but the guards lifted it aside and Alaric steered the cart between the wagons and into the encampment. An almost imperceptible nod to Erman sent him back into the darkness with his riders.

A tall, slim figure stepped out from between two tents and Marcus recognized Sigaric, one of the men who'd accompanied Alaric when they'd met south of the Danuvius. 'Welcome, lord,' he greeted the newcomers with mock ceremony, 'to our little island of civilization in a sea of barbarity.'

'Not the only island, Sigaric,' Alaric assured him. 'And soon we will not be so little.' He turned to Marcus and Brenus. 'You are safe with us. While you are here what is ours is also yours. It is the way of the Goths.'

Marcus nodded his thanks. 'What happens now?'

Alaric beckoned him towards a nearby tent, and didn't object when Brenus followed. He picked up a wineskin and poured into wooden cups, a smaller measure for Brenus, to which he added water. 'Drink, if it is to your taste. You will find it a little more potent than your Roman wines.'

They sat for a while and Marcus felt his heartbeat subside after the strain of traversing the enemy camp. Brenus yawned and curled up in a corner; before a minute passed he was asleep and breathing gently.

'A true warrior,' Alaric smiled. 'He takes his sleep when he can.' He drank from his cup and belched. 'You asked what happens now? The truth is I do not know. I cannot dictate Radagaisus's actions, or read his mind. All we can do is wait and see what he does. From what little I have seen, I believe he is in no hurry to leave here for the moment. He has sent out well-guarded foraging parties to east and west, but much good will it do him. Stilicho's cavalry squadrons have created a desert fifty miles and more wide. He must wait until his foragers return, which will take days, perhaps weeks, and will be disappointed when they come back empty-handed. That is when he must decide. East, towards Aquileia, a ripe enough plum, but with little in between to commend it? Or west, where he would find the riches of Mediolanum difficult to ignore, if it were not for that city's walls, which cannot be taken except by a prolonged siege.'

'I think Stilicho will do everything he can to stop that happening,' Marcus ventured. 'Aquileia would open the door to Ravenna, and an attack on Mediolanum is as much an attack on the Emperor as one on Rome. If there is a move in either direction he would be forced to act.'

Alaric nodded. 'A tweak of the reins here, a touch of the whip there. Yes, he would do that. So Radagaisus will be encouraged to move south, but when and how fast?'

'A raid in force by a mounted vanguard would make sense,' Marcus said. 'Stilicho will leave his destruction of crops and property to the last moment. A few thousand warriors moving at speed would soon chase off those left to carry out his orders. They won't risk their necks to save a few acres of unripe grain.'

'But that would require initiative and imagination,' Alaric said. 'And thus far Radagaisus has shown neither. His speed will be dictated by what lies directly within his reach until such time as necessity or opportunity spurs him into action. Necessity will come when even his personal supplies are drained. That will be when Stilicho must provide the opportunity.' He exchanged a look with Marcus. 'At Bononia.'

XLIV

Ticinum (Pavia)

'Still no sign of any decisive movement?'

'None, general.' Sarus, the young Goth cavalry commander who had allied himself to Rome, struggled to keep his eyes open. His horse soldiers had been given the task of observing the invaders day and night and his strained features showed it.

Flavius Stilicho had set up his campaign headquarters in a modest tent on the banks of the Ticinus river, where the *magister militum* had gathered his forces ready to strike at Radagaisus. A large map pinned to an ash frame was the tent's sole ornament, and the only furniture the general's campaign desk and his cot. Stilicho had managed to bring together three of his Italian legions, but the Emperor had insisted the fourth be left to protect his court in Ravenna. Likewise, though it hadn't proved possible to strip Gaul entirely, the province had supplied upwards of ten thousand fighting men, composed of Imperial units and barbarian *foederati*. All told, eighteen thousand men were camped along the banks of the Ticinus, a substantial army in most circumstances, but not substantial enough to face Radagaisus in a direct confrontation.

Stilicho grunted his disappointment and Sarus continued: 'It is the same as before. His patrols probe westward, but never with any great purpose, and then we push them back. There are minor disturbances within the camp, where one tribe disagrees with its neighbour, or another fouls the nest beyond bearing, but Radagaisus is like a sleeping ox: he snorts, he farts and he stirs, but then he subsides again. Perhaps his sorcerers are waiting for an auspicious day?'

'Then I wish I had one of his sorcerers in my pay,' Stilicho sighed. 'It's been a month now since he emerged from the Alps at Verona. He is a great disappointment, this Goth, begging your presence, Lord Sarus.'

'What about blue smoke?' Valeria asked. 'Have you seen any sign of it in the mornings?' Sarus looked mystified and Stilicho cast her a warning look.

'Blue smoke will be an indication that our spies are at work, Lord Sarus,' Stilicho explained as if it was nothing of importance. 'But they will not display it until Radagaisus is on the move. Once that happens I am to be given word immediately.'

'Yes, lord,' Sarus bowed. He turned to leave, then hesitated. 'Is it possible we have overestimated his need for supplies?'

'Perhaps,' Stilicho conceded, 'but I rather think it is more likely that I have underestimated our own citizens' ingenuity in concealing their produce. That and a Goth's ability to smell it out. Radagaisus stays in position because the countryside provides just enough sustenance to maintain his people for a short time at least. Another reason for his delay is that he had the impertinence to send a letter to the Emperor detailing his demands for retiring from Italia. He will not receive an answer, but he won't move until that fact sinks into his bony skull.'

Sarus left the tent and Stilicho slumped back in his seat. 'He's loyal enough,' he gestured to the doorway. 'But I'd decided it might be dangerous if he was aware that I have people at the heart of Radagaisus's camp.'

'I'm sorry.' Valeria's face twisted into a grimace of regret. 'I shouldn't have mentioned the smoke.'

'You could not have known,' Stilicho said. 'Men call me a master strategist, but perhaps I'm losing my touch. I should have taken you into my confidence.'

'We're all frustrated,' Valeria assured him. 'It hasn't been easy sitting here for weeks on end and knowing Marcus and Brenus face death each moment of every day.'

'Another omission.' Stilicho accompanied the words with a rueful smile. 'I thought making you part of my bodyguard would show my regard for you, but it is hardly an onerous duty. I should have found proper work for you before this.' He rose from his seat and stared at the map as if he could move Radagaisus from his position by the sheer power of his will. 'I truly believe he will move soon. Then you and your squadron will join Lord Sarus and shadow Radagaisus as he moves south. When Alaric has information for me he will send his courier west, where he will be picked up in our net.'

His courier. Valeria suppressed a shiver. Brenus.

'If Sarus is the one who picks him up, what's to stop him killing Brenus if he doesn't know of his existence?'

'Do not take me for a fool, Valeria.' She saw the fire kindle in the dark eyes and understood what made him a power in this land. 'Sarus has orders to bring every deserter or prisoner he catches to me for questioning. He knows to treat them well or he will answer to me.'

'I apologize,' she bowed her head. 'But, unlike you, my concern is for my family, not for Rome.'

Her words brought a bitter laugh from Stilicho. 'How fortunate that you are in a position to make such a choice, and how little you understand me. My wife and my children are my primary concern also, but what will happen to them if I fail Rome?'

They both knew the answer, and Valeria kept silent as Stilicho returned to the map.

'You wonder why I decided to place my army near Ticinum, in the west, when the threat is in the centre?' The question was directed at Valeria, but she understood Stilicho was actually voicing some inner debate and addressing his own doubts. 'Firstly I leave an avenue for

Radagaisus and his barbarians to advance, unhindered, along a path I have chosen. It is also much simpler for me to bring Italia's troops here to meet the legions of Gaul, certain in the knowledge we will be in a position to combine before the invaders bring their strength against us. It is true he has not advanced as quickly as I expected, but he *will* advance, towards Bononia.'

Valeria watched his finger trace a line down the centre of Italia. 'Why would he forsake ease of manoeuvre on the plains for an attack on Bononia?'

'Yes, you see the flaw.' The grey eyes studied her with new respect. 'What must happen is that he is made to believe Bononia is his salvation.'

'But how will you do that?'

'It's simple,' Stilicho said. 'Someone will tell him that all the supplies he needs are within his grasp at Bononia.'

'Someone?'

'All you have to do is get word to Alaric and your brother, they will do the rest. I could send one of my regular couriers, but Alaric is not the most trusting of people. When he sees you, he will know the information came directly from me. You did suggest that you would prefer to be more fruitfully employed?'

'Yes,' Valeria let out a long breath. 'But what I didn't have in mind was being sent like Daniel into the lion's den.'

'There is one other thing,' Stilicho said.

It was another week before they heard Radagaisus was on the move at last. The great horde trundled southwards consuming what little forage, grain and vegetables Stilicho's industrious quartermasters had missed in the fields and barns. In their frustration, the wandering tribes and clans of Goths, Alans and Suevi continued to destroy any home or building they came across. The difference now was that they were first carefully stripped of any timber that could be used in the nightly cooking fires.

'Keep them in sight for as long as it takes to be certain of Alaric's position,' Stilicho advised. 'If he's the soldier I think he is, he'll have his cavalry checking out our units who are shadowing the column, so it may be you can make contact without entering their camp. If not I've assigned three of Sarus's Goths to your squadron. They'll pose as deserters and find a way to get you to his camp. They have no idea who you're meeting, and that's the way it must stay. It's imperative they turn back as soon as you know you're in the right place.'

'I understand.'

'Then may God watch over you,' Stilicho said solemnly.

The troopers of the Ala Sabiniana were waiting outside the perimeter of Stilicho's compound. Zeno helped Valeria into the saddle before mounting his own horse. Only he was aware she intended to venture alone into the heart of the enemy's host and he made it plain he didn't like it. Yet he knew better than to argue. The three Goths Stilicho had assigned to them formed a group a little apart, gentling their horses and ignoring the suspicious glances from the Britons. She was about to order the horsemen into column when a sharp cry alerted her. 'Decurion . . . Lady.'

Leof, who'd remained in Ravenna with Luko to guard Anastasia, limped up the main track of the camp leading a horse that was slick with sweat and breathing hard. Valeria slipped from the saddle and hurried to meet him.

'What is it? Have you had word of Marcus? Is something wrong with Anastasia?'

Leof took a moment to catch his breath. 'It concerns both, lady, but,' he nodded towards the watching men, 'better we talk in private.'

Valeria called to Zeno to stand the men down and led Leof to her tent. 'Tell me?'

Leof hesitated, searching his surroundings with a question in his eyes. Valeria produced a frustrated growl, but reached beneath the cot and pulled out a half-empty wineskin and threw it to him. She allowed him a moment to put it to his lips and slake his thirst.

'Now?'

'We had a visitor at the house the day after you left.' Anastasia and her guards had been living in an annexe of Stilicho's mansion on the outskirts of Ravenna. 'A young aristocrat sent to pass on the compliments of Emperor Honorius to the lady Anastasia. She was flattered . . .'

'Did this young man have a name?'

'He said he was called Julian and he had a Greek look about him. Not that there's anything wrong with Greeks,' he hurried on. 'Naturally, he returned days later to ensure that all was well. By the third time he was suggesting that they could speak more freely alone. We protested for all we were worth, but he was handsome and well spoken and Anastasia assured us we had nothing to fear. He was the Emperor's man, after all. Long and the short of it, he became a regular visitor, and always, we noticed, when General Stilicho's wife was away from home.'

'Christus,' Valeria whispered.

Leof nodded. 'We – that's Luko and me – eventually decided I should follow him, just to make sure he was who he said he was. True enough, he went to the palace, walked in free as you like.'

'But . . . ?'

'But I decided to stay around for a while, and after about an hour he appeared again with someone I recognized, and it wasn't the Emperor.'

'Dulcitius.'

'How did you know?' Leof was evidently disappointed his revelation didn't come as a surprise.

'Who else would it be? One way or the other Dulcitius wants Marcus dead. Just because Stilicho stopped him once doesn't mean he won't try again. We should have known he'd have spies in Stilicho's house. The question is, how much does he know now? What did Anastasia —?'

'I followed them into the city,' Leof interrupted her. 'They thought they were clever, slipping up side streets and through alleyways, but I stayed with them. They met a man in a tavern. One of those you told us to keep a sharp watch for. A Hun.' Valeria closed her eyes. Uldin. What trickery of Hades was this? 'That's when I decided I needed to get word to you even if it meant leaving the lady with only old Luko for protection.'

'Marcus must know about this.' She reached for the tent flap.

'There's more, lady.'

Valeria froze in the doorway. 'Yes?'

'Even before this Julian started calling there was something strange happening,' the Saxon said carefully. 'The lady sometimes made it difficult for us to keep her safe.'

'In what way?'

'She had a habit of disappearing from her room at night.'

'We all need to do that sometimes,' Valeria said.

'This was only when she thought we were asleep, and for longer than it would take to visit the *latrina*.'

'A lover then. One of Stilicho's guards.'

Leof shook his head. 'Luko swears he saw her one night coming from the wing where Stilicho has his private offices.'

Valeria stood for a moment, considering the implications of what she'd been told. 'You will say nothing of this to anyone.'

XLV

Alaric stooped to enter the tent Marcus shared with Brenus. The Tervingi leader's appearance now bore little resemblance to the civilized Goth Marcus had first encountered in the ruined fort. His hair was a mass of tangled curls and his sandy beard covered his chest. His dishevelled appearance helped with his disguise, but like everyone on the march he stank and his clothes and hair were infested with crawling insects.

Marcus knew he looked and smelled little different from the Goth. He and Brenus took turns at picking the lice from their hair and clothes as much to ease the boredom, which had come to seem like a form of captivity, as anything else. They'd discovered that the Goths who surrounded Alaric were a capable set of men, skilled in arms and superb horsemen. Most had none of the trappings that would have been normal for a Roman cavalryman: all wore pot helmets of one fashion or another but only a few owned armour of chain or plate. The others preferred padded leather jackets in the Hun style. Likewise there was little uniformity in the weapons they carried. Sigaric, Alaric and Erman had swords, but the others favoured long, lance-like spears or curved eastern bows that could fire an arrow sixty or seventy paces and always hit the mark. Brenus had taken to exercising with them, and, when they sparred, Marcus noticed that his strength as well as his skill improved with each passing day. The boy became particularly friendly with Erman, who had a reasonable grasp of Latin and the patience to teach him Gothic words and phrases.

'You have a guest.' Alaric stepped to one side and a hooded figure pushed past him. Valeria drew back the hood and sniffed. 'God, this place stinks like a pigsty in summer. Don't you ever wash?'

Brenus cried out in delight at the sight of the familiar features. She stood, clearly enjoying their astonishment, and it was a moment before Marcus found his voice.

'How did you get here?'

'Two of Stilicho's Goths posed as deserters and smuggled me past Radagaisus's outriders.' She turned to Alaric. 'They know only that I was to be guided to a certain encampment, not who I was to meet. We've been watching this army for three days, and trying on the nerves it has been. I've seen slugs move faster and we'd never have located you if it hadn't been for the blue smoke from your morning fires.' Marcus had laid out bread and olives for the evening meal and she frowned when she noticed them. 'Stilicho believes Radagaisus must be running out of food by now, but you seem to be eating well enough.'

'We are only a few score strong and knew to prepare for this situation,' Alaric said. 'Radagaisus convinced himself he was coming to a land of plenty and tens of thousands rely on him to feed them. His advisers try to keep the true scale of the problem from him, but many go hungry and the rest watch their supplies dwindle.'

'You know this for certain?'

'Sigaric has appointed himself spokesman for the western Goths of this host,' Alaric told her. 'He is welcomed at Radagaisus's councils, where he listens to kings and princes, and warlords who would like to be kings and princes, talk themselves hoarse in the hope of getting a decision from their leader. On the first day of the advance, all the talk was of Ravenna, and a switch to the east. On the second the only thing Radagaisus would hear was Cremona in the west, where his wizards predicted trees already hanging with fruit, and fountains of beer for all I know. A week later and here we are still creeping south.'

'There must be no more talk of Ravenna or Cremona,' Valeria said forcefully. 'Nothing awaits you there but empty bellies and a shower of arrows.'

'Then where?'

'Bononia. Every ear of barley and grain of wheat stripped from the fields and hauled from the storehouses of the north now lies in the granaries of Bononia. Great herds of cows, sheep and pigs graze the meadows south of the city ready for the slaughter. The defenders tremble in fear, and the lords of Bononia have renounced the Emperor Honorius and await the arrival of their new overlord, the mighty Radagaisus.'

'Is any of this true?' Marcus demanded.

She gave him a look of scorn he hadn't seen since their childhood.

'True or not, it is what Radagaisus must be made to believe,' she insisted. 'If Sigaric has his ear, so much the better. Your Goths will become Radagaisus's scouts, forging far ahead of the army. Each day they will return with tales from wandering fugitives of the riches of Bononia and the weakness of its garrison. Is there any way Radagaisus can be goaded into moving faster?'

Alaric thought for a moment, then nodded. 'It is possible.' He stooped and marched from the tent, leaving Valeria, Marcus and Brenus alone.

'It is good to see you, sister,' Marcus smiled. 'But I wish you hadn't chosen to risk your neck like this.'

Brenus pushed himself to his feet and bowed. 'Aunt Valeria.'

'No need to be so formal, Brenus,' Valeria said. 'Marcus, we need to talk.'

An inflection in her voice sent a certain message and Brenus was at the tent door even before Marcus could make the suggestion.

'I'll be outside making sure there's no one within hearing distance.'

Valeria smiled her thanks. When he was gone she took a seat on his bedding opposite her brother. 'I need to be out of the camp well before dawn; I only wish it was possible to take both of you with me. Alaric can find another courier.'

'I doubt we would get very far,' Marcus said. 'The Goths are friendly enough and Alaric ensures that I am included in his councils, but everyone knows we are little more than well-treated hostages. For obvious reasons we never leave the camp. I teach Brenus swordplay and talk to him about what it is to be a leader, but he's like a hawk trapped in a cage. All he wants to do is gallop a horse with Leof or Ninian.'

Valeria frowned. 'Why would Alaric need you as a hostage if he's truly doing Stilicho's bidding?'

'He's like a man who always has to have two horses saddled and ready to ride,' Marcus said sourly. 'If the one doesn't suit him he will mount the other.'

'You truly think he's prepared to ally himself to Radagaisus?'

'He might replace Radagaisus if he could,' Marcus considered his words with care. 'Though I doubt even Alaric is capable of bending this undisciplined mob to his will. No, you can tell Stilicho that Marcus says Alaric is keeping his word, as far as is possible. He disappears into the night and practises his wizardry on the other Goth bands who ride with Radagaisus. Some are already pledged to him, but others need a little more persuasion. When the time comes I believe he will be able to fulfil his promise and weaken Radagaisus at the time of most need, but whether it will be enough, who knows?'

There was a weariness to the final words that was so unlike Marcus it concerned Valeria. 'Do not give up hope, brother, for Brenus's sake if not your own. A few more weeks and you will be free and an honoured member of Stilicho's staff.'

'Brenus is not the only one here who feels like a caged bird.' He managed a smile. 'Perhaps you're right and all will be well in the end, but I fear it may not be quite so simple. Let's not forget Uldin and his Huns.'

'No,' she said. 'We cannot forget Uldin.' She told him about Anastasia and her meetings with Dulcitius's agent and Leof's report that the two men had met with the Hun warlord. 'She wouldn't have told him anything deliberately,' Valeria assured him. 'But Leof said he was very persuasive.'

'What could she have revealed that would lead them to me?' Marcus shook his head. 'She knows better than to mention Alaric by name anywhere near Honorius's court and she isn't aware of the details of Stilicho's plan. We saved a Goth lord from the Huns, but what would that tell Dulcitius?'

'You forget that those Huns were Uldin's people and that he sent them to kill Alaric. Do not underestimate Dulcitius, Marcus; he is blinded by his hatred for you, but he is no fool. He may now suspect that Alaric was either on his way to Italia or to Radagaisus, and you met with him, and perhaps even became his friend. He may not know precisely where you are, but he will have his spies among Radagaisus's host, just as Stilicho has. All I ask is that you always have someone watching your back, brother.'

'It's probably nothing—'

He broke off as Brenus put his head through the tent door. 'You should see this, Father.' His voice was breathless with excitement. They followed him out into the darkness, which was broken by a glow on the northern horizon. 'I think something is burning in King Radagaisus's encampment.'

XLVI

A new urgency spread through Radagaisus's camp in the following days. At first light the king's Ostrogoth captains rode from encampment to encampment rousing the tribes and clans into motion. Previously, kings and princes, chieftains and warlords had each made their own decision when to set their followers moving, when to rest and when and where to halt for the night. Now instructions arrived that every tribe should be ready to move at dawn, and none would halt until Radagaisus halted. Bononia was the word on every lip. In Bononia lay all the riches and sustenance of northern Italia, enough to feed every man, woman and child for a month and more. At Bononia, surrounded by plenty, King Radagaisus would issue his demands to the Emperor and Honorius would comply or see his lands ravaged from north to south, east to west.

After the terrible fire that had consumed part of Radagaisus's supply park, Sigaric, on Alaric's instructions, ensured their warrior band was always at the forefront of the advance. Rumour swept the camp that agents of Stilicho were responsible for the blaze that had destroyed the king's wagons, but Radagaisus and his wizards had decided the disaster was an act of the gods brought on by the army's leaden-footed advance. Whatever the truth, Marcus couldn't help noticing Erman's look of grim satisfaction whenever the subject was mentioned.

'People are laughing that Radagaisus's new haste is because he will soon be forced to share their privations,' Alaric told Marcus as they rode south. 'But they are wrong. The flames didn't consume the luxuries he shares with his chosen ones. Those wagons you saw burning contained most of the fodder that keeps every mounted Goth, Suevian, Alan and Hun in the saddle. Horses need grain, and Radagaisus used that grain to wield his authority over the warriors of this host. He will try to keep it secret, but he has lost three fourths of the barley he was hoarding. No amount of grass can make up for that loss. He must reach Bononia, where salvation lies, before the grain runs out or his warriors will be carrying their saddles, not riding on them.'

'What is a Goth or an Alan without his horse?' Marcus murmured.

'Precisely,' Alaric nodded. 'I told your sister this before she left in the night and Stilicho will have heard of it before the day was out.'

'Everything depends on how Radagaisus reacts when he reaches Bononia.'

'There are already grumbles among the tribes that Radagaisus keeps his favourites supplied at their expense. Around the campfires it is whispered that he has no real plan.'

'I wonder who whispers such things?' Marcus said.

'Words are a much underrated weapon.' Alaric produced a wry laugh. 'Stilicho taught me that. They can be used to unite or to divide. A hint or a suggestion to a man troubled over his family's future may be of more use than the threat of a sword.'

'Perhaps Radagaisus knows this too?'

Alaric snorted. 'Such considerations are too subtle for King Radagaisus. He believes only in brute strength.'

Marcus had cause to remember those words later when a dozen warriors of Radagaisus's retinue appeared at Sigaric's compound as night fell and commanded he appear before the king.

'Why him?' Sigaric demanded. 'He's just another arse in a saddle.'

'That is for the king to decide.' The leader of the bodyguards had his hand on his sword hilt and his look said he was prepared to use it, even against an ally.

'Father?' Brenus's voice was little more than a whisper.

'Everything will be fine, Brenus,' Marcus assured his son, though his words sounded hollow even to him. Could it be something to do with the blaze? He felt Erman's eyes on him, but the part-Hun's expression gave nothing away. Marcus turned to the hooded figure who remained seated beside the fire. 'Look after the boy,' he said quietly.

'My word on it,' Alaric whispered. 'I'm sorry. I can do nothing for you now. For your sake and mine do not let the name Alaric pass your lips.'

Marcus went to where Sigaric stood confronting the men at the entrance of the compound. 'Lord Sigaric, I will need someone to speak for me, unless Radagaisus has Latin or Pictish.'

'What did he say?' the guard commander demanded.

'He's a Pict, from over the sea,' Sigaric said, and Marcus hid his relief that he'd picked up on his hint. 'He speaks no Gothic, though he has some Latin.'

'A Pict?'

Sigaric shrugged. 'I don't care where my men come from as long as they can hold a sword. I am his lord, so I will speak for him, though I don't know why Radagaisus bothers with humble folk like us.'

'That is for the king to decide,' the guard repeated. 'You accompany him at your own risk.'

Led by two warriors with torches they walked for what must have been a mile before they reached the flickering glow that marked King Radagaisus's compound. They passed through random groups of tents and circles of wagons, placing their feet carefully to avoid the carelessly ejected waste of their owners. Along the way they witnessed two wailing families burying relatives who'd died of sickness or hunger and Marcus wondered how many similar scenes were being enacted out there in the darkness. The guards made no attempt to bind his hands, which surprised him. It also gave him hope that, whatever the reason for this summons, some ambiguity remained about his status or his guilt.

At last they came to an enormous inner circle of wagons parked tight together to form a defensive barrier. Inside were the tents of the king's closest companions, his advisers and their retinues, who could be counted in their many hundreds, and his personal bodyguard. The tents in turn enclosed a broad open space lit by three great bonfires whose towering columns of sparks gave a hint at why Radagaisus was so content to believe his recent fiery loss might have been an accident. More ominously a smaller pile of logs and brush with a tall stake at its centre remained unlit. Around the perimeter, hundreds of warriors formed a circle, drinking and calling out to each other, or scuffling in mock combats.

The guards led Marcus and Sigaric into the open space and towards a raised platform decorated with two yellowing skulls on poles. Beyond it stood an enormous, richly decorated pavilion, but Marcus only had eyes for the massive figure slumped on a wooden throne at the centre of the platform. Radagaisus looked enormously fat, but Marcus guessed that was an illusion, and that he was actually enormously strong. Beside the king sat a surprisingly delicate, pretty woman in a blue dress, almost like a child's toy compared to her giant of a husband. Two children, a boy and a girl, sat at her feet. Radagaisus wore a tunic of green cloth tied at the waist with a belt of silver links, dark trousers, and leather boots. His hair was long, unkempt and black as a raven's wing, as was his beard which hung to his chest, adorned with gold rings plaited into the curls. Dark, close-set eyes glared out from beneath a heavy brow and fixed on the two men before him.

The guard commander mounted the platform to whisper in Radagaisus's ear, and the great head came up. To Marcus's surprise, the king had a voice entirely at odds with his appearance, deep and melodic, and his words, of which Marcus understood none, had a sing-song quality.

Sigaric answered in the same language, and when he'd finished he turned to Marcus with a troubled look. 'The king says that you are accused of being a traitor. He wishes to know how you answer this charge. I have said I speak for you, but I'm not sure how much good it will do.'

Traitor. Marcus flinched at the dreaded word. Now it all made sense. Valeria had been right. This was Dulcitius's work. He was forced almost to admire the way his enemy had placed his head on the block. The question now was how to remove his neck from beneath the axe. He drew himself up to his full height and met the king's gaze. 'Tell him that I am Cinead, a Pict of northern Britannia, and I want only to wield my sword at his side. I say that any man who accuses me of disloyalty is a liar.'

Sigaric translated the words and Radagaisus nodded slowly. 'And how do you come here, Pict who speaks the Roman tongue as if he was born with it?'

The question was uttered in a perfect conversational Latin and Marcus froze. For a moment the only sound was the fluttering of flames and the crackle of burning branches and he used the pause to take a breath, aware his next words would decide his fate.

'The reason I speak the Roman tongue is that I was born and raised in Britannia just beyond the Wall, where all men must learn it,' he said as if the accomplishment was of little consequence. 'I was captured in battle against the Romans. Our queen, Briga, believed she could defeat them and take the province, but she was betrayed. After the defeat, the Romans drove their prisoners south like cattle. We nobles were sold into slavery and I ended up on a farm outside Mediolanum. I was treated well enough, but I am no man's slave. I killed my owner and fled into the mountains. When your war bands came through the valley where I sought sanctuary, Sigaric's was the first I encountered, and I offered him my sword.'

'You say that anyone who accuses you of treason is a liar?'

'I do, lord king.'

'Yet it is I who accuse you, Pict. Am I a liar?'

A stillness fell over the makeshift arena. 'I believe you have been misled and poorly advised.' Marcus allowed his anger to show. 'Show me my accuser and put a sword in my hand and let the gods decide who is the liar.'

This was no random suggestion. Marcus had witnessed several of

Radagaisus's nightly revelries and Alaric had remarked on the king's fascination with contests of arms. Whoever was accusing Marcus undoubtedly knew his true identity, but for some reason was reluctant to reveal it. For now. If that changed it wouldn't only mean his own death. When Radagaisus dug a little deeper he would discover Alaric, and Brenus was with Alaric. Marcus had to force his accuser into the open now, and take his chances with a sword, to save his son. Radagaisus pondered the suggestion before nodding slowly.

'Bring him forward,' he called.

Two guards emerged from behind the platform with a third man stalking between them. They halted a dozen paces away and Marcus looked upon his accuser for the first time. The flat expressionless features of a Hun, deep-set, spiteful obsidian eyes, a knife-slit for a mouth and that tell-tale scar on his cheek. Bleda. No point in wondering how he'd come here or been able to track Marcus down. If Goths could come and go from Radagaisus's camp as freely as Alaric's men, a Hun could no doubt do the same.

'A Hun?' He spat in Bleda's direction. 'My accuser is a scheming back-stabbing Hun, the filth of the plains,' he took up a theme he'd heard the Goths use round the campfire. He nodded to Sigaric. 'Tell him. He's a coward who is happy to slaughter a village full of unarmed women and children, but will run away before their menfolk return.' He studied his enemy for any reaction, but Bleda only stared back, his expression unchanged. 'I have never set eyes on this abuser of goats. How can he accuse me of betraying my lord king?'

Radagaisus stood and Marcus realized for the first time just how tall he was. 'He says he followed you when you left the camp. You met with Stilicho's horse soldiers.'

A lie, but not one that was easy to disprove. It was Marcus's word against Bleda's, the way Dulcitius had always planned it to be if Radagaisus didn't simply have him killed. The Hun was just as Stilicho had described him, short and squat, muscled shoulders bulging from beneath a stained tunic cut off at the shoulder, and calves like tree trunks straining his leather trews. Nobody had taken Bleda's sword, which hung from his right hip. A smile touched the thin lips and Marcus realized he was anticipating the contest with pleasure. Uldin wouldn't have sent him if he hadn't been certain of the outcome.

'A lie,' Marcus shook his head wearily. 'Not that it makes any difference. Give me a sword and I will kill him for your entertainment, lord king, and then we can get back to killing Romans, the way it should be.'

Radagaisus produced a great booming laugh. 'You have spirit, Pict, I will give you that, and so I will give you a sword. It will be a pity when the Hun kills you.'

'What makes you think he'll do that?'

'Because I have seen him fight.'

XLVII

Bleda was grinning now. He pulled his tunic over his head to reveal a shaggy torso matted with dark hair. An expert with the blade, Stilicho said; well, Marcus had met fine swordsmen in the past and they were all dead. One of Radagaisus's guards handed him a sword in an ornate scabbard. He drew it free and handed the scabbard back, making two practice cuts to test the feel of the weapon and listen to how it made the air sing. It was much slimmer than the double-edged cavalry *spatha* he usually wielded, slightly curved and with a wicked single edge and needle point. Light, but it gave the impression of real strength and the hilt felt good in his hand.

'A good sword, lord king,' he bowed his head. 'I thank you for it.' He turned as Bleda drew his own sword.

And froze.

The dark eyes fixed him like a viper studying a mouse. Bleda was holding his sword in his left hand.

Marcus hesitated, but his mind was racing. He'd known left-handed soldiers among the garrisons along the Wall, and the first thing the drill instructors did was beat that left-handedness out of them. The Roman army thrived on discipline and uniformity. Anyone who was *different* was a liability. A man in a shield line depended on his neighbour to cover his blind spot. He couldn't do that if his sword was in the wrong hand. It was different in single combat. Bleda would only have fought right-handed opponents and his distinctiveness would give him a genuine advantage. Swordsmanship was as much about instinct and insight as skill: a flicker in an opponent's eyes, the twitch of a muscle. All that meant nothing when your enemy acted against every norm.

Bleda sensed his confusion and cried out something in his own harsh tongue.

'He tells you to come and die,' Radagaisus called, before Sigaric could translate.

Marcus took a deep breath and stepped forward to meet the challenge. His eyes never left those of the Hun as he advanced across the downtrodden grass and flattened earth, so he saw the moment Bleda noticed that he'd switched Radagaisus's sword from his right hand to his left. Not just confusion, consternation. Yet that consternation lasted only a moment before it was replaced by resolution and an animal growl from deep in the Hun's chest.

Marcus had no illusions that his sleight of hand gave him any decisive advantage. Certainly he'd practised many times with his blade in his left hand, most recently when he'd been teaching Brenus the finer points of swordsmanship. But exercises against an opponent who wasn't trying to kill you were a far cry from fighting for your life. He'd placed a small doubt in Bleda's mind, nothing more. It had given him, not an edge, exactly, but perhaps a tiny sliver of hope.

Bleda charged without warning, closing in a scuttling, crab-like run. The Hun feinted right with his blade as if for a back cut to Marcus's left, but in the last second he changed to a full-blooded lunge that would have skewered his opponent through the middle. Marcus, tensed and prepared, spun clear, ready for a neck-high back cut of his own, only for Bleda to pull out of thrust and step back. The crowd of Alan, Goth and Suevi warriors roared their approval. Marcus tossed his sword from his left hand to his right and back again and the roars grew louder still. Bleda glared his hatred, snake eyes glittering like black diamonds in the flickering light of the bonfires.

The Hun edged to his right, sword held at shoulder height, searching for an opening. Marcus moved with him step for step, testing the ground as he went, and giving his opponent nothing. A niggling irritation scratched at the back of his mind. Bleda was as light on his feet as a dancer and he moved with all the menace of a prowling wolf. That initial charge had been too laboured, too predictable. This cautious feeling out was unlike the merciless killer Stilicho had described. He almost sensed the moment Bleda tensed to unleash the whirlwind. And pre-empted it with one of his own. Three steps took him across the gap, the beautiful, deadly blade of Radagaisus's sword sweeping up in a smooth arc designed to slice Bleda's flesh from belly to shoulder. Bleda's mind was focused on his own planned attack and it took him a heartbeat to realize what was happening.

His speed saved him, or perhaps Marcus just wasn't as quick as he'd once been. Bleda arched his body back, sucking in his guts, face flinching at the dreadful wound he could almost feel. The sword point slipped by a hairsbreadth from the flesh of his stomach and swept up to score the skin of his right breast bone deep. The Hun cried out at the sting of the blade, but his own sword was already probing for a weakness as Marcus recovered from the stroke. Marcus knew he couldn't give Bleda a single opportunity. Praying the shock of the wound would slow his enemy, he resorted to brute strength, striking one hammer blow after another that Bleda had no choice but to parry or die in the attempt. Marcus drove his opponent back and back, each retreating step punctuated by the ear-splitting clash of iron on iron and the encouraging shouts of the audience. Bleda's eyes darted to right and left seeking some way to regain the initiative, but there was no respite from the relentless attack. Marcus saw the moment the eyes widened as he felt the heat of the flames at his back, where Marcus had deliberately forced him towards the nearest bonfire. The air filled with the stink of singed hair and Bleda's next step took him into the glowing ashes on the perimeter of the fire.

Suddenly the Hun was down, crouched on one knee with the blade of his sword held protectively but uselessly over his head. A dead man.

Marcus moved in for the kill, the sword point searching for Bleda's throat. Too slow. Perhaps the billowing flames or the heat distracted him, or he was wary of Bleda's still deadly potential, but before he could make the killing strike his eyes were filled with fire from the glowing embers his opponent had scooped up with his right hand. Marcus dashed them away but his weeping vision told him Bleda was already on him. Somehow he managed to parry a cut that would have taken his head off at his shoulders, but the act jarred his wrist so the shock of it ran down his arm to his elbow. His fingers could barely feel the sword hilt and he cringed at the next blow that would kill him. Yet Bleda too had suffered in that terrible coming together and his movements were slowed. Marcus switched his sword from left hand to right and as the blades clashed again he managed to force Bleda's upwards, allowing him to stoop beneath it and spin behind his enemy. Bleda roared in frustration, then screamed as Marcus drew his blade across Bleda's lower back, the edge biting deep into the soft flesh beneath the ribs.

Marcus circled his enemy and Bleda stood shuddering at something terrible happening inside him. The sword dropped from the dying Hun's fingers, but he remained upright and Marcus looked without pity into the disbelieving eyes. He turned to Radagaisus, who stood on the edge of his platform with his fists clenched.

'Finish it,' the king said.

Marcus gritted his teeth and drove the point of the sword upwards beneath Bleda's breastbone and felt the moment it pierced the clenching muscle of the Hun's still beating heart. Using all his strength he kept Bleda upright and drove him back until he could feel the heat of the bonfire on his face, and with a roar heaved the twitching body from the bloody iron and into the crackling inferno of logs and branches. He watched as Bleda's hair flared like a torch and his trews became blackened and charred. His head had landed in the fiercest part of the blaze and the flesh began to bubble and the dark eyes melted back into his head.

'You fought well, Pict who talks like a Roman.' Marcus turned to find Radagaisus towering over him. He handed over the sword and the king took it in his giant paw and studied the gore-stained blade. 'The gods say you are not a traitor. Radogast is not so sure. Perhaps a fighter like you I should keep close?'

Marcus shrugged. 'My sword is yours, lord king.' Little blue flames appeared on Bleda's body as fat liquefied, caught light and flared. 'But Sigaric has few warriors and you have many.'

Radagaisus's lips twisted in a lazy half-smile. 'And maybe it is better not to have a viper living under your thatch. But I will be watching you, Pict. Fight well when we meet Stilicho at Bononia and you will have riches and honours. Otherwise,' he nodded towards the blackening corpse among the flames.

Almost in a dream, Marcus walked from the arena with Sigaric at his side and calls of congratulation in his ears. It appeared that a dead Hun, whether he fought beside the Goths, Alans and Suevi or not, was a matter of celebration. It wasn't until they were clear of Radagaisus's compound that he leaned against a wagon wheel and emptied the contents of his stomach on the ground.

Sigaric looked away, but Marcus heard muffled laughter. He recognized two of Radagaisus's guards a few paces back. They continued walking with the pair a short distance behind them.

Sigaric shook his head. 'You won the fight, but Radagaisus does not trust you. He will have men watching you day and night from now on.'

'He told me.'

'But that means you cannot escape before Stilicho closes in on Radagaisus's host.'

'I had the impression that's what Alaric wanted,' Marcus said.

'No,' the Goth shook his head. 'He was going to send you with Brenus once we reach Bononia.'

Marcus wasn't so sure, but he could tell Sigaric believed what he was saying.

'Thank you for speaking for me tonight,' he said.

'I thought I was going to see you die.'

They reached the camp and Marcus went to his tent. Brenus let out a cry and leapt up to put his arms round him. 'I didn't think you were coming back, Father.' He struggled to get the words out and his eyes were wet with tears.

Marcus hugged him back and smiled. 'I told you everything was going to be all right.'

Alaric ducked into the tent and Brenus looked from the Goth to his father. He shrugged and made for the doorway. 'No, Bren, you should stay,' Marcus said.

'What happened?' Alaric said. 'I wasn't sure . . .'

'Didn't Sigaric tell you?'

'I haven't seen him. One of the guards reported you were back.'

'Someone told Radagaisus I was a traitor.'

'Who?'

'A Hun called Bleda. Uldin, or Dulcitius and Uldin, sent him to kill me, one way or another.'

'Bleda, Christ save us,' Alaric gaped. 'And you are here.' He took Marcus's arm and spun him round. 'Where are your wounds? You killed Bleda?'

'Yes. I killed him and threw him on the funeral pyre he intended for me.'

'Then you did the world a service, my friend,' Alaric said earnestly. 'And Alaric. I will not forget this. You won your fight and Radagaisus set you free.'

'But he doesn't trust me.'

'No?' Alaric pursed his lips. 'Then he will be watching you.'

'Me, but not you.' Alaric nodded his understanding and turned to leave. 'There's one other thing,' Marcus continued. 'Radagaisus believes he will have to fight Stilicho to get the food that's stored in Bononia.'

'Then let us ensure Stilicho receives the invitation,' the Goth grinned. 'Brenus,' he turned to the boy. 'Get ready. I will prepare a message for the general. You'll be going out tonight.'

Anastasia trod gently along a corridor lit only by the barely discernible glow of the shielded oil lamp in her right hand. She knew where she was going now so there was no hesitation in her steps. But despite the familiarity with her route, her heart hammered against her breast-bone and the hand that held the lamp shook. She could hardly believe the courage it had taken the first time she'd done this. Not knowing if the halls were guarded – Stilicho's guards, it turned out, were all out-side the villa after dark – or where she was going. She had started with one master, who had promised her a life of wealth and ease in Salona if she did his bidding. Now she had more than one, and had secured a future beyond her wildest imaginings. She almost laughed at Marcus Flavius Victor's blandishments of a life trailing at the tails of a soldier's cloak. How could he have ever believed she would be satisfied to be a common camp follower? But this would be the last time. She had insisted on that. Luko and the others were becoming suspicious.

She turned a corner and reached the door she sought. It creaked slightly as she pushed it open and she felt as if a knife point had been run down her spine. Pitch dark inside, the curtains must be closed, but she knew where the desk was. All she had to do was read the document and carry its contents in her head until her meeting with Julian in the morning. Her knee knocked a stool and she reached out to feel for the edge of the desk. Yes. She took a breath and removed the shield from the oil lamp.

'You!'

Anastasia screamed in terror as the lamp illuminated a face twisted in rage and contempt. She turned to try to escape, but her way was barred by two of Stilicho's personal guard.

'Who put you up to this?' Serena hissed. 'You hesitate, girl? It is of no matter. Stilicho's inquisitors will soon squeeze the truth from you, though I doubt any man will look at you again, without your nose and ears.'

'No,' Anastasia cried. 'I will tell you everything.'

'Very well,' Serena said. 'But your fate is not mine to command. Only Stilicho himself can decide that.'

XLVIII

Bononia (modern Bologna)

Radagaisus's encampments encircled Bononia so tightly not even a mouse could escape the besieged city. Marcus and Alaric had a perfect view of the king's preparations because Sigaric and his band had set up camp opposite the north gate, close to the king's compound. For three days Radagaisus roamed the perimeter with his advisers and his wizards, seeking out some weak spot in Bononia's defences, and every day his frown grew deeper. The depth of his concern became clear on the fourth day, when they watched the king and his wizards pour Bleda's ashes into a stream and break his sword and throw it in after them.

'It is a sacrifice to Godan their war god and Radagaisus's personal deity,' Alaric didn't keep the scorn from his voice. 'He doesn't know what to do. Look at those stone ramparts and the numbers of defenders lining them. He doesn't have ladders tall enough to reach the top or the warriors agile enough to make the climb.'

'A Roman army would be equipped with siege towers and catapults,' Marcus said thoughtfully. 'They wouldn't give the defenders a moment's peace. And all the while a covered ram would be battering away at the gates and tunnellers undermining the walls.'

'That is not the Goth way,' Alaric sniffed. 'We are warriors not diggers.'

'It would make sense to try an assault even if he's not certain of succeeding,' Marcus persisted. 'At best only two or three out of every ten of the defenders is a soldier. Most will be farmers who've sought refuge in the city with their families. There's no telling how they'd react in an attack.'

'And no telling how his warriors would react if the attack failed,' Alaric said. 'His foragers have barely come up with a few sheaves of barley and a couple of stray goats in the last day's march. The majority of his horses are on their last legs and the people have left a trail of abandoned wagons for the last twenty miles because they've been forced to eat the oxen that pull them. Radagaisus knows his warriors are beginning to lose faith. When Stilicho comes, my Tervingi tribes will be the first to desert. The only question is how many will follow them.'

But where was Stilicho?

When he came, it must be from the west, and Sigaric's scouts were on constant patrol to signal the first sight of his army. He would come from the west, pin Radagaisus against the mountains and destroy him. Yet all the scouts had been able to report was the cavalry screen that had flanked Radagaisus's advance since he'd left the Alps.

'Perhaps he is waiting for Radagaisus to attack Bononia?' Alaric chewed his lip and stared westwards.

'He will come,' Marcus assured him.

He must come. Marcus's future depended on it, and more so Alaric's, when he considered it. The Goth had staked everything on Radagaisus's defeat and Stilicho's gratitude in the aftermath. If Stilicho failed him in either part his power would be weakened, perhaps fatally so. It occurred to Marcus that Stilicho could use the invasion as an opportunity to destroy *both* Radagaisus and Alaric. But Stilicho had given Alaric his word. Had he changed so much? And would he sacrifice Marcus to make it happen? Alaric gave him a puzzled look as a bitter laugh escaped his lips. What was it he had said, not so long ago: *I will use any weapon in the furtherance of Rome's defence.*

Away to their left a delegation was mustering outside Radagaisus's compound.

'What's happening?' Alaric demanded.

'King Radagaisus is sending an emissary to Bononia to offer the city generous terms of surrender if they give up their food supplies,' Sigaric informed them.

'We should see this.' The Goth pulled up his hood and led Marcus towards the entrance to Radagaisus's compound, where a crowd had already gathered. By the time the emissary and his escort returned the throng was becoming restive, but the guards pushed their way through to the compound using their spear butts and disappeared inside. Soon after, a messenger appeared in the gateway.

'They are looking for Latin speakers,' Alaric translated. 'As many as they can find.'

Marcus stared at him. 'What's going on?'

'This is your chance to find out.' The Goth pushed him forward. 'This man speaks Latin,' he shouted.

'Bring him here,' one of the guards said. The man's eyes narrowed. 'You're the Pict who killed Bleda the Hun?'

'Yes.'

'Then go inside, the king is waiting to instruct you in your duties.'

Marcus glanced back over his shoulder, but Alaric had already disappeared into the crowd. He did as he was instructed and entered the compound. Radagaisus stood on a dais with his advisers in front of his tent where fifteen or twenty men had gathered. He recognized Marcus and frowned, but otherwise seemed unsurprised at his presence. Marcus noticed he looked paler than normal and appeared tense.

When the crowd of volunteers had built up to about a hundred the king stepped forward.

'I have offered the people of Bononia the most favourable terms for the surrender of the city on condition the authorities give up the food stocks they are holding on behalf of the Emperor,' he announced in his perfect Latin. 'However, the city fathers claim that no such stocks exist and there is no point in my besieging Bononia. They say government troops stockpiled many tons of food and gathered thousands of livestock here until ten days ago, when they drove the supplies and the herds south.' The suggestion that the much heralded bonanza had slipped from their fingers brought a gasp from the assembled men, but the king held up a hand. 'There is no need for panic or concern, enough food for all exists and it still lies almost within our grasp, but I must be certain these people are not duping us. To this end they have offered to allow a hundred of our folk through the city gates, in pairs and under escort. Once inside you will be given free access to every granary and warehouse, private houses and princely mansions. Your task is to test the truth of their claims, to search the warehouses and discover what food remains and what was taken. They assure me of their complete cooperation. If that is not forthcoming I have said I will storm the city, burn it and kill everyone within the gates. You will say nothing of this to any man before you return to me with this information, on pain of death.'

Marcus's mind whirled. Now he saw it all. Stilicho had never intended to attack Radagaisus at Bononia. The city was just a stepping stone to lure his enemy into the mountains. Once they were in the midst of that labyrinth of valleys and hills, it would be all but impossible for Radagaisus to deploy his army against the Romans as a single overwhelming force. With nothing at Bononia, Radagaisus had no choice but to follow the bait south. But what did this mean for Alaric's grand plan and how would the Goth react when he discovered they'd been tricked as much as Radagaisus? Alaric had to know, but Radagaisus's threat made it impossible to contact him. Already they were being herded towards the gate and pushed into their pairs. Marcus was matched with a confused Ostrogoth farmer who clutched his cloth hat to his stomach and clearly wanted none of this.

A line of guards flanked each side of the little column as it was marched out of Radagaisus's compound to the main gate of Bononia. Marcus searched for Alaric and found him among the crowd being kept well back away to his right. He could see the confusion in the Goth's eyes, but what answer could he give? He shrugged and allowed himself to be herded towards the besieged city. They halted just out of bowshot of the walls while a conversation took place between the guard commander and a soldier in one of the two gate towers. Eventually the guards stepped aside and motioned the pairs forward. Marcus was close to the front of the column and he saw the gate open a fraction. As the first pair approached an order rang out from the tower for the others to halt. After a moment the Goths disappeared inside and the second pair were ushered forward.

Marcus and his companion, who introduced himself nervously as Tribi, crossed the threshold minutes later and were taken into the care of a pair of Bononian merchants and an armed guard.

'We are at your service.' The elder of the two traders twitched his nose at the scent of unwashed Goth. 'We will take you where you will,' he assured them. 'Nothing will be hidden from you.'

He led the way through the streets of shops and workshops, apartment blocks and fine town houses, where similar small groups were criss-crossing in front of them from building to building. Emerging into a square, Marcus saw a wooden structure to their left, a large barn or granary. 'That,' he said. 'I would like to inspect that.'

Their guides took them to the door, which proved to be unlocked, and led them inside to be met with the sweet, malty scent of grain. Individual kernels of barley and oats lay scattered on the floor, but the cavernous interior remained echoingly empty. 'This was our own supply,' the elder said with a tear in his eye. 'They did not only take what was brought here. They took everything.'

'Then how do you eat?' Marcus demanded.

'We have food to survive ten days at most,' the man said. 'And even so, we are like enough to go hungry.'

'Show us,' Marcus said.

The elder guided them through the streets, stopping along the way only to visit another empty granary, until they reached a substantial mansion set in its own grounds.

'This is my home,' he said. The mansion was built on two floors and surrounded a small courtyard on three sides. The elder showed them some amphorae of wine in a storeroom, an empty granary and a single goat bleating in a paddock. The kitchen held a few sacks of grain, and his wide-eyed wife and children watched as Marcus inspected them. Not ten days' supply, more like six. Marcus sent Tribi to search the other rooms and he returned shaking his head.

'They are as hungry as we are.'

Back on the street Marcus indicated a dried cowpat, one of many that dotted Bononia's thoroughfares. 'Our king mentioned cattle,' he said. 'What happened to them?'

Unperturbed by the abrupt change of approach, the elder led them up a narrow stairway that carried them to the wall close to the south gate. 'They took them all.' He pointed to a broad grassy swathe on either side of the road, marked by thousands of hoofprints and cut by the wheels of scores of carts. 'To Florentia.'

Marcus had seen enough. He and Tribi walked back through the city to the north gate and out towards the encampments. They made their report to one of King Radagaisus's officials and then Marcus managed to slip away.

He hadn't gone far when Alaric appeared at his side. 'What is it?' the Goth demanded. 'What's going on? There are so many rumours.'

Marcus told him what Radagaisus had said and what he'd seen in the city. 'Stilicho isn't coming and Radagaisus can't stay here,' he said.

Alaric stopped in his tracks with a grimace almost of pain on his bearded features. 'He gave me his word.'

Marcus drew him aside into the space between two tents. 'He was never coming. He always intended to lure Radagaisus into the mountains where he couldn't escape. The question is what it means for you?'

He saw the calculations running through Alaric's mind. The Goth started walking quickly towards Sigaric's encampment. 'I cannot allow my people to be led into a trap with Radagaisus. They must be told to leave now. I'd intended that they would desert Radagaisus and fight at Stilicho's side, but that cannot happen. He will face his enemy with five thousand fewer cavalry than I had planned.'

'You should go with them.' Marcus took his arm. 'What good can you do now?'

Alaric shrugged his hand away. 'I will not run away. Stilicho gave me his word and, despite what has happened here, I have learned to trust that word. If I am not there at the death, what will Alaric and his Goths mean in the grand scheme of things?'

Marcus saw the truth of what he said, but he shook his head.

'The only question is whose death?'

XLIX

Ticinum (Pavia)

'King Radagaisus will reach Bononia tonight or early tomorrow.'
Brenus stood nervously in front of Flavius Stilicho, who was flanked by
his commanders, Sarus the Goth and the intimidating Hun warlord
Uldin. 'My master said to tell you everything is in place as you desired.
Radagaisus's army is ripe for the taking.'

'How would this child know?' Uldin demanded. 'And who is his
master? It could be a trap.'

Brenus's eyes glinted dangerously at the accusation, but Stilicho
raised a hand. 'None of these things need concern you, Lord Uldin.
All you need to know is that I have faith in both the messenger and his
master. I have no doubt Radagaisus and his host are approaching
Bononia.'

'As you intended,' Sarus pointed out. 'Yet you remain at Ticinum
with your army a week's march away while Radagaisus prepares to feast
on all the abundance you have gathered for him at Bononia. We could
have been at Regium now, poised to fall like a stooping hawk on the
Greuthungi and their allies.'

'For once I agree with the Goth,' Uldin said. 'This idleness is unseemly. We have been acting like cattle herders rather than soldiers. It is time to bloody our swords. We should move now on Bononia before Radagaisus has the opportunity to replenish his supplies.'

'Radagaisus will not replenish his supplies at Bononia,' Stilicho said. 'For the simple reason that there are no supplies at Bononia, or what little there is would not feed even a fraction of his great host for a single day. When he reaches the city, the populace will throw themselves upon his mercy, open their empty granaries to him and tell him that Stilicho's men have carried off all that was held there.'

'Carried off to where?' Sarus didn't hide his puzzlement.

'To Florentia, a few tempting days' march south through the mountains. And that, Lord Uldin, is where you will bloody your swords.'

'I know those mountains,' Uldin frowned. 'It will take your legions ten days to follow in Radagaisus's tracks and there are twenty or thirty places he could leave a rearguard to delay us while he attacks Florentia at his leisure. You must know the city is less able to withstand a siege even than Bononia?'

'Oh, I believe Florentia will be able to hold off Radagaisus's army, given that the garrison has been reinforced and its defences strengthened,' Stilicho said.

'For how long against starving, desperate men?' the Hun snorted.

'For a day or two at least.' Stilicho was clearly enjoying his subordinates' confusion.

'A day? Will you fly your army over the mountains, general? Because I can assure you my horses do not have wings.'

'Why would I fly, Lord Uldin, when I can sail? It will take my legions two days to march to Genua, where a fleet awaits great enough to accommodate all, even your wingless horses. Two days' sail to Pisa and a day's march overland to Florentia, where Radagaisus will have spent his time preparing to place the city under siege, only to discover it is his own army which is besieged. Prepare your forces, my lords. My legates have already been alerted. We march at dawn.'

Brenus hesitated, unsure whether he was dismissed or not. He was exhausted, but exhilarated. When he'd left Marcus and Alaric he'd ridden through the night until he'd met a patrol of Sarus's Goths, who'd made their intentions clear with their spear points. Fortunately, he'd remembered the watchword and the atmosphere had instantly changed and he'd been hurried to the general's pavilion.

'Stay, boy,' Stilicho smiled. 'I have more questions for you.'

Sarus and Uldin left the tent whispering to each other, and a slim figure appeared from behind a screen by the rear wall. 'Valeria. Aunt.' Brenus didn't hide his delight.

'You did well, Brenus.' Valeria smiled and rumpled his dark hair. 'Especially under such provocation from the Hun.'

'You heard everything?' Stilicho said.

'Yes, and I was as surprised as Uldin. You tricked us all.'

'I believed it was necessary. No howls of outrage?'

'What? That you had me lie to my brother and placed Brenus in danger for no reason?'

'It was true when I gave you the information,' Stilicho said. 'And I did not believe Brenus would be in any peril. Alaric is a formidable man, and decent.'

'I don't understand,' Brenus interrupted. 'What profit was there in deceiving my father and Alaric?'

'They had to believe, as Radagaisus had to believe, that Bononia was the answer to his prayers. Otherwise . . .'

'Otherwise they might have revealed it when he put them to the question.' Now Valeria didn't hide her scorn. 'Marcus would never have given Radagaisus the satisfaction.'

'But could I take that chance?' Stilicho countered. 'If Radagaisus discovered Bononia was a ruse he would have tried to conserve his supplies and eked out his fodder to allow him to reach Florentia with sufficient to sustain a siege. Now he is a commander without options.'

'You must be very certain of victory at Florentia,' Brenus said quietly. 'I have seen Radagaisus's host and been at the very heart of it. I believe he still has the strength to crush anything that stands in his way, including your legions.'

'Ah,' Stilicho smiled at the boy's presumption. 'But you have not seen my legions fight. In any case, it is my hope and my belief that Radagaisus will be seriously weakened militarily before he reaches Florentia.'

Valeria fixed him with a stare. 'But that depends on Alaric, the barbarian, being truer to his word than you have been to yours.'

'Only time will tell.' Stilicho turned away.

'Why did Lord Uldin call me the wolf's cub when he was leaving with the other man?'

Stilicho froze and Valeria stared at Brenus. 'What did he say?'

'He said he would deal with the wolf's cub now that the wolf was gone.'

'Gone?' Valeria cried. 'What has happened to Marcus?'

'Nothing,' Brenus grinned. 'Uldin sent a man called Bleda to kill him, but Father killed Bleda.'

Valeria almost choked with relief.

'Christ's bones,' Stilicho said. 'That would have been a fight worth seeing. Do not concern yourself, lady. I will keep you and Brenus close. Uldin will not dare to harm you. But Brenus . . . Uldin and Sarus were conversing in Gothic.'

'While I was with Radagaisus, my friend Erman taught me his language and Father taught me swordsmanship.' Brenus shrugged. 'There was nothing much else to do.'

King Radagaisus studied the heights around him. His passage through the Alps had taught him to respect the mountains – in many ways it was miraculous he'd completed the journey with so many followers – and he had never expected to return to them so soon. Of course, these mountains were mere pimples compared to the towering peaks in the north, but they still managed to fill him with something like dread.

He'd never planned to come this far south, into the very maw of Italia. In fact, he sometimes wondered if he'd ever had any plan at all. He'd been driven from his lands far to the east of the Danuvius by the constant Hun raids. Good lands, fertile and well watered, but not worth dying for. When the Greuthungi sought a new home it seemed natural that people had looked to him, a great presence and a renowned warrior, for leadership and protection. As they'd wandered, other wanderers, equally landless, joined them, sometimes individuals, sometimes whole families and clans, and then entire tribes of Alans, Ostrogoths, Visigoths and Suevi. His 'people', as he'd come to think of them, had grown in scale like one of the mountain avalanches he'd witnessed during the spring, and as they grew they created a momentum of their own. It had quickly become clear to him that no single tract of land could sustain such a vast host for any length of time. They would pick it clean for a season, perhaps creating a small surplus to see them through the winter, then move on. Of course, this could not go on indefinitely, any man could see that. They must disperse, or die. But there was no escape for Radagaisus. They called him 'King' now, but he ruled through his council, the tribal leaders, lesser kings, and their meddling wizards and priests. One day the only word a man heard uttered was 'Rome'. If the east would not feed them the Empire's rich lands beyond the Danuvius would provide their salvation. So they'd crossed the river. Even then there'd been no decision whether to move south or north, they'd simply followed the best grazing and water.

And now they were here. Hungrier than ever, and ignored by the Emperor he'd looked to for salvation.

Bononia had been a chastening experience. Faced with those unscalable stone walls and threatening towers, he hadn't known what to do. His vast numbers had meant nothing. Given time he believed he would have found a solution, but they didn't have time. Would it be any different at Florentia? He didn't know and the very thought sent a shiver through him. But what else could they do? The wheel tracks and thousands of hoofprints on the trail were proof that great quantities of food lay not far ahead. They must reach Florentia and take it, or they would waste away.

In truth, the wasting had already begun. When the first warrior band had broken camp and ridden away after the discovery that Bononia contained none of the supplies they needed, he hadn't been too concerned. At least it meant fewer mouths to feed. But they were followed by another, and then another, all western Goths and their Alan allies. Always the most effective warriors he depended on to defeat any Roman army that chose to face him. Eventually, perhaps half his mounted strength had deserted him. The camp followers, the old, sick, women and children, who were only a burden, stayed, because they had nowhere else to go.

A burden that now lay far behind. Time was his enemy, and that meant speed was paramount. A warrior on a horse, even the skeletal, spavined nags that were just about all that remained, could cover the ground at three times the rate of a heavily laden bullock cart. Even a soldier on foot could move at twice their speed. So he had ordered his army to abandon their families and forge ahead at their best pace to take Florentia and its supplies as quickly as possible. It meant the civilians were at the mercy of any cavalry who managed to get past the rearguard he'd left to block the pass, but by the time they caught up with the army there should be food aplenty.

Another glance at the mountainous heights. They protected his flanks, but what did they hide? His scouts assured him that nothing lay between them and Florentia, except a few late-moving farmers seeking the protection of the city walls. But, encouraging though it was, that also begged a question.

Where was Stilicho?

L

Florentia (Florence)

Marcus emerged from the valley with Sigaric's band somewhere near the van of Radagaisus's army, which Alaric now reckoned at thirty thousand horse and foot soldiers all told. The baggage train, with the Goth, Alan and Suevi families who made up another fifty thousand, were two or three days behind, left to make their own way while the warriors rushed ahead to begin the siege Radagaisus hoped would be concluded in days. The cramped confines of the gorge opened out onto a broad plain, and, away to his left, perhaps three miles distant, Marcus identified the smudge of smoke that marked Florentia. But the city wasn't burning. It was preparing.

At the base of that smoke men would be heating oil to boiling point and melting pitch ready to pour on any warrior who attempted to climb the walls. The fires would be surrounded by flammable material ready to be launched from catapults or dropped on any covered rams that attempted to batter in the gates. Florentia wouldn't be like Bononia, where the walls were manned by militia and civilians. Stilicho would have ensured the food and fodder Radagaisus so desperately needed was defended by soldiers skilled in the arts of war and ready to do anything to keep the Goths at bay. They'd be well stocked with arrows and throwing spears, with piles of boulders to hand at regular intervals along the parapet, sourced from the river he could see twinkling to his front.

Alaric had never visited Florentia during his previous incursions into Italia, but he knew of the city from his spies.

'It is not a single fortress, but one inside the other,' he said. 'The outer walls, which encompass the main city, are formidable enough, and extend down to the river, defending the only bridge for miles. The inner walls are higher still and protect what was once the original fort and colony. If Radagaisus believes he will crack this nut in a few days, I fear he has a hard lesson coming.'

'He must believe it,' Marcus said. 'Or he has to accept that he has led these tribes to their destruction. If he doesn't take Florentia his people will starve and his army will melt away.' He turned in the saddle to survey their surroundings. The mountains formed a barrier on all four sides, enclosing a plain twelve or fourteen miles in length and shaped vaguely like a fish, with Florentia at its head in the east. 'Even you must admit that Stilicho, though he duped us both, chose a fine place for his trap?'

'A fine place if he was here to exploit it,' Alaric snorted. 'But where is he? Somewhere up north near Bononia with fifty thousand people and all their carts and baggage blocking the only valley like the stopper in a wineskin. Has he the stomach to slaughter them, do you think? Even that would take days. I curse the day I ever met the man. I've done everything asked of me, but here I am, as helpless as a babe in arms, able only to suck my thumb as Radagaisus goes about his business unhindered.'

A horn blared from the head of the army and announced that Radagaisus was already eager to go about what Alaric called 'his business'. The call summoned Sigaric and the other tribal leaders to a council of war on a hill north of Florentia where the king had raised his banner and erected his tents.

Sigaric returned as they were setting up camp close to the river on the western side of the city. By now they'd had a chance to see the walls, and formidable they were too, lined with spears whose owners stared out implacably at the vast horde that surrounded them.

'Because of the quality of our horses we are to form a mobile reserve in case of any attack on the siege lines,' Sigaric called. The news brought a cheer from the men close enough to hear him. Better to be sitting in the saddle than trying to climb those parapets dodging spears and boiling oil. As he approached Alaric, Sigaric lowered his voice. 'Radagaisus is sending an emissary to Florentia's elders before night-fall. They are to evacuate the city in the morning taking with them the food they can carry, with a guarantee of safe conduct.'

'And if they don't?' Alaric asked.

'There will be no quarter. He will slaughter every man, woman and child when the city is taken.'

'A good offer,' Marcus said. 'But a foolish threat. He has given them a reason to fight to the death, if they needed one. It doesn't make any difference. This is not Bononia. Florentia was never going to surrender without a fight.'

They watched as the tribes settled into their encampments around the city walls. 'They are not as strong as they look,' Sigaric revealed of the walls. 'Florentia is a city that is outgrowing itself. There are several places where buildings span the ramparts. Radagaisus is confident he will prevail before his people reach here.'

'Then may Christ save the people of Florentia,' Alaric said. 'And where in God's name is Stilicho?'

That night Marcus rolled up in his blanket and dreamed of the Wall. Picts in their thousands flooded towards him over the northern hills and he didn't have enough men to stem the tide. Should he reinforce the left or the right? The greatest pressure was against the centre, but surely that was a ruse. If he didn't make a decision soon, it would be too late . . .

'Father.' The voice seemed to come from far away. Was he calling for help from Brenus, his father, or Maximus, his blood-father? It didn't matter, there wasn't enough time. He had to decide. 'Father?'

He opened his eyes and looked into the impossible. 'No,' he said. 'It cannot be. You're safe. A dream, nothing more.' He closed his eyes again, but a hand shook his shoulder, the movement so violent that he grabbed the wrist of his assailant and twisted. He heard a sharp cry and a fist thumped into his face. 'Christus.'

'Never hurt me again, Father. I am not a child any longer.'

'Brenus?' Marcus blinked tears from his eyes and wiped blood from his nose. 'I don't—'

'Stilicho is coming.' Those familiar features, like looking into his own past, the dark eyes gleaming.

'Stay here.' Marcus pulled on his boots and rolled out of his blanket. He was gone for only a few moments before he returned with Alaric. 'Now tell us.'

'When the time comes,' Brenus recounted the words he had learned by rote, 'Radagaisus and all around him must understand that the terms he is offered are as favourable as General Stilicho can give. All will be spared.' He looked directly into Alaric's eyes. 'It is exactly as you agreed earlier.'

'But what does this mean?' Alaric demanded. 'If he is coming as you say, when? What is his strategy?'

'That is all he said,' Brenus shrugged. 'Spread the word. Let all know that an honourable surrender is better than death.'

'You came from him?' Marcus shook his head, still stunned by his son's sudden appearance. 'Where is he now and why did he send you, of all people?'

'Of all people? Because he trusted me to reach you. He discovered I could speak Gothic and he knew I had the ability to pass through the lines.'

'Fool,' Marcus said, meaning Stilicho. 'You could have been killed.'

'There must be more,' Alaric interrupted.

'He landed at Pisa last night with twelve thousand infantry and six thousand horse,' Brenus said. 'It is a hard day's ride away to the west, but I was given two spare horses and told that I must reach you before dawn, that is all I know.'

'Did Valeria agree to this?' Marcus demanded.

'She knew nothing.' Brenus shook his head.

'He used you, a fourteen-year-old boy?'

Brenus stared at him, and for a moment Marcus didn't recognize his son. 'General Stilicho looked into my eyes and said, "Would your father do any less?" What could I reply?'

Marcus turned away.

'There's nothing else?' Alaric persisted.

'Nothing. He's coming and he will be here sometime tomorrow.'

'But the terms are as we agreed?'

'It is what the general said,' Brenus nodded. 'He was very insistent you should know that.'

Alaric bowed his head, already deep in thought. 'Then we should get some sleep. Tomorrow is going to be a day like no other.'

When he was gone, Marcus studied his son. 'You've done well, Bren, but I wish it was otherwise.' He crouched and spread out his bedding. 'Come, share my blanket.'

Brenus lay down and huddled close to his father. 'You don't mind me hitting you on the nose?'

'I fear there will be much more blood than this shed tomorrow,' Marcus laughed, but there was little humour in it.

LI

'Where is Brenus?' Valeria demanded. 'Zeno has searched everywhere and he's nowhere to be seen.'

Stilicho looked up from his deliberations with his legionary commanders and Uldin and Sarus, who would command his cavalry. It was just after dawn on the morning after they'd landed. Stilicho's legions had been on the march through the night in two columns along the left bank of the Arnus river and he'd stopped to rest them in the hills south-west of Florentia. Cold rations today, and no fires to warn of the army's approach. Valeria had spent eight hours in the saddle with Stilicho's headquarters staff and assumed Brenus was out there in the darkness not far away. First light told a different story and now she feared for her nephew's safety, especially after Uldin's whispered threat of a few days earlier.

'General Stilicho has more important things to think about than a stupid boy who's got himself lost in the dark.' The cold-eyed Hun's reaction gave her no reason to doubt her fears.

But Stilicho laid a hand on Uldin's arm and pushed himself to his feet. 'Continue without me for a moment.'

He ushered Valeria to one side. 'Brenus is on a mission for me,' he said quietly. 'A very important mission, as it happens.'

It took a moment for the information to register. 'In God's name, you sent him back to Marcus? He's only a child.'

'Perhaps,' Stilicho made no apology. 'But a very capable one who has shown he can go where others cannot.'

'He was safe with us and now you've sent him into danger.'

Stilicho sighed. 'Some time later today this army of eighteen thousand, including several thousand who are little better than militia, will attack an Ostrogoth host my scouts estimate at almost double our numbers. Still, I am confident of success,' the steely eyes bored into her, 'but that is no guarantee. Perhaps King Radagaisus knows something I don't? Have I lured him into my trap, or am I about to enter his? We have no word of half of his cavalry. They could be out there waiting to ambush us when we emerge onto the plain. No, Brenus is certainly as safe with his father as he would be at my side or yours. I am confident Marcus will look after him. Now come, join my council, and let us consider what may unfold.'

Uldin and the others were crouched on a pebble and sand beach close to where their horses were being watered. No one showed any resentment when Valeria joined the little circle at Stilicho's side. The reason was that they were all concentrating on the lines and circles Stilicho had earlier etched into a patch of sand with the point of his knife.

'Very well,' Stilicho said now, 'I will go over our dispositions once more for my own advantage and that of our guest. Here is Florentia,' he pointed to an oblong to the right of the patch, 'and this is the Arnus. As you can see the river turns east not far from here, which will leave us with a clear path across the plain to the city. Radagaisus's people arrived only yesterday. Their focus will be entirely on their preparations for the siege. They are spread out in a broad half circle around the city, which will hamper their ability to manoeuvre. All of this is in our favour. By the time they know we are there, they will not have time to form up for a proper defence.'

The legate of the First Julia grinned. 'Just what we want, a great steaming pot of confused barbarians – begging your presence, lords – lined up like fodder for our swords.'

313

'Let us not be over-confident, legate,' the general cautioned, 'they are still a dangerous enemy with many formidable fighters. Your First Julia and accompanying auxiliaries will advance on this axis here by the river,' Stilicho drew a line from left to right, 'with our friends from Gaul, the First Flavians, on your left flank, and the Third Julia, Second Constantia and Fourth Italica in line abreast across the plain. Fifth Jovia and Fourth Martia will provide a reserve. Your first duty is to destroy Radagaisus as a fighting force or rout him from the field, your second to relieve Florentia. Now,' he smiled, 'to your units. We will march in an hour.'

The legates scattered to go to their mounts, leaving Uldin and Sarus, whose horse soldiers were in the vanguard of Stilicho's army.

'Now, my lords. It will take some hours for our foot soldiers to march into position. It is my intention that you should use that time to cut off any opportunity for Radagaisus to escape.'

'You will leave him no opportunity to retreat?' Sarus frowned. 'We Goths have a saying: the trapped rat fights hardest.'

Stilicho held his gaze. 'I have told the Emperor that no man who follows Radagaisus will ever be in a position to trouble Italia again. Would you have me break my word, Lord Sarus? No. If Radagaisus is a prudent man he will have left a guard on the route that brought him through the mountains, and where his baggage train advances to join him. It emerges onto the plain here,' he pointed to a cleft on the far side of the valley, 'directly north of this point. Lord Sarus, your Goths will kill the guards and hold that position, aided by Lord Uldin. But Uldin, you must be ready to meet any attempt by Radagaisus to disrupt my infantry while they are manoeuvring into position on the plain.'

Uldin nodded. 'It is a good plan, but better if we had more soldiers.'

'I believe we have as many as we need,' Stilicho said curtly. 'Or I would not be here.'

When the two men had left to return to their regiments, Stilicho returned to his study of the crude map. 'I sense you have doubts?' he said to Valeria.

'Like Sarus, I wonder that you leave Radagaisus with no option but to fight to the death when he has double your numbers.'

'If we relieve Florentia the discrepancy in numbers will be offset by the three thousand veterans I left to hold the city.' Stilicho scuffed his foot in the sand to disperse the map. 'Radagaisus's warriors are hungry and hungry soldiers make reluctant fighters. If Alaric has done what he promised – and all the evidence is that he has – desertions will have reduced the strength of their cavalry by half. They will be cut off from their loved ones, and if I can place my army between them and Florentia I remove their last hope.'

'You make it sound easy.'

'Not easy,' – he called for an aide to bring him his horse – 'but with God's grace we will see victory today. Or if not outright victory, something very like it.'

When Stilicho returned to his tent, a messenger was waiting with a leather scroll case, which he accepted without comment. He broke the familiar seal and studied the contents with a frown that deepened with every sentence he read.

'The little fool,' he whispered. 'Did anyone see her arrive here?'

'No, she was cloaked and hooded throughout the journey as the Lady Serena ordered.'

Clever Serena. 'Good, let it stay that way. Now bring her in.'

The messenger returned with two soldiers Stilicho knew his wife would have chosen for their absolute loyalty. Between them they held a diminutive figure whose features were concealed by a voluminous hooded cloak.

He nodded, and one of the men drew back the hood. Anastasia stood for a moment, blinded by the sudden light, then cried out in terror as she recognized Stilicho.

'Don't be frightened, my dear,' Stilicho said gently. 'You have nothing to fear from me. You are not the first to be led from the path of righteousness by powerful men, and no doubt will not be the last. All that is required is that you confirm the identities of these individuals. My wife writes that you were first in thrall to the Goth, Alaric. Is that true?'

Anastasia clutched her hands together to stop them shaking. 'Y-y-yes,' she stuttered. 'He promised me he would find me a rich husband in Salona if I would agree to travel with the Britons to Ravenna. I believed Victor was only boasting when he talked of his friendship with you, and that I wouldn't have to carry out Alaric's orders to discover your true intentions in the matter of Radagaisus.'

'Then I opened the doors for you?'

Her eyes dropped. 'Yes, lord.'

'How were you to contact him?'

'There was a man in the forum who accepted my messages.'

'Of course. And the others?'

'I only know of Julian – Julian Laskaris – who was kind to me, but he said he was acting on behalf of the Emperor.'

'And you believed him?'

'Yes, lord,' she sobbed. 'He said it would do you no harm. The Emperor had absolute faith in you, all he wanted was for his faith to be confirmed.'

'And your reward for this?'

'A place at the Emperor's court, rank and a country estate.' She brushed away a tear. 'But now all I wish is to return to Salona, lord.'

Stilicho considered for a moment. 'Very well, I'm sure that can be arranged.'

'Thank you, lord.' Anastasia dropped at his feet and clutched his knees.

He bent to prise her loose and nodded to the guards. 'Take her outside, but keep her close.'

When Anastasia was gone, he sat at his campaign desk and picked up a stylus. A wax tablet lay at his right hand and it would have been the work of a moment to arrange a travel warrant and assign her to permanent exile in Salona. But no, it would not do. There was too much at stake, and he had plans for Marcus Flavius Victor that would be complicated beyond measure if he allowed her to walk free.

'Better for all if she simply disappears,' he said, without looking at the courier. 'You know what to do.'

'Of course, lord.' It wasn't the first time he'd been tasked with more than carrying messages.

'Then make it quick.'

Radagaisus had chosen a hilltop town as his base for the siege. Faesulae had only recently been evacuated judging by the food on the tables, which his hungry warriors voraciously consumed as they searched the houses of the town and the villas that dotted the hillside below. Neither the baths nor the fine amphitheatre held any interest for him. What did was the outlook from the summit which gave him a vista across the mile of plain that divided him from Florentia.

From here he had an unbroken view of the inner and outer walls that protected the city and the Goth, Alan and Suevi encampments that surrounded them. Amid the sea of red-tiled roofs great public buildings stood out among the tidy grid of streets: a much larger amphitheatre, the basilica, the forum and a semi-circular theatre. Fine walls of red brick, but in many places houses had been built actually into the fabric of the defences. He already had men felling massive trees to provide rams that would pound the main gates, but it was the houses against the walls that gave him the scent of victory. This was no Bononia. Those warehouses he could see in the outer city were packed with grain and oil and dried meat. From his eyrie, cattle pens were visibly crammed to overcrowding. If he could breach the outer walls he could feed his people for a month and invest the inner fortress at his leisure. As well as the broad trunks, his warriors had been ordered to harvest the longer tree limbs and trim the branches to provide footholds. From the roofs of the houses closest to the walls, the branches would provide ladders up which his men could swarm to take the parapet. Once they took the parapet they would open the gate and the army of Radagaisus would take Florentia.

He had promised the inhabitants slaughter and pillage, but in truth he had no interest in purposeless killing. Despite their refusal of his terms he was minded to be merciful. When the defenders of the inner fort saw their fellow citizens being well treated, they would understand there was no point in risking their lives to defend whatever food remained. He looked up to the sky and judged the position of the sun against its background of blue. His wizards assured him this was an auspicious day for the assault. It would begin soon.

'My king?' one of the lookouts called. Had it begun already?

'To the west, my king,' the man pointed.

Radagaisus's eyes were drawn to the cleft in the mountains where his army had emerged onto the plain. Perhaps it was the first of the camp followers arriving from Bononia.

'Not there, sire. On the plain.'

Radagaisus's heart froze. A long plume of dust advanced at what seemed incredible speed across the parched fields and meadows. Only cavalry moved so quickly. The dust plume obscured their exact numbers, but he knew there must be hundreds, perhaps thousands of Roman horsemen. And where there were horsemen, infantry would follow. 'Godan save us,' he cried. 'Stilicho is here. How . . . ?'

But how didn't matter. What mattered was that he must react. If the horsemen reached the entrance of the valley they would not only block his one escape route, they would have his baggage train and fifty thousand innocents at their mercy.

'Quickly,' he called to a messenger. 'Send word to my cavalry to intercept those people.'

Even as he spoke the words he knew it was too late, but he had to do something.

'The assault, my king,' said one of the Greuthungi warlords, approaching him. 'Should we abandon it?'

'No. It will go ahead as planned. We must have that food.'

LII

'We're to attack their cavalry along with the Alans,' Sigaric announced. Marcus and Alaric had watched the Roman horsemen gallop towards the gap in the mountains and instantly understood their intention.

'Stilicho is closing the door on Radagaisus,' Marcus said.

Sigaric's band numbered almost three hundred and every man was already in the saddle. Alaric pulled his helmet over his thatch of fair hair and drew his sword. The helmet was topped by a plume of red horsehair that fluttered in the breeze like a flame. Sigaric would lead, but there would be no doubt about who commanded.

'You're not going to charge them?' Marcus said. 'In Christ's name, they're our allies.'

'Not yet,' Alaric's eyes gleamed from beneath his helm. 'And they're not Roman. That's Uldin out there, and Sarus. Barbarians, my friend. What else are we to do? Radagaisus will carve out our livers and eat them if we don't act. This is just the beginning, Marcus. To succeed we must be at Radagaisus's side at the end. It's the only way.'

Marcus felt a horse nudge his side and groaned. Brenus wore a Goth's pot helmet and a set of ill-fitting chain armour, his sword was drawn and his expression eager as a leashed hunting dog. 'Wait,' Marcus said.

He looked to Alaric and the Goth shrugged. 'Every man must survive his first fight, Marcus. You know that.' He nudged his mount into motion, with Erman the part-Hun covering his flank, and the Goth cavalry advanced across the plain to meet their countrymen and the Huns they fought beside.

'Father?' Brenus demanded.

Marcus pulled on his helmet and drew his sword. 'Don't stray a blade's length beyond my side,' he growled. They urged their horses to a trot and hurried after Alaric. It hadn't rained for weeks and the ground was powder dry. The dust from the enemy cavalry was visible a mile ahead to their front and, as they rode through fields of ripening wheat and barley, over dried-out meadows, and swerving to avoid the vineyards and orchards that dotted the plain, they kicked up a dust storm of their own.

The Goths rode in long, loose lines, that couldn't be graced with the term formation, and they shifted ahead or hung back as the mood took them. Marcus choked back the urge to order his barbarian comrades to form square or the potentially deadly wedge that a Roman cavalry regiment would have used. A movement to his right drew his attention and he called to Alaric as a second band of horsemen surged up to join them.

'Alani,' Alaric called. 'You can always trust an Alan to look after his horse. Fine warriors and great drinkers. They're too brave for their own good. Four hundred of them. I hope too many don't get themselves killed.'

The Alans soon surged ahead in their eagerness to reach the enemy, but Sigaric kept his men at a steady pace. Brenus would have pushed on into the front rank, but Marcus reached out to grab his rein. 'Stay with me, you young fool,' Marcus snarled. 'Valeria will never forgive me if I get you killed.'

Brenus glared at him, but in a heartbeat the glare turned into a broad grin and his eyes glittered with excitement. The little bastard was enjoying himself. Marcus found himself grinning back at his son, but his heart was in his throat and he mouthed a silent prayer. *God grant us his favour this day, but if only one is to be spared make sure it is him.*

*

A mile across the fields Sarus had seen the dust cloud advancing towards them and signalled to Uldin. The Hun waved his acknowledgement and a bannerman waved a signal that brought the Hun cavalry round in a curving arc to face the threat. Uldin led three regiments of mixed Huns, Vandals and Langobardi, more than nine hundred seasoned riders who shared his joy in blood and plunder, and he reckoned he outnumbered his attackers by at least a third. Mostly, Stilicho used them as scouts, raiders and ambushers, but this was what they lived for, and the Hun warlord felt a visceral joy that took him back to the steppes of his youth. He howled his battle cry and waved his curved sword and the call was echoed from almost a thousand throats.

Marcus heard the great cry and it sent a shiver through him, not of fear, but of anticipation. He could feel the blood fizzing through his veins and he had to force himself to curb his horse to stop it surging ahead of Brenus. Alaric dropped back beside them, with the ever-present Erman at his shoulder.

'Stay close.' The Goth king's eyes blazed. 'Look for my signal and remember that we have not come here to die.'

A good cavalry horse can cover a hundred and twenty paces at a fast canter in less time than it takes to count to sixty. Uldin estimated that his enemy was now perhaps eight hundred paces distant. His leading regiment consisted of archers and spearmen and he signalled for his archers to ready their bows. Six hundred paces and closing fast. His bowmen had a maximum range of two hundred paces and against such a packed target there was no need for aiming. Four hundred paces.

'Let fly.'

Three hundred arrows arced into the sky like a swift-moving haze and as they plummeted earthwards the leading Alan horsemen rode directly into the arrow storm.

'Beware the second flight,' Alaric shouted, and even as the first arrows plunged into the Alans the air darkened once more. At first it appeared the Alans must be slaughtered, but only a few dozen were down, the horses or men killed or injured by fortunate strikes. Most rode on unscathed; others, man or horse, were punctured more than once, but not disabled or dismounted. A terrible cry went up and the Huns and Alans met with a clash of steel fit to burst the ears. Marcus swerved his mount to avoid a downed horse, the rider crushed beneath its weight and reaching up a beseeching hand. Suddenly arrows were falling all around him as the Goths drove into the plunge of the second flight. One clipped his helmet with a sharp clang, another thumped into his saddle pommel. Cries of dismay and pain all around. He risked a glance to his right, but Brenus rode on untouched and he muttered a prayer of thanks. Then they were through and ahead lay an enormous throng of milling men and horses. Swords glinted in the sun as they rose and fell, parried and thrust. Blood misted the air from shattered heads, pierced bodies and gashed limbs.

The ordered mind of a Roman soldier struggled to make sense of the chaos and Marcus took his lead from Alaric and Erman. He called over his shoulder to Brenus to stay close as he followed the Goths into the carnage. Alaric cut at anything or anyone who stood in his way, but it was clear he was trying to avoid the most intense fighting as he concentrated on a banner that flew above a mob of Huns just ahead. Before he could reach it, Uldin's second regiment struck the bloody contest with a force that seemed to make the entire battle pulse. From the corner of his eye Marcus saw Brenus take an excited swing at a Hun who swept by oblivious in pursuit of a fleeing Alan, and he just managed to dip below the blade before it took his head off.

'In Christ's name, it's them you're supposed to kill, not me,' he roared.

When he turned back Alaric was gone, but the banner he'd sought still flew and it was closer now. Marcus parried a slash from a glaring savage in a fur cap, and swept him from the saddle as he rode past with a back cut that severed his spine. That was when he saw Uldin.

'Stay behind me,' he called to Brenus, and forced his way forward, roaring out a challenge.

Whether Uldin heard the cry above the clamour or simply sensed his enemy's presence wasn't clear, but suddenly the dark eyes fixed on

Marcus and his lip twisted into a gap-toothed snarl. Perhaps twenty paces separated them and the two men pushed their mounts through the whirling throng to do battle. Closer, and closer still, but before they could meet, a third horseman charged Uldin from the left, bringing their mounts together shoulder to shoulder and almost unhorsing the Hun commander.

Alaric.

The Goth roared in triumph and swung his blade at Uldin's unprotected head, but Uldin was lightning fast and managed to raise his curved sword in time to parry the blow. Nearby, Erman was exchanging cut for cut with two of Uldin's bodyguards and Marcus intervened just in time to stop a brightly dressed Hun bannerman from stoving his head in with the shaft of his pennant. Without warning, a third bodyguard drove at Marcus from the right, but as he raised his sword to bring it down, Brenus speared his blade up into the Hun's armpit and the warrior reeled away with a cry of agony. Marcus whirled his mount in time to see Alaric and Uldin wrestling together for a moment before the Goth fell from the saddle. Uldin circled his horse, sword raised and grinning as Alaric ducked between the legs of his own mount attempting to avoid the inevitable killing blow. The Hun timed his moment and the blade plunged down.

Marcus was too far away for a proper strike, but he reached out at full stretch and his point lightly pierced the sleeve of Uldin's sword arm. For all that the thrust lacked power, he must have struck flesh because Uldin stayed the blow and clutched at his arm with his left hand. Marcus spun his horse to make room for another attack, but by the time he looked up Uldin had disappeared into the throng.

Alaric was still on the ground searching among the brown grass for his sword, and Marcus stood over him until he recovered the blade. Brenus appeared with the Goth's horse and Alaric swung himself back into the saddle.

'Time we weren't here, my friend,' the Goth said. He called over his shoulder for Erman to follow and they forced their way clear of the fighting, as Sigaric roared at his men to disengage.

'What now?' Marcus asked breathlessly, when they were far enough from the fighting to feel safe from the Hun arrows.

Before Alaric could answer they were interrupted by the blare of a signal horn. Marcus turned in the saddle. Away to his right between the cavalry engagement and the river a long column of armour and spear points glittered in the sunlight as they emerged from the southern hills. One by one they transformed into individual units. Stilicho's legions were here.

Alaric studied the long lines of soldiers for a moment. 'Now,' he said, 'I fear we must return to our friend Radagaisus.'

'Alaric!'

The Goth whirled at the sharp cry from Brenus. Erman was slumped in the saddle and even as they watched he toppled slowly to the ground. Alaric dismounted and ran to the young warrior. Erman wore a leather jerkin over a padded tunic, and Alaric drew back the jacket to reveal three ragged tears, each pulsing blood which had stained his trousers from the waist to his knees. Erman's eyes were closed, blood coated his lips and his breathing was agonizingly laboured. Alaric held his head until, with a final shudder, Erman's last breath was forced from his pierced lungs.

Alaric stayed for a moment, head down. 'I loved that boy like a son,' he said.

Marcus bent and together they manhandled the dead man face down over his saddle.

Alaric patted Erman's body on the shoulder and stared out towards the marching legions.

'We should go now,' he said to Marcus. He turned to Brenus, who stood nearby with tears running unashamedly down his cheeks. 'You must not grieve, my young friend. Erman was a warrior. This was always going to be his end. But never forget. He died for us, and it is up to us to be worthy of his sacrifice.'

LIII

Radagaisus called for his armourer and shrugged on the soft leather tunic he wore beneath his mail to save it chafing his flesh. He stood as the man draped the vest of close-meshed, polished iron rings over his body, feeling the weight settle on his shoulders, and bracing his thighs and calves for the burden. Another strapped his sword belt around his waist and clipped the scabbarded blade into place. His wife, Matasuntha, a princess of the Visi, watched as he stepped into boots banded by thin ingots of bright metal to protect his legs.

'What will you do?'

'What can I do?' he demanded, immediately regretting the anger in his tone. 'Fight, of course. Whatever the outcome we must fight.'

Matasuntha heard the defeat in his voice and bowed her head. She'd listened to the arguments and could see the battlefield laid out below Faesulae like a giant mosaic. Stilicho's legions marched inexorably from the west towards besieged Florentia in a solid impenetrable line. Her husband's great army, torn between attack and defence, milled to and fro, no single part capable of halting or even delaying that steady advance, and no one able to unite the individual components to make a telling blow. A few thousand cavalry might have been able to delay the Romans for long enough to organize a united defence, but the best they had were spent after the attack on the Goths and Huns now occupying the mountain pass that was their only means of retreat. The horses of the rest were so starved they could barely carry their riders' weight.

'If it comes to it,' there was no hiding the gruffness in his voice, but he knew she'd understand, 'Odotheus and your guards will take you and the children into the mountains. You will be safe there for a time . . .'

'And afterwards?'

'Afterwards you must do what you will do.' There was nothing more to say.

His groom brought the great stallion that was one of only two that would bear his weight and he took her hands in his. Despite the anguish that threatened to tear her apart she almost smiled at his awkwardness. Such a fine, great man acting like a boy.

'Farewell, wife, until we meet again.'

'Farewell, husband.'

He kissed her on the lips before placing his silver-gilt helmet over his head, and the groom and the armourer helped him into the saddle. His personal bodyguard rode into place around him and he took the winding road down the mountain without another backward glance.

Matasuntha watched him go. She would not weep. 'Children? Come, we must prepare.'

Every man who rode with Valeria in Stilicho's retinue had fought at Longovicium, but they had never witnessed anything on the scale of the battle for Florentia. Five legions marched, three files deep, in line abreast across the plain, with two more in reserve, and their northern flank covered by the remainder of the Roman cavalry. At three files deep each legion occupied an area of ground eight hundred paces wide. They didn't quite fill the plain at its broadest, but as the terrain narrowed it became clear they would soon overlap the river to the south and the mountains to the north. As the funnel closed little more than a mile from the western flank of Radagaisus's siege lines, Valeria saw the ripple of glittering armour marking the smooth transition from three files deep to four, cutting their frontage by a fourth. Thus far they'd marched unhindered while the Goths, Alans and Suevi tribes beneath Florentia's walls milled in confusion in their thousands, uncertain how to meet the new threat. But that would soon change. Now Radagaisus was truly snared. He must destroy Stilicho and take the city and the supplies so critical to his army's survival or retreat into the barren mountains to the east and face certain starvation. The Goth and Alan cavalry who had attacked Uldin earlier had retired to the lower slopes of the mountains north of Florentia and appeared to have no further interest in the battle. Valeria prayed Marcus and Brenus were among them.

At last the Goths began to respond, pouring from the tented encampments that surrounded the city, but their attacks on the Roman line were uncoordinated and delivered in fragments by individual tribes or clans.

'Fools, but brave fools,' Ninian observed. 'If they don't understand how a Roman army fights, how do they expect to defeat them?'

'Don't underestimate them,' Valeria advised. 'There are still plenty of them and they don't lack courage.'

They watched as a dribble of wounded staggered from the advancing Roman units, to be immediately replaced by the men of the second and third files. As the legions marched on they left behind a scattering of bodies on the dry grass, bloodied Goth warriors and Roman soldiers who would never rise again.

Only to the north of the line, where a force of about five thousand Ostrogoths combined to make a concerted attack on the Second Constantia and the right flank of the Fourth Italica, did Radagaisus make an impression. Valeria saw the line bulge and ripple as the Ostrogoth warriors struck, but it still held. The only breakthrough came at the join between the two legions where a handful of Radagaisus's bravest of the brave fought their way through, only to be cut down by cavalry placed there for just such an emergency. Valeria looked to where Stilicho sat his horse, his face unmoving as the battle unfolded before him.

'He should reinforce the north,' Leof said. 'Those Goths aren't going to give up.'

Valeria saw he was right. The Ostrogoth commander drew his warriors away, only to throw them instantly back into the fray. This time the Second Constantia took a step back, followed by another, and she knew Stilicho only had moments to act, or his entire line might be at risk. Stilicho barked an order and a courier sped off to where the Fourth Martia waited in reserve behind the left of the line. Was he too late? They'd never know, because the commander of the Fourth Italica wheeled his outer files like a closing door to crash into the Goth flank and the pressure was eased. The Goths retreated, re-formed and attacked again, but this attack had none of the ferocity of the previous assaults and they wavered under a hail of javelins from the legionaries of the Martia who arrived in the rear of their comrades.

Sweat poured from Radagaisus's brow leaving him half-blinded, and blood pulsed from a spear wound in the thigh above his protective boots. His bodyguard was close to exhaustion and surrounded him panting and leaning on their spears and axes for support. Not a man was unwounded and a dozen were missing, among the line of fallen the advancing Romans seemed to barely notice.

A few moments earlier he'd been ready to drink deep from the nectar of victory, only for the cup to be dashed from his lips at the last instant. They'd been so close. One more push would have shattered the cohesion of the men behind the painted shields and turned Stilicho's left into chaos. Then the impossible had happened. The Roman ranks to his right had somehow pivoted and crashed into his flank, unnerving the warriors there and forcing him to retreat. They'd gone in again, but now the men were spent, edging backwards from their opponents. Yet his losses so far had been relatively small. Should he disengage entirely and attack another section of the line when they were rested? Did he even have time for that?

He heard a commotion from his left and when he saw what had caused it he knew the true meaning of despair. The Romans had already cut their way into the encampments beneath Florentia's walls, and the city's defenders cheered them on. Thousands of his warriors were streaming away from the battle towards the supposed sanctuary of the heights of Faesulae and more were joining them with every passing second. It was over, at least for now.

For a moment his spirits were so low he considered dismissing his guard and making a suicidal lone charge against the Roman line. Better to die with honour than to endure the humiliation that would surely follow. But that would be to desert the brave men who had followed him here and placed their faith in him. Whatever happened, he would stay and share their suffering.

'We will fall back to the heights and organize a defence,' he called to his chieftains. 'We can hold there and prepare for whatever comes next.'

Whatever comes next. He could see the look on their faces. They were experienced fighters and they knew what this retreat meant. Yet Radagaisus was not without hope. Faesulae was a formidably strong position and he had no doubt he could hold out against Stilicho for as long as his supplies lasted. What if he bled the Romans dry? What if he found a chink in *their* defences that allowed him to use his superior numbers as they should be used. Massed on the hill, he would have more control over the unruly warlords and their hardy fighters. Yes, perhaps it was not over yet.

Someone brought him his horse and he mounted and rode back to the hill calling encouragement to his fleeing warriors.

'This is but a small setback,' he shouted. 'Tonight we will rest and tomorrow we will defeat them.'

A few of the men cheered, but most just plodded on with their heads down, failing even to acknowledge him. He looked back over his shoulder to where the Romans continued to advance at their unhurried, steady pace, the long lines of shields wavering only when they stepped over the Ostrogoth dead. In a way it was more chilling than if they'd swarmed forward to exploit his retreat.

At Faesulae he called his chieftains to him in the town's theatre and issued his dispositions. Every route up the hill would be made impregnable. Each tribe must be ready to support its neighbour in the event of a concerted attack. If they fought with the courage they had shown today the Romans would never take this hill.

Later, as night fell, he limped around the summit inspecting his positions until he was satisfied he'd done everything possible to keep the enemy at bay. Not even a mouse could enter his lines undetected. Below, the Roman campfires formed an unbroken ring around the bottom of the hill between him and the precious, now lost, prize of Florentia's food supplies. The sight sent a shiver through Radagaisus and he drew his cloak closer. There were things, troubling things, he should be thinking about, but his head was dull as a bowl of mud and he drove them from his mind.

In an olive grove not far below the town he found the Goth cavalry who'd fought so well in the opening exchanges of the battle. Orderly horse lines, animals still well cared for and better fed than any of the others he'd seen. They'd managed to withdraw in much better order than most. The men were sharing their rations and no one seemed concerned to see him. Their chieftain – Sigaric? – offered him a crust of bread and a cup of beer and Radagaisus took it gratefully and sat beside the fire they'd set. Opposite was another man he recognized, the Pict who'd fought Bleda. He had a bandage on his forearm and Radagaisus nodded towards it.

'A nick from a Hun arrow,' Marcus said. 'I didn't even notice it at the time.' He spoke slowly as if struggling to find the words and his face was grey with exhaustion. Beside him lay a boy, and another prone figure wrapped tightly in a cloak.

'I watched you today,' the king said. 'If we had more like you I think the outcome would be very different.'

'There were too many,' Sigaric said. 'And the Huns fought well.'

'I'm glad you are here, anyway,' Radagaisus said. 'Your beer is good and we will need men like you in the coming days.' He closed his eyes. 'I think I will stay here tonight, if that does not disturb you too much. I feel as if I am among friends.'

'It would be our pleasure, majesty,' Sigaric assured him, and called for a blanket for the king. When he lay by the fire, with his guards bedded down nearby, Radagaisus noticed that the man in the cloak had moved, but thought nothing of it. As he'd inspected the defences earlier, he'd heard mutterings of complaint and even outright condemnation of his actions. Here, at least, he could count on these men.

That night there were several alarms from tribes reporting the sound of movement below them on the plain, but none of the patrols found any suggestion of Roman preparations for an attack.

At sun-up Radagaisus discovered why. From the edge of the olive grove he looked down to see an ants' nest of activity. Every able man from Florentia must be working on the roughly hewn ditch that now encircled the base of the hill. Marcus and Sigaric joined him to stare down at the incredible labour that had been achieved in a single night, a trench two paces deep and the same wide, with the beginnings of a palisade on the raised far bank.

Radagaisus greeted the sight with a bitter laugh. 'See,' he called to the surrounding Goths. 'The Romans must still fear us greatly if they have to dig a ditch to keep us from them. Soon we will show them they are right.'

'Majesty,' Marcus said quietly, 'that is no ditch, it is the noose around our neck.'

LIV

Radagaisus invited Sigaric to his council the next day in the theatre, and made no complaint when Marcus accompanied the Goth chieftain. The warlords of the Alans, the Goths, the Asding Vandals and the Suevi gathered on the marble seats around him, and Radagaisus gradually became aware that he was surrounded by a wall of suppressed fury. Men he had known as friends either glared at him or looked at the ground refusing to meet his eyes. He had no enemies here, that he knew of, because anyone who became his enemy did not survive for long, but for the first time he truly understood how he had lost their confidence, if not yet their loyalty.

'I have invited you here to discuss the best way to take the fight to the enemy,' he announced. 'Yesterday was a bad day, but we were inches from victory. Today will be a good day.' Murmurs of consternation and disbelief greeted his words and he felt the need to continue. 'This is no time for recriminations or censure, though if that is what you want you will have your chance on another day, when we have swept the Romans from the field.'

'Swept the Romans from the field with what?' Spali, a khan of the Alani, demanded.

'Your people fought well, my lord,' Radagaisus assured him. 'They will fight well again today.'

'Yes,' Spali snarled. A thin, spare man even in normal times, his features were almost skull-like from the one-third rations he'd been forced to impose on his people for the last few weeks. 'They fought well, but others did not.' His eye fixed on an Asding Vandal chieftain called Gaiseric, a notoriously ill-tempered man, whose hand immediately went to his sword hilt.

'They fought well until they ran away,' Gaiseric sneered, 'and left the Asdingi with their arses in the air. If we hadn't covered your retreat you wouldn't be here now, *my lord*.'

Now it was Spali who was on his feet, his bony face purple with rage. Each man had his supporters and there was a moment of uproar before Radagaisus bellowed for quiet.

'Let us be clear, my lords,' the king's chest heaved with emotion, 'division will be fatal to us. We must act as one. Take a moment to control yourselves and consider the answer to my original question.' Spali and Gaiseric settled back onto the marble benches, and the other chiefs followed their example. 'I say again,' Radagaisus continued, 'what is the best way to take the fight to the Romans? Give me the benefit of your wisdom and your experience.'

'Then I respond to your question with one of my own,' Spali said sulkily. 'What am I to offer the men you wish to take the fight to the Romans today?'

'Offer them?' Radagaisus frowned, puzzled by the question. You led men, you didn't offer them anything. 'The opportunity for glory,' he said eventually, and when there was no response: 'All the food that Florentia can provide.'

'No,' Spali shook his head. 'All I can offer them is death.'

'What?' Radagaisus's face crumpled.

'Look around you, lord king.' Spali spoke calmly now. 'The Romans have built their great ditch to pen us in, but that is not all they have done. They know there are only a few routes to where we can launch an attack, and they have ranged their catapults on those places. Narrow ravines where a single well-aimed missile will obliterate a dozen men. We will lose scores if not hundreds before we are even in a position to launch a spear. And when we reach the ditch, then what? The legions are famed for their defence even more than their attack. Our men barely have the strength to climb out of their blankets never mind a mud-slick trench, and all the time being torn by swords and spears, pierced with arrows, and smashed to a pulp by those same catapults. My men are not cowards, they will fight if I ask them to, but I will not ask them to die for nothing. If they die, who will look after their women and children, still trapped and starving on the Bononia road? Not you, lord king, because you are no coward either, and you too will be dead in that ditch.'

'Then let us die together,' Radagaisus forgot his call for calm. 'For what is the alternative? If we stay here the Romans will starve us out.'

Marcus sat, marvelling at the turn the conference had taken, almost as if Alaric was behind a curtain somewhere whispering instructions. Gaiseric's next words did nothing to disabuse him of the notion that the two men had been subject to Alaric's persuasion, if not handed an outright bribe.

'We are already starving, King Radagaisus,' he said. 'All our food and the fodder for our horses, the very clothes off our back are down there,' he pointed to where the besiegers' tents had stood yesterday, now torn asunder and the contents either looted or scattered across the fields around Florentia. 'You were able to bring your supplies to this little eyrie of yours, but we did not have that opportunity. My warriors are down to their last crumbs, and I would wager that what you have in your stores would not feed the host gathered here for a single day.'

'What then?' Radagaisus barked. 'What would you have me do now that the road to an honourable end has been denied?'

'Talk,' Sigaric spoke for the first time. 'I have had men patrolling close to the Roman ditch since dawn. It is the way of these things that those on either side communicate with each other, even if it is only threat and insult. But that was not the way of it today. Every man they spoke to insisted that General Stilicho wants no more bloodshed. He is prepared to offer reasonable terms to see this army remove itself from Italia and return beyond the Danuvius.'

'What terms?' Radagaisus demanded, his suspicion clear.

'I do not know, lord,' Sigaric admitted. 'But there is only one way to find out.'

A murmur of assent accompanied the words, and King Radagaisus knew he'd been defeated for the second time in two days. There would be no attack. Nor any further retreat, because he'd had news that morning that Roman cavalry and infantry now swarmed the hills and valleys to his rear. Yet his doubts remained. What did Stilicho have to gain from offering reasonable terms when he was in a position to destroy his enemy simply by staying where he was?

Marcus could almost see the workings of the king's mind and he nudged Sigaric. 'Naturally our first demand would be that no harm should come to the king and his family,' the Goth said. 'Perhaps you would have to submit to exile, but . . .'

But . . . Radagaisus's head filled with an image of Matasuntha's smile and the adoring faces of his children. Enough.

'Who will carry a message from King Radagaisus to General Stilicho?' he choked out the words.

'I will, though it may mean my death.' Gaiseric, never one to forgo a drama.

'And I,' Spali said.

Radagaisus felt his hackles rise. What was this? 'But neither of you is fluent in Latin,' he pointed out. He searched the benches around them. 'You, Pict. What was your name again?'

It was a moment before the name Marcus had given to Radagaisus came to him. 'I am called Cinead, lord.'

Radagaisus nodded and tugged at his beard for a moment. 'Cinead will carry the green branch and present my message to General Stilicho,' he said. 'You, Sigaric, will translate everything that is said to my lords Gaiseric and Spali.'

He dismissed the council and they spent the next hour discussing the terms Marcus would present. Radagaisus knew he couldn't dictate the fates of every one of his eighty thousand followers to Stilicho. All he could do was ask the Roman to spare their lives and allow them to return to their homelands on receipt of a promise that they would never again set foot in Italia. There would be hostages, of course, to ensure their compliance, and a substantial payment from the treasure Radagaisus had gathered north and south of the Danuvius.

'All this is negotiable, of course. He may demand that some become slaves and that the hostages be kings.' Gaiseric and Spali blinked at that. 'At worst he may have all the treasure. What is not negotiable is that he must guarantee the lives of myself and my family. Without his oath there can be no peace.'

Marcus led Sigaric and the two warlords down the winding track to the plain carrying the olive branch prominently above his head in case the movement attracted a shower of arrows. They reached the slope above the new ditch, with the north gate of Florentia under a mile away to their right front.

'An embassy from King Radagaisus to General Stilicho,' he called to the legionary unit defending that section of trench.

It took an hour before an escort of cavalry from Stilicho's personal bodyguard appeared to guide them to Florentia, where Stilicho had given up his command tent for a substantial house. Marcus had considered involving Brenus in the embassy in some way to ensure the boy's safety, but Alaric insisted nothing should be allowed to jeopardize the final piece of his intricate puzzle falling into place. The fact that it also gave the Goth a valuable hostage should anything go wrong didn't escape Marcus, but he knew there was no point in arguing.

On the way, they passed through the encampments of Stilicho's heavy infantry, but no one gave them a second look as the men concentrated on feasting on the glut of cattle that had been penned within the city. Huge fire pits had been lit and slaughtered bullocks roasted whole over the flames, filling the air with the fragrant scent of cooked beef and reminding Marcus he hadn't eaten meat in almost a month. An echoing rumble told him Gaiseric was experiencing the same feeling and he looked over his shoulder to see the Vandal literally drooling at the mouth at the sight of such bounty.

Within Florentia itself, the populace showed less respect to their former besiegers and they were glad when they eventually reached Stilicho's palatial headquarters.

If the general was surprised to see Marcus as part of the embassy he didn't show it. Neither Uldin nor Sarus had been invited to the talks, but Stilicho sat at a long table flanked by his legionary commanders. He invited Spali to state why they were there, but didn't offer the delegates a seat. It was Marcus who set out the terms for Radagaisus's capitulation and Stilicho listened without a change of expression until the very end, when he tutted and shook his head.

'No,' he said. 'That will not do at all.' Sigaric translated for Spali and Gaiseric and Marcus saw the two men grimace. 'I cannot countenance the return of so many warriors beyond the Danuvius, from where their next likely venture will be to turn north and join the Vandal and Burgundian incursions into Gaul. Still, I have a solution which may be of interest to King Radagaisus. I will accept all of his warriors who are willing into the Roman army, as auxiliaries to be commanded by their tribal leaders, who will serve as Imperial officers, with the benefits and conditions of the same.' The Vandal and the Alan exchanged a glance that confirmed their future careers, and Sigaric said he was sure Radagaisus would agree. 'Naturally their families will also be afforded Rome's protection,' Stilicho continued, and the two men bowed their thanks. 'A portion of these auxiliaries will be required to serve with one or other of Rome's allies, but I am sure that will not be a problem. Any warrior or chieftain who refuses these terms will be sold into slavery, along with their families.'

There was more. The full contents of Radagaisus's treasury were to be handed over, but Stilicho promised to provide food for the entire host, including those destined for the slave pens. Any personal booty taken on Italian soil was to be repatriated and all prisoners to be released. The only proviso was that any warrior found to have abused or otherwise harmed a prisoner would be executed.

Eventually, Stilicho smiled. 'I think that is all. I have already taken the liberty of putting our agreement in writing both in Latin and in the Gothic language.' A clerk appeared and handed Gaiseric and Spali a scroll each. 'If King Radagaisus is in agreement we can conclude the treaty at a meeting between the lines tomorrow.'

Gaiseric cleared his throat. 'There is the matter of the guarantee of King Radagaisus's life and that of his family?'

'Of course,' Stilicho said. 'I assumed that would be taken for granted. He has my oath on it. The only question is where they will spend their term in exile.'

Gaiseric turned away with a sigh of relief, and Marcus made to follow the others from the room.

'Wait, you,' Stilicho called. 'You look like an old soldier. I have a question for you.'

Stilicho waved his generals from the room. 'Are you well, Marcus? God, look at you, a barbarian from your toes to your hairpiece. What have I done to you? Brenus is well?'

'Well enough.' Marcus wasn't sure he was prepared to forgive Stilicho yet for returning his son into peril. 'We'll be glad when it's over.'

'Soon, Marcus. By tomorrow night you will be a Roman again, Marcus Flavius Victor, and reap the rewards you deserve.'

LV

They gathered beneath the midday sun on the flat ground between Florentia and the hill of Faesulae. Stilicho had ordered that a pavilion be set up midway between the city and the mountain, and two thrones placed in the shade inside. To the right of the pavilion the men of the Fourth Italica stood, heads boiling in their metal helmets and sweat pouring inside their mail, thankful they'd been ordered to place their blue and yellow shields at rest in front of them. To the left, Second Constantia, the other legion which had borne the brunt of the fighting against Radagaisus, suffered in similar circumstances.

The king himself sat in the throne at Stilicho's side naming the petty kings, princes, tribal chieftains and warlords who had followed him to Italia, and listening as they pledged their services and those of their followers to Rome. Those followers filled the hillside opposite, watching the proceedings in an eerie, mournful silence that seemed impossible for such an enormous mass of humanity. Radagaisus still couldn't quite believe he hadn't been able to defeat Stilicho with so many fine warriors at his disposal. But that was in the past. For all Stilicho's elegant courtesy he was a king no more, only a penniless prisoner destined for exile. Likewise, he chose not to notice that Sigaric's war band was the only formation from his former army which had been allowed beyond the bank and ditch and within hearing distance of the ceremony.

'You must be looking forward to your rewards, my friend,' Alaric whispered to Marcus. 'You have done Stilicho a great service and he is a generous man.'

'I'm looking forward to a bath more,' Marcus said. He could see Valeria and the survivors of the Ala Sabiniana amongst Stilicho's bodyguard and the thought of renewing the comradeship and companionship he'd had prompted an almost liquid feeling at the heart of him. Soon, he would be back with them, and Anastasia, and looking forward to a future the fates still had to decide. Brenus stood at his side, and he automatically draped a possessive arm over the boy's shoulder, smiling as he felt his son flinch from the gesture of affection. Fifteen now: if this was August, his birthday had passed, forgotten during their time with Radagaisus.

What did the future hold?

Stilicho had hinted at a generalship. There would be lands, honours, an Emperor's favour. A frontier posting, almost certainly, and the never-ending battle to keep the barbarians beyond the Rhenus or the Danuvius.

Was that what he wanted? He hoped not to have to decide until he'd had a chance to discuss it with Anastasia. After all, his future might be hers now.

The ceremony reached an end. The formalities over.

It was almost with disbelief that Marcus heard Stilicho shout 'Seize him' and point to Radagaisus. In a moment the mighty figure of the Ostrogoth king was helpless, pinned between four of Stilicho's guards.

'Get him to his knees,' the general ordered.

'No,' Marcus shouted. But no one was listening.

A great apprehensive murmur went up from the hillside, stilled when Stilicho stepped forward from the pavilion and raised his hands above his head.

'Italia has been invaded.' His shout echoed from the city walls and seemed to reverberate in the very air, but it was doubtful whether even one in a thousand of the warriors on the hill heard or understood. But that didn't concern Stilicho. 'Rome has been wronged, the Emperor insulted and his people dispossessed and murdered. This cannot go unpunished.' He drew the fine sword that always hung at his left hip.

'You promised me my life,' Marcus heard Radagaisus say. Not a plea, just an observation; a recognition that life was not always fair.

'I owe nothing to a barbarian,' Stilicho's reply was cold as an ice house.

'At least spare my family.'

Stilicho raised the sword. The guards had Radagaisus on his knees, arms hauled back behind him. Marcus, watching in sheer horror, had a feeling Radagaisus was stretching his neck to make it easier for Stilicho. He was to be disappointed. Perhaps Stilicho's heart wasn't truly in the murder, or his strength failed him. Perhaps the sword wasn't the weapon it appeared. He brought the blade down in a slicing arc. The first blow seemed to bounce from Radagaisus's broad neck and the Ostrogoth uttered a strangled cry. The second sliced flesh and severed bone and Radagaisus's whole body shuddered. At the third strike, the king's still shaking body voided its bowels. Marcus prayed that he was dead, but the great head, though it hung like an after-thought, was still attached to the torso. It was only at the fourth attempt that Stilicho managed to sever his victim's neck.

Stilicho straightened and Marcus could see his neck muscles bul-ging. The sword shook in his hands and he threw it aside in disgust.

'Find his wife and children and kill them,' Stilicho called to a horse-man on the edge of the crowd, and Marcus noticed for the first time that Sarus had been watching the event.

By now Marcus was halfway to the pavilion, only vaguely aware that his legs were taking him there.

'No, Marcus.' He heard Valeria's shout, but he ignored her.

The four guards saw him come and would have drawn their swords, but Stilicho called on them to stay back 'and get this offal out of here'. He turned to face Marcus and Marcus looked into the haggard fea-tures of an old man.

'Is this what you call honour?' he choked. 'I told him he and his

341

family were safe, and that he had your promise. You made me a liar.' He shook his head. 'Butchery. No man deserves such a foul end. You could at least have given the job to someone who had the courage to do it properly.'

Stilicho's hand flew to his left hip and the sword that was no longer there. 'You go too far, Marcus Flavius Victor. But because it is you and because of the service you have done Rome, I will give you an explanation. I do not call it honour, I call it necessity. What do you think Honorius would have done if I'd let Radagaisus live? He would have had me killed. Me, Stilicho.' His eyes bulged with fury. 'And without Stilicho, very soon there would be no Rome, so do not plague me with your misplaced notions of honour.'

Marcus walked away and Stilicho closed his eyes. 'Marcus,' he called. 'We cannot let the death of Radagaisus come between us. Come to me when your temper has cooled.'

'I want nothing from you.' Marcus didn't look back, so he didn't see Stilicho flinch.

A little way off he found Alaric inspecting Stilicho's sword. 'What will you do?' the Goth asked.

'I don't know,' he admitted. 'Italia has nothing for me now. North, I think. Then Gaul.'

'Not Britannia?'

'From what I hear Britannia is now ruled by a man who wants me dead.'

'Kill him, then,' Alaric said, as if it was the easiest thing in the world. 'If not, come with me to Illyricum, where I am still *magister militum*, I believe. It will be quiet for a while, I think, for I must wait to see if Stilicho can persuade the Emperor to honour his debt. If he can't, maybe I'll be paying a return visit with some of these fine fellows,' he pointed to the warriors on the hillside.

Marcus laughed at the unlikely prospect. 'I'll think on it,' he called as he walked away to seek out Valeria. By now Stilicho had disappeared, but she was waiting not far from the pavilion with Zeno and the others.

'It appears we've been dismissed from the service,' she said. 'I'm still not sure whether that was the most wonderful thing I've seen you do, or the most foolish. What happens now?'

'I don't know,' he admitted as she accompanied him towards the hill where the horses were tethered. 'First, I need to see Anastasia and tell her she's no longer going to be a general's wife.'

Valeria remembered the conversation she'd had with Leof and prayed that her brother would not be disappointed, but she kept silent.

'Father!'

Brenus was sitting on the edge of the ditch. 'Alaric gave me this,' he held up Stilicho's sword with the distinctive gold oath-ring in the pommel. 'Do you think the general will want it back?'

'I don't think so.' Marcus took a seat beside him and held out his hand for the blade. Brenus presented it like a ceremonial gift and he weighed it in his hands. 'A fine sword.' He returned the weapon. 'What will you do with it?'

His son looked thoughtful. 'It is the sword that killed Radagaisus,' Brenus said. 'I do not think there is any honour in it.'

'That is a good answer. Then we will give it to Radagaisus's gods. It is what he would have wanted.'

Brenus nodded. He liked the idea.

'Where will we go now?'

Suddenly it all became clear to Marcus.

'To Britannia,' he said. 'Where we have a proper enemy to kill.'

'What enemy?'

'A man who once offered me an Empire.'

Historical Note

By AD 406 when Marcus Flavius Victor begins his adventure, Britannia had become Rome's forgotten province. Emperor Honorius, who'd abandoned Milan for Ravenna as his capital five years earlier, ruled a western Roman Empire beset on all sides by enemies and his patience with the leaders of the northern outpost was wearing thin. The island's defenders, their efforts unacknowledged and often unpaid, struggled to hold back successive waves of Picts, Scotti and Saxons, and there's evidence that some units had become little more than war bands. An atmosphere of political and military turmoil provided the perfect platform for the ambitious and the unprincipled. One of them was a senior officer called Marcus, who convinced his British soldiers to hail him as Emperor, only to be killed by them a few months later. It seemed to make perfect sense for my own Marcus, who, after all, had convinced his superiors he was following a similar plan six years earlier, to be confused with the real one, which helped set up the opening chapters of the book.

But Marcus's task in *The Barbarian* had always been to rescue his son and be drawn into the great events affecting the Empire proper. The men at the heart of those events were: Honorius, a young man utterly unfit to rule, who would soon lose the provinces of Gaul and

Hispania in quick succession; Flavius Stilicho, the part-Vandal general Honorius relied upon to keep him in power, but whose own power he resented to an ultimately fatal degree; Alaric, king of the Visigoths, or western Goths, the perennial thorn in Stilicho's side who had already invaded Italy; and Radagaisus, king of the Ostrogoths, or eastern Goths, who, while Marcus is making his journey, is leading an army of eighty thousand of his people across the Danube, with his sights on the heart of the Empire.

The growing pressures on the Roman Empire at the end of the fourth century are well known, but the subtleties of the various incursions and invasions of the Barbarian Migrations are less so. We have an image of bearded, fur-clad savages pouring over the Rhine drawn by the wealth of the 'civilized' Roman world, and bent on plunder, rapine and murder, but that wasn't always true, and certainly not in the case of the Goths.

Alaric grew to manhood in the years after the great Gothic victory over the eastern Roman army at Adrianople in AD 378, a battle sparked by what the Goths perceived as Roman treachery. He'd been tried and tested as an ally of Rome sixteen years later at the battle of Frigidus, when the Roman Emperor Theodosius sacrificed the Goths to save Roman blood and then reneged on his promise to give them citizenship. Yet, for all he'd learned never to trust Rome, Alaric knew that the future prosperity of his people depended on citizenship and the sanctuary and illusionary stability of becoming an integral part of the Empire. When Theodosius died, Alaric offered his Goth soldiers in service to the Emperor's eastern successor, Arcadius, and became involved in palace intrigues that made him sometimes an enemy, and sometimes an ally of Stilicho, supreme general of the western armies and protector of Honorius, Emperor of the West. Whether Arcadius ever trusted Alaric is debatable, but he eventually approved his appointment as *magister militum* of Illyricum, and the province's de facto ruler.

Rugged Illyricum was not the homeland Alaric sought for his people, and when his demands for citizenship and fertile lands were refused, he invaded Italy in AD 402, only to suffer defeat at the hands of Stilicho at Pollentia and Verona. Yet the defeats could hardly have been decisive and Alaric's army must have remained intact, because instead of executing his foe, Stilicho came to an agreement that he retire to Pannonia, there to act as a bulwark against further barbarian incursions across the Danube. The decision to essentially ally himself to Alaric, an invader and a barbarian, deepened Honorius's suspicions that Stilicho, who had also recruited Vandals and even Huns to Rome's cause, was becoming too close to his Germanic cousins.

Meanwhile, Radagaisus, of whom little is otherwise known, and the Ostrogothic people had been driven from their lands by pressure from the east, probably from the Huns, savage and merciless horse warriors. As they sought out new lands, they were joined by other fugitive tribes, Alans, Vandals and Suevi, until Radagaisus's horde reached, according to the closest contemporary sources, anything from one hundred thousand to four hundred thousand souls. The majority of these would have been non-combatant old men, women and children, but his military element must have numbered in the tens of thousands. When he crossed the Danube, probably somewhere near Linz, Radagaisus would have had a choice of moving north through the relatively easy terrain of Germania. The fact that he spurned the opportunity and turned south, through the daunting peaks of the Alps, would seem to indicate that, like Alaric, Radagaisus hoped to force Honorius to provide him with a new, fertile homeland where his people could settle. For reasons of narrative pacing, I've compressed a gruelling advance through the Alps and northern Italy that would probably have taken upwards of a year into a few short months.

The final reckoning between Radagaisus and Stilicho came south of the Apennines, at what is now the hilltop town of Fiesole just outside Florence. Stilicho gathered his troops near Pavia and somehow managed to corner the Goths between the mountains and the River Arno. But how did he do it, and why would Radagaisus, with a hundred thousand people to feed, abandon the fertile plains and rich townships of northern Italy for the dubious sanctuary and short rations of the mountains? For me, the most likely scenario was that Stilicho, with far fewer soldiers, devised what would become known as a 'scorched earth' strategy, depriving Radagaisus of supplies when he emerged from the Alps and forcing him to seek subsistence further south. Our two main sources for the invasion, the Roman priest-scholar Orosius and the Greek historian Zosimus, differ on what happened next. Orosius has Radagaisus and his hungry followers caught besieging Florence and forced to take refuge at Faesulae, where they were starved into submission in a few days. Zosimus, on the other hand, hints at a full-scale battle with great slaughter on the Goth side. There's a suggestion that part of Radagaisus's army abandoned him, or that he divided them, allowing, according to one chronicler, 'Stilicho to wheel his Hun auxiliaries and annihilate a third part of the enemy force', with others hinting at infighting and desertions.

I took this suggestion of division among Radagaisus's people as fictional licence to bring Alaric to the centre of these events. There's no evidence he had a personal hand in stirring up dissent among the king's Goth followers, but little doubt that it did happen in some form. Alaric certainly benefited from Radagaisus's defeat, because as well as enslaving many of his enemy, Stilicho recruited still more of the Goth warriors to his cause and most were sent to join Alaric in Pannonia. Uldin the Hun, and Sarus the Goth, who may have been Alaric's brother-in-law, are both historical figures, and Alaric had reason to hate Uldin, who is said to have killed his mentor, Gainas.

Glossary

Adrianopolis – fourth-century battle in which the Goths defeated the eastern Roman army and killed the Emperor Valens.

ala – auxiliary cavalry wing composed, in late Roman times, of three hundred horsemen in ten squadrons.

Alamanni – powerful confederation of Germanic tribes who inhabited the upper reaches of the Rhine.

Alans – eastern tribe involved in the Barbarian Migrations of the fourth century AD.

Alaric – king of the Goths who ruled Illyricum for a time in the late fourth century AD, famous for later sacking Rome.

Albis river – the Elbe in northern Germany.

Andautonia – Roman settlement close to what is now the city of Zagreb, Croatia.

aurochs – very large species of cattle, now extinct.

auxiliaries – originally non-citizen soldiers serving as light infantry and cavalry in the Roman armies. Later, auxiliary units would be composed of locally recruited warriors from nearby tribes.

Bononia – Roman city, now Bologna, Italy.

Branodunum – fortress and part of the Saxon Shore defences at Brancaster, Norfolk.

Brigantes – Celtic tribe inhabiting what is now the north-east of England.

buccellatum – Roman iron rations, very hard biscuits.

Burgundians – Germanic tribe who lived east of the middle reaches of the Rhine river.

Chrysanthus – *vicarius* (deputy governor) of the Roman province of Britannia.

Classis Histrica – the Danube fleet in the late Roman Empire.

comitatenses – the late Roman field army.

Constantinopolis (Nova Roma) – capital of the eastern Roman Empire, now Istanbul.

cuneus (also known as the Boar's Head) – a compact arrow-head formation used by Roman infantry and cavalry to break up enemy formations.

Danuvius river – the Danube.

draco – the dragon standard carried by military units in the late Roman army.

draconarius – bearer of the dragon standard.

dux Britanniarum – commander of the northern military units of late Roman Britain, one of three major commands listed in the *Notitia Dignitatum*, along with the *comes Britanniarum* and the Count of the Saxon Shore.

Eboracum – the Roman fortress and city which is now York.

edilhingui – a high-ranking Saxon nobleman.

Faesulae – Roman hilltop settlement east of Florence, now Fiesole.

Florentia – Roman city which is now Florence.

foederati – mercenary war bands who allied themselves to Rome and pledged their military strength to the Empire.

Fuldaha river – the Vltava river, Czech Republic.

Gaul – a Roman province based largely on what is now France.

Gariannonum – fortress and part of the Saxon Shore defences, now Burgh Castle, Norfolk.

garum – a pungent Roman fish sauce.

Gerulata – Roman fort on the Danube, near Bratislava, Slovakia.

Goths – German-speaking tribe from north of the Danube who migrated across the river and demanded to be part of the Roman Empire (see also Ostrogoths and Visigoths).

hack silver – silver which has been cut from plate into pieces of specific weight.

Honorius, Emperor – ruler of the western Roman Empire.

Huns – feared eastern tribe whose merciless incursions against their western neighbours may have sparked the Barbarian Migrations of the fourth century AD.

Iadera – Adriatic port in Roman times. Now Zadar, Croatia.

insula – Roman apartment block.

Irminsul – a great tree or pillar central to the Saxon religion, that was believed to be the connection between the earth and the Otherworld.

Lake Benacus – now Lake Garda.

Leuphana – settlement on the Elbe near what is now Wittenberge.

Lupfurdum – settlement on the upper Elbe, precise location unknown, but possibly near Meissen.

magister equitum – Roman general in overall charge of the army's cavalry formations.

magister militum – a high-ranking general, military commander of all Roman forces in a province.

magister officiorum – a high-ranking administrative official during the late Roman Empire.

Marcomanni – Germanic tribe who lived in the area which now constitutes Bohemia in the Czech Republic.

Mare Adriaticum – the Adriatic Sea.

Mare Germanicum – the North Sea.

medicus – a Roman doctor.

Mediolanum – Roman city which is now Milan.

Metulum – a city in the Roman province of Dalmatia, close to what is now Siča, Croatia.

Ostrogoths – Gothic tribes from beyond the Danube.

Othona – fortress and part of the Saxon Shore defences at Bradwell-on-Sea, Essex.

Pontus Euxinus – the Black Sea.

praetorium – the commandant's living quarters in a Roman camp or fortress.

prefect (also *praefectus alae*) – Roman military title still in use in later times, cavalry commander (though the term may have had multiple uses).

principia – the headquarters building in a Roman camp or fortress.

Quadi – Germanic tribe who inhabited the area now known as Moravia, in the eastern Czech Republic.

Radagaisus – Ostrogoth war leader who invaded Italy in AD 406.

Ravenna – Italian coastal city where Emperor Honorius fled with his court during Alaric the Goth's invasion of Italy.

Salona – Roman city north of Split, Croatia, now Solin.

Sarus – Visigoth chieftain and rival of Alaric, who became a general in Stilicho's army.

Saxon Shore – Roman military command of the late Empire, consisting of nine forts defending the coastline of Britannia from Norfolk to Hampshire.

Saxonia – homeland of the Saxons, in what is now northern Germany.

solidus – gold coin issued during the late Roman Empire.

Stilicho, Flavius – commander of all the western Roman Empire's armies.

Theodosius, Emperor – last Emperor of the united Roman Empire, died AD 395.

Ticinum – Roman settlement, now Pavia, Italy.

Treva – settlement on the River Elbe near what is now Hamburg, Germany.

tribune – Roman military title still in use in later times, commander of an infantry or cavalry unit.

Uldin – Hun war chief who fought for Stilicho against Radagaisus.

Vandals – a Germanic people who migrated westward into the Roman Empire under pressure from more powerful tribes in the east. In the late fourth century they supplied soldiers for the Empire, including the famous general Stilicho.

Venta Icenorum – capital of the Iceni tribe, located at modern Caistor St Edmund, Norfolk.

Via Istrum – Roman road connecting military bases along the Danube frontier.

vicarius – high-ranking Roman provincial official/deputy governor.

Visigoths – Goths who left their original homeland by the Black Sea to settle in what is now Bulgaria.

Acknowledgements

The Barbarian is my seventeenth novel published by Transworld and I have to thank my editor Simon Taylor for sticking by me throughout the journey. Likewise, my agent, Mark Stanton (Stan) of the North Literary Agency, for his unstinting support over the course of some fifteen years. Once again, the talented production team at Penguin Random House and cover designer Stephen Mulcahey have done a brilliant job of turning the fruits of my imagination into a novel fit for any shelf. *The Barbarian* introduced me to two of history's great characters, neither of whom turned out to be as I'd formerly imagined them. For the detail of Flavius Stilicho, I have to thank Ian Hughes's book, *Stilicho: The Vandal Who Saved Rome*, while *Alaric the Goth* by Douglas Boin gave me an insight into the man who wasn't the enemy of Rome some histories would have us believe. Simon Macdowall's *The Goths* and *Empires and Barbarians* by Peter Heather provided the fine detail of the life he lived. As with *The Wall*, Mike Bishop's peerless *Roman Military Equipment from the Punic Wars to the Fall of Rome*, with J. C. N. Coulston, and *The Late Roman Army* by Pat Southern and Karen R. Dixon helped me navigate through the military life of Marcus Flavius Victor's time.

CALIGULA

Can a slave decide the fate of an Emperor?

Rufus, a young slave, grows up far from the corruption of the imperial court. He is a trainer of animals for the gladiatorial arena. But when Caligula wants a keeper for the emperor's elephant, Rufus is bought from his master and taken to the palace.

Life at court is dictated by Caligula's ever shifting moods. He is as generous as he is cruel – a megalomaniac who declares himself a living god and simultaneously lives in constant fear of the plots against his life. His paranoia is not misplaced however: intrigue permeates his court, and Rufus will find himself unwittingly placed at the centre of a conspiracy to assassinate the Emperor.

'Jackson brings a visceral realism to Rome in the days of the mad Caligula'
DAILY MAIL

'Light and dark in equal measure, colourful, thoughtful and bracing'
MANDA SCOTT

'A gripping Roman thriller'
SCOTLAND ON SUNDAY

CLAUDIUS

Rome AD 43. Emperor Claudius has unleashed his legions against the rebellious island of Britannia.

In Southern England, Caratacus, war chief of the Britons, watches from a hilltop as the scarlet cloaks of the Roman legions spread across his land like blood. He must unite the tribes for a desperate last stand.

Among the legions marches Rufus, keeper of the Emperor's elephant. Claudius has a special role for him, and his elephant, in the coming war.

Claudius is a masterful retelling of one of the greatest stories from Roman history, the conquest of Britain. It is an epic story of ambition, courage, conspiracy, battle and bloodshed.

'What stands out are Jackson's superb battle scenes . . . I was gripped from start to finish'
BEN KANE

'If I were Conn Iggulden or Simon Scarrow, I'd be rather worried by the new Scottish kid on the block'
THE SCOTSMAN

HERO OF ROME

AD 59. And the warrior queen Boudicca is ready
to lead the tribes to war . . .

Rome's grip on Britannia is weakening. Emperor
Nero has lost interest in this far-flung out post of his empire.
Roman cruelty and exploitation has angered its British subjects;
the Druids are on the rise, stoking the fires and spreading
the spark of rebellion among the British tribes.

It falls to the Roman tribune Gaius Valerius Verrens to lead
the veteran legionaries of Colonia in a last stand against the
rising tide of rebellion and Boudicca's seemingly unstoppable
rebel army. For a single act of violence has ignited the Britons'
smouldering hatred into the roaring furnace of war . . .

Hero of Rome is the first novel in Douglas Jackson's Gaius Valerius
Verrens series. The story continues in *Defender of Rome*.

'A splendid piece of storytelling and a vivid recreation
of a long-dead world . . . the final battle against Boudicca's
forces is as vivid and bloody as anyone might wish'
ALLAN MASSIE

THE WALL

AD 400. Rome and its Empire are failing . . .

And veteran cavalry commander Marcus Flavius
Victor knows his time is running out.

Through a combination of military prowess, brutality and bribery,
Marcus has spent years keeping the Pictish tribes at bay.

He's feared by his enemies, loathed by his superiors,
but it is his strength of will that has kept the disgruntled,
poorly paid garrisons of Hadrian's Wall in place.

And now he's embarking on a final tour of the forts along
the Wall. Each one holds memories, old friends, rivals, even
enemies and yet as his journey progresses, it becomes clear
that this is much more than a routine inspection.

What exactly *is* Marcus Flavius Victor's objective? Is he
preparing for a bloody civil war because he wants the province for
himself . . . or is he raising an army that could save Britannia?

**'A tour de force . . . cements his reputation as
not just one of Scotland's best historical fiction
writers but one of our best writers'**
DAILY RECORD

THE

CODEPENDENCY
WORKBOOK

SIMPLE PRACTICES FOR
Developing and Maintaining
Your Independence

KRYSTAL MAZZOLA, MEd, LMFT

callisto publishing
an imprint of Sourcebooks

Published by Callisto Publishing LLC C/O Sourcebooks LLC
P.O. Box 4410, Naperville, Illinois 60567-4410
(630) 961-3900
callistopublishing.com

Printed and bound in China
OGP 2

To Ethan: Our relationship is the most rewarding and tangible proof of my recovery. For many years, I wouldn't have been able to accept the profound love, respect, and support you provide me or have been able to return this to you. Thank you for being my partner, and best friend, in life. I love you.

Contents

INTRODUCTION   VIII

HOW TO USE THIS WORKBOOK   X

PART I: UNDERSTANDING CODEPENDENCY AND CBT   1

Chapter 1: Defining Codependency and CBT   3

Chapter 2: Identifying Self-Destructive Patterns   23

PART II: YOUR PATH TO SELFHOOD   41

Chapter 3: Set Your Goals   43

Chapter 4: Challenge and Replace Your Negative Thoughts   53

Chapter 5: Identify Your Triggers   77

Chapter 6: Problem-Solving in a Codependent Relationship   93

Chapter 7: Manage Conflicts and Emotions   109

Chapter 8: Reduce Stress and Calm Your Mind   129

JOURNAL PAGES   150

RESOURCES   158

REFERENCES   160

INDEX   164

Introduction

Welcome!

I am so happy you picked up this workbook, because I know that means you are seeking active guidance to recover from codependency. Your journey has likely been filled with self-doubt, confusion, heartache, and anger, and I congratulate you for taking this step. Your willingness to start this workbook means you've stopped looking outside of yourself to change your life and started going within to create this change. Your recovery has already begun.

I am a licensed marriage and family therapist who is both personally in recovery for codependency and professionally supports others in this process. Before we dive into your recovery, I want to tell you a bit about myself. I was born to a teen mother who was deeply enmeshed with her own mother, who has Borderline Personality Disorder. These relationship complications, growing up in an alcoholic home, and not knowing my biological father due to his serious and untreated mental illness contributed to my development of codependency. I have also been fascinated by healing and positive growth since I was a child. I began my recovery work informally through reading and journaling, and then formally, working with massage and mental health therapists. I was on my way to being interdependent for a long time but felt stuck for years in my patterns around romantic relationships. When I finally engaged in trauma therapy, I was able to resolve those last symptoms. Having been on both sides of recovery, I can say it truly is worth all the work necessary to do it. The sense of self-assuredness, trust, and peace I feel daily is personally and professionally rewarding. I am deeply grateful when I'm allowed to support a person's recovery journey.

Whenever I work with someone in their codependency, I always utilize Cognitive Behavioral Therapy (CBT) at some stage of treatment. This approach is essential to creating meaningful and lasting change, as it looks at the ways thoughts and behaviors can either support or detract from their recovery. I can say that without exception, all people in their codependency frequently think thoughts that intensify their distressing emotions, such as anxiety, resentment, and shame. These thoughts contribute to unhelpful ways of behaving, such as not communicating our needs directly or over-involving ourselves in the lives of others.

This CBT workbook will help to change personal thinking and behavior patterns that reinforce codependency. I deeply believe this book, along with other resources, will allow you to live in recovery. Have you heard the old cliché, though, that things get worse before they get better? This is true in therapy, time and again. It feels more emotional initially to directly address the thoughts and behaviors that reinforce codependency, as well as why it developed in the first place. If you find that you are struggling with uncomfortable feelings at first, you may find the support of a therapist beneficial.

Finally, I have written this book from a place of recovery in my own codependency. Therefore, I have no agenda about what you do with this information, only the sincere hope that it is a helpful tool in your recovery. I have insights into what skills will support your recovery, but your personal values and goals will influence your outcome. For example, if you are in a marriage with an addicted person, you will not be "forced" to leave. Instead, you will be asked to clarify your needs and explore how you may be reinforcing your codependency. Then you will learn skills to assert your needs, set boundaries, and change your own thinking and behaviors, so that you may live interdependently.

I deeply respect and admire you for your courage to change. Your willingness to pick up this book highlights that you have already begun to find your path toward recovery. Most people in codependency are unwilling to seek support from others, either because they do not see that their own issues contribute to their problems or because they don't want to be a "burden." I know for a fact that recovery from codependency is possible, both because I live in this reality and because I witness people recover all the time in my therapeutic practice. I sincerely wish you peace while you complete this workbook. I am excited for you to experience recovery. You are so worth it!

How to Use This Workbook

In this section, I will explain the outline of the book to act as an introductory guide to the process.

Part I provides an overview of codependency and its symptoms. You will also learn more about types of addiction and the addiction cycle. Part I provides a brief overview of both codependency and addiction. They often occur simultaneously, though not always, so it's important to have a clear understanding of both conditions. If you'd like to learn more, I encourage you to read my first book, *The Codependency Recovery Plan: A 5-Step Guide to Understand, Accept, and Break Free from the Codependent Cycle.* This workbook is a companion to that book, so you will find many of the concepts I reference briefly explained there in more detail. I also provide recommended resources in the back pages of this book for other concepts discussed here. Part I includes a quiz to better understand your current personal level of codependency. As you practice the skills in this book, I invite you to take the quiz again to see how you are progressing.

Part I is mostly informative, rather than practice-oriented, but you may still find yourself feeling strong emotions. This is completely normal. One of the core symptoms of codependency is minimizing as well as denying your feelings and perspective about how much certain situations affect you. Healing often feels more uncomfortable at first. Chapter 8 outlines many coping skills you can use if you find you are struggling with your emotional reaction to the material. You may also benefit from therapy with a licensed mental health professional. This is especially true if you are struggling with a mental health condition, addiction, or a history of trauma. Also, if you find that you feel stuck despite your honest effort and commitment to the guidance in this book, please consider professional support. A mental health therapist can be an ally in this journey; they will remind you to be self-compassionate, reinforce the skills you learn here, and ensure that you are not overlooking any thinking or behavioral patterns that prevent recovery. In the resource section, you will find some options to find a therapist in your area.

Part II will ask you to be introspective. I ask you to contemplate what you want to accomplish from completing the workbook and its activities. Chapter 3 will ask you to envision what living in recovery looks like to you. I want to encourage you to dream big here, as these wishes for the life you want to create are an intrinsic part of your authentic self. Whenever you tap into your authenticity, you move closer to living in recovery from codependency. These dreams will highlight your long-term goals. You will also be asked to identify the smaller steps—short-term goals—that will enable you to reach your big goals. I ask that all your goals are specific here, as research proves that setting clear goals facilitates greater change, and I want that for you.

Part II provides information on CBT skills, with activities that reinforce these skills to support removing codependent symptoms and patterns. You will follow an archetypal couple in their codependency from chapters 4 to 7 to help clarify these concepts and skills. In each chapter, you will read examples of how a person can implement each skill. Finally, you will be given the opportunity to practice and apply what you have learned to your own life. Each time you complete such an exercise in a chapter, you go deeper into your recovery! Please remember, though, that each skill will require contemplation and practice for it to feel natural and automatic. This is not a failure; it is a fundamental part of the recovery journey. You will benefit from returning to these exercises as issues arise in your life.

Chapter 4 explains common negative thinking, also called cognitive distortion, that reinforces your codependent symptoms, patterns, and overall sense of distress. You will also learn how to change your thoughts to be based in fact in order to reduce your stress. This cognitive restructuring process will allow you to think more clearly, and therefore respond more effectively when problems arise. No matter the goals you identify in chapter 3, thinking in a more positive and reasonable way will help you reach them more effectively. Becoming aware of and restructuring your thoughts is a fundamental CBT skill that requires effort and practice. You may find that even after learning this skill, you automatically think in negative ways. This is completely normal. The work is to practice restructuring so that, over time, you will naturally think in more supportive ways.

Next, in chapter 5 you will learn what triggers cause you to react, rather than respond effectively. Knowing your triggers allows you to face and conquer your fears, then plan ahead so that you are able to respond differently than how you typically do. You will learn two skills in this chapter: exposure therapy and response prevention. Both are important skills to learn how to respond effectively when you face a problem. I will give you examples and the opportunity to practice.

Once you have learned how to think in a more supportive way and to react to your triggers less often and less intensely, you will be ready to learn how to effectively solve problems in chapter 6. You will integrate the skills you have already learned in order to ensure that you are less reactive and don't distort the facts of a problem. Learning how to solve problems is an important skill in codependency recovery. It is empowering to learn that you do not have to defer to others to manage the struggles in your life. When you are able to respond maturely to problems, you will see how capable you truly are of handling whatever life throws your way. You will trust yourself more—a necessary step in developing self-love.

You will now integrate everything you have learned thus far to manage conflict in your relationships. Chapter 7 will teach you that you are capable of asserting your needs clearly and kindly, rather than denying them. This will help you be heard, as this method reduces defensiveness in any person you are having problems with. You will see how the case study couple integrates all the skills in an example provided. This will be the last time they will be referenced. Numerous other examples will highlight the layering of necessary skills. Finally, you will have the chance to practice for yourself.

Your hard work culminates in chapter 8, where you will learn techniques to better manage stress in your life. Many people in codependency are not sure how to care for themselves when they are upset, and this chapter will be your gentle guide. I encourage you to practice the skills explained with an open mind. As you read this chapter, you may find yourself thinking things like "Oh, I've already tried that" or "That won't work for me." If so, I encourage you to try again, because coping skills require practice to highlight their efficacy. Furthermore, some skills work better than others for certain emotions or situations, and you can't know this without allowing yourself the chance to explore.

I am so excited for your work to begin. Please remember that I believe in you completely. Throughout this writing process, I kept thinking about you, dear reader, and the courage and strength you will demonstrate as you read this book and practice the skills. You are so capable!

Part I

UNDERSTANDING CODEPENDENCY AND CBT

In part I of this title, you will be provided with the basic building blocks necessary for a deeper understanding of codependency and CBT. In order to attain this understanding, we will provide an overview of codependency, addiction, various symptoms, and the addiction cycle. A quiz has been provided in order to help you better understand your own level of codependency. While this section is more informative than practice-oriented, you may still find you have strong emotions. This is completely normal.

Chapter 1

Defining Codependency and CBT

This chapter will give you a clearer understanding of what codependency is, since there is often confusion around this subject. I will give a brief overview of the addiction process here, as codependency and addiction are often co-occurring, for the individual or in their partner. Finally, I will describe Cognitive Behavioral Therapy (CBT) and why this model will support your recovery. While reading this chapter, it's important that the primary recovery goal of interdependence is clear. When we recover from codependency, we become interdependent. World-renowned codependency expert Pia Mellody explains interdependence as the process in which we rely on ourselves, as adults, to take care of our basic needs and wants, while accepting support from others to meet needs that only they can provide. When we live interdependently, we allow others to care for themselves while offering the same support. We care for others rather than carrying them.

Defining Codependency

The definition of codependency is often unclear even when we identify with the term. As I described in *The Codependency Recovery Plan: A 5-Step Guide to Understand, Accept, and Break Free from the Codependent Cycle*, this confusion is due in part to the fact that codependency is not included in the *Diagnostic and Statistical Manual of Mental Disorders* (DSM-5). This manual directs the understanding and diagnosis of mental health disorders and their symptoms in the United States for mental health professionals. This exclusion of codependency from the DSM-5 means that no definitive explanation exists of codependency and its symptoms.

Although I spent years struggling in and then recovering from codependency, as well as professionally supporting others, I also struggled for a long time to clearly define it. I was still always struck by how this concept clearly resonates deeply with those experiencing it, even without an official clinical definition. My personal and professional observations revealed one clear unifying factor and led to my own definition: Codependency is the process in which people's focus on the world is external, so they seek their worth, and proof of their worth, from others rather than using an internal compass. Their focus is on "other worth," instead of "self-worth." A person who is codependent doesn't believe in their inherent value, so they believe they need external measures to "prove" their merit. In contrast, interdependency occurs when a person is focused internally first, because they trust in their inherent worth. They have a healthy sense of self and self-respect, so their actions reflect self-awareness, maturity, and integrity.

Caring about others is not the problem; the issue is the degree to which one self-neglects in the name of loving someone else. We are designed to care and connect with others in interdependency; however, as codependency expert Melody Beattie states, "Codependency occurs when these normal caring and connecting behaviors go too far." Codependency is a pervasive condition and a lens through which we see the people in our life and our experiences.

Understanding and identification of codependency has expanded significantly as more people have gained expertise in the subject. We now understand that codependency is a cluster of symptoms that exist in a person. Whether they are in a romantic partnership or not, the codependent process exists within them. Of course, codependents often attract one another, as their symptoms can play off one another perfectly. It is common for a codependent person to date someone they believe is toxic without realizing that they are contributing to toxic cycles because of their own thoughts, insecurities, and behaviors.

Codependency has two presentations. The first, with which we are more familiar, consists of people-pleasing and caretaking, while in the second presentation, people may be selfish and entitled. This second group of people may act in such a self-centered way that they may easily be confused with a narcissist. Beattie asserts that these codependents "expect life to be easier than it is." Mellody says that instead of feeling insecure or worthless, a person in their codependency may believe that they are better than others. This presentation of codependency, while not uncommon, doesn't often drive people to seek recovery, as it tends to be less overtly painful and costly to the individual. Those around them suffer more clearly and are likely to exhibit the first presentation of codependent described. Therefore, most of this workbook will focus on the caretaking and people-pleasing form of codependency.

Codependency often develops because of trauma in one's childhood. In fact, Pia Mellody defines codependency as a disease of immaturity caused by childhood trauma. When discussing trauma, it's important to note that the word "trauma" stems from a Greek word meaning "wound." While it's common for people in their codependency to resist blaming their parents for their struggles, most people in codependency can agree that they had some wounding experiences growing up. While rare, it does happen sometimes that one had a "good enough" childhood and codependency began from adulthood trauma such as a sexual assault or infidelity. However, codependency is a separate issue from post-traumatic stress disorder (PTSD). PTSD has its own cluster of symptoms, as well as a physiological aspect not present in codependency.

Some very common childhood traumas contribute to codependency development, such as growing up in an alcoholic or addicted home or having a parent with serious and unmanaged mental illness. Another factor that can lead to codependency is having to play a role in your family growing up, rather than being allowed to be your authentic self. In *The Codependency Recovery*

Plan, I outline why families rely on roles and what the specific roles are in much greater detail. In short, the more troubled your family was, the more likely it is that you had to play a specific role. These include the "Placater," the person who learns that they must exist to comfort others rather than expressing/coping with their own emotions; the "Hero," seen as the perfect child, whose mistakes are typically blamed on another family member; the "Scapegoat," the imagined source of all the family's struggles and the person most often blamed for any issues; the "Lost Child," often invisible and neglected by the family; and finally, "The Mascot," the imagined source of comic relief and joy in the family. People can play overlapping roles in a family. One can be the Scapegoat to their father but the Hero to their mother, which will further confuse their sense of self and self-worth. You may or may not relate to these roles, but whatever your personal wounds from childhood or adulthood, I will say this with certainty: Your codependent behaviors make sense given your history.

RELATIONSHIP CODEPENDENCY

Codependency exists with or without addictions present and whether an individual is in a relationship or not. It can manifest in any relationship, including between a parent and child, siblings, and friends. However, in a romantic relationship, the codependency that manifests may be so intense that it qualifies as "love addiction." It should be noted that, like codependency, love addiction is not in the DSM-5. Stanton Peele first brought the concept to popular awareness in the 1970s with his book *Love and Addiction*. Peele wrote, "Love is an ideal vehicle for addiction because it can so exclusively claim a person's consciousness. If, to serve as an addiction, something must be both reassuring and consuming, then a sexual or love relationship is perfectly suited for the task." Interestingly, when anthropologist Dr. Helen Fisher conducted studies on the brain chemistry of love, she found that tremendous quantities of dopamine and norepinephrine are at play when falling in love. Dopamine helps motivate us to seek what's rewarding, and it plays a key role in experiencing pleasure. Norepinephrine increases heart rate and is part of the rush and restlessness of falling in love. These same chemicals are experienced in massive amounts during cocaine use, although the "high" of falling in love can last much longer. Knowing this allows us to see how addictive a relationship can be.

Pia Mellody describes love addiction as the process that occurs between a "love addict" and a "love avoidant." The "love addict" creates a fantasy version of their partner and struggles to see their true character. In their obsessive fantasy, they often turn this person into their meaning in life or their "God." They will often feel "high" from their fantasy and obsess about how to be with the object of their desire. They may even wish to "merge" with them so they may be rescued from their own life. The "love avoidant" may present as a more self-involved presentation in their codependency. They are not genuine, and they hide who they are, creating walls that may even reinforce the love addict's fantasy. They equate love with being needed, and they feel attracted to—yet simultaneously resentful of—the "love addict." Therefore, they will create distractions outside of the relationship, like work or sex addiction, to prevent the love addict from getting "too close."

ADDICTION CODEPENDENCY

Historically, codependency and addiction have been considered interwoven disorders. The term "codependent" first emerged in 1979 to describe how life becomes "unmanageable" for someone in a relationship with an alcoholic. Prior to the identification of codependency, addiction treatment professionals observed that families would often display behaviors that actually prevented or complicated loved ones' recovery. While the understanding of codependency emerged from addiction treatment, we now know that they are separate processes.

Codependency can exist without addiction; however, the two still frequently overlap for two main reasons: First, being in a relationship with an addict or alcoholic is often attractive to a codependent person, because an addiction can demand much of the codependent's time, energy, and focus. They consistently have a moving target to prove their worth: how well they can care for the addict and get them to change. Second, it is painful living in codependency, so one may develop a behavioral or substance addiction to manage this pain. It is common for a codependent person to minimize their own addiction issues. Their typical external focus makes the codependent believe that other people cause their substance abuse or other behaviors by making them feel angry, disappointed, or neglected. They believe that other people are the problem, rather than the codependent's own choice of coping mechanism.

A person in addicted codependency plays the role of the enabler or the addict. The enabler, like the Placater, focuses primarily on protecting the person in their addiction from its natural consequences. They protect in the name of love, doing things like covering for a drunk friend after a car accident and saying they were the driver. This prevents the addicted individual from feeling the full gravity of the costs of their addiction, and actually contributes to the addiction. The addict may use their addiction as a mechanism of controlling others through their addiction. For example, an addict may control their partner, insisting certain topics such as finances never be discussed, lest the addict be "forced" to drink. The person with the addiction may manipulate their partner into taking care of all the household responsibilities or childcare. The addicted person may threaten that if the partner doesn't stay quiet about their concerns, they will have no choice but to use or drink recklessly due to their disappointment.

A Broad Look at Addiction

Addiction and codependency often—although not always—coexist, so it is important to have a clear understanding of addiction to understand codependency. As Pia Mellody asserts in *Facing Love Addiction*, "a person with an addiction is probably also a codependent; and conversely, a codependent most likely has one or more addictive or obsessive/compulsive processes."

Addiction, like codependency, is an often confusing and unclearly defined psychological concept, further complicated by how addiction is often stigmatized. Conversations around addiction have been moralistic and racist from the beginning of American history. Dr. Benjamin Rush, one of the men who signed the Declaration of Independence, called alcoholism a "disease of will." This narrative unfortunately holds strong, and there are still people who believe addicts are simply weak-willed people, too lazy or bad to stop using. This belief contributes to the false idea some codependents harbor: that their loved one is *consciously choosing* their addiction and would recover if only the codependent was "enough." Of course, as codependency itself is often a process of denial and minimization (see more in chapter 2), such a misguided view of addiction may reinforce the already existing denial of a codependent. It is common for those in codependency to feel justified in abusing a substance or behavior, but to judge another for that same process.

Our understanding of the nature of addiction is fortunately now more scientific than moralistic. Research shows that over time the brain changes from substance abuse, and addiction is now referred to as a brain disease. The American Society of Addiction Medicine's definition is:

> *"Addiction is a primary, chronic disease of brain reward, motivation, memory, and related circuitry. Dysfunction in these circuits leads to characteristic biological, psychological, social and spiritual manifestations. This is reflected in an individual pathologically pursuing reward and/or relief by substance use and other behaviors. Addiction is characterized by inability to consistently abstain, impairment in behavioral control, craving, diminished recognition of significant problems with one's behaviors and interpersonal relationships, and a dysfunctional emotional response. Like other chronic diseases, addiction often involves cycles of relapse and remission. Without treatment or engagement in recovery activities, addiction is progressive and can result in disability or premature death."*

Addiction is currently framed as a brain disease that involves increased use despite increasing and ongoing consequences due to that use. It should be noted that the DSM-5 avoids the term "addiction" and instead labels addictive processes as "Substance-Related Disorders." The DSM-5 clarifies that "the essential feature of a substance use disorder is a cluster of cognitive, behavioral, and physiological symptoms indicating that the individual continues using the substance despite significant substance-related problems." Consequences of continued use can include problems at work, school, or home, such as losing a job, dropping out of school, or increased fights at home over the use or behavior. "Whatever we're addicted to initially made us feel better, but eventually begins to make us feel worse," Pia Mellody writes.

American journalist Maia Szalavitz, who is in recovery for addiction, advocates for addiction to be seen as a learning disorder, rather than a brain disease like Alzheimer's. In fact, through her research, she found that all addiction theories state that learning is a fundamental aspect of the development of addiction for the brain. She says the importance of "seeing addiction as a learning disorder allows us to answer many previously perplexing questions, such as why addicted people can make apparently free choices like hiding their drug use and planning to ensure an ongoing supply, while failing to change their habits when they result in more harm than good." This approach is good news for recovery: If someone's brain can learn to prioritize the addictive substance or behavior, then their brain can unlearn this process as well. The learning disorder view of the brain disease of addiction supports what many health professionals know to be true: People can, and do, genuinely recover from addiction.

The DSM-5 does not include behavioral addiction, such as gambling, and the American Psychiatric Association asserts that there is not yet sufficient peer-reviewed data to establish the diagnostic criteria. However, as many can attest to the experience of codependency despite its exclusion, I believe that the same is true for behavioral addictions. The word "addiction" originates from the Latin word *addicere*, which originally meant "to speak to," but evolved to mean "enslavement to another." *Addicere* was used to describe the "debt slaves" in the Roman Empire, people who lost control of their lives as they acquired gambling debts. Interestingly, rather than being a new concept, it can be stated that a behavioral addiction—gambling—is the first recorded addiction.

Addiction is clearly a major issue in the United States. Statistically, whether you are in codependency or not, you are highly likely either to know someone struggling with addictive processes or to struggle with one yourself. In the latest national survey in 2018 from the Substance Abuse and Mental Health Services Administration (SAMHSA), which includes people aged 12 or older, 20.3 million people had a substance-use disorder. The rates of Americans who use substances but don't qualify for a disorder are much higher, with an estimated 164.8 million people having used tobacco, alcohol, or illicit drugs. This is 60.2 percent of the population, which means it is more common for people to use substances than to not do so in this country.

Prescription drug use is an issue of escalating concern, and few have not heard of the "opioid crisis" in the United States. In 2017, according to the latest data from the Centers for Disease Control and Prevention (CDC), there were 70,237 drug overdose deaths in the United States in 2017. This means that in 2017, 192 people lost their lives to a drug overdose *every single day*. Of these deaths, 68 percent involved an opioid (in prescription and/or illicit form).

As stark as these numbers are, none of this data includes statistics for those struggling with addictive behaviors such as food addiction, even as we can see evidence of this in the "obesity epidemic." About 93.3 million Americans, or about 40 percent of the population, are obese. This is a major public health concern, as obesity increases risk for a variety of health conditions, including type 2 diabetes and heart disease. Food can be an attractive coping tool; as Ulrich-Lai et al. (2010) reveal, foods high in sugar relieve stress similarly to the way sexual activity does.

It is crucial to note that many studies show that trauma is a common element in addiction and codependency. Khoury et al. (2010) found high rates of lifetime dependence on various substances (39 percent alcohol, 34.1 percent cocaine, 6.2 percent heroin/opiates, and 44.8 percent marijuana) in a highly traumatized population. Furthermore, the more severe the substance use, the more likely the person was to experience PTSD symptoms due to childhood emotional, physical, and sexual abuse. Hirth et al. (2011) highlight the specific connection between trauma and food addiction, finding that young women who have PTSD consume fast food and soda at higher rates than those young women without the diagnosis. Fast food is highly accessible in the United States, which makes it an easy substance to abuse. Finally, Mason et al. (2014) discovered that women with six to seven PTSD symptoms were more than twice as likely to struggle with food addiction than women without these symptoms. Addiction is an increasingly unhelpful coping style to self-medicate emotions.

SYMPTOMS

The DSM-5 states that a substance-use disorder consists of "a pathological pattern of behaviors related to the use of the substance," and includes 11 behavioral signs and symptoms. Two or more of the symptoms must have been met within the last 12-month period for a professional to diagnosis an individual with a substance-use disorder. If someone has two or three symptoms, the substance use is considered mild; four or five is moderate; and a person displaying six or more symptoms is diagnosed with a severe substance-use disorder.

The symptoms for a substance-use disorder include taking the substance in increasing amounts, especially as a tolerance develops. High tolerance means that one must take more of the substance to achieve the desired effect. Craving a substance is also a sign of a substance-use disorder. A person may use for longer periods of time and thus neglect their responsibilities. It is not uncommon to see people drop out of school, call in to work "sick," or frequently run late in their addiction. Interpersonal problems are another symptom of addiction, such as conflict in a marriage over the addicted partner being unavailable to parent their children. A person may also skip other activities they once enjoyed or stop engaging altogether. Using in a way that is dangerous to self or others, such as driving drunk, is another sign of a substance-use disorder. Other physical or psychological consequences include depression or damaged organs. Trying repeatedly to cut back use or to quit but failing is another sign of addiction. Finally, if a person quits and experiences withdrawal, this is another symptom of a substance-use disorder.

TRIGGERS

Triggers are emotional, social, environmental, and behavioral cues that reinforce a desire to use. Environmental triggers include going to a bar or seeing paraphernalia used to abuse the substance, such as a pipe. Emotions, including positive ones such as wanting to celebrate, are often triggers. In love addiction, engaging in fantasy thoughts is a trigger. It is important to note that sometimes traumatic triggers can lead to a desire to use. These triggers can be emotional or sensory (smells, textures, sounds). For example, if someone was sexually assaulted by a smoker, cigarette smoke may trigger their traumatic response of fight-flight-freeze. The overwhelming distress of these triggers can lead to the addictive process to try to cope. In addiction treatment, it is important to learn to cope with triggers effectively to prevent relapse.

THE ADDICTION CYCLE

Not everyone who abuses a substance or behavior will struggle with addiction. Some key risk factors for addiction are the age of first use or developmental stage, genetics, and a history of trauma. Personality also plays a role, as extremes in character, i.e. being reckless or especially fearful, can lead to addiction. Impulsivity is common. The DSM-5 highlights how some people have lower levels of self-control, perhaps due to "impairments of brain inhibitory mechanisms," which may predispose them to addiction.

ABUSE VS. ADDICTION

It is not uncommon for humans to turn to a substance or behavior to cope with life's distresses. However, when a person overly relies on substances or harmful behaviors to cope, an abuse cycle can develop. The overt behaviors may look similar in both the abuse and addiction phases. However, in abuse, it will be easier for a person to stop if desired. In addiction, the brain has undergone significant changes that make it more difficult or impossible to stop.

INITIAL USE

A person will never develop an addiction without first use of the substance, engagement in the behavior, or, in the case of love addiction, the first interaction with the object of fantasy. The timing of this interaction makes a crucial difference. Research shows that if a person waits until an age after complete brain development, typically in their twenties, to begin using substances, it is highly unlikely that they will develop an addiction.

TOLERANCE

Eventually, a person may need to use or engage in the addictive behavior for longer amounts of time and at greater doses to get the desired effect. High tolerance occurs when the brain changes in response to the drug. One of the most tragic examples of tolerance is in opiate addicts who overdose after some sober time. A person may relapse and choose to inject the same amount they were using prior to abstinence, when they had increased tolerance. Tolerance drops after sober time, however, so this dose can lead to accidental overdose death because the body/brain is no longer adjusted to such a high dose.

WITHDRAWAL

Withdrawal is a negative emotional or physical state in the absence of the substance. It happens because the brain now depends on having the substance in the body to function. Many people have the image of a person physically withdrawing from drugs, such as heroin. Emotional withdrawal is less obvious; it often takes the form of anhedonia, meaning a person cannot feel pleasure from activities that most find enjoyable. This process may last for months to years. Love addiction also has a withdrawal phase, which can lead to depression. Some people in this phase of their love addiction can benefit from antidepressants.

PHYSICAL CRAVINGS

Cravings occur as part of the learning process, in which the brain has been conditioned to seek the reward it associates with the addictive behavior or substance. The brain "tells" the addicted person to acquire the substance or engage in the behavior it believes it now needs.

DEPENDENCE/EMOTIONAL OBSESSION

Moving from abuse to addiction involves the learning pathways of the brain. Dependence can be physical, because the brain has adapted around the use to be functional. Emotional dependence results when someone feels they must cope in a specific, addictive manner to manage the distress of life. It's not uncommon for a dependent person to be obsessed with thoughts of acquiring the substance or engaging in the behavior and planning to make this happen. According to Pia Mellody, a person in love addiction will "focus almost completely on the person to whom they are addicted; they obsessively think about, want to be with, touch, talk to, and listen to their partners, they want to be cared for and treasured by them."

RELAPSE

Relapse is a key feature of the addiction process. Up to 60 percent of people will relapse, eventually returning to the addictive substance or behavior, even when they have attempted to abstain. When this happens, other approaches, such as developing new coping skills, may be needed to fully recover. For example, a person may relapse after an intense fight with their spouse. This can highlight the need for better self-soothing and coping skills, such as deep breathing or journaling, plus communication skills to prevent relapse in the future.

ADDICTION CAN TAKE MANY FORMS

We have discussed in this section that addiction can be either substance-related or behavioral. Most basically, if a behavior or substance gives a person a desired feeling—such as relief, numbness, or euphoria—it can become highly attractive and lead to abuse, and then addiction. Commonly abused addictive substances include alcohol, cocaine, and opioids (both prescription and illicit versions such as narcotic painkillers and heroin). Common behavioral addictions include food addiction (typically overeating or binging on high-fat, high-sugar foods), sex addiction (which can include reckless sexual activity), infidelity, compulsive pornography use and masturbation, and addiction to technology/social media (compulsively checking and updating one's social media).

Defining Cognitive Behavioral Therapy (CBT)

The initial image of therapy that pops into many people's minds is of a patient on a couch describing their childhood while the therapist takes notes. Entering my office for the first time, clients often remark in surprise that I ask them to take a seat rather than lie down. My clients also commonly say that they had a good childhood and don't want to dig into the past. While there are countless therapy models, it's clear to me that the one still most often portrayed in popular media is psychoanalysis, the therapeutic approach developed in the early twentieth century by Sigmund Freud. His model is centered on the belief that all people experience trauma as infants because of the inherent helplessness of the experience. Psychoanalysis then seeks to make conscious how this affected one's desires and impulses unconsciously, thus allowing the patient to move to catharsis. This approach is vastly different from other more commonly used models today.

Therapy models provide a clear and comprehensive framework to facilitate positive change in clients. There has been a push in the psychology field for decades to ensure that models can be proven effective by research; these are the evidence-based or empirically validated treatments. Cognitive Behavioral Therapy (CBT) is one of the most famous of these empirically validated treatments. Dr. Aaron T. Beck, a fully trained and practicing psychoanalyst, created CBT in the early 1960s. He wanted the medical community to accept psychoanalysis as legitimate and knew that for this to happen research would need to prove its efficacy. He created a series of experiments to prove the benefits of psychoanalysis. However, his research revealed the need for a different approach from psychoanalysis to treat depression, focused on the distorted thoughts and beliefs, or cognitions, that are a primary feature of depression. CBT treatment focuses on solving one's current problems by changing the unhelpful thinking and behavior patterns that reinforce them.

CBT's fundamental principle is that events in life trigger our thoughts, which impact our emotions, which then influence our behaviors. These behaviors add up to our life circumstances, which may or may not be problematic. How we think and feel about a life event—or "trigger"—will impact our lives and relationships. Any event can be interpreted in countless ways, either to help the individual cope or to add to their distress. The CBT cognitive model addresses the thoughts, beliefs, and behaviors that contribute to our psychological problems. Simply put: When we change our thoughts and our actions, we change our lives.

In CBT, the therapist works to empower the client so that they may be able to solve their own problems moving forward; this is why the treatment model is designed to be short-term. From the very beginning, the therapist helps the client identify the current thoughts that reinforce the presenting problem—the problem that brings a person to therapy, such as anxiety or social concerns. The therapist shows the client how the thoughts reinforce the presenting problem, as they lead to problematic behaviors. For example, a person may feel that they are "awkward" (thought/core belief), which makes them nervous in social situations (feeling), which causes them to avoid eye contact and pause excessively throughout conversation (problem behaviors). The person may continue to believe that they are "awkward," even though it is this false belief combined with the resulting feelings and behaviors that creates this socially uncomfortable reality.

Some thoughts become central to a person's view of themselves, others, and the world. These thoughts, or "core beliefs," create a schema in which the person organizes the events of their life and work through often negative filtering. For example, a person may have a core belief that they are "dumb." This schema will support them in organizing their world based on this belief. They will focus on times that they failed a test or were passed up for a promotion, but will dismiss times that they excelled academically and professionally. Negative filtering is an example of a cognitive distortion, or an error in thinking. These thinking mistakes tend to be consistent and systematic.

CBT therapists work to identify a person's personal cognitive distortions to support them in empowering themselves to challenge these false ways of thinking that reinforce distress and unhelpful behaviors. Chapter 4 will outline these cognitive distortions in detail to support you in identifying—and challenging—your personal ones. Therapists also help the client identify their core beliefs and begin to notice exceptions to them. This allows a client to think differently about themselves or their life, which reduces their suffering over time.

WHO CAN BENEFIT FROM CBT?

While CBT was first developed to treat depression, it has since been adapted to treat many presenting issues, including anxiety, PTSD, and addiction (both substance abuse and behavioral addiction). CBT can even address couples' issues. No matter the population that CBT is adapted to treat, the guiding principles remain consistent. Fundamentally, CBT always addresses the importance of identifying those of one's thoughts that negatively impact mood and behaviors, with the goal of changing these thoughts so people can feel—and cope—better.

Since Beck first developed CBT, he and countless other researchers have sought to prove that it works to support immediate and ongoing change in a person's life. Research consistently shows that CBT effectively addresses many presenting problems and that many people maintain their gains over time. The simpler question may then be, "Who can't benefit from CBT?" While consistently proven to support recovery for a wide range of psychological disorders, CBT is, of course, not the only treatment. Some people may only respond slightly to CBT and benefit more from a different modality. In my experience, cognitive models greatly support mental health and addiction recovery, as they support the development of new and healthier ways of thinking and coping with life's distress. Sometimes, however, core beliefs are difficult to completely change through a cognitive model alone. In these cases, I find that a trauma modality, like Eye Movement Desensitization and Reprocessing (EMDR), can support a person in changing their negative cognition to one that is more positive and life-enhancing.

WHAT ARE AUTOMATIC THOUGHTS?

Every person has countless thoughts every day; some are functional, while others reinforce our distress. In CBT, an automatic thought is one that simply pops into your head without any effort. For example, if someone bumps into you at the grocery store, you may automatically think "Watch it!" This thought reinforces anger, which causes you to scowl at them. Some thoughts are consistent and may even feel like permanent features of your personality. Cognitive distortions are automatic thoughts that we consistently think that are not based in fact and add to our distress. For example, you may believe that you are just a glass-half-empty kind of person, while you may simply have many negative automatic thoughts.

WHY CBT FOR CODEPENDENCY?

CBT emphasizes that common filters and cognitive distortions reinforce one's presenting concern—in this case, codependency. I will explore these filters and distortions in detail in later chapters, but all of these problematic ways of thinking can be seen in codependency. Codependents often have frequent errors in thinking that reinforce their pain, their resentment, and the codependency itself. For example, it is common for a codependent to believe that it's bad or selfish to have any self-interest, and as a result they will feel guilty when they experience a normal urge to engage in self-care. Many people will cope with this guilt in unhealthy ways by stuffing it, denying their need for self-care, and overcompensating for the guilt by fixating on others' needs.

In CBT, we see that an event will trigger a thought. A person who is codependent will experience most life events much differently from an inter-dependent person. An example of such an event is walking into a kitchen where the sink is overflowing with dirty dishes. A codependent person may think, "This always happens to me! My family thinks I'm the unpaid maid." This thought can lead to feelings of anger and resentment. The codependent will then act on these feelings in a specific way—they may "accidentally" break their wife's favorite mug when putting it in the dishwasher and then feel justified in this behavior. An interdependent person, on the other hand, will have a much more balanced view. They may walk into the kitchen and think, "Wow, the kitchen is a mess! I know that my wife had an early meeting today, though, and my son didn't get home from his job until late and still had to study for that test." They may feel annoyance at the reality of dirty dishes, but they won't take it personally and won't feel the need to act out. They may instead realize that they have time to clean up the dishes today but will ask for a family meeting to avoid this experience in the future.

Much of the codependent cycle centers on the unhelpful thoughts that reinforce it. Codependency's external focus can trick us into believing that we are helpless and victimized by others, but this is a false belief. The reality is that unless we are in an abusive, controlling, or violent relationship, we make choices as adults that affect our lives. We feel stuck because of these false beliefs that lead to maladaptive behaviors and reinforce the situations that make us feel bitter and resentful. We recover when we remember the truth, which is that we have options, make choices, and are responsible for our choices and behaviors.

CBT is a wonderful model that helps us recover, as it helps us notice our thoughts and beliefs that reinforce our codependent symptoms and behaviors that lead us to feel "stuck." We realize that we can interrupt this process through mindful attention to our current cognitive distortions and false beliefs and then explore alternative ways of viewing situations. This is very empowering! CBT highlights that we always have a choice in how we react, unless of course our nervous system becomes hijacked, and then sometimes the best we can do is take a time-out. (See more about that in chapter 6.) In codependency, we often are compelled to feel or act in a certain way because someone "made" us do it. When we use the CBT tools, we no longer have to feel controlled by others. If we choose our actions, then we choose the state of our life. We will no longer be victims, and we can make positive changes in our own lives.

CBT is a skills-based therapy that seeks to empower the client so they can be their own source of positive change maintenance. One way this happens is by the therapist asking for accountability in the therapy process in the form of therapeutic homework. Research has shown this is a valuable component of CBT treatment. A meta-analysis of the impact of homework on efficacy in

CBT treatment (Mausbach, Moore, Roesch, et al.) that included 23 studies with 2,183 subjects in total found that when patients fully engaged in the homework portion of treatment they had greater improvement rates regardless of what symptoms led them to seek treatment (i.e., depression, anxiety, or substance use). This is great news when completing a workbook!

It is important to give yourself grace throughout your recovery process. An important CBT principle is that all behavior makes sense, as it all serves a purpose. We developed codependent thoughts and behaviors for honest reasons, often due to trauma. We can have self-compassion when these old ways of thinking and behaving continue to present themselves.

Your willingness through this process will serve you well. Burns and Nolen-Hoeksema (1991) found that when patients were more willing to learn positive coping strategies, they more readily recovered from their depressions. You are your best ally in your recovery process, and your willingness to contemplate all workbook prompts, to journal, and to practice the new skills provided will help you recover much more quickly and in a lasting way.

WHEN TO SEE A THERAPIST

This workbook, while a great resource in your codependency recovery work, cannot substitute for therapy when you need it. If you are struggling with suicidal thoughts, it is very important to seek professional support to reduce this type of thinking. If you are experiencing intense depression or anxiety, professional support will help you recover more effectively. Addiction will also complicate codependency recovery, and a therapist can help you manage the addictive cycle. Finally, if you have a trauma history, you may benefit from a trauma therapy like EMDR. In addition to therapy, there may be times to consult with a psychiatrist, including any experience of intense suicidal thoughts and symptoms of depression or bipolar disorder. The combination of psychiatric treatment and therapy is ideal for some.

Chapter 2

Identifying Self-Destructive Patterns

Codependency often includes many self-destructive patterns of thought and behavior that reinforce our pain, resentment, and sense of being less than others. This workbook is your guide to changing these patterns. In this chapter, we will first build awareness of the specific ways in which you may continue to reinforce your codependency. This insight will better prepare you to specifically target your codependent thoughts and behaviors and move toward recovery.

Codependent Qualities

Codependent schemas—or belief systems—and thoughts exist within the self, although some relationships highlight or even exacerbate these symptoms. While each person's codependency may manifest in unique ways, it stems from some common qualities. Codependency always includes distorted thinking, or, to use the language of CBT, cognitive distortions. I will describe these distortions in detail in chapter 4, but some common errors of thinking in codependency are personalization, all-or-nothing thinking, and "should" or "must" statements. Codependents often personalize others' negative behavior as a reflection of their worth, rather than considering alternative reasons for it. All-or-nothing thinking is like black-and-white thinking, where we get stuck in believing that there are only two options in a situation, rather than remembering that life occurs on a continuum. Finally, "should" or "must" thinking involves believing that you know best how others should behave, while exaggerating how bad it will be if they don't behave according to these expectations.

A common example in codependency that integrates all three of these distorted thoughts is deciding that a loved one must stop using substances, and that their only option for this is total abstinence, which they will achieve by entering residential drug treatment. When they are not willing to do this, we may believe that it's because they don't love us enough. Otherwise, they would enter drug treatment and stop using altogether. Since they are unwilling, we believe that we are destined for failed relationships because we are clearly unlovable. Intimacy problems are fundamental to the codependent experience. We cannot have healthy and intimate relationships while consistently personalizing others' behaviors and trying to control them based on our own measures of what is best for them. Let's look at some of the more common key qualities often included in codependency.

LACK OF SENSE OF SELF

When I hear someone say, "I don't know who I am," I know with certainty that they are struggling with codependency, even if I don't know their specific symptoms. A key symptom of codependency that I hear time and again is people feeling they've lost themselves, or never knew who they were in the first place. This often develops from having to play a role within a dysfunctional family system growing up that robs us from connecting with our authenticity. Experiencing serious trauma can further disconnect codependents from our sense of self, as our focus becomes survival-oriented, rather than on expansion and exploration of self and the world. A common manifestation of this appears when a codependent makes a new friend or starts dating someone new, when we will often feverishly research and adopt the new friend or partner's hobbies. A person in their codependency may not be able to identify their authentic interests, or even true beliefs regarding politics or spirituality, for example.

In codependency, people will often define themselves by their roles—mother, employee, business owner—rather than knowing who they are authentically. They may also be driven to perfectionism in these roles to prove their worth. This externally based sense of self is fragile, and if something changes in their life, such as losing a company or a relationship, they may feel suicidal, as they feel they are truly losing themselves and their reason to live. This lack of self-awareness is commonly coupled with a lack of self-worth, which can contribute to suicidal thoughts and feelings. These thoughts may be active—having a plan and intent to die, or passive—not having any plan, but feeling that it would be okay if they just happened to be in a fatal car accident, for example. Common thoughts of suicide, however, are to be taken seriously. If you are having thoughts of suicide, please seek professional support as soon as possible.

Finally, when someone does not have a clear grasp of who they are, they will often not realize, or they will minimize, how things truly impact them. They may accept others' version of reality over their own gut instinct and may even feel bad or sick about questioning others. For example, if they suspect their partner of cheating with a coworker, a codependent person may feel they are wrong or bad to even have this thought. This can make them especially vulnerable to manipulation or gaslighting.

LACK OF SELF-RESPECT

Self-loathing and the resulting lack of self-respect are fundamental to the codependent experience. This lack of self-respect may manifest as physical and emotional health risk-taking, such as sleeping with a new partner without discussing safer sex or risking finances by supporting an adult family member who is in their addiction.

Codependents do not fully believe in their worth. If they did, they could not behave in ways that seriously risk their health and wellbeing. People in codependency typically feel like they are not "enough"—not lovable, pretty, smart, rich, or fit enough. However, please remember though, that as American culture has such pervasive marketing of perfection it may be difficult to fully escape this type of thinking, even in recovery.

A few cognitive filters reinforce this symptom of feeling less than others. One is failure, or the belief that we can't do anything right. Another is worthlessness or defectiveness, a belief that we are inherently broken or damaged. Finally, helplessness reinforces total dependency and the belief that we can't cope because of our own anxiety and/or inadequacy.

NEED FOR APPROVAL

With approval seeking, someone primarily behaves to receive approval or to fit in and lives inauthentically to do so. When someone self-describes as a "people pleaser," they are revealing that they are struggling with codependency even when they aren't familiar with this concept. A people pleaser consistently prioritizes others' wants, needs, and even perceived expectations over what they personally need to gain approval. Complicating this is that they may be so externally focused that they may not even know what they need. If they do know what they need or want, they will frequently believe any self-interest or self-care is bad and selfish, leading to feeling inappropriate guilt. We feel appropriate guilt when we violate our own values system, and this teaches us to live with integrity. You will feel appropriate guilt when you lie, for example, if you value honesty. Inappropriate guilt is feeling a sense of responsibility to make amends when you did nothing wrong. Having basic needs and wants is a basic human right and experience and this cannot be "wrong." Your needs and wants are crucial, as they will help you to know who you are authentically. Your emotions, thoughts, needs, and wants are not burdens. In fact, someone treating you as if your emotions—not behaviors—are a problem is abusive. In healthy, interdependent relationships, others can tolerate and accept our emotions, thoughts, and needs, even if they differ from their own, and will seek compromise and negotiation.

Two common CBT cognitive filters in this symptom are abandonment and approval seeking. A person with abandonment as a schema believes that others are unavailable to them and that they will leave them when someone better comes along. Therefore, they may work hard to prove that they are worth staying for, emotionally and physically, such as by doing all the household tasks like cooking and cleaning.

LACKING THE ABILITY TO NEGOTIATE

Displeasing others feels life-threatening to many people in their codependency. The feeling that others could be irritated, inconvenienced, or, worst of all, angry at us feels like something to avoid at all costs. Many people in their codependency also lack self-awareness, so they may notice feeling resentful, but will not be able to directly identify their needs. Finally, if a codependent person does know what they need, it is common to feel guilty about it. As a result of these issues, many people in their codependency won't advocate for themselves.

Since codependents often abdicate their basic rights and control over their lives to keep others around or happy, they often feel trapped or held hostage to others' wants, needs, or expectations of them. They will then feel resentful of those in their lives. Resentment is always a sign that we are not advocating for a need or a boundary that we personally have, due to a lack of awareness, fear, or shame (believing you don't have a right to your needs).

Some negative schemas described in CBT that may be present with this symptom are emotional inhibition, emotional deprivation, or subjugation. Emotional inhibition occurs when we suppress our feelings and avoid open communication with others to avoid disapproval. Emotional deprivation is the belief that others will be unwilling or unable to meet even our basic and appropriate needs. This schema can prevent us from negotiating for ourselves, due to the belief that other people will consistently fail us anyway. Subjugation is when we feel forced to deny our emotions or needs, due to the belief that others will attack or leave us if we do express ourselves.

NEED TO SAVE OTHERS FROM BAD CHOICES

By definition, people in their codependency focus externally rather than internally. Therefore, we often find it more comfortable to fixate on how others can improve their lives rather than looking at our own behaviors and the consequences of these actions. This obsession with how others behave often has at least two purposes for the codependent: to show "love" and to make the codependent person feel better and more "in control." As I discussed in *The Codependency Recovery Plan*, a central paradox in codependency is that the more someone focuses on controlling others, the more out of control they will feel, since no person can change another.

While commonly coming from a place of care and love, others will often resent the codependent attempting to "save" them, as these efforts often come off as self-righteous. It is a very personal process to identify, explore, and become willing to change our own behaviors. Codependency centers on denying, minimizing, and rejecting the truth and reality of situations. We may think that we know who someone is more than they do; for example, that they are more ambitious than they really are and they just need to find their passion. Or we may want to prevent our loved ones from experiencing any discomfort as a result of their choices. The reality is that our loved ones will make choices that will lead to distress for them at times. This is part of their personal journey, and we are not responsible for it. We cannot prevent this, or even help speed up the process of them "learning their lesson."

Finally, as part of this external focus on others' choices, we will often minimize our own unhealthy behaviors or decisions, and rationalize or justify why we make them. This process prevents our personal recovery, as we cannot change unhealthy behaviors if we don't acknowledge them. Of course, at the same time, it's common to deny others this grace of minimizing or rationalizing. Two CBT negative schemas present in this symptom are enmeshment/undeveloped self and unrelenting standards. In enmeshment, a person feels that they must be fused to another. Therefore, they may feel completely justified to control another's decisions, as it genuinely feels like they are making decisions for both of them. Perfectionism often ties into unrelenting standards. In this schema, we strongly believe that there are a right and a wrong way to do things—based on our own values—and believe it may be catastrophic if things are not done in the right way.

CODEPENDENCY QUIZ

1. *You just started dating someone a couple of months ago, and you just had your first weekend away together. You feel things went wonderfully, but upon returning your new partner discovers his youngest child is being bullied and asks for a few days to deal with this before seeing you again.*

    a) You understand, but (without his request) email him a list of counselors and articles on bullying to help him.

    b) You totally understand—it must be so painful and stressful to discover this. You let him know that you are happy to see him when he can, and that you are available to talk/text if he likes while the dust settles.

    c) You act accepting at first, but then become angry that he is putting you on the back burner. You have needs, too! Send him a text about how he needs to figure out how to balance having a relationship with being a parent, because this isn't fair to you.

    d) You are convinced that over the course of this trip he discovered something about you that he hates and this is his way of preparing to break up with you.

2. *You are proud of yourself, as you finally have an emergency fund, which you have spent a long time saving up for. Shortly after reaching this goal, your brother calls and tells you he was arrested for drunk driving and doesn't have the thousands of dollars for an attorney.*

a) You let him know how stressful this is and how you hope he will go to treatment. Give him the money, but only half of what he is requesting, as you want to have a little money still in your savings account.

b) You tell him no. You have been afraid for a long time about his reckless drinking habits. Let him know that it's unfortunate that he got himself into this dilemma, but you are hopeful he will accept the full weight of this consequence and learn from it.

c) You think, "Of course this would happen just when I finally have a safety net," but give him the money. Moving forward, you track how he is spending his money and make comments every time you see him about how he can afford to spend in this way.

d) You give him the money because he's your baby brother. You know he can't ask your parents, as they are on disability. You are obligated to him.

3. *You can tell your boyfriend is stressed. When you ask him what's wrong, he tells you he doesn't want to talk about it.*

a) You drop it, but struggle to stop thinking all night that maybe he's angry because of something you did wrong.

b) You say you understand, but that you care, and say you would love to talk to him if he wants to do so later.

c) You get mad! You are his girlfriend and he's obligated to tell you what's wrong. Let him know that he's supposed to tell you everything.

d) You think that the relationship must be over if he's completely shut you out like this.

4. *Your husband called your child names after another night of binge drinking.*

    a) You talk to your husband about your concerns about his drinking but stop talking about it when he tells you that it won't happen again (even though he doesn't tell you how he plans to prevent this).

    b) You tell your husband that you know you can't make him change, but also that you can't tolerate living with verbal abuse and you are responsible for protecting your child, even if it's from their other parent. Ask if he is willing to attend couples' therapy with you to prevent this from happening again.

    c) You don't talk to either of them about the incident directly but "accidentally" knock over the liquor shelf when you are dusting.

    d) You talk to your son about how his dad has a lot of stress right now and come up with a plan with your son so he can avoid angering his father in the future when he is drinking.

5. *You are a divorced parent when the "man of your dreams" comes along. He is everything you ever hoped for in a partner. There is only one problem: He is moving halfway across the country. You know your parents would love to have your children with them, and they wouldn't even have to move schools.*

    a) You don't move but you leave your children with their grandparents whenever you can get a long weekend to go visit him. You justify getting into a little debt for this traveling as your self-care.

b) You know that it's not appropriate to disrupt your children's lives for someone you just met. You can continue dating and, if things work out, you can reevaluate in a year or so.

c) You stay, but tell your children the sacrifices you make for them any time they upset you.

d) You are convinced that if you don't move with him, he will find someone else because he's so perfect. You need to work on this relationship to give your kids the perfect father figure, so you leave them with your parents and make the move.

6. *You finally get the courage to break up with your toxic partner when they message you asking to meet up.*

a) You excitedly text them back and make plans for tomorrow. Then you do some journaling because you feel conflicted. At this time, you remember why this relationship was unhealthy for you, so you text them back to cancel.

b) You tell them via text that you wish them well, but no longer want to engage with them.

c) You ignore the message and feel joy every time you think about how you finally have the upper hand.

d) They deserve the chance to be heard, so you meet up with them. You are so excited when they tell you they will finally change (even though they've told you this before) and reunite with them. Your friends and family will just have to understand!

7. *While going through your finances to prepare your taxes, you discover a large amount of money is missing from your joint savings account with your wife. When you confront her, she confesses that she has been betting online and just needs a little more time to win the money back.*

    a) You tell her you understand that she wants to earn this back, but that you can't risk losing any more money, so you must go to the bank and remove her name from the savings account.

    b) You ask your wife when this problem started and if she is willing to seek support for this. If not, seek guidance from an attorney about how to protect your assets, as you don't want a divorce, but you also don't want to risk your financial health.

    c) You tell her that you knew she would betray you, just like everyone else has done.

    d) You accept that she needs more time to win the money back. It's the least you can do for her, considering she puts up with you and your faults.

8. *You have an especially hard day: a fight with your daughter, a poor review at work, and getting stuck in traffic for over two hours. Now you just discovered you have an outstanding medical bill that you owe hundreds on, which you were not planning for. When you get home:*

    a) You feel sorry for yourself for a while and vent/overeat/drink/watch TV/go on social media a little too much, but then regroup and take a nice bath and go to bed early.

b) You remember that difficult experiences are just a part of life and that while they piled up today, you have many good days, too. Take a walk with your dogs as you normally do and prepare a nice balanced meal. Engage in your normal healthy rituals as usual.

c) You obsess about all the ways your daughter has disappointed you and send her a lengthy email about it.

d) You ruminate all night about how your life is a failure because you are a failure.

9. *Your best friend consistently cancels plans with you and cuts you off when you are in emotional distress. A mutual friend observes this and shares that this must be painful.*

a) You agree. It does hurt a lot, but you are unsure how to bring it up.

b) You thank your friend for her support, as this has been bothering you. Let your friend know that you are going to discuss this issue privately with your best friend, which you do. You let your best friend know clearly what your needs are moving forward and pay attention to if your friend is being more respectful or not when you decide what to do next.

c) You tell your mutual friend that it's okay, because you are secretly having an emotional affair with your best friend's husband.

d) You tell your mutual friend that she is wrong. It's okay that your best friend is like this because she always has so much going on, and you are lucky she makes any time for you.

10. *You are on your way to see a concert, which you planned a month in advance with a good friend when you receive a text message from your husband asking you to come home so he can avoid his addiction.*

   a) You go to the concert. You have waited for months for it, and you don't want to disappoint your friend. However, tell your husband you will call him every 20 minutes to give him moral support.

   b) You tell your husband that you feel empathy for how stressed he must be right now, but that you will not break your commitment. Remind your husband that he can call his sponsor, but also know that you are not responsible if your husband relapses.

   c) You go home. You resent that he wants you to be his babysitter and make rude comments and faces at him all night.

   d) You return home. This is not the time to be selfish.

QUIZ RESULTS

If you answered mostly A's: Your level of codependency is low, or you have already been doing codependency recovery work and it's paying off. However, there are still a few ways you are likely working on improving, such as knowing your needs, asserting yourself, and letting others manage their own lives. This workbook will support you in developing more tools to fully enter recovery.

If you answered mostly B's: Congratulations! You live primarily in an interdependent state. In other words, you are in recovery from codependency, if you experienced it previously. You will likely have less to relate to from a place of deep pain throughout this workbook. You will still benefit from the exercises, as our lives can always become more expansive, abundant, and joyful.

If you answered mostly C's: You are likely still struggling with codependent symptoms on an ongoing basis. If you relate to these answers, you are behaving in a passive-aggressive manner. This means that you struggle to get your needs met by directly letting others know what you need, so you indirectly seek ways to hurt them back for the ways they've hurt you. They may not even be aware they are hurting you, because you likely don't communicate directly about it. Moving forward with this workbook, please consider the automatic thoughts (chapter 4) that reinforce this way of behaving, as I know they cause great pain for you, and probably for your loved ones, as well. Please know that you have a right to your needs and that others may still be unable to meet them. You can assert yourself and tolerate the discomfort of being told "no" when it happens. This workbook will help you.

If you answered mostly D's: You are likely struggling in your codependency on an ongoing basis. Your codependency likely comes from a place of feeling not good enough, so you try hard to compensate for your perceived brokenness by making yourself useful to others. Of course, every human being has a finite of amount of resources (energy, time, money), and you will likely burn yourself out and then resent others, which causes you to feel like a victim. This type of thinking is probably contributing to your automatic thoughts (detailed in chapter 4) that reinforce your belief that you are less than others. You are not. You have equal worth and value. Your behavior simply enables others to take advantage of all that you offer.

Selfhood

Selfhood connects to being an individual and accepting the self as separate from others' identities. When people discuss the value of being authentic, it is an encouragement to live connected to our selfhood. We experience selfhood when we are who we are outside of our roles, obligations to others, or even cultural or familial expectations. You may be a real estate agent or a father, for example, but selfhood goes beyond that. We are people with complex histories who behave the way we do based on the thoughts and behaviors we acquired honestly. We are a unique combination of characteristics—strengths and flaws, attitudes, temperament, needs, desires, passions, and dreams—that make up who we are as individuals. This is our selfhood.

Codependency disconnects us from our authenticity; therefore, it's totally normal to be unsure of who you are as you begin this workbook. The skills taught here will help you identify your values, your needs, and the belief systems that may be preventing you from fully self-actualizing. Self-discovery is empowering. As we learn who we are, we will trust and like ourselves more, which leads to more self-care, and eventually self-love.

Part II

YOUR PATH TO SELFHOOD

Now that you have completed part I, it's time to move forward and practice a few CBT skills. These activities have been specifically created in order to support removing codependent symptoms and patterns. Additionally, you will follow an archetypal couple in their codependency from chapters 4 to 7 in order to help drive home the concepts and skills you are about to learn. In each chapter, you will read examples of how a person can implement each skill. Finally, you will be given the opportunity to practice and apply what you have learned to your own life.

Chapter 3

Set Your Goals

This chapter will help you become more self-aware, which is essential to recovery from codependency. You must know who you are, including your needs, wants, and values, so you can live authentically rather than in reactivity to others. Furthermore, we must gain self-awareness so we can cultivate self-love. While it's a cliché, it is true that we can only give and receive love to others to the degree that we love ourselves. The path to self-love begins by building a relationship with ourselves. After all, it is nearly impossible for most people to deeply and unconditionally love a stranger. This chapter will help you learn who you are so you can become a friend to yourself.

The Importance of Setting Goals

I know that you are likely still feeling disconnected from yourself, but you picked up this workbook for a reason. What motivated you to explore codependency recovery now? The answer to this question will help to reveal what motivates you and point you toward the goals that you will now identify.

Setting goals is valuable for two important reasons: Goals give insight into your genuine self, *and* they help you effectively recover. When you get in the driver's seat of your car, you typically have a clear destination in mind and you can map out the best route. Without this internal sense of direction, you would often be lost. Goals clarify the steps you should take to recover. They highlight your values and originate naturally from a place of hope. I find that your goals are typically are already within you; they are intuitive and will come to you with ease. It's insecurities, criticism, and fear that hold you back from working toward them, or even saying them out loud.

Goal-setting theory examines why some people perform better than others with equal intelligence and skill. It reveals that in addition to intellectual and literal capabilities, motivation affects human accomplishment. Locke and Latham (1991) studied goal setting and task performance. They found that goals must be specific to be effective. A vague goal can lead to some less than desirable outcomes. For example, if someone says they want to stop working so much, they may cut back hours at work without addressing the underlying reasons for their workaholism, possibly to avoid their family and self-care. They may then replace this unhealthy behavior with another fixation, such as marathon training. This may look healthier on the surface, but it still allows them to abuse their bodies with their obsession and stay away from home.

Specific goals allow you to be intentional about your change *and* assess yourself accurately. Research has found that when a person sets vague goals such as "I will do my best," they perceive themselves as accomplishing more than they are actually accomplishing. The specific goal of wanting to lift more weight can be better assessed than the vague goal of becoming "stronger." The person with the specific goal can see when they are literally lifting more weight and can appropriately motivate themselves to continue. If a person just wants to be stronger, they may be able to lift a lot more weight but may stop at 50 pounds rather than 68 pounds. They will never discover their true potential, due to the human tendency to positively evaluate ourselves with vague goals.

SHORT-TERM GOALS

You likely have big-picture goals for your recovery, such as finally knowing who you are, being able to say "no," or having a healthy relationship. These goals are fundamental to a satisfied life. However, short-term goals—or goals you would like to accomplish soon—are also necessary. Any goal that you can fully accomplish in less than a year is considered short-term. Sometimes these goals can be reached in a day, or they may take a little longer, such as a week or a month. Short-term goals often lay the necessary groundwork for completing a long-term goal. For example, one may have the long-term goal of graduating from college. This goal consists of many smaller short-term goals, such as completing the college application by the end of next month. This short-term goal can be further broken down into even smaller and shorter-term goals, such as reaching out to references one day and writing the rough draft of the personal essay on another day. Short-term goals are empowering; they allow you to work toward your big dreams in more attainable steps. As they can be accomplished quickly, they will show you how capable you are and will reinforce your ability to complete your long-term goals.

LONG-TERM GOALS

Long-term goals are your dreams in life, or what you most want out of it. In codependency, a common long-term goal is to be able to love yourself. Because of their personal significance, these goals may seem lofty or even impossible, but as short-term goals reveal, they can be broken down into smaller tasks. I once heard that change happens very slowly, and then all at once. This deeply resonated with me, because day after day in my therapy office I see clients planting seeds toward their larger goals. Working toward goals in therapy can initially be dissatisfying, as the results of one's efforts are not often revealed quickly. One day, though, a person is finally capable of integrating all the skills they have learned to live a life in recovery.

Let me highlight this: Change toward your long-term goals will not typically be evident at first. For example, if you want to be able to forgive your parents, it may not feel like you are making any progress on this for some time. But if you set smaller goals toward this, such as practicing self-compassion through encouraging statements, doing trauma work with a therapist, or writing a letter to your parents in your journal to honestly acknowledge your feelings, you will likely find that one day, forgiveness will arrive. Use your long-term goals as inspiration as you work toward them and remember why you are working so hard, but then acknowledge that it is truly a process. If you stay committed to recovery and to your smaller goals, you are on your way to a deeply rewarding life.

READY TO BEGIN?

Now, please contemplate the specific direction in which you would like to guide your life. While perhaps cheesy, really think about what "living your best life" would mean to you. Take a moment to journal about the life you hope for, in as much detail as possible. Think about your professional life, your physical and mental health, finances, and relationships. Your best life may include being debt free, having supportive people in your life, or accepting your body no matter its size. Also, if you notice you are struggling with an addiction of any kind, you may want to envision your life without this unhealthy way of coping. Imagine replacing this coping mechanism with something healthier for you, such as being able to talk to a friend or take a walk instead of engaging in your addiction. This is your chance to dream. I encourage you, for a moment, to try to imagine the world through the eyes of a child when you dream about your recovered life, rather than censoring yourself. No dream of yours is too grand or silly. Your dreams are profoundly meaningful and highlight who you truly are.

Step One: Journal Your Concerns

This workbook is your recovery ally, and in this section, I want you to honestly explore your concerns. Is there anything weighing you down as you explore your codependency and look toward recovery? This is a safe space for you, and no one else needs to see it.

Prompt 1: When you described your best life, you could identify the following barriers (examples: lack of education, time constraints, financial concerns):

_____

_____

_____

Prompt 2: Sometimes even when we want something positive, we are afraid of the negative consequences of change. We may fear losing a relationship or that others won't like us if we show them who we truly are. I encourage you to identify at least one thing that you notice you are afraid of in the event that you do recover.

_____

_____

_____

Prompt 3: Imagine a person who is unconditionally supportive of you. What advice would they give you so you could plan to manage the barriers you identified in Prompt 1? What insight or encouragement would they have about your fears from Prompt 2?

_____

_____

_____

Step Two: Set Your Goals

It is important that you set both long- and short-term goals for yourself, as described previously, to most effectively recover. Now you will contemplate these goals.

Prompt 1: The three big-picture, long-term things I most want to change are:

_____

_____

_____

Prompt 2: Now identify a minimum of three smaller, specific ways you could work toward each long-term goal in Prompt 1.

For example:

1. *One thing I most want is a community of supportive friends.*

   - Work with a therapist to reduce my social anxiety
   - Participate in the social events hosted at work, such as potlucks
   - Volunteer in order to meet others with similar interests

_____

_____

_____

Prompt 3: Identify one even smaller goal that could be accomplished within one week's time toward one of these smaller goals from Prompt 2. Then hold yourself accountable and practice this one thing within the week.

For example, perhaps in Prompt 1 you want to reach the long-term goal of honestly saying that you love yourself. Your short-term goal may be to develop a self-care plan to cultivate self-love. Your even shorter-term goal may be to identify that you want to go to a yoga class, then find a studio by your work and sign up for it later this week.

WHAT HAPPENS IF YOU SLIP?

Human beings are intrinsically imperfect, so making mistakes is a part of the change process. I know that many people in their codependency struggle with perfectionist attitudes, so I want to state this explicitly: Plan to make mistakes. If you have been working toward a goal and notice that you are starting to slip, that is normal. Use this regression as information. Notice what thoughts, behaviors, or circumstances contributed to your regression, but then move forward. The most important part of changing is that we continue to get back on track whenever needed. The most important thing is not to get stuck in any perceived failure. You may have unhelpful thoughts that prevent getting back on track, so in the next chapter you will learn how to change your thinking patterns to support your recovery.

Moment of Reflection

In this chapter, I asked you to deeply consider who you are through the lens of your goals. You also learned about the importance of setting specific goals to truly have the life you most desire. Barriers and insecurities can impede our recovery work, so you were also asked to identify and plan around these. The act of identifying your goals paves the path to transformation. You are cultivating greater self-awareness by knowing what life you most want to create for yourself. This is a powerful process that requires patience. The larger goals understandably take more time, so keep your vision in mind for your recovered life, while setting and working toward smaller goals to feel accomplished, empowered and capable. I genuinely believe in you!

Chapter 4

Challenge and Replace Your Negative Thoughts

Now that you have identified your goals, you can identify and challenge the negative thoughts that prevent you from fully living in recovery. During this phase, you will learn to be more mindful of your unhelpful thoughts and find new ways to think about your emotions, relationships, and life events. This process of learning to think differently is called cognitive restructuring. In chapter 2, we identified some core belief systems, or schemas, related to codependency symptoms. I encourage you to refer back to this section if desired so you may note what schemas you relate to (if you have not already done this). This will help inform your exercises throughout this chapter. In the next section, you will learn about other patterns of thinking that reinforce codependency.

Case Study

You will now meet an archetypal codependent couple and you will follow them throughout this workbook. This example will allow me to better explain the concepts and exercises. Please note, this case study is to provide clarity and is not all encompassing. Your personal experience of codependency may or may not exist in a romantic relationship. This workbook will still prove useful to recover from all codependent relationships, whether romantic, platonic, or familial.

Manish, 43, and Jade, 38, have been married for three years after dating for two years. Jade had a string of failed relationships throughout her twenties. She would always blame herself when they ended because she believes she's "not enough." She grew up in an alcoholic home, and her mother often blamed her as the cause of her father's drinking. Jade tried her best to get good grades, stay quiet, and keep the house clean when her mother was working to support her and her father. However, no matter her efforts, she still "failed," because her father continued to drink. She was relieved to meet Manish, who said he was ready to settle down after years of a bachelor lifestyle. Jade felt validated that she was finally enough, as Manish chose her after dating many other women. In reality, Manish proposed to Jade because he loved how she showered him with attention. She always seemed to be able to prioritize him: cooking his favorite meals, keeping the house clean, and giving him sexy surprises, all while managing her job as a paralegal. The only downside for Manish was that sometimes Jade would nag him about his drinking. He responded that he deserves to relax after working hard. Jade would back off and rationalize that his weekends of binge drinking were okay, even if he was disrespectful when drunk. After all, he has a successful job, unlike her father.

Jade's "acceptance" of Manish's drinking didn't take away the nagging pain in her stomach when he did drink. She never knew what he was going to do, like say something condescending to her in front of his friends or be overly flirtatious with another woman at a party. Manish's drunk behavior triggers her feelings of being "not enough," which makes her depressed. She stops showering Manish with attention when depressed. This upsets him because he believes Jade is obligated to care for him, and it triggers unconscious feelings of neglect, as his own mother abandoned him. When this happens, he drinks heavily to cope. Seeing how sad Manish is always seems to help Jade get out of her depression; he needs her, and this is a reason for her to get up in the morning. The cycle then repeats.

Identify Your Negative Thoughts

Beck discovered that patients struggling with a mental health disorder tend to have negative and automatic thinking patterns. These negative thoughts can be verbal or visual, such as visualizing a car crash every time you get in the car. Very simply, this negative thinking reinforces one's core issues, such as depression, addiction, or codependency. These thoughts are not based in fact; rather, they are distortions of reality, and are therefore referred to in CBT as cognitive distortions. This skewed reality intensifies distress and contributes to the likelihood that a person in codependency will react ineffectively. I detail 10 common distortions below. As you read these, I encourage you to highlight which patterns of thinking you notice in yourself. After you gain awareness of this, you will be able to be more mindful when you are thinking in an unhelpful and inaccurate manner.

The 10 common cognitive distortions are:

1. ***All-or-nothing thinking:*** *This is extreme thinking in which one sees themselves, others, and the world in black-and-white terms. They see only two options when interpreting a situation. For example, "If I make a mistake, I'm a total screwup." In reality, most things exist on a continuum. A clue that we are engaging in this thinking is using the terms "always" or "never," both of which are rarely true. Codependents commonly engage in this type of thinking when they believe that they "always" care for others who "never"*

show up for them. This type of thinking prevents considering options for our thoughts and reactions.

2. *Discounting the positive:* A person using this specific mental filter overlooks, denies, or minimizes positive experiences or qualities. They may attribute achievements to luck only while discounting the hard work it took to accomplish what they did. A nice gesture may not count, because it was "owed" to them for the caretaking they did. This type of thinking prevents the feelings of joy and gratitude that energize and sustain us.

3. *Catastrophizing:* This cognitive distortion is also called a fortune-telling error. It happens when a person believes they can predict the future, but their prediction is extremely negative. They also tend to exaggerate how badly they will cope if the worst happens. The actual outcome in both circumstances is likely to be a lot less extreme. This type of thinking intensifies anxiety and can often lead to avoidance, procrastination, and passivity. In codependency, people sometimes catastrophize by thinking, "I can't let others know what I really feel or they will hate me. And if they hate me, I won't be able to handle it."

4. *Personalizing:* This distortion, common in codependency, occurs when a person mistakenly believes they are the reason for another's behavior, even when there are other, more plausible reasons, and they are not responsible at all. For example, a person may spend the day wondering what they did wrong if another person is rude. When someone personalizes, they overlook other possible causes of another person's behavior, like that they may be tired, sick, or irritated with someone else.

5. *Overgeneralization:* This thought happens when a person draws an exaggerated and cynical conclusion that goes far beyond what's actually happening. For example, a person may overgeneralize by thinking, "I'm going to die alone," when they had just one bad date.

6. ***"Should" or "must" statements:*** *This thinking occurs when a person has a fixed expectation regarding their own or others' behavior and exaggerates how bad it will be if these expectations aren't met. In the case study, we can see that Manish believes Jade "should" constantly be available to meet his needs for him to feel loved. He then feels abandoned when she fails to meet this expectation.*

7. ***Labeling:*** *This is when a person judges themselves or another person for an event or a quality in an extreme manner. Internally directed labeling reinforces shame. For example, a person may think they are a dumb loser if they fail a test, when really they struggle in one subject but do well in other classes. Labeling directed at others prevents deeper understanding. A person may think, for example, that their friend is a "heartless jerk" after discussing politics, when this friend is really very supportive.*

8. ***Mind-reading:*** *Another distortion very common in codependency, mind-reading occurs when a person believes they know what another person is thinking and/or feeling without considering other options or asking them. This evaluation is usually inaccurate and negative. An example is believing that your romantic partner clearly doesn't care about you if they are silent when you share a story, when they may actually be listening, but uncertain as to how to respond.*

9. ***Emotional reasoning:*** *This is when a person believes that if they feel something it must be true, while in reality, emotions are subjective. Not all people feel the same way about the same things. A person may think that because they feel as though others don't like them, this must be true. Many people may like this person, but this false reasoning causes them to misinterpret social interactions.*

10. ***Mental filtering:*** *This is when a person ignores the big picture and focuses on the negative details of a situation or person,*

intensifying distressing emotions. They may say they had a bad day, when in reality they are noticing only the things that upset them and not the positives, like great weather. This is different from discounting the positives previously, as in mental filtering a person does not notice the positives at all.

These distortions greatly affect our views of self, others, and the world, and they always contribute to more suffering. Distorted thinking leads to more distressing emotions. These emotions then influence our behavior in usually unhelpful ways, either for ourselves or in our relationships. These reactions may include picking a fight or refusing to tell someone what we need. We can then have more cognitive distortions based on how we choose to react, which contributes to a cycle of feeling stuck and hopeless.

In the following section, you will be given three exercises to help you notice with greater clarity how thoughts impact emotions and actions, an important element of cultivating deeper self-awareness. For this exercise, you will need to identify basic emotions. It is very common in codependency not to be able to clearly identify our emotions and to have a limited vocabulary for them, so I have provided some basic emotion vocabulary here to assist you with this exercise:

- **Anger; includes annoyance, irritation, and frustration**
- **Sadness; includes disappointment**
- **Grief**
- **Fear; includes nervousness, anxiety, uncertainty, and fright**
- **Guilt**
- **Shame; includes embarrassment and the feelings of worthlessness and being "not good enough"**
- **Happiness; includes joy**
- **Gratitude**
- **Hope**
- **Loving/loved**
- **Excitement**
- **Passion**
- **Stress; includes distress**
- **Calm; includes peace and acceptance**

SITUATION EXERCISE 1

Manish and Jade are attending a mutual friend's wedding. Manish tells Jade that he wants to ensure he can relax throughout the evening after a stressful work week, so he will be drinking prior to the event. Consider the following three thoughts Jade could have and how they would affect her mood and behavior.

Thought #1: Great, now I'm going to have to monitor him all night instead of having fun, so he doesn't embarrass us.

> EMOTIONS: Anger, Resentment, and Anxiety
>
> REACTION: "Babysit" her husband all night by counting his drinks and watering them down when he gets up to spend time with others or use the restroom. Unable to focus when good friends come over and want to chat with her, because she's keeping an eye on Manish.

Thought #2: Why am I not enough for him to relax and have fun tonight without alcohol?

> EMOTIONS: Shame and Anger
>
> REACTION: Stuff her emotions while he's drinking at home. Feel embarrassed at the wedding about her own imperfect marriage. Make passive-aggressive comments about their friends' relationship being so much better than "some other peoples'" relationships during the ceremony.

Thought #3: I'm not excited that he will likely be drunk before we even arrive, but I can't control that. I'm going to focus on reconnecting with friends tonight rather than on what he may do.

> EMOTIONS: Disappointment, yet calm/acceptance
>
> REACTION: Breathe through her upset. Accept that he is allowed to act in any way he wishes. Spend time with friends rather than "babysitting" him throughout the evening.

Now you will have the opportunity to identify the likely emotional and behavioral outcomes for each thought for two situations. You can journal each response in the space provided.

SITUATION EXERCISE 2

Darnell's mother, Ruth, calls him multiple times a day since she divorced her second husband, whom she started dating when Darnell was a teenager. She sometimes even calls in the middle of the night. Darnell's own father died when Darnell was only seven, and prior to passing, he instilled in Darnell that he is now the man of the house, responsible for his mother. Darnell therefore ensures that he is always available to his mother, but this is taking a toll, as his sleep is disturbed by her calls and it's affecting his work. He's especially exhausted one night when she calls and asks him to come over to be with her.

Thought #1: I need to be stronger and suck it up. I'm the only man in my mom's life now, and she needs me more than ever.

EMOTIONS: _____

REACTION: _____

_____

Thought #2: I never realized that my mother is so weak until now. Can't she keep it together for one night?

EMOTIONS: _____

REACTION: _____

_____

Thought #3: I understand that she's having a hard time, but I realize I can't get behind any more in my sleep or at work. Eventually it will become too much for me, and I won't be able to support her. I need to find a way to support my mother while also taking better care of myself.

EMOTIONS: _____

REACTION: _____

_____

SITUATION EXERCISE 3

Mila and Erin, both 26, have been friends since they were toddlers, as their moms are best friends. Lately Erin has been very flirtatious with Mila's fiancé, José. Worse still, José seems to enjoy and encourage the attention. Mila wants to talk to Erin about this but has been having one of the following thoughts.

Thought #1: Wow, I'm really losing it. Erin and José are my best friends. Of course, I want them to be close. What's wrong with me to be upset about them being friends?

EMOTIONS: _____

REACTION: _____

_____

Thought #2: I don't want to create problems for my mom with her best friend. I had better keep my mouth shut and just keep reminding José that his needs are met at home by having sex with him more often.

EMOTIONS: _____

REACTION: _____

_____

Thought #3: I have a right to be concerned about them flirting, and even if Erin is offended, it's important that I bring it up with her to avoid unnecessary stress, anxiety, and judgment.

EMOTIONS: _____

REACTION: _____

_____

YOUR TURN!

Please identify a current situation that causes automatic negative thoughts for you. Then, follow the outline below.

1. Describe the situation:

_____

_____

_____

2. What thoughts are you having about this situation? Please identify any cognitive distortions.

_____

_____

_____

3. What emotions does this thinking cause?

_____

_____

_____

4. In what ways have you behaved (or do you want to behave) because of these emotions?

_____

_____

_____

5. What are the effects of this behavior on your self-image and your relationships?

_____

_____

_____

Challenge Your Negative Thoughts

By now, you have identified at least some of your mistaken thinking that contributes to intense negative emotions. You may be wondering how to "watch your thoughts" now, so that you can challenge them.

I have good news: Every error in thinking that you engage in can be challenged so that you will feel less distress. A good way to start this process is to begin to observe when you are having a strong emotional experience. When you are feeling intense emotions about something, you may be engaging in automatic thinking that's exaggerating the way you feel. At this point, pause and explore what skewed thoughts you may be having. Next, begin to challenge this thought to feel less distress.

Cognitive restructuring is the process of challenging negative thinking. Renowned psychologist Albert Ellis described it as "disputing irrational belief," and created a systemic way to do this that was integrated into CBT. Ellis' method highlights that irrational beliefs (IBs) can be changed to rational beliefs (RBs) and that this change in thinking will improve functioning. RBs are "self-helping," whereas IBs are "self-defeating." A key component of challenging your negative thoughts is to assess the facts of a situation that lead to your distorted thoughts. Ellis would ask, "What is the evidence to support your distorted thought?" For example, a person may believe others will reject them if they speak up, the common cognitive distortion of catastrophizing. They can challenge that belief by asking, "What proof is there to support this belief?" Another way to challenge negative beliefs is to consider the consequences of refusing to give up your negative thinking, using a process called pragmatic questioning. This person may think, "What will happen in my life if I continue to believe that rejection is certain if I assert myself?" This belief will prevent them from speaking openly and directly about their needs, so their needs will continue to be unmet. They will continue to be unhappy and resentful because they refused to speak up. Finally, a person can also shift their thinking from absolutes to preferences, while reinforcing their ability to cope with disappointment. In the same example, a person may think, "I prefer to be accepted by others all the time, but this may not be possible. I can learn to tolerate rejection of all kinds so that I may live authentically."

Now that you know the steps to challenge your negative thinking, please consider what cognitive distortions you think commonly. In my professional experience, prior to cognitive restructuring, most people frequently engage in at least three of these thinking mistakes. It's not uncommon for someone to think nine or all ten of these thoughts. When I was training to become a therapist and first learned about cognitive distortions, I realized that I engaged in nine out of the ten on an almost daily basis. There is no shame in having a lot of mistakes in your thinking. You came by it naturally.

Rather than judging yourself for these thoughts, I encourage you to celebrate that you have more awareness of them now. This is an accomplishment, and is a sign that you are recovering. There is a reason you developed these mistaken thoughts. In the case study, we can see that Jade personalizes Manish's drinking, and when we remember her childhood, it makes sense. Her mother explicitly blamed her for being responsible for her father's drinking. Of course, as a little girl, Jade had no way to control her father's choice to drink. This is also true of her husband's choice to drink; she is not responsible for how he chooses to cope or behave, even though she is affected by it.

At this time, you will be provided two examples of how to restructure your thoughts.

CHALLENGE NEGATIVE THOUGHTS EXERCISE 1

Your spouse sends a text message in the middle of the day that throws you off course. They are blaming you for getting their morning off to a rough start because you woke them up when you were getting ready, and this is their one day off work. You think, "Great, the whole day is ruined now. I wanted to go out with them and have fun tonight, but now we can't!" and become overwhelmed.

Try taking the following course before allowing yourself to react:

Challenge #1: Reality check. Consider what evidence there is to support your thought that because they are angry the whole day is ruined.

"I realize he's angry, and now I'm hurt and defensive. Even though he's angry and may decide to stay in that mood all day, I'm still capable of having a pleasant day. I'm still at work and I can still do nice things during my day, such as going to lunch with a coworker. Maybe I can talk to him in a manner that helps de-escalate things."

Challenge #2: Pragmatic questioning. Consider the consequences of indulging your negative thought. Contemplate how these consequences detract from your short- and long-term goals.

"If I continue to think that my whole day—and our whole night—is ruined because my husband is angry right now, then it will be ruined because I won't do anything productive to help myself or my relationship. I will stay miserable, which prevents learning how to cope in healthy ways with whatever life throws my way."

Challenge #3: Put things in perspective. Remember that you have preferences but don't need to get attached to things being a certain way.

"I would prefer if we can manage this situation to have a nice date tonight, but that's out of my control. However, I can decide to find ways to cope so my day is better."

CHALLENGE NEGATIVE THOUGHTS EXERCISE 2

Daniela and Matias, both 19, have been dating for a couple of years when they get into a fight about moving in together. Daniela tells Matías that she's not ready to move out of her parents' home yet. Matías keeps arguing, because he keeps thinking to himself, "If she's not ready now, she will never be ready to live with me! She should be ready by now!"

Challenge #1: Reality check. Consider what evidence there is to support Matías's thought that she should be ready to live with him, and that if she's not ready right now, she will never be.

"We are both only 19. Neither of us has a full-time job, and we are both in school. It may be true that we aren't yet ready to handle the financial responsibilities of living together. I also know that Daniela's family is really religious, and maybe she's afraid of what they will say or think if we live together before we are married."

Challenge #2: Pragmatic questioning. Consider the consequences of Matías indulging his negative thought. Contemplate how these consequences detract from his short- and long-term goals.

"If I continue to think that Daniela should be ready, then I'm going to judge her for not being ready. I really want to be a good husband eventually—unlike my dad—so it's important that I learn to understand her rather than judge her. If I continue to think this means we will never live together, I may feel hopeless and break up with her, which is the last thing I want to do."

Challenge #3: Put things in perspective. Remember you have preferences but don't need to get attached to things being a certain way.

"I would prefer to live together now, but I can learn to accept that she's not ready. I can ask her what would make her feel more comfortable with living together so we can work toward the goal of sharing a home eventually."

YOUR TURN!

You will now challenge your own negative thoughts. Please consider the prompts below to work on restructuring your thoughts. The more you practice this when you're less distressed, the more capable you will be of doing it when you're emotional.

Prompt #1: Consider a social situation that triggers your negative thoughts, including any cognitive distortions.

Challenge #1: Reality check. Consider what evidence there is to support your thought.

_____

_____

_____

Challenge #2: Pragmatic questioning. Consider the consequences of indulging your negative thought. Contemplate how these consequences detract from your short- and long-term goals.

_____

_____

_____

Challenge #3: Put things in perspective. Remember that you have preferences but don't need to get attached to things being a certain way.

_____

_____

_____

Prompt #2: Consider a situation in your family that triggers negative thoughts, including any cognitive distortions.

Challenge #1: Reality check. Consider what evidence there is to support your thought.

_____

_____

_____

Challenge #2: Pragmatic questioning. Consider the consequences of indulging your negative thought. Contemplate how these consequences detract from your short- and long-term goals.

_____

_____

_____

Challenge #3: Put things in perspective. Remember that you have preferences but don't need to get attached to things being a certain way.

_____

_____

_____

Replace Your Negative Thoughts

Negative automatic thoughts are often rigid and extreme, which intensifies distress. Cognitive restructuring highlights that the reality of a situation is often much more tolerable than our initial perception indicates. Putting things in perspective, you notice that you have options in the way you think about a situation. This shift helps you to think in more helpful ways.

Your new thoughts will be more supportive, as they will integrate the reality of a situation. This balanced approach helps you feel less overwhelmed, and maybe more hopeful or empowered. These replacement thoughts show you how to respond to situations, rather than unconsciously reacting to them. Supportive thoughts are a healthy coping skill. Every time you find a new way to think about something that's more empowering, you are deepening your recovery.

Modifying your thoughts has numerous components, but first you must identify the negative thought. You then practice cognitive restructuring to find an alternative and more supportive cognition. Throughout this chapter, I have emphasized identifying cognitive distortions. This is because, in general, these distortions have a corresponding supportive thought. For example, when catastrophizing, you can remember that outcomes are usually not so drastic. Or, when discounting the positive, you can remember that both negative and positive events happen, and you can give them at least equal weight.

Numerous strategies help to create a replacement thought. These strategies include investigating the evidence to support our negative thought as we did in cognitive restructuring. You can then think in a more neutral or encouraging way. For example, you may think, "I'm a bad person if I take time for myself." When you explore this belief, though, you may notice that you respect others who practice self-care. You may also notice that they are less stressed than you are. So, you may replace the initial thought with, "Even though I feel guilty when I practice self-care, I know it's a way to start feeling less stressed. I will take time to take care of myself regularly, and I can learn to cope with my feelings of guilt."

When exploring facts, you may notice sometimes that there is some accuracy in your original thought. The thought can still be replaced to be more positive, however. At these times, it's important to remember that most things in life exist on a continuum. While it may be true that others may be uncomfortable or even angry if you set boundaries, it is also highly unlikely that everyone in your life will reject you for this. You may choose to think, "Some people may not like when I set boundaries, while others may respect me more for it. Even though I'm uncomfortable when others are upset with me, I must tell people what my needs and limits are so that I can be less resentful."

Finally, if you struggle to find a replacement thought, try imagining others going through the same situation with the same negative thought you have. Sometimes we can see reality more clearly when it feels less personal. Let's say that you have just been put on a performance plan at work, and you think that this is confirmation that you are dumb. This may feel deeply true. If you envision that your best friend has just been put on a plan at work and feels dumb, you may see the reality that this is only a sign of one issue at work. You will remember that your supervisor gave you positive feedback, but is concerned about your sales numbers. Then you will recognize that you are smart enough to create a plan to improve your sales technique, such as talking to colleagues or reading books. The new thought is: "I am disappointed that I have been put on a performance plan, but this is an opportunity to grow. All people have areas where they do less well, but I can develop skill with practice. I am capable."

With enough practice, you will eventually stop thinking so negatively in the first place. However, it's important to be patient with yourself, as this takes quite some time. A great way to help your mind have fewer automatic thoughts is by developing a mindfulness practice, which will be outlined in chapter 8.

REPLACE NEGATIVE THOUGHTS EXERCISE 1

You will now be given examples to teach the action steps required to replace your thoughts.

You are about to send out a group email invite to a holiday dinner you are planning when a negative feeling creeps in. You begin to picture the dinner as a disaster: Your spouse will show up late and inebriated, your family will disapprove, and relatives who don't get along will create problems. Your dream of a lovely holiday has quickly turned into a scenario of dread and disappointment in your mind. How can you turn this feeling around?

Step 1: *Recognize. Acknowledge that a negative thought has entered your mind.*

I'm noticing that I'm afraid my holiday dinner will be ruined. This will then ruin the holidays! I'm catastrophizing and overgeneralizing.

Step 2: *Respect your emotion and go through the process of cognitive restructuring from the previous section.*

It's okay that I'm nervous. I love the holidays and they really matter to me. I can't control my spouse, but I know that my family has been supportive of me while I work things out in my marriage. They may be stressed if my spouse is late and drunk, but they can be understanding. After all, my brother and his wife worked things out after she had an affair, and my family has been accepting of them. If I choose to keep worrying about a ruined dinner, I know I will put more pressure on my spouse to "behave," which often backfires.

Step 3: *Replace.*

Using the thoughts identified in step 2, create a new perspective of the problem. Find a more balanced viewpoint.

I am worried about the holiday dinner not going smoothly because of my spouse, but even if the worst happens, my family will continue to accept me and respect my need to make my own choices. It is one dinner, and the holidays consist of numerous events. I can still have a pleasant holiday season.

REPLACE NEGATIVE THOUGHTS EXERCISE 2

Late one night, Manish reaches for Jade and suggests that they have sex. She declines, saying she's tired. Manish feels rejected and starts to view his body negatively. He thinks to himself, "Of course she doesn't want to have sex with me. I'm gross. I shouldn't have had those fries earlier today."

Step 1: Recognize.

I'm noticing that I'm taking Jade's lack of interest in sex personally right now.

Step 2: Honor emotion and practice cognitive restructuring.

I'm feeling embarrassed and insecure. However, Jade has expressed to me in the past that she doesn't have a high sex drive. One side of fries isn't going to make me disgusting.

Step 3: Replace.

Sometimes, people are not interested in sex, and that does not mean that their partner is disgusting. She's told me many times that I am attractive to her, but I am noticing I'm feeling out of shape since I've stopped working out. I can start working out to feel better about my body, but I can also tolerate rejection.

YOUR TURN!

Now it's time to replace your own negative thoughts. In this section, you will find prompts to help with this process.

Prompt #1: Please go back to the social situation you described in the section for challenging your thoughts. Consider the facts and how you put the thought in perspective. Now create a new replacement thought. For example, "Just because I don't have friends now does not mean it's impossible to make friends. It just takes effort and patience."

_____

_____

_____

Prompt #2: Please go back to the situation described in the section for challenging your thoughts related to your family. Consider the facts and how you put the thought in perspective. Create a new replacement thought. For example, "I tend to focus on how others take from me, but overlook when they support me because I often refuse that help. People in my life do want to help, but I need to accept that support."

_____

_____

_____

Moment of Reflection

This chapter has guided you through identifying, challenging, and replacing your negative thoughts. When you think in less distressing ways, you can cope more effectively. Consider how your balanced perspectives support your short- and long-term goals. I know you are likely still working on self-awareness, but know that your automatic negative thinking does not define you. These tendencies developed for a reason and are not your true essence. When you begin to think in a more balanced way, you clear out your self-sabotaging chatter and start to hear your true self more. Please continue to work on noticing, challenging, and replacing your negative thoughts. You will be more empowered to behave differently and to truly enter recovery.

Chapter 5

Identify Your Triggers

Many people are anxious in their codependency—about their thoughts, about their fears of rejection, and about their lack of self-awareness. In this chapter, I will ask you to contemplate the situations that produce anxious feelings, called "triggers."

Triggers are often situational, such as the thought of public speaking leading to feelings of anxiety. Basically, anything that causes you to feel distressed and respond in a hurtful way to yourself and others is a trigger. Consider the situations, people, and things that overwhelm you and lead to negative and obsessive thoughts.

You will learn to manage your triggers better in this chapter. Exposure therapy, a process of identifying your triggers and exposing yourself to them over time, is one way to do this. While reading this, you may feel anxious. I understand; however, exposure therapy is a crucial component of recovery using CBT. Avoidance of the things that scare you causes initial relief, but it perpetuates your fear by reinforcing your negative beliefs about the trigger. If you never face your fears appropriately, you will feel stuck. The good news is that by gradually facing your fears, you can become less sensitive, or even desensitized, to a trigger.

The Origins of Fear

Fear originates in your amygdala and initiates the fight-or-flight response to protect you against a threat. This response leads to various physiological changes, including the slowing of your digestive system to send blood to your muscles, allowing you to run or attack as necessary. The hippocampus and prefrontal cortex then allow you to assess if the threat is truly dangerous. Just because something triggers a fight-or-flight response doesn't mean it's life-threatening.

Exposure therapy is a progressive process. The first step is to consider your anxiety triggers, such as dating, setting boundaries, or even swimming in public. Perhaps you want to stop being so self-critical so you can go swimming during your next family vacation instead of sitting on the shore. You will identify smaller tasks that will help you get there, including swimsuit shopping, asking for assistance from a salesperson while trying on a suit, swimming at a small gathering, and going swimming at a public pool. You will rate how anxious you think you will be completing each of these tasks. Once each task is accomplished, you will evaluate how anxious you actually were. This process, along with self-assessment, will reinforce how capable you are of facing this fear—and overcoming it!

Response prevention is another wonderful tool to manage triggers. When you know your triggers, you learn to behave differently by considering different ways to think and act in advance. This process involves developing an effective action plan when next faced with your trigger and making the internal commitment to follow through on this new strategy. I engaged in response prevention with my triggers around problems with my car by understanding that I can't avoid them, as I drive almost daily. I considered my options—carrying a spare tire or jumper cables in my car or having a roadside assistance membership. Knowing that car issues are distressing to me and that I have no interest in learning how to resolve them myself, I chose the membership. I also began to save in case of a pricey care emergency. I felt so accomplished the first time I put my plan into action, pulling out my phone to call for assistance without any of the usual panic or tears when I had a dead car battery. I waited patiently for the tow truck knowing I had the money to take care of it. In this chapter, I will outline examples to engage in response prevention after exposure therapy examples.

A NOTE ABOUT TRAUMATIC TRIGGERS

Please note, *traumatic* triggers are different than the triggers described in this chapter. Traumatic triggers exist because certain situations, items, sounds, smells, or physical sensations remind your body and brain of a trauma you have endured. For example, if a person was sexually assaulted by a cigarette smoker, they may have the physiological response of panic when they smell cigarette smoke. Key signs that a trigger is traumatic are dissociating (a feeling like you are floating in a fog or have left your body) or having a panic attack. If you notice that you have these triggers, I urge you to seek a therapist who specializes in trauma so that you can learn to manage these triggers with formal support. Exposure therapy can work with trauma, but it is not recommended to do this process on your own. If you feel uncomfortable, but the trigger is not tied to trauma and is manageable, you can complete these exercises on your own.

CASE STUDY AND EXPOSURE THERAPY EXAMPLE 1:

Jade has been responsible for the household tasks since she and Manish first started living together. She noticed from the beginning that Manish asked her what she was making for dinner and, after eating, excused himself without offering to clean up. Jade wanted to keep Manish happy, as she felt lucky to be with someone she saw as better than her in many ways. She didn't want to upset him and give him an excuse to dump her. Over the years, when she gets resentful, Jade rationalizes that since Manish earns more money, even though she works full-time, too, she owes this to him. However, she now wants to pursue a longtime dream of starting her own catering company. She knows that she is going to need to work long hours to meet this goal. She has decided that it's time to talk to Manish about renegotiating their division of labor, but she is terrified.

Jade decides to practice exposure therapy to work up to talking to Manish about their household tasks. She sets aside some time and identifies the following:

Part 1: She makes a list of ways she can challenge herself to speak up, allowing herself to work toward this conversation. These include:

- I need to tell my mom that I can't visit her this year for the holidays, as I've decided to work.
- I can tell my coworker that he needs to stop taking credit for the work I am doing.
- I can journal what I want to say to Manish and then tell my best friend about it to practice.
- The next time I'm at a restaurant and they make a mistake on my order, I will ask for it to be fixed rather than just eating it.

Part 2: She will assess how anxious she imagines she will be when she pursues each one of these tasks. She will use a 0 to 10 scale, with

*10 being the most anxious. Jade will also note any predictions she has
about how this will play out.*

- Talking to my mom is stressful and she probably won't be understanding, but I know she will get over it. I'll likely be a 7 with my anxiety.
- I have never asked anyone to not take credit for my work, and my coworker will likely be defensive. I usually just work behind the scenes anyway. This sounds super scary. I'd say my anxiety will be a 9.
- My best friend is really supportive, and I imagine she will just listen and let me talk. I'll probably only be a little anxious because of imagining how Manish will react when I speak to him, so I think my anxiety will be at a 3.
- I think the restaurant server will give me some attitude that I didn't order correctly. My anxiety will probably be a 5.

*Part 3: Over time, Jade will expose herself to the trigger of asserting
herself so she can desensitize herself to the anxiety of it. This will
enable her to talk to her husband. She will then assess in her journal
how true her predictions were. If any of her predictions were false,
she will cross them off. This will help to reinforce that her predictions,
while often negative, are also often inaccurate. She will be less likely
to experience the fear that her negative predictions cause her in
the future.*

EXPOSURE THERAPY EXAMPLE 2:

*Grace is in a relationship that she knows is going nowhere. She would
eventually like to get married, but her boyfriend, Bryan, has told her he has
no interest in marriage. He has been out of work for the last five months,
and she has been working overtime every week since then to ensure that all
their bills are paid. When she asks Bryan to look for work, he says that he's
looking but there are no decent jobs currently available. Last week, he told*

her that he had a job interview in the afternoon, but when she unexpectedly came home early from work, he was playing video games. He told her that he didn't feel like going to the interview. She wants to break up with him but is terrified of being single. She's always had a boyfriend but is now ready to learn how to be more independent.

Part 1: *Grace wants to be single, but she is scared. If she breaks up with Bryan, she will be single and living alone for the first time. Due to this fear, she finds ways to challenge herself to work up toward breaking up with Bryan and being single:*

- I have been invited to join a book club at work but have been afraid of meeting new people. I will follow up and join this book club.
- My friend Lia is single and lives alone. I will talk to her about how she manages this.
- I have always relied on my boyfriends for my hobbies, but I have always wanted to get into Pilates. I will attend a class.
- I will go out to a movie and dinner by myself.

Part 2: *Grace will assess what she thinks will happen and how anxious she thinks she will be on a 0 to 10 scale.*

- I think I will be a 6 going to the book club, as I will only know one person there. I think I will be awkward and that people won't want to talk to me.
- Lia will probably be a little passive-aggressive about me "finally" being single but will talk me through the process. I'll probably be a 4 because of her attitude and my anxiety about living alone.
- If I go to Pilates alone, others in the class will probably judge me for not having friends. They will probably also point out my lack of skill in the class. I will be an 8 on my anxiety scale.
- I will get sad looks from others at dinner by myself. The server will feel sorry for me and keep asking if anyone else is coming to join me. My anxiety will probably be at a 9.

Part 3: Grace will complete each task over time and cross out any inaccurate predictions to reinforce that she may be wrongly predicting how awful being single will be.

- ~~If I go to Pilates alone, they will probably judge me for not having friends. They will probably also point out my lack of skill in the middle of the class. I will be an 8 on my anxiety scale.~~
- ~~I think I will be a 6 going to the book club as I only will know one person there. I think I will be awkward, so people won't want to talk to me.~~
- ~~I will get sad looks from others at dinner by myself. The server will feel sorry for me and keep asking if anyone else is coming to join me.~~

At this point, Grace will feel more empowered that she can do things independently and feel better prepared to be single.

YOUR TURN!

Now consider your anxiety triggers, especially a situation or a person that you have been avoiding due to your fear. Some examples are: enforcing rules and consequences with your child, asking for a raise, public speaking, or dating after a long break. After identifying the trigger you are avoiding, please go through the following exercise to desensitize yourself to it.

Part 1: Journal about the situation you are anxious about and what your ultimate goal is in this situation. Identify at least three tasks that will help you work toward this larger goal.

_____

_____

_____

Part 2: Contemplate what you think will happen when you perform each task, and how anxious you will be on a 0 to 10 scale, with 10 being most anxious.

_____

_____

_____

Part 3: Review what actually happened and cross out any false predictions you made.

_____

_____

_____

RESPONSE PREVENTION EXERCISE 1:

Rudy's mother is a consistent trigger for him. She has been highly critical of him and fixated on her own needs ever since he was a little boy, never satisfied no matter how he has tried to support her. After years of feeling sick about their relationship, he decided to cut her out of his life. Since they live in different cities, he never worries about bumping into her, but he does get triggered when she occasionally decides to contact him. When she reaches out, he becomes enraged. He then stops working out, binge eats, and picks fight with his partner, Simon. Rudy knows that his mother's ability to disrupt his life so intensely is a destructive cycle. Knowing that it's just a matter of time before she reaches out again, he decides to plan ahead.

Rudy's Response Prevention Plan

Step 1: *Consider the trigger(s).*

Hearing from my mom via mail, email, or phone call.

Step 2: Think about his old ways of reacting.

Get really angry, stop going to the gym, eat a lot of fast food, get irritated by every little thing Simon does.

Step 3: *Consider the thoughts that reinforce these actions.*

Why can't it be enough? Why can't I be enough? I hate her. I can't stop her.

Step 4: Consider new ways of looking at the situation.

Just because my mother is so negative and unhappy doesn't mean that I am the problem. She was this way even before I was born. I can't fix her. I can't fully prevent her from finding ways to contact me if she's that motivated, but I can stop her from getting such a rise out of me when she does.

Step 5: Visualize the trigger, imagine thinking these new thoughts, and contemplate how you would respond differently to cope better.

Okay, I see my mother emailing me something negative. I will think: "It's not my fault that she's this way. I can't fix her, but I am not powerless. I can cope with life better than she does." I will remember that I'm not obligated to respond.

Next, I will take a deep breath and close my laptop. I will take a walk around the block to clear my head. I will call Simon and ask if we can have a nice dinner out later. He will definitely like this idea, as he loves going out. I will talk to him over a relaxed dinner about my feelings. I will ask him to help me commit to working out tomorrow. I will preregister for a workout class so that I'm more motivated to go to avoid getting charged for not attending.

Rudy will keep this plan in the back of his mind now and tell Simon about it, as he is a support for Rudy. When his mom reaches out again, Rudy will be better prepared to handle this trigger in a healthy way.

RESPONSE PREVENTION EXERCISE 2:

Sophia's husband, Marcus, has cheated on her three times, but always says he's going to stop. Every time Sophia discovers the infidelity, she feels like she is dying and that her life is meaningless. She becomes intensely depressed and has needed to be hospitalized once for her thoughts of suicide. Another time, she attacked Marcus physically, but no one knows about this, because Marcus said he deserved it. Even though she's hopeful he won't cheat again, Sophia knows that it's important to plan how to respond differently if it does.

Sophia's Response Prevention Plan

Step 1: *Consider the trigger(s).*

Finding proof that he is cheating, such as finding condoms in his suitcase when he goes away for work, seeing a message pop up on his phone, having someone call me to tell me they know about an affair, or unusual expenses on our credit card.

Step 2: *Think about her old ways of reacting.*

If he's not home, I will call him nonstop and leave angry text messages on his phone that "I'm done" with him. I will shake, weep, and feel weak. I will then take more Xanax than I am prescribed and drink a bottle of a wine. I will feel too tired to engage and go to bed.

When I see him, I will start to tell him all the things I hate about him, throw things at him, and once I even hit him.

I will get overwhelmed and start thinking about suicide.

Step 3: Consider the thoughts that reinforce these actions.

It's my fault that he keeps cheating on me. Men can't be faithful, and I'm stupid and weak for expecting otherwise. I'm not important to him and he's my life, so I should just die.

Step 4: Consider new ways of looking at the situation.

It is not wrong of me to want my husband to be faithful to me, as I am to him. I have a right to need and want monogamy.

Step 5: Visualize the trigger, imagine thinking these new thoughts, and contemplate how you would respond differently to cope better with the trigger.

Okay, I imagine finding proof of the infidelity. I know my stomach will drop and I will feel sick. I know I might immediately think about dying, but I will remind myself that I have more reasons to live than my marriage. These reasons include my patients at work, my mother, my dog, and my hope for the future. I will need to let myself cry without feeling weak. I will tell myself that "It is okay to cry when I am feeling so betrayed." If needed, I will take a Xanax as prescribed. After I'm done crying, I will get up and take a shower to feel refreshed. I will then get my bag and go stay at a hotel for a night to clear my head. I will write a note for Marcus that I discovered the affair and need some time. I will ask him not to contact me, and I will block his number for the night. While at the hotel, I will call my mom for support. In the morning, I will figure out what I want to do next.

If he's home, I will get up and walk out of the house to get some fresh air. I know I will need to leave immediately; otherwise we are likely to fight, and this is destructive for me. I will call my mom on my walk and let her know what has happened. I will ask if she can pick me up since she lives in town. If my mom is unavailable, I will get a cab and go to her house and just wait so I don't do anything destructive.

In both scenarios, I will leave a message for my therapist to see if I can get an emergency session this week.

Sophia will prepare to follow through with her plan by setting aside some cash to stay in a hotel as needed. She will keep an emergency bag packed in her closet to have ready to go if needed. She will also make sure that she keeps her phone charged so she can use it to call her mom. Additionally, she will let her mom know in advance of her plan so her mother is aware of the support Sophia is requesting and her mother is prepared to follow through. Finally, she will identify a therapist and start meeting with them in advance so she will have the option for an emergency session.

YOUR TURN!

Consider a situation or a person that triggers you and that will likely happen again, such as fighting with your spouse or getting negative feedback at work. Please complete the following to create your response prevention plan:

Step 1: Consider the trigger(s).

_____

_____

_____

Step 2: Think about your old ways of reacting.

_____

_____

_____

Step 3: Consider the thoughts that reinforce these actions.

_____

_____

_____

Step 4: Consider new ways of looking at the situation.

_____

_____

_____

Step 5: Visualize the trigger, imagine thinking these new thoughts, and contemplate how you would respond differently to cope better with the trigger.

_____

_____

_____

Moment of Reflection

In this chapter, you learned two important methods to manage the triggers that prevent you from taking healthy action. When you practice exposure therapy and response prevention, you allow yourself to live more in recovery. Life will always have stressful moments, situations, and people. It's how you choose to respond that makes the difference between living in codependency and in recovery. Please consider the goals you identified in chapter 3 and whether any triggers are preventing you from accomplishing them. If so, please complete one or both practices outlined in this chapter to move past this barrier. As you identify more triggers and complete the techniques in this chapter, you will live more and more peacefully. When your life feels more stable and peaceful, rather than chaotic, it is a clear sign that you are living in recovery. I look forward to this practice for you.

Chapter 6

Problem-Solving in a Codependent Relationship

In this chapter, you will learn how to effectively solve problems that arise in your relationships. Prior to using this workbook, you have likely already tried numerous ways to solve your relationship problems, without much success. Without examining your thinking mistakes or triggers, some of your problem-solving thus far has likely been destructive. This type of problem-solving may actually reinforce issues. Luckily, CBT has a method for constructive problem-solving, and it's a skill set you can learn.

Effective Problem-Solving

CBT outlines the steps for effective problem-solving as the following: identify the problem; consider your options; choose a solution; and then implement it. When identifying the problem, it's crucial to be as specific as possible so you can brainstorm potential solutions with more clarity. While brainstorming, please remember that there is no bad idea. If you feel particularly stuck, feel free to ask someone you trust for possible solutions. Please remember to turn to someone, though, who won't resent you if you choose a different option—a possible outcome in codependent relationships. Then, you may review the pros and cons of the potential solutions if needed to decide what to do. Finally, choose a short-term solution that you can implement immediately. This immediate solution may not be the one that's needed to manage the problem long-term, but it's a place to start creating change. For example, you may want to get a ride home first if stranded somewhere because your partner isn't answering their phone; in the long-term, you will need to create a plan to prevent this issue in the future.

You will likely also want to consider your long-term solutions so you can make progress toward and implement those. Once you have addressed the problem, you may choose to review the outcome of your interventions in order to enhance your problem-solving skills.

It's important to clarify that when problems are completely solvable—such as needing a cab to the airport because your spouse is drunk—the problem-solving focuses on fixing the problem. However, if the problem cannot be fully resolved or is outside of your control—stopping your partner from drinking alcohol—you need to focus primarily on addressing your feelings about and reactions to the issue.

Jade believes that Manish's "drinking problem" is her primary problem, but when she goes through the CBT problem-solving process, she realizes that the real problem is the way he behaves disrespectfully when he drinks excessively, rather than the drinking itself.

Clearly determine the problem: Manish dismisses what I say and is flirtatious with other women when he drinks excessively.

Brainstorm: For an immediate solution, Jade can speak to Manish about her concerns with more specificity now that she has more clarity about the problem. She can also seek support quickly through Al-Anon. For a long-term solution, she may choose to go to individual therapy to help her manage her feelings, thoughts, and reactions to Manish if he drinks excessively. She can also implement a long-term response prevention strategy. Jade can invite Manish to attend couples and/or individual therapy himself for support on managing this problem. She can learn communication skills to assert herself as needed with Manish.

Take action: Focus on immediate solutions first. Jade is still unsure what to say to Manish about the problem, so she finds an Al-Anon meeting she can attend tomorrow after work. She also does some research and finds a therapist for support who specializes in codependency. Next, she focuses on long-term solutions. She purchases a book on communication for couples to get some ideas. Finally, she commits to going to therapy for at least three months for support in managing the problem.

PROBLEM-SOLVING EXERCISE 1

Leonor, 54, and Peter, 49, were married last year. Shortly afterward, Leonor's father passed away and left her a large sum of money. Peter is pressuring Leonor to invest in his company, as he "just needs a little" to get him through the "slump" in his business. Peter shares that he "just" needs $20,000. Leonor is stalling, as she feels uncomfortable. She doesn't want to waste her father's hard-earned money and doesn't know anything about Peter's company's financials. He started this business years before they met. Peter is getting pushier, telling her that she must not believe in or love him if she can't support him when he needs it. He says he would take care of her if the roles were reversed.

Clearly determine the problem: Peter wants Leonor to invest money in his company. She is not comfortable with this but is not telling him directly. He is getting pushier, so she feels more overwhelmed and confused.

Brainstorm: For an immediate solution, Leonor can speak to Peter about needing to see his company's financial information before investing. Leonor can ask to attend a meeting with his accountant. She can also make an appointment with her financial adviser to help give her some clarity. She can let Peter know she feels hurt that he is equating her love for him with investing in his company. She can simply tell him no, or invest even though she's uncomfortable. Long-term solutions are to seek couples therapy to navigate financial issues in the relationship or to become a formal investor with a legal contract in his company. Leonor feels overwhelmed, so she makes a pros and cons list to evaluate her current options. She feels that there are many downsides to telling him no, as she isn't even sure that's what she wants to do. She knows it's important to communicate in a healthy relationship, so she sees more pros to talking to him than cons. She sees no cons in speaking to her adviser. Despite the pros, Leonor also has numerous concerns about getting his financial information first. Couples therapy is an option, but not one she wants to implement first. She knows that he may be offended by this offer without her trying to solve it with him individually first.

Take action: Leonor decides to talk to Peter tonight about her concerns that he is feeling unsupported by her when she feels responsible to her father regarding the money he left her. The outcome of this conversation will help her evaluate how to solve this problem long-term. She discovers that Peter is upset when she discusses her concerns, and he emphasizes that all money they earn or acquire when married belongs to both of them. Leonor then continues to feel coerced. She decides to ask if he is comfortable sharing his company's financial information so she can learn more, with his accountant present. He declines. At this point, Leonor realizes that she has a firm boundary, which is not to invest money when she is not fully informed about her investment. She decides to tell Peter that she is unable to invest in any company—including his—without full knowledge of her investment, with legal protection. If Peter struggles with this decision, she can recommend couples therapy to help them navigate their concerns while respecting each other's boundaries.

PROBLEM-SOLVING EXERCISE 2

You have been married for six years. Both you and your husband work full-time. You have noticed that, ever since you married, the overwhelming major-ity of household tasks have fallen on your shoulders. It seems as though if you don't do it, it just doesn't get done! When you have mentioned this to your husband in the past, he has shared that you simply notice things before he does, but if you ask him to do it, he will. You resent this for two reasons. One is that you hate asking others for help, as it feels so vulnerable. The other is that he lives in the home, too. Can't he simply see a mess in the kitchen or laun-

dry that needs to be done? You decide not to talk to him about this again for a while and go back to doing almost everything yourself. It feels like less work to do it yourself than to nag your husband anyway. However, you have started to work on your codependency recovery, and you realize that this problem in your home needs to be addressed.

Clearly determine the problem: Ever since you and your husband moved in together, you complete most of the housework. He has offered to help, but you haven't wanted to ask him constantly to do various tasks. Therefore, you continue to do the work yourself and resent him. This is exhausting you and negatively affecting your friendship with your husband.

Brainstorm: For an immediate solution, you can ask your husband to clean up the dishes tonight after dinner. You could also talk to him about your feelings tonight directly. Another option would be to draft a chore sheet and put it on your fridge. You could hire a housekeeper ASAP. For a long-term solution, you need things to be more equitable in your marriage from now on. You could draft a list of all tasks in the home and negotiate a weekly task schedule with him. You could ask him every day to help. You could practice asking for help in general from others, to help you ask him. You could hire a housekeeper to come consistently and share the fee with your husband.

Take action: Focus on your immediate solutions first. When you consider creating a chore sheet for him to use moving forward, this does not seem fair or equitable. In fact, you see that it's quite patronizing, and you don't need to take your resentment out on your husband. You can change the dynamic instead. Therefore, you decide to talk to your husband tonight about how hard it is for you to ask for support around the house. You decide you want to tell your husband that you want to find an equitable solution that meets both of your needs. You will share that you want to focus on a long-term solution. You can let him know that you have heard and appreciate his offers to help over the years, but that *you need to have a clear plan of action, as it's a lot of work to delegate tasks. You offer to create a list together of all the chores that need to be done around the home, and how often. Then you can each volunteer to do various tasks that you feel more comfortable or skillful at doing, so that it feels fair. For example, you know that you feel more comfortable cooking than your husband, so it makes more sense for him to clean up after meals. You can also find solutions for some professional cleaning support together that fit your budget, to have some balance. For example, you can have your groceries delivered to save you both the work of this task. Finally, you can create a calendar to hang in your kitchen that outlines the tasks and who is responsible for each for the month.*

PROBLEM-SOLVING EXERCISE 3

Mila and Erin, both 26, have been friends since they were toddlers, as their moms are best friends. Mila has always trusted Erin. However, Mila has noticed that since she and her fiancé, José, became engaged six months ago, she has felt weird around Erin. She couldn't quite put her finger on why until recently. Last week, when out with Erin and José for drinks, she excused herself to use the restroom while Erin stayed behind. When Mila was walking back, she saw José and Erin sitting close; they were laughing and had their heads next to each other's intimately. When they noticed her, their body language changed to be more distant, and they stopped talking. Mila acted like she hadn't noticed anything, but felt sick to her stomach afterward. She has not known how to address this issue. She tells herself that she may just be insecure and that she will upset them for no reason.

Clearly determine the problem: Mila feels different around Erin since she became engaged. She doesn't know why, but does know that when she stepped away to use the restroom, she saw her best friend and fiancé sitting and conversing in a manner that appeared intimate. She also knows that they distanced themselves when they saw her. She does not know what this means, but does know that they felt comfortable communicating intimately when she stepped away and did not want to behave in this manner in front of her. Mila knows part of the problem is that she feels she could be wrong about her suspicions and will push Erin and José away if she reveals them.

Brainstorm: For an immediate solution, Mila could validate her observation first—that their behavior was odd, even if it was harmless. Mila can validate that she's not being "crazy" or insecure by noticing odd behavior. She could also talk to her mother, who knows Erin and José very well, for some suggestions about how to address this. Mila could also journal about her feelings to help give her clarity. She could draft—but not send—a letter in her journal to José and Erin, to help her find the words on how she wants to talk to them. Mila knows that to manage this problem long-term she needs to talk to both Erin and José, even though she's terrified. Mila could talk to them separately or together to address this.

Take action: Focus on your immediate solutions first. Mila is overwhelmed and is second-guessing herself, so she chooses to find a supportive mantra for herself. She does this by first journaling her feelings. She discovers that she keeps using the words "wrong," "stupid," and "crazy." Her mantra, which arises from noticing her thought distortions, is: "I have the right to share my perspective with others." Defining and using the mantra makes her feel more empowered, but she still doesn't know what to say to Erin and José yet. She decides to draft separate letters in her journal to Erin and to José, as she has close—but different—relationships with each of them. In her journal, she discovers she wants to know why their behavior changed when she returned from the restroom. She reminds herself that this really happened, and she repeats her mantra: "I have the right to share my perspective with others." Mila concludes that for her feelings to be resolved long-term, she must speak to Erin and José together. If she speaks to them separately, she's afraid that she won't trust the *responses of whoever she speaks to second. Her mind may tell her that they conspired together for a response. She honors this truth and plans ahead for that. She knows that Erin is coming over tomorrow night for dinner with José and her. She plans to talk to Erin and José then. Mila will create another letter detailing what to say to them directly, as she knows that she may lose her words if she doesn't write them down. Mila will tell them what she observed. Based on their responses and reactions, Mila will go through this problem-solving exercise again as needed. For example, if they become defensive, she knows that she will need to go within herself and develop another strategy to address this issue.*

PROBLEM-SOLVING EXERCISE 4

You have signed up to take night classes at your local community college in hopes of bettering yourself and getting ahead in your career. Because you and your spouse share a car, you have both agreed to a plan: Your spouse will drop you off on campus and pick you up each night 10 minutes after your class gets out. Your spouse is currently 40 minutes late and is not responding to your calls or text messages. You check the GPS location of your car through a cell phone app and see that it is at a local dive bar a mile away. It is dark out and you are feeling nervous that you are stuck at the college while your spouse is drinking.

Clearly determine the problem: Your spouse has broken a promise. They are not responding to your calls or texts. You are stuck without a ride at the college. You feel unsafe as it is now nighttime.

Brainstorm: For an immediate solution, *can you call a friend and ask for a ride? Can you call a cab or a rideshare? Could you walk to the bar?* For a long-term solution, *do you trust that this will not happen again? What* steps should you take to make certain that you are not placed in this position again? One strategy is to drive yourself to the college from now on, and your spouse can plan around this on the two nights a week you have class. Or you could plan to take a cab on your school nights.

Take action: Focus on your immediate solutions first. *You don't want to walk to the bar, as this could create a big fight. You don't have the money for a cab or rideshare. You text a couple of your friends and one answers back; you secure a ride home.* Next, focus on your long-term solution. *What should you say to your spouse to prevent this from happening again? You can't afford to have two cars, or to take a cab two nights a week to campus and back home. Find a plan that meets your financial needs while ensuring you are able to make it safely home when you attend school. You and your spouse agree that you will take the car on your school nights.*

PROBLEM-SOLVING EXERCISE 5

You are a single parent, as your partner left when your daughter, Becca, was only a toddler. It's been hard work raising her over these last eight years, and you often sacrifice for your daughter. The last time you bought yourself clothes was when you got a new job two years ago. Despite the sacrifice, things are always tight financially. Therefore, whenever your mom can watch Becca, you pick up extra work shifts. Becca seems irritable one night, so you ask her what's wrong. She tells you that you never show up to her soccer games like the other moms and that you never remember what's going on in her life. She reminds you that just last week you forgot her best friend's name. It makes you feel sick with guilt and anger that you are still failing no matter how much you sacrifice. However, you tell her that you appreciate her telling you how she feels, and that you will figure out a solution.

Clearly determine the problem: Becca is upset that you are not showing up for her soccer games and that you are forgetful about the things that matter to her.

Brainstorm: For an immediate solution, you could take some time off work, as you have some PTO saved. Or you could dismiss her concerns and explain to her that this is just the reality for single parents. You could sleep less so you can spend more time with her at night. You could also talk to your supervisor about flex time. Long-term, you know that you need to plan to stay engaged to prevent her from feeling emotionally neglected. An option for this is to plan special time for the two of you monthly. Or you could ask her to keep a journal that you share, updating each other about your lives. You could also plan to attend soccer games consistently, which would require a change to your work schedule. Finally, you could quit this job and try to start a work-from-home venture.

Take action: Focus on your immediate solutions first. *It is important to you to show Becca that she is your priority as her parent. However, you need to keep your current job, as you rely on this income. Additionally, you already are often sleep deprived, so cutting back on sleep isn't a healthy option. You have been saving a few PTO days "just in case," so you plan to talk to your supervisor tomorrow about scheduling these as soon as possible. You won't be able to afford a vacation, but you can surprise Becca with a "staycation." You will spend this time watching her favorite movies, baking (which she loves), and just talking. You know this isn't a* long-term solution, *so you let Becca know that you want to spend quality time with her consistently. You may not always have the quantity of time you prefer, but you can have quality time together. You tell her that Sundays—which you always have off—will be your special day together. There may be work to do at home, but you can share it, so you have some time to relax on Sunday evenings together. You want her to know long-term that you do care about her life. Therefore, you tell her that you want to write letters together. On your "staycation" with her, you go to a discount store to buy a special journal. In this journal, you will take turns writing to each other about what's going on in your lives and your dreams and fears. Becca can also ask you any questions in the journal that she feels too nervous to ask you directly, and you will answer them there.*

PROBLEM-SOLVING EXERCISE 6

Chantel and Phillip have been together for five years when they decide they are ready to buy a home. They decide to set up a joint bank account to save for this goal. They have been cutting back on eating out, various subscriptions, and other extras. Chantel is quite proud that they have saved nearly $11,000 in six months. The sacrifice is paying off, and she likes checking the bank account to remind herself of this. One Monday morning, Chantel logs in to the bank account site to discover that the savings account is down to $6,000. She begins to panic—this must be a mistake. However, she starts to review the charges and sees that Phillip used this account for thousands of dollars in transactions over the weekend. She sees charges for bars, clubs, and stores. She knows that he was out of town for his friend's bachelor party, but she never thought he would spend so much, especially on the account that they are sharing to save for a house.

Clearly determine the problem: Phillip spent almost $5,000 on his weekend trip with friends. This money came from a shared account which they had agreed to use only to save to purchase a house. They each had a debit card for this account which they had agreed would be for dire emergencies only. Philip broke his promise to her and spent almost half of their savings.

Brainstorm: For an immediate solution, Chantel needs to address this with Phillip. She can call him or text him while they are both at work, or she can wait to talk to him tonight. She needs to discover if all this money is truly gone. Maybe he is waiting for money back from friends? She can address the money, his breaking of a commitment, or both issues at once. Long-term, she needs to be able to restore trust in Phillip, that he cares about this commitment to buy a house as much as she does. They also need to prevent spending that isn't necessary on this account. He could get rid of his debit card, or they both can.

Take action: Chantel focuses on her immediate solutions first. She decides to wait to contact Phillip. She knows that he will be home from work before her and she can talk to him there. She doesn't want to have such a serious discussion when they are both at work. She takes her lunch break to identify what she wants to say. She decides to address both the broken commitment and the loss of money in one discussion, as these issues are interconnected. She talks to Phillip that night about her concerns. Long-term, she wants to prevent spending their savings, and she shares the need to come up with a plan for this. Chantel proposes that they both get rid of their debit cards to prevent spending from this account until they purchase a home.

YOUR TURN!

You have learned how to constructively solve problems. It's now your chance to practice this skill. At this time, please identify a situation that has you currently feeling stuck or stressed, and then go through the exercise below.

Clearly determine the problem:

_____

_____

_____

Brainstorm: For an immediate solution, what options do you have? For a long-term solution, what steps should you take to make sure that you are not placed in this position again?

_____

_____

_____

Take action: Focus on your immediate solutions first. Next, focus on your long-term solution and strategize how to implement it.

_____

_____

_____

Moment of Reflection

Few experiences in life are more immediately empowering than learning to solve problems effectively. This is a skill you can cultivate, and the more you practice it, the more skillful you will become. The good news is that life is full of opportunities to practice constructive problem-solving! The more effectively you solve your problems, the more you will trust that you can handle whatever life throws your way. Trusting yourself is a cornerstone of living interdependently. Speaking of interdependence, please remember that asking for support in brainstorming solutions when you feel stuck is a part of effective problem-solving. You are capable of implementing a plan of action that meets your needs, but you do not have to do it all alone. And if the initial plan doesn't work out as you hoped, that's okay. The flexibility to try a new strategy as needed is an important part of this process.

Chapter 7

Manage Conflicts and Emotions

In this chapter, you will learn how to better manage your emotions when there is discord in your relationships. The goal is to teach you how to cope with your distress so that you can effectively express your needs while also being able to listen to the needs of the other person. This dual approach will allow you to more effectively manage conflict.

A Universal Relationship Truth

It is important to understand a universal relationship truth: Differences in personalities are unavoidable no matter how close two people are, so disagreement is inevitable. A clear sign of recovery is when you are able to tolerate the distress of conflict so that you may find deeper understanding between yourself and the other person. I know it feels counterintuitive, but effective conflict resolution actually deepens intimacy. It is deeply vulnerable to share your needs with someone and risk being told "no." However, your needs are a core part of who you are authentically. No one can truly know you without your willingness to share your needs.

It is essential, though, to communicate your needs in a clear, specific, and kind manner. In other words, it is important to develop an assertive communication style. Often, in codependency, people communicate in ways that are unclear (passive), unkind (aggressive), or a combination of these qualities (passive-aggressive). I describe these forms of communication in more detail in *The Codependency Recovery Plan*, if you would like to learn more. Most basically, though, it's essential to communicate directly and with kindness. This gentle approach helps prevent escalation of conflict and assists with repair afterward.

Knowing how to resolve conflict is a fundamental quality of healthy interdependent relationships. In codependency, it can be terrifying to even imagine conflict due to a mistaken belief that this will lead to complete rejection. However, in interdependency, we know that conflict is inevitable in any relationship, so we don't spend our energy fixated on preventing any discord. Rather, we learn how not to escalate conflict when it does occur *and* how to repair things once there has been a disagreement.

Amazingly, we now have over 40 years of research regarding what makes relationships stable, healthy, and lasting. John Gottman, with Robert Levenson, began research on predictors for divorce in 1975. Eventually, they created a "love lab"—an apartment where couples were observed by cameras doing what they would do on a Sunday at home. Data was also collected on each person's physiological responses to their interactions. This research revealed many qualities of both stable relationships and those that are likely to end in divorce. Those with healthy, stable qualities were deemed *masters* of relationships, while the latter group—those with the qualities likely to contribute to divorce—were called *disasters*. Conflict was inevitable in both groups, but it is how conflict was managed that was remarkably different.

Whether one is masterful in their relationship skills or not, all people become physiologically overwhelmed when danger is perceived—when a partner is irritable, expresses different needs, or has negative feedback for us, for example. When we become physiologically overwhelmed, the fight-or-flight process is activated. Heart rates increase and breathing becomes shallow. At this point, we are flooded, and this prevents the ability to think clearly, listen effectively, or have empathy. We are often defensive when we are flooded, and we may repeat ourselves. Flooding is a natural human process and has nothing to do with codependency.

Once flooding occurs, it is essential to focus first on soothing yourself to move out of this state, rather than continuing a conversation. If you try to continue a discussion when you are flooded, nothing productive will happen. I am positive that you can identify numerous examples of this in your life. Once you are flooded during a disagreement, it is important to take a break. Having a formal time-out agreement with your partner is a great strategy to help prevent escalation in your fights moving forward. You can discuss this strategy when you are not having a disagreement, clearly outlining what you will say when you need a break, i.e. "I need a moment." Then, you decide where each of you will go in the house and for how long, which should be between 10 and 30 minutes to allow yourself time to calm down. Choose a place in your house to meet back up to try to discuss things again, when time is up and you are calmer. One of the behaviors that most greatly predicts divorce is called *stonewalling*—when a partner completely shuts down, stops listening, or leaves when there's disagreement. People stonewall when they are flooded; the formal time-out prevents this behavior that deteriorates relationships while still allowing time to calm down.

When you take a break from conflict, it is essential to actively calm yourself down with coping skills. The next chapter will give you numerous ways to do this. Once you have calmed down, you then return to the discussion. During this discussion, you will clearly express your needs, while also expressing understanding for the other person. To best express understanding, you must listen to them, rather than focusing on what you want to say. In this process, you will use the words they use to describe their feelings, needs, and perceptions, and will also use empathy to imagine what they are feeling. This approach is outlined in the examples below. You must be willing to accept the other person's right to their own reality. It is codependent to fixate on changing others and trying to convince them that they are "wrong," which will only push people away, rather than supporting closeness. Everyone has the right to their views and values; therefore, the task of repair is to negotiate. This is a healthy, interdependent process focused on mutual give-and-take.

The last time Jade addressed Manish's drinking, he told her that he saw her point. He shared that it would help him to stop drinking for a while. He's been wanting to lose weight and he does not need the alcohol anyway. Jade feels relieved. One night, he comes home late after a work dinner. She can see that he is drunk by the way he is walking, and she can smell the alcohol on his breath. Jade feels overwhelmed and angry. She tells him that she thought he was going to stop drinking. Manish becomes irritable and tells Jade to stop being such a nag. She becomes defensive immediately and argues that she's not nagging. She's only reminding him of his promise. Manish responds that he doesn't have a drinking problem—his only problem is her. He tells her that he is sick of having to change to make her happy. He also shares that she used to be fun, but he doesn't know who he is married to anymore.

Jade feels hurt and angry, but does not want to engage in a fight with Manish. She has learned that fighting back at him doesn't solve anything and is also very draining. She also knows that since Manish is drunk, he won't remember much of anything they discuss. Jade has been working on her recovery, so she knows she has a right to let Manish know how he's affecting her while also knowing that she needs to wait to talk to him to be heard.

EMOTION AND CONFLICT MANAGEMENT EXERCISE 1

Jade took a break to manage her reactions. She needed to calm down first so she could go through the steps outlined below.

Step 1: Recognize her own needs.

Jade needs Manish to be honest and accountable. If he wants to stop drinking, great. If he wants to revisit this, okay. But first, she needs him to keep his word. Second, she needs home to feel safe, and she needs to be able to express her concerns without being verbally attacked.

Step 2: Communicate with emotions in check.

- Allow herself time to respond.
  Jade knew nothing productive would happen if she argued with Manish when he was drunk. Therefore, she spent the night in their guest room. She journaled to calm down and considered Manish's perspective so she will be less defensive when she speaks to him later, when he's sober.

- Pay attention to her feelings as she expresses her words.
  Jade outlined what was important to say. She asked to speak to Manish the next day when he was sober. She noticed that her breathing was fast, so she took a deep breath to help herself not get flooded. She continues to breathe deeply to help manage her anxiety.

- Pay attention to the emotions of the other person—validate!
  Jade acknowledges for Manish that she knows he is feeling nagged and probably feels angry about this.

- Be aware and remain respectful of yourself.
  Jade needs Manish to be more honest with her about his drinking, because it makes her feel anxious. She lets him know that sometimes he

has behaved disrespectfully when he's drinking, so now she can't help but be on guard when he's drunk. She lets him know that he has the right to drink if he chooses, but that she needs him to be honest about his drinking so she can be prepared and plan how to cope with her anxiety about it.

- Be aware and remain respectful of the other person.
  Jade reminds herself internally that Manish has the right to drink if he wants, regardless of her feelings. She can validate that he is in control of what and how he drinks, and that she just wants to prevent disrespect and manage her anxiety about this.

Step 3: *Say your piece, and release.*

- Recognize that she has the right to express her reaction.
  Jade has the right to share her thoughts, feelings, and needs with Manish and to share her response based on this perspective. She can let him know what she heard him say while also letting him know what she thinks about his response.

- Understand that once she has put it out there, she can let go.
  Jade has shared her concerns about potential disrespect due to Manish's history of treating her this way when he is drunk. She cannot control what he does with this information, but she knows that she is living with integrity by being honest about her feelings and needs. She can revisit this process moving forward based on what conflicts arise again, but until then she must find ways to cope so she can let this go for now.

EMOTION AND CONFLICT MANAGEMENT EXERCISE 2

You and your partner are newlyweds after dating long distance because of their military service. You are very excited for your first holiday season together. You love spending time with your family and continuing all the traditions you've had since you were a child. You let your partner know your plans to spend time with your family this Christmas. You add that your mom is so excited to see you both. Your partner shares surprise at this statement, as they have already committed to spending time with their family.

Step 1: *Recognize your own needs.*

- What do you need at this time? You realize that you need to ensure that you have time with your family for the holidays.

Step 2: *Communicate with emotions in check.*

- Allow yourself time to respond.
  You notice your initial disappointment and anger. You had a certain vision for the holidays, and your partner is messing with this! However, you take a deep breath and remember that they are your family, too, so you must figure this out together.

- Pay attention to your feelings as you express your words.
  You tell your partner: "I feel disappointed, as I already committed to my family, too."

- Pay attention to the emotions of the other person—validate!
  You let him know that "I understand that you probably feel frustrated, too, since we both just assumed that we would spend Christmas with our own families."

- Be aware and remain respectful of yourself.
  "I know we need to figure this out together. I need to ensure that we do spend some time with my family for the holidays. It's really important to me to keep up with family traditions. I also want to make sure that we figure out our traditions before we have kids."

- Be aware and remain respectful of the other person
  "It sounds to me like you also want to see your family for Christmas."

Step 3: Say your piece, and release.

"I'm hoping we can find a plan that works for both of us."

- Recognize that you have the right to express your reaction.
  Your partner responds that they already bought tickets for both of you to
  see their side of the family for Christmas. You say, "I'm disappointed that
  we didn't communicate about this sooner. In the future, please include
  me before making travel plans. I feel sad because I don't want us to waste
  the airline tickets now, so I know that we have to find another time to see
  my family for the holidays."

- Understand that once you have put it out there, you can let go.
  Now, you must find a way to cope with your own disappointment. You
  choose to do this by doing an activity you love, such as painting, and
  then calling your best friend.

EMOTION AND CONFLICT MANAGEMENT EXERCISE 3

*Harry, 24, and Jazmin, 22, just started dating two months ago. Harry has
noticed that Jazmin does not offer to pay when they go out, not even once. At
first he dismissed this, as they had just started dating, but he is now feeling
concerned. He wants to date Jazmin exclusively, but does not want to feel
taken advantage of moving forward.*

Step 1: Recognize his own needs.

Harry realizes that he needs a relationship to be equitable. He makes more
money than Jazmin, but he wants her to contribute financially in a fair way to
their meals out and activities.

Step 2: Communicate with emotions in check.

- Allow yourself time to respond.
  Harry realized this need after his previous date with Jazmin. He doesn't have plans to see her again for a few days. He decides that he will talk to her on their next date and prepare what he wants to say prior to this.

- Pay attention to your feelings as you express your words.
  Harry knows that he may come across as angry, as he's starting to feel resentful. He knows that he needs to focus on keeping his body language relaxed, so he will have this conversation when they are sitting down. He will also make sure to breathe and pause as needed.

- Pay attention to the emotions of the other person—validate!
  Harry lets Jazmin know that he loves the time that they are spending together and is hoping they can date exclusively. He shares that he knows they have only recently started to date, without any commitments up until now. He shares with Jazmin that he has enjoyed treating her and that he has never asked her to contribute before.

- Be aware and remain respectful of yourself.
  While acknowledging that Jazmin may not have meant to offend him at all, he lets her know that moving forward, he hopes they can invest more fairly into their dates.

- Be aware and remain respectful of the other person.
  Harry adds that he knows that as Jazmin is still in college, she does not have as much money as he does. He shares that his idea of fairly splitting costs would be her willingness to cover costs for low-expense meals, like when they get fast food.

Step 3: Say your piece, and release.

Harry shares that he is hoping they can have a committed and fair relationship.

- Recognize that you have the right to express your reaction.
  He waits for Jazmin's response. She shares embarrassment, but also understanding. She lets him know that she wants the same things from

the relationship as he does. Harry shares his appreciation of her understanding and excitement over their new relationship status.

- Understand that once you have put it out there, you can let go.
  For now, this negotiation is over. Moving forward, if issues with inequality come up again, Harry can use this outline. For now, he can let go.

EMOTION AND CONFLICT MANAGEMENT EXERCISE 4

Tess and Beckett started dating five years ago. When they first met, Beckett let Tess know that he and his mother, Rachel, are very close. He shared that they talk every day. Initially, Tess was excited to finally meet a man who valued his mother. However, over the years, she has been frustrated when Beckett is unavailable to her due to his calls to his mother and when he doesn't stand up for her when his mother is critical of her. Tess was hopeful that after they married and had their own kids this would change. However, it hasn't, and she now notices that her mother-in-law has become critical of Tess's parenting style. Tess and Beckett have a two-year-old son, Victor. Just yesterday, during Rachel's visit, Tess felt that tensions were reaching a boiling point. Rachel told Tess that she thinks she is "too soft" on Victor and that he is going to fail in life because of it. Tess just nodded, because she felt overwhelmed.

Step 1: *Recognize her own needs.*

Tess recognizes that her primary need is to have her parenting style respected by Rachel, but she also needs Beckett's support in addressing this issue.

Step 2: *Communicate with emotions in check.*

Tess wasn't able to tell Rachel how she felt in the moment because she felt overwhelmed. She distracted herself by cooking when she was initially overwhelmed.

- Allow herself time to respond.
  Later that night, Tess thinks about what to say to both Beckett and Rachel. She realizes that she wants to talk to Beckett first.

- Pay attention to her feelings as she expresses her words.
  Tess finds a chance to talk to Beckett the next morning over coffee. She takes a deep breath and lets him know that she needs to parent their children based on her and Beckett's values, without Rachel's criticism. Even though she is anxious about upsetting him and Rachel, she needs to let Rachel know her concerns.

- Pay attention to the emotions of the other person—validate!
  Tess validates how important Beckett's mother is to him—and the whole family. She acknowledges that he may have some of the same values as his mother, but that she wants to hear it from him directly so they can negotiate how to parent together. She lets him know that he may feel he's put in the middle, but that she respects his relationship with his mother and knows how important Victor's grandmother is to him, too.

- Be aware and remain respectful of herself.
  While validating Beckett, Tess lets him know that she does need her parenting choices to be respected.

- Be aware and remain respectful of the other person.
  Beckett lets Tess know that he wants to be there when she talks to Rachel to help it go smoothly. Tess shares that she wants to address her concerns herself because she wants Rachel to know that she's okay with being direct; Tess also accepts Beckett's preference.

Step 3: *Say her piece, and release.*

Now that Tess knows what Beckett needs, she can let go of needing his support, as he is willing to support both her and his mother.

- Recognize that she has the right to express her reaction.
  Tess shared her willingness to have him there, while reminding him of her needs.

- Understand that once she has put it out there, she can let go.
  Tess has discussed her concerns with Beckett, and they have negotiated a plan to talk with Rachel together. Tess can let go of her need for his support—she has it.

EMOTION AND CONFLICT MANAGEMENT EXERCISE 5

Beckett wanted to be present when Tess spoke to Rachel. He shared that he just wanted to be present and only intervene if things escalated.

Step 1: *Recognize her own needs.*

Tess noticed that she needs for Rachel to not criticize her parenting style.

Step 2: *Communicate with emotions in check.*

Tess found a time to talk to Rachel the next day when her son was napping, so they would not be distracted. She knew that if they were distracted, she would be more anxious. Beckett was present, so Tess mentally reminded herself that he was there for support.

- Allow herself time to respond.
  Tess had given herself a chance to consider her needs and already had spoken to Beckett. She then had the night to contemplate what to say to Rachel.

- Pay attention to her feelings as she expresses her words.
  Tess knows that she tends to speak too fast when she's anxious, so she continues to remember to "slow down."

- Pay attention to the emotions of the other person—validate!
  Tess remembers to be as gentle as possible, to try to reduce defensiveness. She shares that she knows Rachel loves the family so much and wants the best for everyone.

- Be aware and remain respectful of herself.
  While acknowledging Rachel's love, Tess states that at times she has different values from Rachel's that influence her parenting. She tells Rachel that parenting is hard work, and she would appreciate support rather than criticism.

- Be aware and remain respectful of the other person.
  Tess acknowledges that as Victor's grandmother, Rachel may have opinions about how he is being raised. If Rachel has serious concerns, she invites Rachel to address them privately with Tess and Beckett. She asks that Rachel communicate assertively, rather than in a critical manner.

Step 3: Say her piece, and release.

Now that Tess has let Rachel know her needs and her willingness to have a dialogue, she needs to accept Rachel's right to respond.

- Recognize that she has the right to express her reaction.
  Once Rachel responds, Tess has the right to share her response to negotiate. Rachel lets Tess know that she doesn't want to come across as critical, but that she thinks boys should be raised to be strong men. Tess thanks her and lets Rachel know that she agrees that all children should be raised to be emotionally strong, but they may define this differently at times.

- Understand that once she has put it out there, she can let go.
  Tess has addressed her concerns, and her work for now is to let go. If another issue arises in the future, she can go through this exercise again, but for now, it's over.

EMOTION AND CONFLICT MANAGEMENT EXERCISE 6

It is your first family vacation since you remarried earlier this year. You have three children from your previous marriage: Lexi, 16; Rory, 13; and Lili, 6. It's been five years since you and their father divorced. Overall, the divorce was as smooth as such a thing can be, and you are grateful to their father for that. Your new husband, Simon, has never had children before, but has understood that he's their stepdad now, and there will be an adjustment phase. Earlier today, when getting ready for the day's activities, Lexi became angry when Simon asked her to help prepare the beach bags. She told him that he's not her father, and she isn't obligated to do anything for him.

Step 1: *Recognize your own needs.*

You need your children to respect the new parenting dynamic.

Step 2: *Communicate with emotions in check.*

- Allow yourself time to respond.
  You are upset in this moment, but notice that you are still thinking clearly and don't feel overwhelmed, so you can move forward.

- Pay attention to your feelings as you express your words.
  You notice that you feel sad and irritated. You can feel these emotions in your body, so you breathe deeply. You tell Lexi, "It is important to me that Simon is respected as your stepfather."

- Pay attention to the emotions of the other person—validate!
  "I know that you are 16, and it is strange to have a new parent figure now. I also know that you are really close to your dad, and in no way is Simon taking his place."

- Be aware and remain respectful of yourself.

  "At the same time, Simon is my partner, and he is going to be involved in your parenting. It is important that this is respected because it is still my job—and now Simon's—to guide you into adulthood."

- Be aware and remain respectful of the other person.

  "Perhaps we can find ways to adjust to having a new parent figure. We should have a family meeting with your siblings to make things clear moving forward."

Step 3: *Say your piece, and release.*

You take a breath and wait for her response.

- Recognize that you have the right to express your reaction.

  Lexi says that things feel really unfair right now. You validate her again telling her that you know change is stressful and that your first priority is still being her mother.

- Understand that once you have put it out there, you can let go.

  You understand that you now have a plan to have a family meeting. It may take time for Lexi to stop struggling with the change, but for now you can move forward.

YOUR TURN!

Please consider a conflict in your life and go through the exercise below.

Step 1: *Recognize your own needs.*

- What do you need in this situation?

_____

_____

_____

Step 2: *Communicate with emotions in check.*

- Allow yourself time to respond.
  Pay attention to your feelings as you express your words.

  Notice your breathing at this time and how your body is feeling to notice your emotions.

- Pay attention to the emotions of the other person—validate!
  Listen and express understanding.

- Be aware and remain respectful of yourself.
  Stay clear on your needs.

- Be aware and remain respectful of the other person.
  Stay clear on their needs.

_____

_____

_____

Step 3: *Say your piece, and release.*

- Recognize that you have the right to express your reaction.
- Understand that once you have put it out there, you can let go.

_____

_____

_____

Moment of Reflection

Assertively addressing your needs helps you to connect with your true self, while validating others deepens understanding in your relationships. You have likely had numerous conflicts in your relationships in which you felt stuck, but the process outlined in this chapter will reduce conflict, prevent escalation, and help create greater intimacy. Moving forward, please remember that conflict is inevitable. It is proof not that you or another person are wrong but that you have different needs or values. You can negotiate by being honest about what you need, while respecting another person's views. This creates interdependent relationships. To achieve this, you must first be willing to honor what you are feeling, to soothe yourself so you can use these skills. In the next chapter, you will learn how to cope with your feelings in more effective ways.

Chapter 8

Reduce Stress and Calm Your Mind

Life will always include stressful situations. No amount of planning, self-help, or therapy can prevent problems in life. Often, in codependency, we may deny this truth, causing us to think and behave in ways that reinforce pain, anger, and stress. An interdependent person accepts the truth that life has stress, so they focus on cultivating positive coping skills rather than fixating on problems. They learn to tolerate uncomfortable situations and emotions so their reactions don't worsen things. Whenever I contemplate codependency recovery, I imagine a tree that is so grounded that when the weather is stormy, even while the branches sway, it's never uprooted. In this chapter, I will support you in developing the skills necessary to respond (rather than react) to stress, so that you, too, may stay grounded no matter what is happening around you.

Mindfulness to Stay Grounded

This chapter will focus heavily on mindfulness to achieve this goal of staying grounded. Mindfulness means to focus completely on the present moment with acceptance rather than judgment. It is acknowledging life for what it is, rather than what you wish it would be. After all, getting mad about reality doesn't change reality. Mindfulness is the opposite of multitasking—it is truly doing one thing at a time. When your mind wanders, as it will, you will simply bring your attention back to the present moment. Mindfulness is a practice; you focus on the present, your mind wanders, and you return to the present again, repeatedly. This process does take time and effort, since most people focus more easily on the past and future.

Learning to be mindful requires commitment and ongoing practice. A lot of people initially resist this practice, so you are not alone if you feel that way. This is not easy work, and it can feel quite tedious at first. However, I encourage you to practice anyway, because learning how to be mindful will get you out of fixating about what's wrong with you or others and feeling the unnecessary stress of thinking the present is "wrong."

Countless studies have revealed a plethora of emotional, relational, and cognitive benefits of mindfulness. Davis and Hayes (2011) reviewed numerous studies on mindfulness, and they found that a key benefit is emotional regulation—the ability to stay grounded no matter what happens. Additionally, the more mindful you become, the higher your threshold for distress. This means that many of the things that currently bother you just won't anymore. You may still get flooded at times, but it will certainly happen less often. Furthermore, it's proven that if you do get overwhelmed, a mindfulness practice will allow you to calm down faster. Amazingly, you can create a new baseline for yourself, where you are genuinely a calmer person. Over time, you won't have to think about the practice of mindfulness, as this focus on the present will be more natural for you. Finally, mindfulness reduces rumination—that obsessive thinking about what upsets you—and allows you to have more empathy when experiencing conflict. As you saw in the last chapter, this will allow you to resolve conflict effectively.

Developing a mindfulness practice can begin simply. It is about focusing on what is happening right now, both within and outside of you. For example, when you are eating, do only that. Focus on your food—how it tastes, looks, and smells—as well as your physical sensations, such as feeling hungry and satiated. Or, the next time you are waiting in line, resist the urge to pull out your phone, and simply observe your surroundings instead—what you hear, smell, and see. Tune in to your physical sensations as well. This is very helpful in managing your reactions to stress, because all emotions originate in the body. When you know what your emotions literally feel like, you will be able to cope with them more effectively. There is an exercise for this in *The Codependency Recovery Plan*. You can practice mindfulness with others by actively listening to what they say, rather than planning what to say next. Finally, meditation is a healing mindfulness practice that will be explored later in this chapter.

EXERCISES TO REDUCE STRESS

Below, you will learn skills that you can begin using today to help manage, and even prevent, stress. As you read, please identify the skills you would first like to practice.

Reducing Stress Skill 1

Breathing is a powerful stress management skill that you can use anywhere and at any time. Your body and your breath are always with you, and learning how to use the power of deep breathing will greatly reduce your stress. When you are in fight or flight, your breathing becomes shallow as your sympathetic nervous system is activated. For people living with chronic stress like codependency, this shallow breathing can become the default breathing pattern. It is normal to need to relearn how to breathe deeply. If you don't truly breathe deeply into your diaphragm, you actually reinforce the feelings of stress that come with being in fight or flight. Later in this chapter, I will guide you through a mindfulness meditation to ensure that you are practicing diaphragmatic breathing.

When you practice diaphragmatic breathing, you activate your parasympathetic nervous system. When you are in this state, your body moves out of fight or flight and thereby relaxes. Therefore, when you are stressed, you can use your breath to tell your brain to "relax." Studies on deep breathing reveal that it lowers anxiety, depression, and stress. It has also been shown to help us sustain our cognitive attention, which may reduce feelings of fatigue and burnout.

Example:

When Kate was growing up, she felt like she had to walk on eggshells around her angry, alcoholic mother. Now, whenever she even perceives someone as irritated with her, Kate gets overwhelmed and fixates. Kate is at the grocery store when someone makes a comment about how rude she is for blocking the items they need with her cart. She moves her cart instantaneously, but feels unable to move otherwise.

Skill #1: Kate pauses and scans her body. She notices that her stomach feels sick and her upper body is completely tensed up. She also notices the urge to cry.

Skill #2: Kate remembers diaphragmatic breathing and does a couple of cycles.

Skill #3: She scans her body again and notices that her stomach and upper body are beginning to relax, although not completely. She takes another deep breath to deepen her relaxation. She now notices that she is able to move again.

Skill #4: Kate reminds herself that she was not intentionally disregarding others in the store, and it's okay to make mistakes. She is now able to continue with her shopping without fixating.

Reducing Stress Skill 2

It's okay to need a break from your emotions and thoughts when you are overwhelmed. Perhaps it's not the right time to address the stressful situation, or it feels like too much to process initially. When this happens, many people's automatic urge is to suppress their emotions, to "stuff" so that you don't let yourself think about the problem or feel the corresponding emotions. This is a coping strategy that may feel better at first, but is ultimately destructive. Most people will eventually notice that they are exploding or imploding if they repress their emotions for too long. An explosion may look like yelling at a partner when you just can't take it anymore. An implosion is where you eventually hurt yourself. You may get overwhelmed by your feelings and deal with it by calling into work, cutting yourself, or drinking too much. In extreme cases, the refusal to feel your emotions can lead to the need for hospitalization to avoid hurting yourself or others.

It is still possible to use this suppression tactic positively, although it's essential to do it consciously. This is done by acknowledging that you need time and then creating a strategy to follow up later. A helpful strategy for consciously quieting your emotions and thoughts is to visualize any container that works for you, such as a box, a food storage container, or a jar with a lid. When you visualize this container, imagine putting all distressing thoughts, feelings, and physical sensations into it. Then, make the commitment to address whatever you contained later, maybe in your next therapy session, or this weekend with a friend.

Example:

This morning, Manisherson noticed that Becky seemed to be irritated. He asked her repeatedly what was wrong, and she kept saying, "Nothing." He hates when she won't communicate with him! When he's driving to the hospital where he works, he notices that he is alternating between how mad he is at Becky for being difficult and how nervous he is that he did something wrong. When he notices this, he does the following:

Skill #1: He breathes deeply for three breath cycles when he's stopped at the next red light.

Skill #2: He chooses to use a coping thought: "I can tolerate this, even though it's uncomfortable."

Skill #3: Letting go. He understands that there is nothing he can do to resolve this until tonight, as both he and Becky will be working all day.

Skill #4: Once in the parking lot at work, Manisherson visualizes a wooden chest with a lock. He breathes deeply as he puts images from this morning's conflict into it. He also puts his anger and anxiety into it, along with the physical tension he feels in his chest and hands. He takes another deep breath as he locks the container. He makes the commitment to follow up about this tonight.

Skill #5: Distraction through mindfulness. He focuses on his work throughout the day, and when his mind wanders, he comes back to his patients or paperwork.

Reducing Stress Skill 3

You can reduce stress by choosing to create positive thoughts to encourage you. Many of us become critical of ourselves and others when we are overwhelmed, which reinforces our distress. You can interrupt this by using positive coping thoughts. These thoughts may change depending on the situation, or you may notice that you want to create a mantra of sorts. For example, you may consistently feel weak, so you can create the thought, "I can handle this." If you have a go-to coping thought, consider envisioning a symbol or image that represents this. For example, if you think "I am strong," you may envision a person lifting weights. If you identify an image, I encourage you to find a picture of it to either keep as your phone wallpaper or hang in your home to support your recovery.

Example:

Nia, 34, has been living with Dante, 44, for three years. Lately, she has been worried that he is cheating on her, as he has started going to the gym at night. She hasn't felt ready to talk to him about it, but is terrified that if he is cheating, her life is over.

Skill #1: Mindfulness. Nia observes that she is thinking about her fears constantly. She decides to scan the room and identify six colors she sees.

Skill #2: She practices a breathing exercise she learned in yoga called alternate nostril breathing (note: this will be explained later in the chapter).

Skill #3: Now she can think more clearly, and she wants to encourage herself. She creates the coping thought: "Even if I find out he is cheating on me, I would survive. I'm stronger than I give myself credit for." She repeats this to herself when she begins to obsess.

Skill #4: Because of her coping thought, she realizes that she is capable of talking to Dante. She goes through the exercise she learned in chapter 7 to do this.

Reducing Stress Skill 4

In the last chapter, letting go was mentioned as part of the conflict management process. Letting go, or detachment, is to focus on the present without judgment or expectation. It is the process of accepting life for what it is. The quintessential mantra for this is "It is what it is." When you cannot change what troubles you, letting go is a powerful skill. You can still care about what is going on, but you accept reality to lower the stress in your life. A simple example is to imagine being stuck in traffic. A person who is attached to their expectations may think, "I can't believe this is happening to me! I'm going to be late now. I can't believe how awful these drivers are—this is such crap!" This person will keep themselves angry with their fixation on wishing things were different. A mindful person who practices acceptance would notice, "Wow, my body feels tense now that I have to sit here, and I know I will be late. However, I cannot change the traffic; it is what it is." This person will feel much less stress than the person who is fixating. This isn't to say that you won't still have feelings about the situation when you are practicing letting go, but it does reduce your stress. The mindful person will still notice stress when they are stuck in traffic, but because they accept it, they can find helpful ways to cope. They can listen to an audiobook or use this opportunity to practice their breathing exercises, for example.

Example:

Kirsten's adult daughter, Kim, has refused to talk to her for a year. She has sent many messages to Kim trying to get her to talk to her; however, she gets no response when she sends letters, and her electronic communications are now blocked. Kirsten is in deep emotional pain about this and continues to fixate on how to get Kim to speak to her. But now, after entering recovery, she decides to practice letting go. She knows that she will still feel grief, but when she finds herself fixating on how to get Kim to talk to her, she reminds herself that only Kim can decide if she will speak to her again. "It is what it is," she tells herself, while breathing through it. She then focuses on coping with her grief by journaling, crying, or meditating. This process, while it doesn't remove the grief, allows her to reduce her suffering by not fixating on how to change reality when she can't.

Reducing Stress Skill 5

When many people think about yoga, their initial image is of someone highly flexible twisting into complex poses. While physical flexibility may be cultivated, the primary focus of yoga is on the breath, or *pranayama*. *Prana* means "life force energy." West et al. (2017) studied the impact of yoga on 31 women with PTSD. They discovered that all participants reported feeling more empowered after the study. Many were able to accept the past more, partially due to yoga's focus on the present moment. Finally, some participants felt more compassion toward their bodies, which led to greater self-love.

Since the first focus is on the breath, yoga is for anyone who wants to practice their breathing. If you have mobility issues or a disability, yoga can be adapted. The breath is linked to *asana* or practicing a pose. You breathe in on one movement and breathe out with another. When you struggle with a pose or your mind wanders, you come back to the breath. There are many ways to start practicing yoga, including going to a local gym or yoga studio or working at home. There are many wonderful yoga instructors on YouTube, so you can try it for free. I highly recommend checking out *Yoga with Adriene*; she has a wide range of videos for every skill level and of varying lengths, making it easy to fit it into your schedule.

Example:

Brian is having a stressful day at his company. It seems that no matter where he turns, a customer or an employee has a complaint. He is getting overwhelmed and resentful, so he decides to take a yoga break.

1. He goes into his office and puts a sign on the door not to be interrupted.

2. He doesn't have his yoga mat with him, so he doesn't want to lie on the floor, but he knows that is not a problem.

3. He decides to practice tree pose to ground himself, so he takes off his shoes.

4. He finds a clear space on the ground and stands tall. He focuses on his feet and brings them close together. He makes sure all parts of his feet are connected to the earth.

5. He shifts his weight to his left foot and lifts his right knee. He breathes into this change and makes sure that he is grounded on his left foot. Keeping his chest lifted assists with this.

6. He is not able to lift his right leg all the way up to his inner thigh, so he bends his right leg and anchors it into the side of his left calf. He takes a few deep breaths as he focuses on his desk chair, which helps him maintain balance.

7. He repeats this practice on the other side and is then ready to return to his day.

MEDITATION

When you practice these meditations, please find a quiet place where you can be undisturbed for at least 10 minutes. Beginning a meditation practice may sound intimidating, but it's simply focusing on the present moment. When your mind wanders during these exercises, just move your attention back to the instructions.

Mindfulness Meditation

You will now focus on your breath to stay present in the moment and support your body in being able to fully relax. If your mind wanders, please allow yourself to come back to the present moment and your breath.

1. *Allow yourself to find a comfortable seat where you can sit up straight.*

2. *Place one hand on your belly and one on your chest.*

3. *Take a deep breath in and out, while noticing which hand rises more; you may need to take a few breaths to fully assess this, so please allow yourself this time.*

    a) If the hand on your chest rises more, then we will practice deep diaphragmatic breathing to assist your body in fully relaxing.

    1. Imagine a deflated balloon of any color in your belly, just below your rib cage.

    2. Now, pull in your breath through the nose.

    3. As you breathe deeply, imagine the breath being pulled deeply into your belly to expand your balloon. Allow the balloon to expand, if only a little.

    4. Once you have the breath in your balloon, please hold it for a moment.

    5. Now, slightly relax your jaw, and push the breath out of the balloon through your mouth.

6. Great job! Let us practice again.

7. Take another deep breath in—pulling deeper and deeper, expanding your balloon a little more this time. Wonderful.

8. Holding it at the top, pause for a moment.

9. Now, relax your jaw and push out all the stale breath deep within your belly being held by this balloon. Really push it out. You no longer need this old energy inside of you.

10. Great. Relax into your body and notice what you physically and emotionally feel. If you notice you are a little light-headed or dizzy, this is completely normal at first as your body adjusts to breathing deeply. Take a few breaths that feel normal and usual to you for a moment.

11. Now we will practice diaphragmatic breathing one more time.

12. Take the deepest breath you've taken so far, pulling it deep into the balloon to expand it as much as possible today. Hold the breath until you must fully release. Push your breath completely out of your belly. Take a few gentle breaths, focusing on how you feel. Please know you may practice this any time you wish.

b) If it is the hand on your belly, great! This is diaphragmatic breathing. But please still practice taking four deep breath cycles as described previously.

If you noticed that your breathing was shallow, please practice this breathing exercise at least once a day to assist in your body in staying emotionally regulated. In the beginning, you only need to practice for three or four breath cycles. Please be gentle with yourself as you adjust to diaphragmatic breathing. When you are no longer dizzy or light-headed, you may add to the breath cycles you practice. Great times to practice include on a work break or right before bed, as it will help you drift off into sleep.

If you noticed diaphragmatic breathing came naturally to you, wonderful! You are still able to practice deep breathing daily to ensure that you are allowing yourself to relax as deeply as possible to reduce stress.

Guided Meditation to Prepare for a Difficult Conversation

For this meditation, please have a journal or notebook readily available.

1. *Take a deep breath in through your nose and pull the breath into your belly.*

2. *Hold the breath for a moment and then fully relax your jaw to release your breath.*

3. *Now repeat this for a few more breath cycles.*

4. *With each inhalation, imagine that you can breathe in peace, holding it in your belly for a moment at the top.*

5. *With each exhalation, breathe out tension, stress, and fear.*

6. *Now please begin to focus on what your specific needs are at this time.*

7. *Your needs are worth celebrating and honoring.*

8. *They are a core part of who you are.*

9. You have a right to your needs.

10. And the responsibility to share them kindly.

11. See your needs as a seed of light within your belly.

12. Holding on to this image, begin to visualize the person with whom you need to communicate now.

13. They are standing in front of you.

14. Take a deep breath and see this person surrounded by a soft white light and with compassion in their eyes.

15. They value you and want to know what you need; they may not be able to meet your needs exactly, but they do care.

16. They are committed to creating a plan that will honor both of you.

17. Knowing this truth, take another deep breath in and fully exhale.

18. Begin to see the seed of your light—your needs—in your core again.

19. As you focus on your needs, this seed of light begins to sprout.

20. See this seed unfurling into a beautiful flower that extends into your heart space.

21. This flower has green and pink petals with a soft golden glow around it.

22. *Take a deep breath, connecting with this beautiful flower in your heart.*

23. *As you breathe into your heart, you will begin to notice how to express your needs.*

24. *You will hear exactly what to say, so that your message is loving for you and for the other person.*

25. *You can show yourself love by expressing your needs . . . while also embracing the love you have for another.*

26. *Take a deep breath, feeling the gratitude of having this clarity.*

27. *You know now what to say.*

28. *Continue to breathe, as you know this message will stay with you until you can deliver it to the other person.*

29. *Place your hand on your heart, sealing this message in and knowing that this flower will stay within you.*

30. *Thank the other person for being a part of your journey.*

31. *When you are ready, please take a few deep breaths and begin to wiggle your fingers and toes.*

32. *Slowly open your eyes.*

Now take your journal and write down the messages or insights you had so that you are fully prepared to have this conversation.

Mantra Meditation

Mantra meditation is using a word, phrase, or sound to help your mind stay centered. It's a wonderful tool if you find that you struggle to stay mindful. The mantra acts like an anchor so that when your mind wanders, you can use it to ground yourself back to the present. Yogic mantras are chanted sounds that were first described in ancient Indian scriptures, and each has a different meaning. *Mantra Yoga and Primal Sound: Secret of Seed (Bija) Mantras* by David Frawley is a good resource if you'd like to learn more about yogic mantras. You may be familiar with the yogic mantra "Om" (pronounced AUM), which is said to be the first sound from which creation, including all other sounds, emerged. Numerous studies have been conducted on how the use of Om affects meditators. It has been shown to reduce breathing and heart rates—the opposite of what happens when we are flooded.

Research shows that you may also choose a word or phrase to benefit from mantra meditation. It is important to practice using your mantra consistently to benefit from it. To begin, please take some time for yourself. Consider the mantra that you want to focus on, such as "Om," a word like "safe," or a phrase such as "I trust myself." Make sure to pick a mantra that resonates with you. You may want to journal about your meditation goals to assist you in revealing an anchor word or phrase.

Once you have identified your mantra, please follow the guidance below:

1. *Find a comfortable seat where you may have some peaceful time alone.*

2. *Have your mantra in mind or written in front of you to help anchor you.*

3. *Take a deep breath in through your nose, into your belly, and out through your mouth.*

4. Say, chant, or repeat your personal mantra quietly in your mind three times.

5. Pause and notice how you feel physically and emotionally and whether you were able to focus on the mantra. If or when you notice distractions, please bring your attention back fully to your mantra.

6. In this moment, your mantra and grounding yourself into its truth are the only things that matter.

7. Take another breath and allow yourself to say, chant, or repeat your mantra until your mind wanders.

8. Then, come back to your mantra and repeat it at least three more times.

Yoga Meditation

Now you will have the opportunity to practice a form of *pranayama* called alternate nostril breathing. It will help you relax and can even reduce headaches, but it is normal to feel confused by it at first. Please give yourself the grace to feel silly or odd, but to practice anyway.

1. Please find a comfortable seat in a chair or sit cross-legged on the ground.

2. When you are seated, please keep your core engaged so that you are sitting tall, making sure that your shoulders are looped back, rather than slouching forward.

3. Now take some normal breaths to center yourself.

4. Great. Now take your right hand and fold your index and middle fingers toward your palm.

5. If you are noticing that holding your hand in such a way is difficult or distracting, please do not worry. Simply take all three middle fingers and fold them into your palm. You may use your pinky and thumb for this.

6. Otherwise, hold your right hand with your index and middle fingers folded, and take your right thumb to your right nostril, sealing it. Inhale through the left nostril and pause. Now take your ring finger and seal the left nostril. Exhale now through the right.

7. Inhale through the right, and then seal this nostril with the thumb.

8. Exhale through the left.

9. Inhale now in the left nostril, and then seal with your finger.

10. Breathe out through the right, and then inhale.

11. Pause and seal your right nostril with your thumb, then exhale through your left.

12. Now inhale through your left. Pause and seal with the finger.

13. Exhale through the right nostril and then inhale.

14. Move the thumb to the right, and exhale through the left.

15. Now inhale through the left, pause and seal with the finger.

16. Exhale through the right nostril and then inhale.

17. Wonderful work! You may relax your hand now and ground back into your body. Check to ensure that you are sitting up straight and then move your shoulders up and back. Breathe into your body, noticing how it feels now that you gave it loving attention.

Moment of Reflection

This chapter has given you skills to cope with stress more effectively. You have learned to practice mindfulness through diaphragmatic breathing, yoga, and meditation. Please practice at least one form of mindfulness daily so you can create a new baseline of calm. This will empower you to think more clearly and not overreact when stressed. You have also learned the values of containing an emotion if necessary, distraction, and self-encouragement. Finally, you have integrated these skills with letting go. Practicing these skills daily leads to incredible self-empowerment. You will know that while you cannot control life, or your emotions when they arise, you are fully capable and in control of your response.

You have now reached the end of this workbook, and with the use of the skills you have learned throughout it, you are entering codependency recovery. At this time, please reflect back on your goals and acknowledge your accomplishments. Remember, though, that recovery is a lifestyle rather than a destination. Reviewing the skills you have learned to more deeply integrate them into your life is an ongoing part of the journey. Please come back to the different chapters as you need to practice them again and again. You will find some lined pages just below to reflect on the insights you have gained from the meditations or to identify strategies to begin integrating these skills into your daily life. You are so capable!

Journal Pages

Resources

If you would like to learn about the history of codependency, its symptoms, and recovery, I recommend the following books:

The Codependency Recovery Plan: A 5-Step Guide to Understand, Accept and Break Free from the Codependent Cycle by Krystal Mazzola

You're Not Crazy—You're Codependent: What Everyone Affected by Addiction, Abuse, Trauma or Toxic Shaming Must Know to Have Peace in Their Lives by Jeanette Elisabeth Menter

You may also find the comprehensive reading list on both codependency and love addiction found here at the Center for Healthy Sex very helpful: https://centerforhealthysex.com/sex-therapy-resources/other-resources/reading-list/love-addiction-and-codependency-books/

If you would like to learn more about addiction, I recommend reading:

Unbroken Brain: A Revolutionary New Way of Understanding Addiction by Maia Szalavitz

The Addiction Recovery Workbook: Powerful Skills for Preventing Relapse Every Day by Paula A. Freedman, PsyD

If you would like to learn more about trauma, I recommend reading:

The Body Keeps the Score: Brain, Mind, and Body in the Healing of Trauma by Bessel van der Kolk MD

If you would like to learn more about mindfulness, I recommend reading:

The Power of Now: A Guide to Spiritual Enlightenment by Eckhart Tolle

Full Catastrophe Living (Revised Edition): Using the Wisdom of Your Body and Mind to Face Stress, Pain, and Illness by Jon Kabat-Zinn

If you would like to improve your romantic relationship, I would recommend reading:

The Science of Trust by John M. Gottman PhD

Passionate Marriage: Keeping Love and Intimacy Alive in Committed Relationships by David Schnarch, PhD

Free coping skills:

You will find meditations, lectures, and a list of community resources for meditation at tarabrach.com

Free yoga videos—and paid courses if you want to learn more—are at yogawithadriene.com

CBT worksheets for a variety of concerns and skills, including cognitive restructuring, may be found at https://www.therapistaid .com/therapy-worksheets/cbt/none

Therapy resources

The Substance Abuse and Mental Health Services Administration has a helpline for addiction treatment referrals and information at 1-800-662-HELP (4357). This line operates 365 days per year, 24/7.

Their website at samhsa.gov provides information on treatment resources for both mental health and substance abuse concerns.

You may learn more about mindfulness-based CBT at mbct.com and find mindfulness-based CBT therapists at accessmbct.com

Psychology Today offers a comprehensive and free directory to find a therapist in your community (and zip code). You can search based on specialties, accepted insurance providers, and specific areas in your community: https://www.psychologytoday.com /us/therapists

You will find information on therapy to improve relationships and recover from codependency at healthyrelationshipfoundation.com

References

Chapter 1:

American Addiction Centers. "The Addiction Cycle: Phases of the Chronically Relapsing Disease." Edited by *Editorial Staff.* https://americanaddictioncenters.org/the-addiction-cycle. Accessed 10/20/19.

American Psychiatric Association. *Diagnostic and Statistical Manual of Mental Disorders: DSM-5.* Arlington, VA: American Psychiatric Publishing. 2013.

The American Society of Addiction Medicine. "ASAM Releases New Definition of Addiction." *ASAM News*, 26, no. 3, (2011).

Beattie, Melody. *Codependent No More: How to Stop Controlling Others and Start Caring for Yourself.* Center City, MN: Hazelden Publishing, 1992.

Beck, J. S. *Cognitive Behavior Therapy: Basics and Beyond* (2nd ed.). New York: Guilford Press, 2011.

Burns, D. D., & Nolen-Hoeksema, S. "Coping Styles, Homework Compliance, and the Effectiveness of Cognitive-Behavioral Therapy." *Journal of Consulting and Clinical Psychology*, 59, no. 2 (1991): 305–311.

Centers for Disease Control and Prevention. "Drug Overdose Deaths." https://www.cdc.gov/drugoverdose/data/statedeaths.html Accessed 10/20/19.

Fisher, H. "Lust, Attraction, Attachment: Biology and Evolution of the Three Primary Emotion Systems for Mating, Reproduction, and Parenting." *Journal of Sex Education & Therapy*, 25, no. 1 (2000): 96–104.

Hales, C. M., Fryar, C. D., Carroll, M. D., Freedman, D. S., & Ogden, C. L. "Trends in Obesity and Severe Obesity Prevalence in US Youth and Adults by Sex and Age, 2007–2008 to 2015–2016." *JAMA*, 319, no. 16. (April 24, 2018): 1723–1725.

Hirth, J. M., Rahman, M., & Berenson, A. B. "The Association of Posttraumatic Stress Disorder with Fast Food and Soda Consumption and Unhealthy Weight Loss Behaviors Among Young Women." *Journal of Women's Health* (Larchmt), 20, no. 8 (2011): 1141–1149.

Kenny, Dianna T. "A Brief History of Psychoanalysis: From Freud to Fantasy to Folly." *Psychotherapy and Counselling Journal of Australia.* (Sept. 1, 2016.): 1–26. http://pacja.org.au/?p=2952.

Khoury, L., Tang, Y. L., Bradley, B., Cubells, J. F., Ressler, K. J. "Substance Use, Childhood Traumatic Experience, and Posttraumatic Stress Disorder in an Urban Civilian Population." *Depression and Anxiety*, 27, no. 12 (Dec. 2010): 1077–1086.

Mason, S. M., Flint, A. J., Roberts, A. L., Agnew-Blais, J., Koenen, K. C., & Rich-Edwards, J. W. "Posttraumatic Stress Disorder Symptoms and Food Addiction in Women by Timing and Type of Trauma Exposure." *JAMA Psychiatry*, 71, no. 11 (November 2014): 1271–1278.

Mausbach, B. T., Moore, R., Roesch, S., et al. "The Relationship Between Homework Compliance and Therapy Outcomes: An Updated Meta-Analysis." *Cognitive Therapy and Research*, 34, no. 5 (October 2010): 429–438.

Mazzola, Krystal. *The Codependency Recovery Plan: A 5-Step Guide to Understand, Accept, and Break Free from the Codependent Cycle*. Emeryville, CA: Althea Press, 2019.

Mellody, Pia. *Facing Love Addiction: Giving Yourself the Power to Change the Way You Love*. San Francisco, CA: HarperOne, 2003.

Mellody, P., Miller, A. W., & Miller, K. *Facing Codependence: What It Is, Where It Comes From, How It Sabotages Our Lives*. New York: Harper & Row, 1989.

Peele, Stanton, with Brodsky, Archie. *Love and Addiction*. New York: Taplinger, 1975.

Rosenthal, Richard, J., & Suzanne B. Faris. "The Etymology and Early History of 'Addiction'," *Addiction Research & Theory*, 27, no. 5, (2019): 437–449, DOI: 10.1080/16066359.2018.1543412.

Riggenbach, Jeff. *The CBT Toolbox: A Workbook for Clients and Clinicians*. Eau Claire, Wisconsin: PESI Publishing & Media, 2013.

Substance Abuse and Mental Health Services Administration. Key Substance Use and Mental Health Indicators in the United States: Results from the 2018 National Survey on Drug Use and Health (HHS Publication No. PEP195068, NSDUH Series H54). Rockville, MD: Center for Behavioral Health Statistics and Quality, Substance Abuse and Mental Health Services Administration, 2019. Retrieved from https://www.samhsa.gov/data/.

Szalavitz, Maia. *Unbroken Brain: A Revolutionary New Way of Understanding Addiction*. New York: St. Martin's Press, 2016.

Ulrich-Lai, Yvonne M., Christiansen, Anne M., Ostrander, Michelle M., Jones, Amanda A., Jones, Kenneth R., Choi, Dennis C., Krause, Eric G., Evanson, Nathan K., Fura Amy R., Davis, Jon F., Solomon, Matia B., de Kloet, Annette D., Tamashiro, Kellie L., Sakai, Randall R., Seeley, Randy J., Woods, Stephen C., & Herman, James P. "Pleasurable Behaviors Reduce Stress Via Brain Reward Pathways." *Proceedings of the National Academy of Sciences*, 107, no. 47 (Nov 2010): 20529–20534; DOI: 10.1073/pnas.1007740107.

Chapter 2:

Beck, J. S. *Cognitive Behavior Therapy: Basics and Beyond* (2nd ed.). New York: Guilford Press, 2011.

Mazzola, Krystal. *The Codependency Recovery Plan: A 5-Step Guide to Understand, Accept, and Break Free from the Codependent Cycle*. Emeryville, CA: Althea Press, 2019.

Mellody, P., Miller, A. W., & Miller, K. *Facing Codependence: What It Is, Where It Comes From, How It Sabotages Our Lives*. New York: Harper & Row, 1989.

http://www.schematherapy.com/id73.htm COPYRIGHT 2012, Manishrey Young, Ph.D. Unauthorized reproduction without written consent of the author is prohibited. For more information, write: Schema Therapy Institute, 561 10th Ave., Suite 43D, New York, NY 10036 Accessed 10/20/19

Chapter 3:

Locke, Edwin, & Latham, Gary. "*A Theory of Goal Setting & Task Performance.*" *The Academy of Management Review*, 16, no. 2 (1991). DOI: 10.2307/258875.

Mazzola, Krystal. *The Codependency Recovery Plan: A 5-Step Guide to Understand, Accept, and Break Free from the Codependent Cycle*. Emeryville, CA: Althea Press, 2019.

Chapter 4:

Beck, J. S. *Cognitive Behavior Therapy: Basics and Beyond* (2nd ed.). New York: Guilford Press, 2011.

O'Donohue, William T., & Fisher, Jane E. *Cognitive Behavior Therapy: Applying Empirically Supported Techniques in Your Practice, 2nd Ed.* Hoboken, NJ: John Wiley & Sons, 2004.

Riggenbach, Jeff. *The CBT Toolbox: A Workbook for Clients and Clinicians*. Eau Claire, Wisconsin: PESI Publishing & Media, 2013.

Chapter 5:

Beck, J. S. *Cognitive Behavior Therapy: Basics and Beyond* (2nd ed.). New York: Guilford Press, 2011.

Fullana, M., Cardoner, N., Alonso, P., Subirà, M., López-Solà, C., Pujol, J., et al. "Brain Regions Related to Fear Extinction in Obsessive-Compulsive Disorder and Its Relation to Exposure Therapy Outcome: A Morphometric Study." Psychological Medicine, 44, no. 4 (June 2018), 845–856. doi:10.1017/S0033291713001128.

Javanbakht, Arash, & Saab, Linda. "What Happens in the Brain When We Feel Fear: And Why Some of Us Just Can't Get Enough of It." *Smithsonian Magazine* (October 27, 2017). https://www.smithsonianmag.com/science-nature/what-happens-brain-feel-fear-180966992/.

Chapter 6:

Beck, Aaron T., & Clark, David A. *The Anxiety & Worry Workbook: The Cognitive Behavioral Solution*. New York: Guilford Press, 2012.

Beck, J. S. *Cognitive Behavior Therapy: Basics and Beyond* (2nd ed.). New York: Guilford Press, 2011.

Chapter 7:

Gottman, John. *The Marriage Clinic: A Scientifically Based Marital Therapy*. New York: Norton, 1999.

Gottman, John. *The Science of Trust*. New York: Norton, 2011.

Mazzola, Krystal. *The Codependency Recovery Plan: A 5-Step Guide to Understand, Accept, and Break Free from the Codependent Cycle*. Emeryville, CA: Althea Press, 2019.

Chapter 8:

"Alternate Nostril Breathing." Yoga with Adriene. Accessed 12/6/19. https://yoga withadriene.com/alternate-nostril-breathing/.

Davis, Daphne, & Hayes, J. A.. "What Are the Benefits of Mindfulness? A Practice Review of Psychotherapy-Related Research." *Psychotherapy*, 48, no. 2 (June 2011): 198–208. DOI: 10.1037/a0022062.

Frawley, David. *Mantra Yoga and Primal Sound: Secret of Seed (Bija) Mantras*. Twin Lakes, WI: Lotus Press.

Kumar, S., Nagendra, H., Manjunath, N., Naveen, K., & Telles, S. "Meditation on OM: Relevance from Ancient Texts and Contemporary Science." *International Journal of Yoga*, 3, no. 1 (January 2010): 2–5. DOI:10.4103/0973-6131.66771.

Ma, X., Yue, Z. Q., Gong, Z. Q., Zhang, H., Duan, N. Y., Shi, Y. T., et al. "The Effect of Diaphragmatic Breathing on Attention, Negative Affect, and Stress in Healthy Adults." *Frontiers in Psychology*, 8 (June 6 2017): 874. DOI:10.3389/fpsyg.2017.00874.

Mazzola, Krystal. *The Codependency Recovery Plan: A 5-Step Guide to Understand, Accept, and Break Free from the Codependent Cycle*. Emeryville, CA: Althea Press, 2019.

Moran, Susan. "The Science Behind Finding Your Mantra and How to Practice It Daily." *Yoga Journal* (March 20, 2018). Accessed 12/5/19. https://www.yogajournal.com/yoga-101/mantras-101-the-science-behind-finding-your-mantra-and-how-to-practice-it.

Novotny, S. "The Science of Breathing." *IDEA Fitness Journal 4*, no. 2 (February 1, 2007). http://www.ideafit.com/fitness-library/science-breathing.

Shunya, Acharya. *Ayurveda: Lifestyle Wisdom*. Boulder: Sounds True, 2017.

West, J., Liang, B., & Spinazzola, J.. "Trauma Sensitive Yoga as a Complementary Treatment for Posttraumatic Stress Disorder: A Qualitative Descriptive Analysis." *International Journal of Stress Management*, 24, no. 2 (2017): 173–195. DOI: 10.1037/str0000040.

Index

A

abandonment, 27
addiction
    behavior, 10–11, 13, 14
    cycle of, 1, 3, 12, 14
    food, 11, 15
    food, as to, 11, 15
    forms of, as many, 15
    learning disorder, as a, 9–10
    looks like, as to what, 8–9
    love, 6–7, 8, 12, 13, 14
    overlap, defined, 7
    sex, as to, 7, 15
    substance, as abuse, 7, 9–14, 15
    trauma, as common element, 5, 11
alcoholic
    addiction and, 10
    codependent and the, 7, 54, 59, 112, 132
    disease of will, 8
    response to, 94
    trauma and, 5, 11, 15
American Psychiatric Association, 10
American Society of Addition Medicine, 9
anger
    avoiding, as a plan, 31, 134
    feeling of, 59, 102, 115
    thought, as response to, 18, 58, 129
approval seeking, behaviors of, 26–27
authentic self
    awareness of, 39, 43, 64, 110
    knowing, as, 26
    role playing, as lose to, 5, 25
automatic thoughts
    defined by, as not, 75
    negative as, 36–37, 55, 62, 64, 70–71
    responsive, as, 18

B

Beattie, Melody, 4, 5
Beck, Aaron T., 16, 17, 55
behavior
    caring, connecting and, 4
    compulsive, as, 8, 15
    harmful, 13
    maladapted, 19
    problematic, 7, 9, 12, 16, 18
    rationalize, as to, 28
    unhealthy, 28, 44, 46
Burns, David D., 20

C

calm
    acceptance, as, 59
    down, as in cool off, 111, 113,130
Centers for Disease Control and Prevention
    (CDC), 10
Codependency Quiz, 29
    results, 36
codependent
    addiction and, 8
    approval, as searching for, 26–27
    attract, as to other codependents, 5
    authentic self, as missing, 25, 28
    childhood, as usual beginning, 5
    control, as in need for, 28
    defined, 4, 7
    emotions, as unclear, 58
    family role in, 6
    patterns, as destructive, 23, 28
    people-pleasing, as, 27
    perfectionism and, 25
    schemas, as beliefs, 24–25
    self-respect, as lacking, 25–26, 28
    therapy, when needed, 20
    thoughts, as often false, 18–20, 25

Cognitive Behavior Therapy (CBT)
  codependency and, 18–20
  defining, 15
  evidence-based, 16
  problem-solving, as, 16–17
  skills based, is, 19
  therapist, when to see, 20
cognitive distortion
  catastrophizing, 64
  cynical, 56
  expectation, as unmet, 57
  filter, as in mental, 58
  judgmental, 57
  mind-reading, inaccurate, 57
  negative filtering, 17, 24, 56
  outcomes, as positive, 70
  personalizing, as to behavior, 56
  positive experience, discounts, 56
  reasoning, as emotional, 57
  restructuring, 65
  thinking, all-or-nothing, 55
  thoughts, as automatic, 18
cognitive restructuring, 64
communication
  assertive, as style of, 110
  avoidance of, 27
  passive-aggressive, as, 110
  speaking up, fear of, 64, 80
  understanding, expressed by listening, 112
conflict
  breaking from, 111
  empathy in, 130
  resolution, 110, 113–122
control
  being in, 28
  lack of, 9, 10, 13, 27
  others, as from, 19

  partners or family, as of, 8, 65, 72
core beliefs, 16–17, 18, 53

D

depression
  intense, as needing therapist, 20
  relief from, 16–17, 20, 132
  substance abuse and, 12
  thoughts, as from, 55
  withdrawal and, 13–14
diabetes, type 2, 11
Diagnostic and Statistical Manual of Mental Disorders (DSM-5), 4
dopamine, 6
drug use
  overdose from, 10–11
  prescription, 10, 15
  tolerance to, 13
  treatment for, 24
  withdrawal from, 14
dysfunction, 9, 25

E

Ellis, Albert, 64
emotion and conflict management
  exercise 1, 113
  exercise 2, 114
  exercise 3, 116
  exercise 4, 118
  exercise 5, 120
  exercise 6, 122
  reflection, 126
  your turn (exercise), 124
emotions
  basic, as every day, 58, 77
  distressing, 58, 75, 78, 133
  exercises, to improve, 113–122

intense, 6, 14, 20, 64
negative, as, 13, 26, 56
strong, as, 1, 64, 121
enmeshment, 28
excitement, 58
exposure therapy, 80
example 1, 80
example 2, 81
your turn (exercise), 83
Eye Movement Desensitization and
Reprocessing (EMDR), 18, 20

F

false beliefs, 19
fear
facing your, 77, 78, 81
hindering, as, 44
losing, of, 25, 47
origins of, 78
rejection, of, 64, 77, 110
fight-or-flight response, 12, 78, 111,
131, 132
Fisher, Helen, 6
flooding, as overwhelmed, 111

G

gaslighting, 25
goal
dream, big, 45, 46
long-term, 45–46, 48, 66–69, 75
mistakes happen, 49
setting, 44, 50
short-term, 45, 48
Gottman, John, 110
gratitude, 56, 58, 143
grief, 58, 136
guilt
feelings of, 18, 27, 70, 102
inappropriate, as, 26

H

happy, making others, 27, 29, 80, 112
heart disease, 11

I

integrity, 4, 26, 114
interdependency, defined, 4
irrational beliefs (IBs), 64

J

journal pages, personal, 150
journal your concerns, 47

L

Levenson, Robert, 110
love
addiction, 6–7, 8, 12, 13, 14
avoidant, 7
self, as of, 38, 43, 48, 137, 143
showing, 28

M

manipulation, 8, 25
meditation
guided, for conversation, 141–143
mantra, 144–145
mindfulness, 139
yoga, 145–147
Mellody, Pia, 5, 7, 8
mental health
diagnosis of, 4, 55
services, 10, 159
mindfulness
benefits of being, 130
meditation for, 132, 139
present, as to being, 130, 131, 148
thought control, as to, 134, 135, 13071

N

narcissist, 5
negotiate, 27, 119, 120, 126
Nolen-Hoeksema, Susan, 20
norepinephrine, 6

O

obesity epidemic, 11
other worth, 4

P

passion, 28, 38, 58
Peele, Stanton, 6
people-pleasing, 5, 27
perfectionism, 25, 28, 49
post-traumatic stress disorder (PTSD), 5,
  11, 17, 137

problem-solving
  behavior, as disrespectful, 95
  exercise 1, 96
  exercise 2, 97
  exercise 3, 99
  exercise 4, 101
  exercise 5, 102
  exercise 6, 104
  reflection, 107
  your turn (exercise), 105
psychoanalysis, 15–16

R

resentment, 18, 23, 27, 59, 98
response prevention
  exercise 1, 84
  exercise 2, 86
  reflection, 90
  Rudy's plan, 85
  Sophia's plan, 86–88
  your turn (exercise), 88–89
responsible
  children, as protecting, 31, 60
  choices made, as for, 19, 65
  others, as not for, 28, 35, 56, 65, 97
role playing, in families, 6
Rush, Benjamin Dr., 8

S

sadness, 58
schemas, belief systems, 24, 27
self-care
  avoiding, 44
  guilt, feelings of from, 18, 26
  practicing, 31, 38, 48, 70
self-destructive patterns, 23

self-neglect, 4
self-reflection, 50
  case study, 54–55
  negative thoughts, identify, 55–57
  negative thoughts, replace, 53
self-respect, lacking, 4, 25
self-righteous, 28
self-worth, 4, 6, 24
self, sense of, 4, 6, 24–25
set your goals, 48
shame, 27, 57–58, 59
situation
  exercise 1, 59
  exercise 2, 60
  exercise 3, 61
  your turn (exercise), 62
stonewalling, 111
stress
  overwhelming, feelings of, 12
  reducing, 129, 131–137, 141
  traumatic, 5, 12, 79
stress reducing exercises
  reducing stress skill 1, 131
  reducing stress skill 2, 133
  reducing stress skill 3, 134
  reducing stress skill 4, 135
  reducing stress skill 5, 137
  reflection, 148
substance abuse
  addiction and, 7, 9, 13–15
  America, high rate of, 10
  disorders of, 9–12
  help with, 10, 159
  symptoms of, 12
  triggers, 12
Substance Abuse and Mental
    Health Services Administration
    (SAMHSA), 10
suicide, thoughts of, 20
Szalavitz, Maia, 9

T

therapist
  when to see, 20
therapy

exposure, 79, 80
thought changing, 64
    challenge negative thoughts exercise 1, 66
    challenge negative thoughts exercise 2, 67
    negative, as to replacing, 70
    reflection on, 75
    replace negative thoughts exercise 1, 72
    replace negative thoughts exercise 2, 73
    your turn (exercise), 68, 74
thoughts, as distorted
    all-or-nothing, 55
    catastrophizing, 56
    discounting the positive, 56
    emotional reasoning, 57

labeling, 57
mental filtering, 57–58
mind-reading, 57
overgeneralizing, 56
personalizing, 56
should or must statements, 57
toxic cycles, 5
trauma
    defined as, 5
    therapy, as EMDR, 20
triggers, 12
    identifying, 77
    traumatic, 79

Acknowledgments

I want to express gratitude to some individuals who allowed me to create this workbook.

First, I want to thank Caleb Mitchell, who truly helped me understand how to not believe every thought I think. For that, I'm deeply grateful. My recovery—and this workbook—would not be possible had you not helped me fully live into that lesson.

Next, thank you to my professors at the University of Oregon in the Couples and Family Therapy Program; especially Jeff Todahl, Marc Zola, and Tiffany Brown. As a therapist in training, you helped me understand the value of being clear in therapeutic models to guide my work so that my clients and I have a clear path to recovery. Thank you from the deepest place in my heart for supporting me in not only accomplishing my dream of being a therapist, but also guiding me so that I'm effective while living my dream.

Thank you also to Nana Twumasi. I'm so glad I got to work with you again. I deeply appreciate that you understood my needs during this process so that this workbook could be completed from the highest place of integrity.

Although this book is dedicated to Ethan Wood, I want to thank you again. You provided both tangible and emotional support to me throughout this process while I also ran my practice. Thank you for always understanding and supporting my vision in this world to help others. For you, every day, I'm deeply grateful.

Finally, I want to thank every single person who will engage with this workbook. Your dedication to growth and recovery truly makes this world a better place. Thank you.

About the Author

Krystal Mazzola, MEd, LMFT, is a licensed marriage and family therapist, author, and entrepreneur. She founded her therapy practice, The Healthy Relationship Foundation, with the commitment to help individuals, and couples, recover from codependency and mental health issues to have healthier lives and relationships. Krystal is the author of *The Codependency Recovery Plan: A 5-Step Guide to Understand, Accept and Break Free from the Codependent Cycle*. She gained her professional expertise by training with pioneering expert on codependency, Pia Mellody, when working at The Meadows. Krystal is personally in recovery from codependency, PTSD, and depression. She attributes her recovery, in part, to her belief that healing is always possible; it just requires commitment and practice. When she is not writing or working at her company, Krystal enjoys learning, gardening, spiritual pursuits, and spinning. She lives in Scottsdale, Arizona, with her boyfriend and their cat. You may connect with her on her website: www.healthyrelationshipfoundation.com.